DEVIL'S KITCHEN

DEVIL'S KITCHEN

CANDICE FOX

TOR PUBLISHING GROUP

NEW YORK

DEVIL'S KITCHEN

A Forge Book
Published by Tom Doherty Associates / Tor Publishing Group
120 Broadway
New York, NY 10271

www.torpublishinggroup.com

Forge® is a registered trademark of Macmillan Publishing Group, LLC.

The Library of Congress Cataloging-in-Publication Data is available upon request.

ISBN 978-1-250-34575-2 (trade paperback)
ISBN 978-1-250-87598-3 (hardcover)
ISBN 978-1-250-32970-7 (ebook)

Our books may be purchased in bulk for promotional, educational, or business use. Please contact your local bookseller or the Macmillan Corporate and Premium Sales Department at 1-800-221-7945, extension 5442, or by email at MacmillanSpecialMarkets@macmillan.com.

First Edition: 2024

Printed in the United States of America

0 9 8 7 6 5 4 3 2 1

To Andy, Loraine, Tim, and Anna

DEVIL'S KITCHEN

ANDY

.

We know you're a cop," Matt said.

Andrea had been waiting for those words. All the way out to the forest, as they pulled off the highway and onto the thin dirt road. The unsteady headlights between Matt's and Engo's shoulders cast the trees in a strangely festive gold. The killing fields. In a way, Andy had been waiting for the words a lot longer than that. Every morning and every night for almost three months. The potential for them clinging to the lining of her stomach like an acid.

We know.

Now she was kneeling on the bare boards of a run-down portable building in the woods, the sound of boats on the Hudson nearby competing with the moan of skin-peeling wind. The corrugated-iron roof rattled above all their heads. The property—a massive, abandoned slab of woods that probably belonged to some absent billionaire who'd had ideas of building a house here once—was dead silent beyond the little shack. Andy knew she was in a black spot on the river's otherwise glittering edges, so close to safety, yet so far away. Ben was breathing hard beside Andy, sweating into his firefighting bunker uniform. The reflective yellow stripes on his arms were trying to suck up any and all available light. There wasn't much. Matt, Engo, and Jakey were faceless silhouettes crowding her and Ben in. Strange what a person will long for at the end. A sliver of light. To breathe the sour air unfettered, as Ben did. They'd taped her mouth.

Matt put his gun to Ben's forehead, nudged it hard so that his head snapped back.

"You brought a *fucking cop* into the crew."

"She's not a cop! I swear to God, man!"

"I *raised* you," Matt growled. "I found you in a hole and I dug you out and this is how you want to play me?"

"Matt, Matt, listen to me—"

"Benji, Benji, Benji." Engo stepped forward, put his three-fingered hand on Ben's shoulder. "We *know*. Okay? It's over. You got a choice now, brother. You admit what you've done, and maybe we can talk about what happens next."

"*She's not a cop!*"

I'm not a fucking cop! Andy growled through the tape. Because it's what she would say. Andrea "Andy" Nearland, her mask. She wouldn't go down quiet. She would fight to the end.

Engo came over to her and tried to start in with the same faux pleasantries and soothings and bargains and she flopped hard on her hip, swung her legs around, and kicked out at his shins. He went down on his ass and she let off a string of obscenities behind the tape. Andy had always hated Engo. Andy the mask. And the real Her, too. Jake got between them. Little Jakey, who had until now been hovering in the corner of the dilapidated portable and gnawing on the end of an unlit cigarette, muttering worrisome nothings to himself.

"Get her back on her knees."

Jakey came over and helped her up. His hand was clammy on her neck.

Don't fucking touch me!

"Benji," Big Matt said. "There's an out here. I'm *giving you* an out. You gotta take it."

"I don't—"

"Tell us that you turned on us. That's all you have to do, man."

"She's not a cop!"

"Just tell us!"

"Matt, please!"

"Tell us, or I'm gonna have to do this thing. I don't want to do it. But I will."

Andy looked at Ben. Met his frantic gaze. She saw it in his eyes, the scene playing out. Andy taking the bullet in the brain. Her body ragdolling on the floor. Ben next. All the vigor going out of him, like his plug had been yanked from the socket. Matt, Engo, and Jakey strapping firefighting helmets onto their dead bodies and lighting the place up around them. Driving back to the station car parked at Peanut Leap. They'd make the anonymous call to 911. Then respond to Dispatch when the job came over the radio.

Hey, Dispatch, we're up here anyway. Engine 99 crew. We took the station car for a cruise and we have basic gear on us. We'll head out there while the local guys get organized.

It would look like an accident. The crew had taken the station car out for a spin, parked to watch the lights on the river and sink beers, and picked up a run-of-the-mill spot-fire call. They'd rolled up to the property, spotted the portable that had probably served as a construction-site office once, starting to smoke out. Ben and Andy had taken the spare gear from the back of the car and rushed in ahead of Matt and the rest of the crew, no idea that the blazing building was full of gas bottles and jerry cans that some local cuckoo had been hoarding.

Kaboom.

A tragedy.

Oh, there'd be an inquiry, of course. Wrists would be slapped—about the rec run with the station car, the beers, the half-cocked entry. There would be whispers, too. Especially after what happened to Titus.

But then everybody would cry and forget about it.

Matt and his crew did that: they made people forget.

Andy watched Ben weigh his loyalties. His crew, against the cop he'd brought in to destroy them.

"I don't want to do this, Ben," Matt said. The huge man's voice was strained. He shifted his grip on the gun. "Just tell us the truth."

The wind howled around the shack and the boats clanged on the river and Little Jakey started to cry.

BEN

·

Fire is loud. It calls to people. Probably had been doing that since the dawn of time, Ben guessed. When it was old enough, when it had evolved through its hissing and creeping and licking phase and was a good-sized beast learning to roar—that's when they came. Stood. Watched. Felt the heat on their cheeks and felt alive and part of something, or some hippie shit like that.

By the time Ben's boots landed on the wet sidewalk of West Thirty-Seventh Street there were huddles of people in darkened doorways across the street and gawkers hanging out of apartment windows above them. The pinprick white lights of phone cameras. He hardly noticed, was hauling and dumping gear onto the concrete, his mind tangled up with the next eighteen steps. Engo had a cigar clamped between his jaws and was drenched in sweat, started stretching the line.

"This is a mistake," Ben told Matt as the chief jumped down from the engine. The flashing lights were making Matt's angry red neck stubble a sickly purple.

"It'll be fine."

"A fucking fabric store?" Ben ripped open the hatch on the side of the engine and started grabbing tools fast and efficiently. A looter in a flood-lands Target. "It's a tinderbox."

"The building is right on our path. It was the best way in."

Clouds of singed nylon were pouring out of the building above them. "It'll go up. And Engo and Jakey won't be able to—"

"Stop bitching, Benji."

Ben stopped bitching, because you didn't bitch too long at Matt. By now, two windows on the third floor of the fabric store had blown out and the crowd in the street had doubled. The windows were glowing up there, not just the ones that were blown. Ben had been doing this ten years, longer. The window glow told him the fire was big enough that it was probably into the foundations.

He tanked up, slapped on his helmet, shouldered a gear bag, and went in. Engo was in front, of course, his chin up, the hose hanging over his arm like a great limp dick. A guy walking into a fancy museum. Engo made a show of marching into fires like that, like it was all routine. Like nothing was a big deal. *What happened? Granny left the iron on?* Ben had seen the guy step over bodies as if they were kinks in a rug. His tank was unhooked because smoke worried him the way water worried fish.

Ben dropped his hose, split from Jakey and Engo, and went down the stairs while they went up toward the fire. Things passed before him, curiosities his mind would pick over later as he tried to sleep. Walls of buttons in a thousand shapes and colors. Giant golden scissors. Cutting tools and rulers. There were stacks of leather lying folded on shelves, colors he hadn't imagined possible. He was glad they'd decided to set the spark device that ignited the fire on the third floor. It was all fur and feathers on the basement level—this part of the store was going to vaporize when it caught.

Ben dropped his bag and helmet. The bag was so heavy with tools it shook the floor, made a jar of pins jump off the nearby cutting counter. He took a knife from his belt, slit a square in the carpet, raked it back, and exposed the boards. Lifting up six floorboards with a Halligan tool took fifteen seconds. He dropped his gear bag down onto the bare earth below the building and slipped in after it, landing right on top of the concrete manhole. He didn't have a pit lid lifter but the Halligan did the job, slid nicely into the iron handle of the forty-pound manhole cover. He adjusted his mask, worked his jaw to make sure it was sealed tight before he popped open the cover and stepped down into the blackness.

Something about being surrounded by toxic gas makes a guy breathe harder. He'd thought about that for the first time as he hauled bodies for overworked paramedics in COVID times, then while putting out car fires while the NYPD doused the streets in pepper spray during the George Floyd days. It had occurred to him again now in the dark, working his way along the disused, hand-bricked tunnel beneath West Thirty-Seventh Street, he thought of the hydrogen sulfide swirling in the air around him, built up from decades of moss and sewage and whateverthehell percolating in the old, sealed subway access. It made him suck on the oxygen like a hungry baby at the tit.

He didn't use the flashlight down here. Engo had tried to argue that H_2S wasn't that flammable, and an LED didn't spark like that anyway, but

Ben wasn't going to turn that corner of New York into Pompeii because he didn't like the dark. He had about eleven minutes to get where he was going, do the job, and get back again. The blindness would make the timing tight. The radio crackling in his ear canal with the voices of the crew behind him made him twitchy.

"Engo, you on-site?"

"Yeah, boss. We got a nice little campfire here."

"Ben?"

"Checking for a secondary ignition site," Ben lied. His voice felt trapped behind the mask.

"We better black out the whole block," Matt said. *"We don't know who shares a distributor."*

Ben fast-walked, imagining Matt on the street, ordering the backup crews, who were probably already arriving from Ladder 98, to shut down the power to the whole Garment District. The guys from 97 and 98 would probably think that was over the top, that blacking out the singular block would do. But Matt needed to make sure that not only the fabric store was powered off, but also the jewelry store on West Thirty-Fifth, where Ben was heading.

Left, right, left, he reminded himself. Just like the marching call. He turned the last corner, walked for three minutes, his gloved fingers trailing the wall, all sorts of landscapes passing under his boots, most of them wet and squelching. He found the steppers he was looking for—rusty iron rungs concreted into the wall—dropped his gear bag, and went up. His arms were shaking as he lifted the second manhole cover. Nerves.

It had been a year or more since they'd done a high-end job like this, something that required blueprints to be memorized and on-site scouting in the lead-up. A dry spell ended. Ben didn't like these kinds of jobs; scores they *needed*. Don't rob when you're broke. That was a mantra he'd always believed in. Desperation makes guys stupid, dissolves trust. Because at the end of the day, did Ben really know for sure that Matt had gotten the best fence for this take? Someone who could move what they stole tonight without making ripples? Or had Matt settled, because the crew chief had three ex-wives with their hands out and a bun in the oven with baby mama number four? And did Ben really know for sure that Jakey had double-checked on all the construction sites in the Garment District for late-night workers who might be in the tunnels? Did Jakey know the local police response times? Or was the kid into the horses again? Was he hocking old PlayStation games to fend off loan sharks?

Ben realized, as he hauled his gear up through the manhole and into the two-foot-tall crawl space beneath an apartment building on Thirty-Fifth, that he didn't trust his own crew on a job anymore.

And that was bad.

But there were worse kinds of mistrust.

There was the one that had made him write the letter to the detective.

Ben lifted the manhole cover back into place, raked his oxygen mask off, and lay panting on the compacted dirt floor. The crawl space was as black as the tunnel, but years of working in roof cavities and basements and tunnels and collapsed buildings had given Ben the ability to maneuver in the dark like a night creature. He found the flashlight on his belt, clicked it on, and got his bearings. Wide, raw-cut floor beams stretched into the nothingness just inches above where he lay. They'd probably been built when they still called this place the Devil's Arcade, and it was an army of prostitutes and bootleggers, and not fancy types shopping for diamonds, stamping over them. Ben started crawling west, found a gap in the brick foundations that separated one building from another, and kept on. A hundred yards from the manhole, three buildings over, the subsurface power-distribution board belonging to the jewelry store was just where he expected it to be, bolted to a brick strut.

He pulled wire cutters and a charge tester and the bug from a vest strapped under his turnout coat, started working the board to insert the bug. Sweat ran into his eyes. His mind kept trying to wander away from what his fingers were doing and drift two blocks over to the fabric store, to twenty-three-year-old Jakey, shoulder-to-shoulder with an eight-fingered, potbellied psychopath who wanted to die in a blaze of glory. The two of them battling a decidedly glorious blaze. The men trying to let the magnificent thing eat through enough cotton and satin and jersey and whatever else to give Ben the time he needed to do what he had to do; but not so long it would become a monster and turn and eat them, too.

Ben finished installing the bug in the jewelry store's security system and was shifting around to crawl back to his gear bag and tank and the manhole three buildings away when he heard a woman's voice.

"Hello?"

Ben froze. Instinct made him flatten on the dirt like a threatened lizard.

His toes were curled in his boots. His eyes bulged and his lungs expelled all the air that was in them. He heard the floorboards somewhere to the right of where he lay creak with footsteps.

The radio in his ear crackled.

"*Engo and Jakey, you got it in hand?*"

"*Yep. Yep. We got it.*"

"*It don't look like it from here.*"

"*I said we got it.*"

"*Ben, give me an ETA. They need you up there.*"

Ben didn't breathe. Whoever was in the jewelry store above him walked across the boards right over his head. He heard a muffled snap, and then, even through the layers of carpet on the boards above him, he saw the glow of a light.

"Fuuuuuuck," he mouthed.

"Hello?"

"*Ben, give me a sitrep,*" Matt insisted.

He didn't speak. Slowly, achingly, he lifted his hand from the dirt and reached for the radio on his shoulder. He clicked the transmit button twice, the code for trouble.

There was a long pause. Ben counted his breaths. The counting made him think of time. Seconds ticking off. With a recognition so filled with dread it sent a bolt of pain through his spine, he remembered the PASS alarm on his belt and reached down and shook the safety device so it wouldn't sound a pealing alarm at his immobility. Sweat was dripping off his eyelashes.

"*Two for hold, three for abort,*" Matt finally said. Ben could hear the tightness in his chief's voice. He clicked the radio twice.

Another three minutes. Ben counted them. The woman in the jewelry store moved some stuff around, opened and closed a cabinet.

"*Ladder 98 crew are comin' up to join you, Engo,*" Matt said. Ben could hear the quiet fury in his voice now.

"*Tell those pricks we got it!*"

"*I'm telling you to haul ass!*" Matt said. "*They're comin'!*"

Ben swore under his breath. It probably sounded to anyone monitoring the radios that Matt had been talking to Engo, encouraging him to get the fire under control before another crew came in and claimed the knockdown of the fire. But Ben heard the real message. Matt was telling him to haul ass out from under the jewelry store and back to the fire before the guys from 98 geared up and entered the site, climbed to the second floor, and asked where the hell Engine 99's third guy was.

Or worse, they came looking for him. In the basement, maybe, where he'd opened up the hole in the floor to access the tunnel.

The light clicked off above him. Ben guessed whoever was in the store had decided the sound she heard wasn't a person. He counted off ten breaths, then slithered for his life back to the manhole, tanked up, and popped the cover and dropped his gear into the shaft.

He was sprinting so hard down the home stretch his fingers almost missed the steppers on the wall under the fabric store. He grabbed on and yanked himself to a stop, almost slipped in the toxic sludge. Ben climbed to the top of the ladder, shouldered open the manhole, got out and threw it back into place, then heaved himself up through the hole he'd cut in the floor. His body was screaming at him to just lie there, take a minute. Three-quarters of his oxygen tank was gone just from his own panicked breathing. The air in the mask tasted rubbery and thick. Soon it would start shuddering on his face, a sign he was about to max out. He rolled over instead, got up, and dragged a heap of furs to the edge of the hole. He lit them with a cigarette lighter and bolted up the stairs.

He arrived in the foyer as the Ladder 98 guys were marching up the stairs to the second floor. Ben came up behind them. He couldn't think what else to do. A guy he didn't recognize whirled around on him.

"Da fuck?"

"We got a secondary ignition site in the basement," Ben said. The Ladder 98 guys looked at each other for a moment, probably trying to decipher how the hell a secondary fire could start on the basement level of the building when the main fire was on the third floor. And what the hell Ben was doing down there looking for a secondary site before his own crew had taken hold of the primary site. But they shook it off. They probably guessed Engo was behind the split in manpower, and they'd all seen stranger things happen with ignition sites. Fires creeping through walls and popping up in two apartments on opposite sides of the same building. Fires reigniting two weeks after they were put out. Fire had no rules. It was the only magic left in the world.

"Go to your crew," the 98 guy said. "We'll take the basement."

Ben watched them go. He could see flames licking up the walls of the basement stairwell. Just as he'd predicted, the basement was already just a room full of ash and memories.

It was 4 A.M. and they were in the squad room before anybody could talk about it. Matt's crew had a room of their own, mainly because nobody from the other crews could stand the idea of Matt coming in and sitting down to watch the TV and them having to sit there with him like there was a full-size lion lounging on the end of the couch. Ben and the guys, they all stank. Ash and sweat and monoammonium phosphate. Engo was in his armchair nursing his paunch, a wet basketball under his T-shirt. Matt was throwing shit around in the kitchenette. Jakey stood by the door, wincing like he was expecting to be the next thing picked up and hurled against the wall.

"Who *the fuck* was she?" Matt bellowed.

"How do I know?" Ben shrugged. "Hard to make her out through the floorboards."

"It was *your* job to watch the ins and outs." Matt turned and stabbed a sausage-sized finger at Engo. "You said nobody would be there."

"So somebody pulled an all-nighter," Engo said. "What do you want from me? I watched the store for two months. Nobody ever stayed past nine."

"*Did* you watch the store?" Ben piled on. "Or did you sit in your car eating burgers and jerking off?"

"This guy." Engo shook his head sadly at Ben.

"'Member that time you landed that nineteen-year-old on Snapchat? You let those security guards creep up on us at the Atrium."

Engo sat grinning at him.

"What if we'd put you on watch duty at the fabric store instead of the jewelry store? Huh?" Ben asked. "What if someone pulled an all-nighter there, and you didn't notice them? We could have had a civilian on the second floor when the fire started. Or in the basement, when I was cutting through the goddamn floor."

"You're really mad, huh?"

Ben held his head.

"Would it help you feel better if you took a swing at me, babycakes?" Engo tapped his stubbled chin. "Because you're welcome to try."

"Jesus Christ."

"Yeah. That's what I thought."

"We can't go on with this job." Ben's hair was still plastered to his skull with sweat. He thought about giving up and going home to bed. He made one last appeal to Matt. "The 98s saw that I was split off from my crew. They'll know something was up. They're going to wonder why I went looking for a second site when the primary site was getting so out of control."

"It was never out of control," Engo said.

"If I hadn't got back when I did, you and Jakey would be sandwich meat between the third and fourth floors of that place right now."

"You're delusional."

"It was into the foundations!"

"No it wasn't."

"Maybe we should think about it," Jakey piped up, already glowing red in the neck and cheeks like a parakeet. "Because there was, uh . . . You know. There was the radio call, too. 'Hold or abort.' That'll be on the record. That's not good."

"We're not pulling the pin on this job," Matt finally said. "We're too deep."

"We've been deeper before and walked away," Ben reasoned.

No one spoke.

"The woman. What if she figures the noises under the carpet were rats?" Ben asked. "Maybe she sends a pest guy down there."

Matt was white-knuckling the kitchen sink, staring out the window at the training yard. "Some dumbass rat guy's not going to know anybody else was down there messing with the electrics. He'll be looking for rats, not bugs."

"'Rats, not bugs,'" Engo laughed. "That's funny."

"What if she *doesn't* figure it's rats," Ben said. "We hit the jewelry store in three weeks, and she remembers the noises she heard under the floor. Reads about the fabric-store fire in the papers. Sees it was the same night she heard the noises."

"So we wait a month," Matt said.

"We can't go ahead," Ben insisted. "A job this size has got to be perfec—"

"*I said we're doing it!*" Matt grabbed a mug off the counter, gripped its rim and handle and sides like a baseball. Like a grenade. "You got a hearing problem I don't know about, Benji?"

He didn't answer. No one did.

In the end, Ben just shrugged, because he was tired and he didn't need a coffee mug to the temple right then.

And what did he care, anyway? They were all going to jail, whether it was a month from now or sooner.

He was staring into his plate of eggs at Jimmy's when she came in. Ben's hands were still shaking. Had been all morning. But he couldn't figure out if it was last night's near-miss under the jewelry store or The Silence, as he'd come to think of it. The great big Nothing-At-All that had happened since he'd left a handwritten letter on the windshield of a car belonging to a homicide detective from the South Bronx.

Eighteen days. Not a phone call. Not an email. Not a sound.

He poked his eggs with his fork and listened without really listening to the people bustling in and out of the diner, their moaning about the heat. A Ferris wheel of possibilities was turning in his head, each carriage a different explanation for why nothing had happened since the letter. Maybe the guy had figured it was a prank. Maybe the wind had swept the envelope off his car. Maybe his girlfriend and her kid going missing had fucked Ben's brain up so bad that he'd imagined the whole damn thing—choosing the detective, writing the letter, putting it on his car. He'd been so jacked, walking there and placing the envelope under the windshield wiper, that he barely remembered doing it.

Maybe it was much worse than any of those things.

Maybe Engo or Jakey or Matt had followed him the day he left the letter. Maybe they'd taken it off the windshield. Read it.

Maybe they *knew*.

His fork was doing Morse code on the edge of his plate. One of Jimmy's guys banged a fry basket into the hot oil and the fork leaped clean out of Ben's hand. He had to stop thinking about it. He looked at Jimmy's terrible clumsy handwriting on the greasy whiteboards above the fry station and picked off items and tried to think about them instead. About salad. About burgers. About soup.

Ben stared at his eggs.

The woman had to say his name a couple of times before he heard her.

"Benjamin Haig?"

He looked over. The woman was sitting on the stool next to his, her hand on the countertop near a steaming coffee. He had no idea how long she'd been sitting there, got the feeling that it might have been a while. Her bobbed blond hair was slicked behind her ears and she was watching him through navy-blue reading glasses. His rattled brain took down some things about her. She was beautiful. She was expensively dressed. She was a stranger. That was all he got.

When the woman knew she had his attention, she unfolded the newspaper on the counter in front of her and set about scanning the headlines.

"I'm here about the letter," she said.

ANDY

.

She felt, rather than saw, the reaction. Her words sent a bolt of electricity right though Benjamin Haig, seizing the air in his chest. Raw seconds passed, in which she read the paper and he tried to come to terms with what was happening. When she looked up again, he'd collected himself a little. But the fork was being white-knuckled in his fist and all the muscles in his neck were wire-tight.

"Detective Johnson sent you?" he asked his eggs.

"No," Andy said. "He got your letter and passed it on to his superiors. I was called in about five days ago."

"Oh good." Ben's wild eyes flicked to her. "So fifty goddamn people know about this already."

"No, you just—"

"I'm out." He shoved his eggs away and stood. He was bigger than she'd anticipated. Broad-shouldered and roped with muscle. "I don't need this."

"Yeah, you do." She turned back to her paper. He'd stopped by her chair, and she could smell him. He hadn't showered after the fabric-store fire from the night before. He reeked of chemicals and body odor and grief. "If you want to find Luna and Gabriel, you need this, Ben."

He thought about it. Then walked back to his stool, slipped onto it, slow and numb. People had noticed the tension between them. Of course they had, it was bouncing off the countertop like welding sparks. But they went back to their own business soon enough. Andy sipped her coffee. It was good.

"Detective Johnson knew this was too big for him," Andy said carefully. "He went directly to his superior, who kicked it over to the FBI. An agent there, Tony Newler, reviewed the situation and made a decision to call in a specialist. I'm that specialist."

"If the crew find out I've flipped"—Ben eased the words out—"I'll be dead. You get that? They will kill me. It'll happen on the job, or I'll just disappear. I'll end up in a hole up north somewhere. No one will ever find my body."

"Do you think that's what's happened to Luna and her child?" Andy kept her tone neutral. She flipped the newspaper to read the bottom half of the cover. The front page was about the fabric-store fire. "Do you believe your crew put them in a hole somewhere?"

"I don't know! That's the whole point."

They sat in silence for a while. Jimmy's people yelled out order numbers and scraped the griddle. Andy took her phone out, eventually, and zeroed in on the photograph she had taken of Ben's letter.

"'I am worried that my girlfriend might have discovered something about what the crew and I have been doing,'" she read. Ben kept his head low. "'Either the last job we pulled, or one of the ones we did in the past. I am worried she and her son might have been killed to silence them.'"

"You don't have to read me the letter," Ben said. "I wrote it. I know what it says."

"'My efforts to find Luna and Gabriel have come to nothing, and the police officers handling her case are not taking it seriously. I am—'"

"'I am willing to cooperate to help police solve a number of high-level criminal cases if police will help me investigate my fellow crew members.'" Ben worked his jaw. "Yes I know. I wrote it. I read it a thousand times before I handed it in."

"Those cases," Andy said. "They're burglaries."

"Why would I say that to you now?" Ben leaned back on his stool, exhausted. "You haven't given me anything."

"Reading between the lines, it looks like you're talking about burglaries," Andy said. "You talk about 'valuables.' You call them 'jobs.'"

"I don't know why we're doing this here." He looked around.

"We could do it in an interrogation room, if you like." She smiled, flipping to the sports.

She felt his eyes on her.

"So what are you, then? An agent?"

"I'm a specialist."

"I wanted Johnson. I picked him on purpose," Ben said. "He's not connected to anybody in Midtown. And he solved that . . . that murder last year. The waitress. Everybody said she'd just gone back home to Mexico. I read about it in the paper."

"I told you. Detective Johnson isn't trained for this."

"For what?" Ben was leaning in. The smell again. "What kind of specialist are you? I don't even know your name."

"You can call me . . ." She gave it a few seconds of consideration. Never more than that. "Andy."

"What are you, FBI or something?"

"I need to get this straight, Mr. Haig," Andy said carefully. "You believe one or all of your crew—Matthew Roderick, Englemann Fiss, and Jacob Valentine—may be responsible for their murders. That Luna found out about what you'd been doing and the crew got worried she was going to go to the police. They decided to silence her. The kid was collateral."

She turned to him. His head was down now, grimy fingers raked up into his dark hair, his elbows splayed over the eggs. She knew that putting the situation so plainly was making him question the whole thing. But she wanted him to question it. Really examine what he was doing. Because she needed him fully on board, not with one foot still on the pier.

"Matt wouldn't kill a kid," Ben murmured, almost to himself. Andy could barely hear him. "He's got six of his own. One on the way. He talks a lot of shit but he wouldn't . . . But Engo. Engo, maybe. If Matt ordered it, then . . ."

"You don't believe it was something else," Andy pressed. "You fully believe it was one or all of them?"

Ben thought. For a full minute, he was completely still, staring at his plate.

Then he nodded.

"I'm going to just go ahead and assume you're talking about high-stakes robberies in this letter." Andy put her phone down. "But you haven't been specific enough about which cases you'll cooperate on. And is it just burglaries that we're talking about? I notice that you don't mention Titus Cliffen when you talk about your past crimes. Was he not part of your crew?"

Ben didn't speak.

"Titus was killed in a workplace accident," Andy went on. "Did he find out about the crew, too? Was he murdered? Is that why you're so convinced Matt, Engo, and Jake might have had a hand in what happened to Luna and Gabe?"

Ben just shook his head. Exhausted, angry.

Andy sipped her coffee, ran some things through in her mind. Approaching Ben in the café had been the final big-ticket item on her list. She had decided to take the job. But that just meant starting a whole new list. Phase Two. The Entry. She opened the newspaper and turned it to the back and folded it again so the apartment listings were on top. The last sip of coffee wasn't as good as the first. Dish-soap residue in the bottom of the cup. She stood, and Ben sensed her movement.

His head snapped up. "Wait."

"You've got some things to do." Andy held his eyes with hers. Because it was all business now. Not a curiosity. And she needed him to feel it. "You need to get this under control."

"What?"

"This." She gestured at his face, his body. The complete package. From the perspective of the gawky diners, she probably looked like an ex telling a guy to clean up his life. Maybe she'd give him a second chance if he did. "The shaky hands. The twitchy eyes. You need to get your head together, Ben. Shave off the grief beard and pick yourself up. Because when I come back into your life, you're going to need to be a man who's finished grieving. A guy coming to terms with the idea that his girlfriend just took the kid and ran off home to Mexico."

"I don't understand." Ben shook his head. "Where are you— When are you coming back?"

"It's better if you don't know," she said. "Or you'll be expecting me."

She dropped some bills on the counter. He had the look of a dog being abandoned on a roadside.

"And take a shower, for God's sake."

The callout was for a kid, so that had gotten everybody hustling. Always did. A guy could be three minutes from the end of his shift, his replacement already in-house an hour earlier, shooting the shit with the day crew in the hall between squad rooms, his mind already in his bed at home. Then a child-in-peril callout comes in, and he's hard-nosed and hungry like it's his first minute on the job. Ben remembered they were about midshift when they got the alert from Dispatch. Sundown. A kid was stuck outside the 7-Eleven on Eighth and Thirty-Ninth. Jakey was so geed up he was grinding his teeth in the back of the engine. Even Engo looked awake.

The excitement shorted out pretty quick. It was clear from a block away that the kid wasn't in any real danger. A crowd hadn't formed on the sidewalk, and traffic was still moving. Matt parked the engine, got a measure of the situation, then went inside the store to buy a Coke. Ben got a glimpse of the mother. Curvaceous, beautiful, Latina. So he pushed ahead of Engo before the guy could say something awful in greeting. The woman was standing over the kid, her face taut and veined with stress.

"Fire department," Ben said. "What's goin' on?"

"Aw, Jesus." The mother straightened and gestured to the kid, let her hands slap loudly on her painted-on jeans. "This kid. This kid! I'm gonna have a goddamn heart attack out here. I stopped to check my phone for five seconds—five seconds! And look at this. Just look! Jesus Christ!"

Ben assessed the predicament. The boy of maybe three years old was bent at the waist. His head of close-cropped black hair was thrust through a U-lock, that U-lock connecting a rusted bike body to a rack. The rack was bolted to the sidewalk. There were thousands of bike carcasses like this one chained to racks all over the city, even more in the Hudson, rented or bought cheap by tourists and then abandoned after they flew out. It had been picked over for everything that could be repurposed or hocked by the homeless. Now only the trapezium-shaped midsection of the bike remained, its heavy-duty U-shaped lock hanging around the neck of its tiny human attachment. The kid was drenched from the neck up in vegetable oil, and there was a half-empty bottle standing nearby, an attempt by someone to grease him up and slip him loose. The kid was growl-crying. Big snot bubbles. If everybody hadn't been so upset, it might have been funny, the tiny pudgy man sentenced to time in the medieval stocks.

"He stuck his head through there while you weren't looking?" Ben surmised.

"It just—it just—it happened so fast."

"It's okay." Ben felt bad for the lady. "It's an easy fix."

"Why do they have this sitting here?" The mother slapped both hands to the sides of her head now, raked her curls back from the sweat on her face. "Who leaves half a goddamn bike chained up like this? Why the huge lock if you're not gonna come back for the bike?"

"Ma'am—"

"Why doesn't the city come and cut this thing off?"

"Quit your complainin'," Engo snorted. "This is on you, not the city. You should have kept an eye on your kid, lady. You're in New York, or hadn't you noticed?"

"Engo."

"What?" Engo gave the woman a look-over. "Okay—so today the kid got his head stuck in a bike rack. Lucky you, missy. You don't change your ways, and tomorrow they'll be scraping him off the underside of a taxicab. Or pullin' his corpse out of a manhole."

"I was watching him!" the lady barked. "I-I-I had to take a call from my boss!"

"So your job is more important than your kid now?"

"Engo! Fuck, man!"

"What can I say? I just—I see this all the time." He took off his helmet, gave the sigh of the disenchanted. "Modern mothers addicted to their phones. It's sad, is what it is. There's a whole generation bein' raised without—"

"Man, what the fuck are you sayin' to me right now?" The lady came at Engo. Ben just managed to get an arm around her in time. "Who even is this guy? You're gonna come here and-and-and judge my parenting? I called you for help! Who the hell do you think you are?"

"Stop, stop, stop, stop." Ben took the mother by the shoulders as gently as he could. "Jakey, cut the kid free, will ya? Engo, fuck off."

He took the lady to the mouth of an alley where she could still see her kid. Jakey had been soothing the child and seemed to just about have him smiling already. He went to the engine to get a Hurst tool and Engo stepped in to take over clown duty and ruined all Jakey's good work. Ben's main concern was the woman. She dumped her huge handbag at her feet and kicked it hard.

"Listen." Ben put his gloved hands up in surrender. "Listen to me. This kind of stuff happens. All right? Okay? This is nothing. The kid is fine. You want to hear about bad mothers? You wouldn't believe the—"

The lady burst into tears.

Then she fell into his arms.

As a firefighter, Ben had been hugged by strangers a million times. He understood it. Emotions were high wherever he went, and the uniform—the heavy jackets and the helmets and the huge heatproof boots—tickled that corner of the brain reserved for football mascots and superheroes. But when Luna Denero hugged Ben that day, a padlock fell off an old, rusty iron door somewhere inside him. It was a door he'd been pulling on and struggling with, breaking and bending keys in, for much of his adult life. Suddenly every inch of his skin was on fire. Humiliation and exhilaration and desire and horror. He did something that surprised himself then. Instead of stiffening and waiting for it to be over like he usually did, he seized the moment and wrapped his arms around her and rocked her a little, feeling like the luckiest son of a bitch in New York.

He held her for maybe twenty seconds, and in that time, five guys in the steady flow of foot traffic glanced over at the firefighter hugging the Latina beauty with the huge brown eyes and cheeks for weeks and gave him a glare that sent pain waves right down to his balls. Then she broke it off, thumbed her mascara back into place, and was just as dry and hard and put-together as she had been when she'd tried to scratch Engo's eyeballs out a minute earlier.

Jakey was cutting the U-lock off the screaming kid with the hydraulic Hurst tool. Engo was trying to scare off the crowd, who had started gawking and filming now that there were flashing lights and uniforms to look at. Matt was standing at the open door of the engine, an elbow on the high seat, guzzling the Coke and watching the fray.

"Where's my handbag?" Luna asked.

Ben looked down at the ground, at the spot at the mouth of the alley not three feet from them where the woman had drop-kicked the bag.

It was gone.

He'd found the bag.

It had taken him most of the night, and he'd walked all over the city. Afterward, he'd felt pretty clever about it. If his parents hadn't been no-good junkies and his mind hadn't been poisoned against the police from before he was even out of the womb, he would have made a passable cop. Ben had returned to the 7-Eleven after his shift, got a printout of the skinny figure in the ball cap captured by the store's CCTV scooping up the handbag from the alleyway and walking away without even slowing his pace. He'd stared hard at the image: the young man bent double, reaching for the bag, twelve people in the frame and none of them seeing the grab. Ben figured the guy was a seasoned thief. He'd shown the picture around all the local scumbags, paid out a couple of hundred bucks in bribes. The CD peddlers near Central Park couldn't help him, and neither could the elders of the homeless communities in the Financial District. He struck out with the men and women in red uniforms standing in Times Square, the ones hawking tickets to hop-on, hop-off bus rides for tourists. He quizzed the sellers of knockoff handbags spread out on sheets on the sidewalk, the guys with sunglasses stands, the ice cream and kebab truck drivers. He focused on the shoplifters taking breaks outside the stores on Fifth Avenue for a while, kids sweating in their big jackets and baggy jeans. For a sizable bribe, these skinny youths had helped him dig up some TikTok footage of the crew cutting the boy's head free of the U-lock, and he'd gotten a better image of the thief from that.

About 2 a.m. he had a name. At 3 a.m. he had an address. At 4 a.m. he'd knocked on the asshole's door and dragged him out into the stuffy hallway of his walk-up in the projects in a yet-ungentrified corner of Brooklyn. Ben had thrown the guy clean through the drywall beside his apartment door and back into his own living room. At 5:30 a.m. Ben was dumpster-diving for the handbag in trash cans outside a diner back at Times Square.

Luna was trying to hustle the kid out the door of her apartment in Dayton and get him off to daycare when Ben came walking down the hall at about 7:30 a.m., the bag strap clutched in his fist and a big dorky grin on his face.

BEN

·

He stood in his bathroom now shaving his "grief beard," which he hadn't even known was a thing until he really looked at it. Patchy, dark stubble, creeping too far down the neck to be anything but accidental. Ben's father had sported a grief beard, was a walking wilderness with two dead eyes peering through it as far back as Ben could remember. He'd shave it off periodically to look for work, and it would shock the neighborhood every time, get people speculating, like when the front yard of an abandoned house is suddenly shorn down to the roots in the early morning by people unseen. Ben remembered a few times as a kid he'd wondered if someone new had moved in there behind his father's eyes. Then he'd watch him go back to the needle and realize it was just the same old guy.

He looked at the prickles in the sink, realized one had fallen on Gabriel's toothbrush. He picked up the brush, removed the particle of hair, rinsed it, and put it back on the edge of the sink where the kid had left it, instead of in the cup by the mirror where it belonged. He spoke to them then, quietly yet fervently in the solitude of the apartment bathroom, the same words he always said when the bad thoughts pricked at him. Of Gabe and Luna lying entwined in a grave somewhere. Or their ashes being scattered along lonely shores by river winds.

"I'm gonna find you," Ben said.

ANDY

·

ony Newler pulled into the parking lot in Greenpoint and cut the
engine, just sat there looking through the windshield at Andy like
he expected her to go over there and get in. She didn't. Working
undercover jobs for the last fifteen years had made her wary of tight
spaces, even when she completely trusted the company. But this was the
first time she'd laid eyes on Tony in ten years, and the mere sight of him
was making her itch in weird places. Palms of her hands. Sides of her neck.
Allergic to him.

He got out, came around, and sat on the hood of his car, which was nose-
to-nose with hers, ten feet away. He'd put on a few pounds and his hair was
white at the temples. She guessed that's what too many press conferences and
cadet graduation banquets did to you.

"Blond, huh?" he said, huffing a little surprised laugh, trying his hand
with friendly and light. Andy shifted, told herself not to touch her hair. Her
scalp prickled. She didn't do "friendly and light." Not with him.

"Is that for this job, or from the last one?"

"The last one," Andy said. She glanced over at the next lot, a hire place
for construction vehicles. Razor wire and bright orange lights and yellow
diggers dripping with grease. "I'm not set up here yet."

"What *was* the last job?" Newler asked.

"Pedophile in a daycare center." Andy resisted the urge to pluck at the
front of her shirt. Sweat was tickling its way down her ribs. "I went in as a
broke divorcée, new in town."

"Where was that?"

"Michigan. It was for the local PD."

"Huh, interesting."

She waited.

"It's just—I heard you were mostly working private undercover jobs."
Newler shrugged. "I knew you weren't doing anything for the bureau. But

you always hated working with police departments. Too many swinging dicks."

She didn't comment on that.

"Did you catch the guy?"

"Them," Andy said. "I caught them. Can we get on with this?"

Newler folded his thick forearms. She remembered the long sigh. The guy could sigh for five seconds straight. "I guess I should have thought to offer you something involving kids. All those times I tried to get in contact with you, and you didn't answer. You've always been a sucker for kids."

She dug her hand into her jeans pocket and pulled out her car keys.

"Okay, okay, okay." He held his hands up in surrender. "Tell me what you've got."

"Luna Denero worked for a snooty art college in SoHo. She taught pottery classes. She lived out in Newark with the kid, Gabriel. Met Benjamin Haig on the job."

Andy paused to let a squad car with sirens blaring pass behind her on the service road between the two parking lots. The red lights in Newler's eyes made her queasy.

"She was last seen heading to work," Andy continued. "Night classes. She'd drive the kid to the grandmother's place, five minutes away, then fight the traffic to Lower Manhattan."

"Who saw her last?"

"Haig," Andy said. "They'd been living together a couple of months at that point. In a relationship eight months all told. He said in the letter to Detective Johnson that he was home sick with stomach flu that night. Luna left the apartment with Gabriel. No red flags. But she never made it to her ex's mother's place, and never made it to the studio. The car's still missing."

"Who raised the alarm?"

"Ben," she said. "He woke up at midnight, found she wasn't there, and blew up her phone and the studio phone with calls looking for her."

"If he was home sick, why didn't he take care of the kid that night himself?"

"You haven't looked at the case?"

"Not in detail," Newler said. "I gotta be honest with you, I'm not here for the kid and the mother. I'm here for the robberies he talks about in the letter. That's the only thing that got this case to bureau level. That's the meat in the sandwich."

Andy sighed.

"Doesn't mean I'm not curious. Who doesn't love a puzzle, am I right?"

Andy didn't bite.

"So why didn't he—"

"He was *real* sick," Andy said. "Sick enough that he didn't go in for his shift at the firehouse, which from what I can tell is out of character. The guy hasn't had a day off work since he came out of the womb."

Newler thought. A stray cat slunk into the edge of the parking lot, followed a trail of weeds in the cracked pavement, keeping an eye on Andy and Newler toe-to-toe between their vehicles. Andy watched the cat disappear through a gap in a wooden fence.

"I'll look closely at Haig," Andy said. "But I don't see him throwing himself on his own sword like this if he killed his girlfriend and her child."

"Why not?"

"The letter says he's been pulling jobs with his crew for the last ten years. The main two, Matt Roderick and Englemann Fiss. Jake joined later," Andy said. "He hints at them being big jobs."

"So . . ."

"So the guy grew up in foster care. Which would make him prone to hoarding. He almost certainly has a runaway stash somewhere. They probably all do. If Ben just snapped and killed Luna and Gabriel, he would have run. He wouldn't stick around and rat out his whole team."

"Hmm." Newler shrugged. "Could be the other way around, though. Maybe the woman and the kid have run from *him*. You said he blew up her phone when she didn't come home right away. Maybe he's such an abusive, possessive asshole that he's ratting out his crew just to hunt them down."

Andy said nothing. Newler seemed to read the silent codes in the air. "Just guessing." He shifted awkwardly. "What about the ex? The kid's father?"

"Dead. Cancer," Andy said. "The ex and his family were the only avenue of investigation the initial detective looked at after he'd given Haig a good sniff."

"Who was the initial detective?"

"Guy named Simmley."

"Don't know him."

"Luna's brother-in-law used to chop cars for a cartel. Simmley liked that as a storyline for all this. The ex's brother and the cartel he belongs to don't like Luna's new life—the fancy job in Lower Manhattan, the white boyfriend raising her kid. Simmley looked at the disappearance for about two weeks, then told Haig that's almost certainly what happened. Luna got snatched up by the cartel, smacked around a bit, and told to go the fuck home across the border where she belonged."

"And Haig didn't believe it," Newler said.

"No."

"Sure wasn't going to offer an alternative theory."

"He gave it a shot," Andy said. "He pointed his own crew out to Simmley. Said so, in the letter. Didn't say they were thieves. Just said there were some dangerous people there. Simmley didn't bite."

"Do you think Haig's right? That it's someone in his crew?"

"Maybe. Plenty of contenders there." Andy looked at the skyline. "Matt Roderick is a classic hothead. As you know, Englemann Fiss has been picked over before about his wife's disappearance in Aruba. Jake Valentine doesn't seem dangerous, but he's weak. He'd do what he was told."

"How long are you going to need?" Newler asked.

"There's no way of telling."

"Look," Newler sighed. "It's like I said. I'm not here for the woman and her kid. I'm here for the robberies. There are some big, big open cases which might lend themselves to being solved here. Millions of dollars lost. So I can justify the cost to the bureau of bringing you in and all the off-the-books stuff that'll be required. But I can only do that if you hit pay dirt early on the heists."

Andy didn't answer.

"There's a specific case we're interested in," Newler continued. "Guy's penthouse apartment was robbed in Kips Bay. Looks like the safe was cut from the floor with a tool . . . a Hurst machine. It's like the Jaws of Life. Forensics specified the model used. There was also a fire in the building two floors below this same apartment, only six months earlier."

Andy listened.

"Now the guy, the owner of the apartment"—Newler flicked a hand—"he was some Singaporean gangster asshole. So there was money there. A lot. A headline-making amount, if we can close the case. But it gets better. We think an off-duty cop, Officer Ivan Willstone, ran into the thieves in the side street behind the building as they were loading the safe into a van. They shot him dead."

"Right."

"If I can solve *that* . . ." Newler's eyes glittered. His words trailed away, the enormity of it snuffing them out. Andy didn't need him to finish. She could see it, too. The political glory on offer. "I'll give you anything you need to find those fucking guys that shot that cop."

Andy folded her arms.

"I assume you've made the initial contact. Did Haig say which—"

"Tony."

"Of course. Of course. You're not even in yet." Newler stared at the horizon.

"If you jump too early," Andy warned, "you'll have him on nothing. If you're patient, and smart, I'll give you the crew for the heists, the cop shooting, maybe the mother and child."

Newler's face broke into a smile. "Maybe it'll be Christmas for everyone, and you'll wrap up that murder in Aruba as well."

Andy didn't speak, didn't smile.

"Well. It's a tricky one. Plenty there to tempt you back in." His eyes traveled up her body. "I just wish I'd found something like this earlier. Ten *years*. It's too long."

"Is it?" She knew her lip had twitched as she spoke, and she blazed with anger at herself now. She straightened, shook herself off. "I'll need fifty grand up front."

"Fifty! Jesus!"

"You don't get to question my process," she snapped. "That's what it costs. I need papers. I need an apartment. Clothes. Research. I'm going to have to spend some time with an expert, get myself trained up."

"I can get ten without saying what it's for." Newler shook his head. "But beyond that, the bureau will want to know who I'm working with and what I'm doing."

"Well I guess you'll just have to dip into your personal account," Andy said pleasantly. "Because that's what this is, right? This is personal. The only reason you would bring in a specialist on a case like this is because you want to engineer the story about how it was solved. You'll tell no one I'm involved, take everything that I've gathered at the end of the job, and you'll claim it as your own work. You and a couple of handpicked cronies you let ride on your coattails will look like heroes. You'll be riding the political clout this generates long after you're in the grave."

"Something like that," Newler sighed. "People have done worse things."

"Uh-huh. Including you."

"For fifty fucking grand, I want my *grandkids* riding on the political clout I get from this." A flash of ferocity in his eyes. "This can't fail, okay? So you can't—"

"Oh no." She held a hand up. "No, no, no. Don't use your next breath to tell me you need to babysit me through this."

"Well—"

"I'm not gonna come crawling to you every ten minutes because I'm broke," she said. "I'm not checking in with you at all until this is over, in fact. It's too risky."

"Well that's not going to work for me." Newler shook his head. "I wanted to see you once a week. Like I said. I have to remain involved, even if this is all off the books. You're unpredictable. You're heavy-handed at times. If you want to be smart about this, you'll let me take overwatch, like we did in the old days."

She stood. "Good luck with the next guy."

"All right! All right." Newler pinched his brow. "All right. Jesus. You are . . ."

He looked at her, and Andy stood there with her jaw vise-tight and her eyes lasering through his skull, daring him to give a word to what she was these days. What she had become since the last time they'd been together. There were so many words available, and she could see them dancing on the tip of his tongue. But Newler knew her. The real *her*. So he kept his mouth shut.

"Just be careful," he said.

Andy got in her car and drove away before she did something she'd wanted to do for a decade.

BEN

·

I t was the color changes that told him it was bad. It was a second-due job. Third and Thirty-Seventh. Ben was hauling himself up the stairwell of the apartment block by the rickety wooden handrail, ninety pounds of equipment hanging off him, when he noticed the wallpaper darkening. It was a subtle thing. A slow tanning from white to beige. But he knew as he kept stomping upward that the little blue flowers on the paper were cooking from the heat of the fire on the first floor as surely as if they were in an oven. Soon the wallpaper would peel as the glue reliquefied. Then it would blister like human skin. Then it would burn. The fire was in the walls, which for a place built in the eighties, probably under the Mafia's Concrete Club, meant every soul on the floors above him was in peril.

He split off from the stairwell on the third floor, kicked in an apartment door, and crashed through the home, knocking over a coffee table, trudging clean through a pile of laundry to bust the window out with the handle of his axe. He was on ventilation duty with Jake while Engo and some Ladder 2 guys fought the blaze below. Everybody should have been out, but Ben never counted on that. People ignored alarms. They slept with AirPods or earplugs in. They panicked and huddled into closets or under beds.

Right on cue, he met Jake in the hall, and a frail figure joined their gathering, swimming out of the swamp-thick smoke in his plaid boxer shorts. The old man was carrying a saucepan of water, his thin arm trembling with the effort of holding the pan aloft.

"Fire!" he stammered. He raised a shaky finger toward his own apartment. "I think there's a fire! But I can't—I can't—I can't—I can't see it!"

"Jake." Ben flicked his head. Jakey took the saucepan from the old man's hand and set it down on the carpet, scooped the guy up like a babe in his arms, and started carrying him down the stairs. Two years' extended probation and the kid was still like that. Gentle with civilians. Polite and respectful, even when they were all at risk of being flash-fried to a crisp. But the microsecond it would have taken to bat the saucepan out of the guy's hand instead might have counted for something. Jake would lose that gentleness, Ben supposed, as he trudged on. It would go, the first time he had to punch a woman in the head to knock her out because she was gripping onto a grand piano in a flaming house like it was her child, refusing to leave it behind. If Jake didn't get tired of Matt extending his probie signoff until he was in his goddamn midforties and quit, Jake was going to have to wrestle grown men to stop them climbing into burning cars after their kids. He was going to have to push old ladies off ledges. The tenderness in him would be boiled bone-hard.

On the fourth floor, a woman in a headscarf rushed toward Ben out of nowhere, almost slamming into him. "Come! Come this way, please! We need help!"

"Ah, shit!"

He followed, angry, calling in to the ground team as he went.

"Matt, the fourth floor is crawling with civilians!"

"Well, you're cut off. Second floor is about to flash. So stop venting and start an evac."

Ben stumbled into the dark apartment and went to the nearest window facing north. He looked down and saw Jake handing the old man off to ambulance workers. It was like a concert out there; lights, noise, upturned faces, open mouths. The woman in the scarf was pulling at him. In a bedroom he found another woman crouched in a corner with a bundle in her arms.

"He's not breathing!"

Ben raked his mask off to get a better look. The carpet all around them was steaming. Hot air in his throat. He tried to grab at the baby but the woman twisted away.

"He's not breathing! He's not breathing! Oh my God!"

"Give it to me!" Ben made another swipe at the kid. He'd seen this before. People so desperate for help, they couldn't see that that help was right in front of them. "Give me the kid! Jesus Christ!"

"Mom, give him the baby! He's a fireman!"

"He's not breathing! Help! Help me!"

The woman put the baby on the carpet, started pounding on the bundle with her open hands like she was trying to shove clothes into an overpacked suitcase. Ben grabbed her by the shoulders and threw her aside. The infant's lips were the blue-gray of the ocean.

"Fuck this." He took the child to the window and shoved it open. On either side of him, ladders were accessing other apartments, people crawling down them, aided by firefighters. There was no time. He clicked his radio, tucking the newborn under his arm like a football.

"Matt!"

It was all he needed to say.

The fire chief caught his eye, even from so far below, even through the smoke and mist and light and chaos. Matt tore his gloves off. Ben waited until his boss had gotten into position between two police squad cars, legs set, eyes wide. The women were screaming and begging and clawing at Ben. One of them got her hand up under the collar of his jacket and raked her nails down his neck. The other was hanging off his shoulder. He barely noticed.

Ben held his breath, stepped back, and threw the baby out the window.

The bundle seemed to hang in the air.

The crowd roared—a wave of collective horror.

Matt made the catch.

He accepted the bundle into his chest like a seasoned quarterback.

On the sidewalk, crews from uptown were unrolling the air safety cushion. The ground was awash with yellow and red, men from the crowd emboldened by the baby toss darting in to hold the edges of the cushion alongside the firefighters.

The two women were hugging each other. Ben grabbed the nearest one by the shoulders.

"You're next," he told her.

Microseconds. That's what it all came down to in the end. Ben knelt on the wet sidewalk beside Matt as they worked on the baby, and Ben wondered whether the microseconds Jake had spent putting the saucepan on the floor instead of smacking it out of the old-timer's hand meant that the man had sucked in one more mouthful of smoke than he should have. He wondered whether that breath could have damaged anything inside him. Darkened a corner of his lung tissue, or killed a handful of brain cells. Had Jake made the decision to exchange a microsecond of unnecessary politeness for a day, or an hour, of the old man's life?

Would the microseconds it would have taken Matt to hand the CPR duty on the baby over to the paramedics make the difference between life and death for the child? How long would a handover take? One beat on the tiny chest? Two? Were those the deciding beats on that small, blue, grape-sized heart? Ben didn't know. Once Matt had started resus on the kid, he just kept doing it. Ben held the infant's delicate head in his bare palms, keeping it tilted and safe from the concrete, while Matt pumped the tiny chest with two thumbs. Ben tried not to think about Gabriel's head in his hand, the weight of it as he set the kid down in his bed after he fell asleep on the couch.

He realized he was looking at Matt only when his boss glanced up at him. Lightning passed between them.

Matt worked. His huge hands swaddled the baby's torso, encircling him completely from armpits to hips. There were five people in the huddle around the child: two paramedics, Ben and Matt, and some guy from the crowd who might have been a doctor. Their heads were bent together, now and then touching. Sweat dripped on the kid's onesie. Ben had flashes of memories from when he was a child. Five boys examining a skinned knee. The voices trapped in the hot and humid press of bodies were growling with frustration and urgency.

How long has it been?

Who's got the count?

Come on, buddy. Come on.

You got this, Matt.

Shut up. Shut up. You're distracting him.

You're doing good, Chief. Keep going.

I got the count. It's been four minutes.

Jesus, fuck. Come on, kid. Come onnnnn.

The deciding beat came.

The baby squeaked and vomited foam, arching its back. The eyelids fluttered. The huddle broke. Matt handed the infant to the medic nearest to him, who rushed it to a waiting stretcher. He marched off toward the engine, his head down and his shoulders up. Ben knew better than to follow.

McSorley's was out. So was Plug Uglies. Anywhere that FDNY were known to hang out, because that would bring the inevitable parade of local civilians who had seen the apartment-block fire or heard about it and were now wanting to buy them drinks as payment for inside stories. They wouldn't even ask—they'd send drinks over, and the tall tables would be littered with flat undrunk beers, and husky stockbrokers would be peppering them with stupid questions and wanting selfies. *Did anybody die? How did it start? Who threw the baby?* Offering up their own tales of heroism and terror when a Himalayan salt lamp shorted out and destroyed a patio table.

Matt was sitting across from Ben now on an unlucky wooden stool in some cozy but crowded place off Hudson Street, well out of the zone of the apartment fire, a place too narrow to suit firefighters, who tended to be loud and broad-shouldered. Matt was looking like he'd strangle the next person who asked him anything about anything. Ben didn't even know where they were. There was an Irish flag over the bottle shelf and sawdust on the floor. That's all that counted. He was sitting there looking at his open palm on his lap where the baby's head had lain.

"You need to fuck something," Matt said.

Ben looked over. Glowing embers in Matt's eyes.

"What?"

"*I* need you to fuck something." Matt tapped his chest. "Because you gave me some kinda look while I was working on that baby back there. And the next time you do that I'm gonna knock your teeth in."

"I didn't give you a look."

"Yeah you did." Matt gripped his beer. "It was a look like maybe you were wondering what kind of man I was."

Synapses were snapping in Ben's brain, frantic warnings about the shark in the water, circling beneath him. He slid around on his stool and faced his boss. He needed to focus, shake off the slowness the whiskey had brought into him.

"I wasn't giving you any kind of look, Matt."

The chief said nothing, just glared.

"Or maybe I was looking at you trying to figure out if you were pissed about me throwing the baby out the window." Ben tried to laugh. "Jesus. I just threw a *baby* out a *fucking window*, Matt. I'm recovering here. I'm trying to pan what the fuck I'm going to say when Command hauls my ass over the coals for that."

"You yeeted a baby out a window!" Jake wandered up, hearing the tail end of Ben's words, swinging his arm around Ben's neck. "I still can't believe it!"

"Fuck off, Jake," Ben growled.

Jake fucked off.

"It wasn't that kind of look," Matt said.

"What was it then? You tell me."

"It was a look like maybe you think that me or somebody else on this crew had something to do with Luna and Gabriel being gone."

"Christ, do we have to get into this?"

"If that's what you're thinking, you need to come right out and say it."

"I'm not saying that. I've never said that."

"I didn't kill your goddamn girlfriend, or her boy," Matt said. There were muscles in his jaw pulsing beneath the stubble. "I just spent ten minutes trying to drag a kid back from the light at the end of the tunnel. You think I could kill one?"

"I have never said—"

"I'm tired of you moping around." Matt's eyes flashed under his heavy brow. "Sitting there staring at your hands like you're Lady fucking Macbeth."

"Who?"

"Whatever happened to that woman, wherever she is, it had nothing to do with this crew."

"'That woman'?" Ben told himself to ease off but didn't. "Her name is Luna."

"I know."

"You had her at your house."

"You've been looking at us all weird since she left," Matt said. "There's something in your tone. You keep bringing up Engo's ex, what maybe happened to her. Then I see you staring at me while I'm working on that baby back there."

"You're talking crazy."

"Everybody on that scene was looking at that kid except you."

"I can look at whatever the fuck I want, Matt."

"Luna is gone, Ben. She ran off on you." Matt reached across the table and seized a handful of his shirt, got chest hairs with it. "She. Ran. Off. On. You."

"Okay," Ben replied. Because a guy says what he has to when his leg's in the jaws of a great white. "Okay, Matt."

"Fuck something. Get it out of your system."

"I got it."

The door jangled open. A bunch of twentysomethings rolled loudly in. Ben felt his clean-shaven face and thought about the woman who called herself Andy. It had been a week. She'd not wanted him to expect her, and yet every time a door opened or a phone rang he hopped. Jake seemed to know the frat boys who had just arrived, grinned and went over, shaking hands. The probie had two beers in him by Ben's count. He was half a glass away from being anybody's man.

Engo hooked an arm around Ben's neck. "Don't look now, buddy boy," he sang stomach-ulcer-stink into Ben's face, "but you've got nibbles on the liiiine."

Ben followed his gaze. At the back of the bar, a woman was shooting pool by herself. He didn't recognize her until her eyes lifted from the three ball she was lining up and locked on to his.

Andy.

The beer glass slipped out of Ben's fingers, popped and shattered on the floor.

The bar erupted. Engo slapped his back, hard. "Smooth, man."

"Don't worry." Jakey was tottering back over, handsy, patting Ben's chest like he was comforting a nervous dog. "You're just out of practice, that's all. Don't panic. Nobody panic! We can do this. I can be your wingman. I can—"

"Fuck off, Jakey."

"Order her a cocktail," Jake slurred. He pointed to the chalkboard behind the bar, almost took Engo's head off with his yacht-boom arm. "I know some good ones."

"Don't buy her a drink. Get *her* to buy *you* one. Go over there and make her do it."

"No, no, no, that'll never—"

"It's what they want. They're all feminists now."

"You don't know what you're talking about."

"Both of you get your fucking hands off me." Ben pushed them away. They were like dance moms prepping a toddler for a pageant. "I don't need you to hold my dick."

Ben walked to the back of the bar. Past the douchebag frat boys. Past the music machine. He was stiff-legged, awkward. She didn't look anything like she had when he'd first seen her. She seemed to have spent every second since they'd met working out and starving herself. Her arms were toned and her forearms and hands were veined from lifting. Her hair was black and pulled back into a ponytail over one of those punky shaved undercuts. She looked less like she was going to disembowel a guy in family court now, and more like she was going to hold a guy down and tattoo something on him.

Halfway across the bar Ben wondered if he had been supposed to approach or not. But when he met her eyes, she was smiling at him, head cocked, inviting.

"What is this?" Ben asked. "What are we doing?"

"We're meeting for the first time." Andy stood her pool cue on its end and leaned on it, appreciated him. "Try to look less like you're meeting with your parole officer, will you?"

Ben shielded his eyes. "We—They—Engo and Jakey . . . they think you're trying to pick me up right now."

"I am trying to pick you up right now."

Ben stared at her, uncomprehending.

"So don't blow it," she said. *"Smile."*

Ben breathed, jammed his hands in his pockets, forcing a smile. It ached on his face.

"Great. Now jerk your thumb toward the bar," Andy said. "Like you're asking if you can buy me a drink. Glance at my tits."

"This is crazy."

"Do what you are told." She was smiling, but the words were icy. "Now."

He did. The question came out robotic and flat and stammering. *Would you-would you-would you—* She nodded. He went to the bar and came back with two whiskeys, neat, because that was what his body was screaming for and he couldn't think what to order for her. When he looked back at the crew, Jakey was slapping his palm to his forehead and gesturing madly at the cocktail list. Engo was shaking his head, disappointed.

"We can't do this." Ben leaned in close to Andy, stared unseeing at her breasts like he'd been told to. "I can't pretend you're my . . . my girlfriend, if that's what you're thinking. They'll never believe it."

"You're going to have to make them believe it, Ben," Andy said. "And I said *glance*."

His eyes shot up to hers.

"How else do you think I'm going to help you pin these guys?" She was so close to him now, he felt like his blood was boiling beneath the surface of his skin. "I need to get into your world. Into *their* world. If we're going to find out what happened to Gabriel and Luna, you and me are going to need to be in close quarters *every day*. And telling the crew you've hired a personal trainer isn't going to cut it."

"I expected you to just, you know . . . investigate from the outside."

"That's not the kind of specialist I am."

"But I've had no warning."

"That's the best way to do it," she said. "Now touch me."

Ben could feel Engo's and Jakey's eyes on him. He forced a hand up, stroked his knuckles down the back of her arm.

"Not bad." Andy smiled. "Now tell me a story. Tell me about this." She reached up and touched the scratch on his neck. The mother of the baby, her fingernails under the collar of his jacket. He looked at the ceiling and told the story. Facts only, his brain spinning. She drank her whiskey and hung on his every word.

"Now shrug humbly," she said. "Like it was no big deal."

He did.

"My turn. I'll tell a story. You listen. And would it kill you to laugh at something I say? We're flirting. We're not planning your return to Sing Sing."

"Who the hell *are* you?" he asked. Her hand on the edge of the pool table was right by his. He tried not to flinch when she lifted it and hooked a finger into the hem of his jeans, in the hollow of his hip, right by his dick. "This is what you do? You just come into people's lives and—"

She laughed. He laughed with her. It hurt worse than the smile.

"—pretend to be someone you're not? That's your specialty?"

"Kind of." She gave a cute little shrug. That finger was tracing his body inside his jeans to the small of his back. "Now put a hand on my waist."

"Aren't we moving too fast?"

"It's a one-night stand," she said. "For now."

"What does that mean?"

She kissed him. His reality split. On the one side, his body caught on and did what it was supposed to do; got hard, drew her in, grabbed her ass with one hand and tugged her hips to his and dived deep and tasted her. That half of the moment was fueled by a blessed relief—loneliness and fear and alcohol and memories of Luna. On the other side of his mental divide was a frantic awareness of everything happening around them. Engo and Jakey cheering and being stupid across the bar. Matt burning like a human fireball in the corner while one of the young frat boys talked at him, the rest of the douchebags rumbling around the room like fresh-caught mustangs trying to escape a corral.

She pulled away sharply. It was Matt's voice that did it. Ben looked over, saw the big man was standing, Engo and Jakey crowding one of the douchebags in. They divided the young guy off from his herd as skillfully as hyenas. The hunt was on. Andy was pushing a phone into Ben's ribs, trying to get his attention back.

"Put your number in here," she said. "Before you have to go."

He did, handed the phone back to her. Matt was towering over the douchebag, the stocky, shaven-headed kid with his hands up, trying to back off, finding himself boxed in. Ben went there. The little guy's friends were all standing at the bar, speechless, their beers in their hands. Ben was only thirty-eight. But it seemed like he was remembering a time forgotten, when young men rushed into a fight whether they knew what it was about or not. Ben had been so drunk and angry at the world in his late teens he'd sometimes accidentally rushed into frays without knowing any of the combatants, just so he could get the skin off his knuckles before he went home.

"What's the problem?"

"Listen"—the little shaven-headed guy was wasted but wide-eyed—"I-I-I-I was just trying to tell him; I know who he is."

"So what?" Ben yanked the kid out of the triangle of hyenas. "Fuck off, son."

"My uncle is in the job."

"Great." Ben walked him toward the door. "Nobody cares."

"I just wanted to buy Matt a drink. To-to-to show respect."

"He's got a drink."

"I'm going to the academy next year. I applied."

"Buddy." Ben was gripping the guy's biceps so hard he was bending and twisting to try to loosen it. "I'm telling you. Stop talking. Start walking."

"I didn't mean no offense!"

"I'm warning you."

Engo and Jakey and Matt were at their heels.

"I just want to be a part of it, that's all." The young guy stumbled. Ben righted him. "I want it more than anything. That's why I joined. I've seen

Matt around. I thought if I introduced myself, maybe he'd remember me, and after I've done my training I could be a part of his crew. Some of the old guys told me about him. I know Matt was there on 9/11."

Ben stopped.

The numbers. The kid had said the magic numbers.

All Ben could do then was drop the douchebag and get out of the way. Matt picked the young man up by the shirt like a rag doll and punched him so hard he flew six feet across the room, hit the door like he'd been rammed by a bus. Twenty people in the bar; nobody did a thing. Matt dragged the kid into the street to beat the snot out of him. Ben and Jakey and Engo followed, because that's what you did.

An hour later they were all standing on the corner of the empty block smoking, nobody talking, three-quarters of the crew thinking that maybe the young buff with the hard-on for Matt probably hadn't deserved a four-way beatdown. That buffs, firefighter groupies, had always been a thing, long before 9/11. It was just something that came with the job. But Ben also knew that they had a choice: they could hand out a real beating to someone stupid enough to approach Matt about 9/11 once a year, or they could go softer with someone about it once a month. Putting a guy in the hospital—that was gossipworthy, for guys on the job and members of the public both. While crews around Manhattan were constantly approached by print journalists, podcasters, documentarians, 9/11 truthers, kids doing high school assignments, buffs, and naive tourists and asked about that day, Matt almost never was, because he'd built a reputation. Carefully, deliberately, one overhanded beating at a time.

Ben's phone dinged in his pocket and Engo's eyes lit up like headlights. "Is it her?"

Ben pulled his phone out. "Yeah."

Jakey went to the wall two stores down from the bar and put his hand on the bricks and threw up on the sidewalk. Matt was just standing there on the corner, looking at his hands like Lady fucking Macburnie or whoever the hell it was.

"What does it say?" Engo tried to lean in. "Are there pics?"

"No pics." Ben put his phone back in his pocket. "She just wants to meet. See ya."

"Fifty percent of women in America under the age of thirty report having had a girl-on-girl experience," Engo said.

Ben looked at him. He had no words. A cab was crawling up the block. Ben stuck his arm out and prayed.

"It's true, man. Google it."

ANDY

.

Ben walked into his apartment, turned the corner sharply, and went right to the fridge in the bright kitchen full of hanging plants. He stood drinking a cold beer in the open doorway, staring at nothing, a good thirty seconds passing before he came to himself and thought to get a bottle for her. He brought it over to the table with an awkwardness that was painful to watch.

"Okay, so you're my girlfriend." Ben collapsed into the chair across from Andy. "What now?"

Andy couldn't count how many times over the last fifteen years she'd sat in the apartments and houses of hapless men like this, watching them struggle for purchase while her plan unfolded around them. Ben was wandering in a darkened wood full of land mines, only her hand guiding him along. Men didn't like to be guided.

"Now you tell me everything you know about Luna Denero and her son Gabriel," Andy said. She sipped her beer.

"Look. I'm so tired right now." He rubbed his eyes. "I'm so confused, and so tired."

"Forget that," she said. "Your crew is supposed to believe we're banging each other's brains out tonight. Tomorrow morning, you go in for your shift looking like the walking dead, or you'll blow our story."

"Right." Ben gave his cheeks a slap. "Okay. I get it."

He got up and walked across the stylish but small apartment, slipped a black spiral notebook out from a bookshelf crammed with pretty pottery, overwatered succulents, and paperbacks. He smacked the notebook on the table in front of her. "This is everything I have."

"I've read it."

Ben stared at her.

"I broke in here a week ago, while you were on duty. I came across your notebook in the first hour." She gestured to it. "You've recorded all your efforts to find Luna and Gabriel in your atrocious handwriting, both before and after you tried to get police to take the case seriously. It's all there. The CCTV footage you dug up. The people you spoke to. What they said."

He kept staring. So she threw him a bone.

"It's not bad."

"Who the hell *are* you?"

"We need to get deeper."

"No, wait, back up." Ben sat and pushed his beer aside, tapped the notebook. "You read this? You *broke in* here? You went through our things?"

"Ben," Andy said, "I needed to know that you hadn't done it."

His tight features loosened. He looked baffled. There was blood in his hairline from trying to drag Matt Roderick away from the kid who'd said *those numbers* at the bar. Andy pictured the brawl in the steamy street. "I didn't do it."

"Sure. I believe that now," Andy said. "But I needed to see for myself."

"Why?"

"Because what you're sacrificing to find Luna and Gabriel wasn't enough to convince me."

"It wasn't?" Ben scoffed. There was no humor in it. "I'm going to go to *jail*. I'll be a snitch. Do you have any idea what that's like?"

"Assuming that you are talking about high-level burglaries, with full cooperation and good behavior, I'll be surprised if you see a decade on the inside, Ben. Different story if you'd killed Luna and Gabriel. You'd be looking at life without parole. And for the killing of a small child? You wouldn't last twenty-four hours before another inmate took you out. Not in a New York prison."

Ben was silent. Watchful.

"Why would I do that? Why would I burn my crew just so I could try to get away with something like that?"

"Because it happens. Because trying to get away with it is easier than running. I've seen men throw in their own family members to avoid prison or life on the lam," Andy said. "I've seen men walk the streets, participate in searches, hand out thousands of flyers in the hopes of finding wives and children they know for a fact are rotting in shallow graves in lonely oil fields."

He winced. "So you came here to look at our lives. Rummage around in our stuff. See if I was capable of doing that."

"Yes."

"And what were you looking for, exactly?"

"Broken doorknobs. Holes in the walls. Scary drawings hidden in the mess in Gabriel's bedroom. Evidence that the kid kept a hiding place." She shrugged. "Business cards from women's shelters tucked away in Luna's makeup cases."

He stared at his beer.

"Instead, I found love notes," Andy said. "Saved up in her underwear drawer. Mostly from you to her. Goodbyes while she slept and you went out on night shift. I found Gabriel's hairs behind your headboard. Too curly and fine to be yours or Luna's. You must have let the kid crawl in there when he had nightmares."

Ben shifted in his chair, rubbed his brow so he could hide his eyes.

"I also searched your own apartment in West Harlem, the one you sublet." Andy drank from her beer, stared into it. "Even though you've got a tenant there. I'm thorough."

"So I'm off the hook, then?" he asked.

"You've kept this place like a time capsule. Like you truly believe they'll walk in the door any minute."

"It's still possible," Ben said. His words hung in the air, thin and unconvincing. When he spoke again his voice was thick. "I just want to find my fam—"

Andy kept her face neutral.

"My girlfriend and her boy."

"So help me do my job."

"But I don't know if I can do what you're asking." Ben put his hands out, offering up his wide and callused palms. "I'm not an actor. What we did in that bar tonight? That was me half drunk and making it up as I went. The guys are going to see through us, okay? They know me. They know when I'm acting weird."

"They'll put it off to nerves about the new relationship," Andy said. "And you'll back it up by telling them how nervous you are about the new relationship."

She pulled a slip of paper from her back pocket and pushed it across the table toward him. "This is our text script for the next few days. It's only a couple of days' worth, just to get you started. Establish a tone."

He looked at the paper. Dates, times, little messages. Him and her. The first message would come from him to her later that morning. He'd just woken up. She was gone. He wanted to know if she got home safe. If maybe he could see her again.

"Do not get creative," Andy said. "Text those words. At those times. Nothing else."

"This is crazy. How do you know how to do all this stuff?"

"Practice."

"What if I slip up?"

"You won't slip up," Andy said.

"How do you know?"

"I'm guiding you."

He sat back. Dropped his hands to his lap.

"It's time," Andy said. "Tell me about them. Everything you know. Until the moment they went missing."

BEN

.

He told her everything. About how a hard upbringing in New Jersey and the teachings of her tough-love, old-school Mexican parents had meant Luna Denero didn't fall for the returned-handbag trick. Because she'd gone to sleep every night of her childhood hearing from her father about the kind of things that could happen to a person on the streets of Guanajuato, and from her mother about the same kind of things, only in Sonora. So she wasn't going to let some grinning white boy, some Captain America wannabe, threaten what they'd set up for her. Her parents had worked their way through the US naturalization process like two people crawling on their naked bellies over a desert of broken glass. She had the schooling, the safety, the American dream, and getting it for her put them both in an early grave.

So Ben dropped two grand—two *grand*!—on pottery classes in SoHo because that's what it cost to sit in a rose-gold and pastel studio with a bunch of middle-aged women and learn to turn out misshapen cereal bowls under Luna's mentorship. He hadn't been so out of place in a long time, sitting on the tiny stool with his hairy knees up around his shoulders, his finger calluses dragging lines in the slick mud. Clay water spattered over his sneakers and flecked in his hair. In the class were a Hollywood actress, a retired judge, and a modeling-agency exec, and those ladies were all convinced he was the bodyguard of one of the others.

Luna thought it was hilarious. But it still took him six weeks and twelve soul-destroying pieces of tableware before she agreed to go to coffee with him.

That coffee was a head-spinning, heart-soaring hour of exhilaration, a festival of delights in which Ben knew exactly what to say at all times, made her laugh, made her hang on his every word, told her stories that made her cry and gasp, caught her looking at his ass while he paid for the drinks at the counter. He'd never performed so well on a date in his life, and it was for the simple fact that he'd spent six solid weeks struggling with wiggling, spinning clay and coming up with lines, jokes, stories, questions for her that would show how much he liked her. How carefully he'd been listening to her and watching her, because he knew that okay, maybe some women had a thing about firemen but all women—*all women*—thought being really listened to was sexy as hell.

He'd hoped in the way that kids hope—wishing on stars and pennies and eyelashes—that this magnificent date was his ticket in.

And it was.

He knew it was, because after the coffee date he asked her to come to dinner with him in Chinatown. She came, and walking beside her, his big eyes dazzled by the red lanterns hanging along the street, was the boy Gabriel.

Ben dated Luna and Gabriel. There was no other way of putting it; his efforts to impress Luna turned to ash when Gabriel got tired in the afternoon and turned against him, calling him a meanie, hiding from him behind Luna's skirts, occasionally treating Ben to a full-arm slap upside the head. Luna never sided with Ben against the child, not once, not ever, and he loved that about her so much it made his mind fill up with pain. It was a hurtful sorrow for his boyhood self, at all the losers his mother dragged through the household in those years after his father left, guys who would beat and belittle him or decide to employ new "household rules" his mom wouldn't question. The guys who punished him by making him do push-ups until his arms didn't work, or run laps of the yard in the heat until he passed out. The guys who weren't so creative, who just took their belts off and whupped the shit out of him.

Ben was a willing punching bag for Gabriel, but after a while of gritting his teeth and bearing it, the punching bag became a jungle gym. Then a lounge chair. A cradle. There came rituals. Gabriel couldn't go to sleep until Ben said good night—over the phone or in person or whatever. He couldn't use the apartment block elevator until Ben had cleared it of ghosts.

So Ben became Gabriel's fount of knowledge about the world, his walking encyclopedia. Ben would answer so many questions over the space of a day that his voice became hoarse and his mind tangled and sputtered like old Christmas lights.

And then, six months after he'd met her, Ben was sleeping on his stomach beside Luna in the bed in her big, bright room under the city sunrise. He was practically living there, and he was so accustomed to the sound of Gabe thumping down from own his bed and running up the hall to Luna's bedroom that Ben's stomach braced with pure muscle memory, anticipating the little boy launching himself up onto his back. The kid wriggling and noodling around and talking and playing hiding games between Luna and Ben as they sat up against the pillows and tried to drink coffee without being bumped and spilling it everywhere.

Those were the good days. The days full of light.

Of course, there were problems.

Luna had been eight months pregnant with Gabriel when her ex, Tomas, died, so she was fucked up from trying to welcome one love of her life into the world while she ushered the other one out. Tomas's death had dissolved all the bad things about him, as death did with most people, so Ben was up against the memory of this guy who apparently never got angry or came home drunk or trashed the kitchen. Luna was afraid of getting serious, of losing someone again, of stirring things up with his family, who hadn't been the most comforting people in the world when her ex died. Tomas's family were indeed interested in the kid only as far as they wanted to know who Luna was going to replace Tomas with. They had ideas, and they felt entitled to express them. The separation had been enough. Now this. Luna thought Tomas's people were half convinced she'd given him the cancer. Like she had the power to corrode a guy's esophagus with pure selfishness.

And Ben, in turn, had his complications. His parents were deadbeat junkies, and he'd almost destroyed himself rescuing his kid brother from the clutches of the foster care system when he learned of the boy's existence. Ben was geared to rescue people, because it helped him live out the fantasy of being rescued himself from the violent and chaotic crack house he'd been raised in. Luna didn't want to be rescued. And she didn't need some messed-up guy with fantasies of a perfect family getting confused about whether he actually loved her, or he just wanted to play Mommies and Daddies with somebody.

"She had problems with my half brother, Kenny," Ben said. There were two and a half empty beers on the table. Andy was still cradling her first. "They didn't get along."

"Why?"

Ben waved a hand. "It's complicated."

"And the ex's brother," Andy pressed. "Edgar. She didn't get along with him, either?"

Ben nodded, looked at the glittering skyline.

"He has cartel ties, is that right?"

He didn't seem to hear, was rubbing his eyes furiously.

"Maybe I'm crazy," he said instead. "But you know, I've been a fire-fighter for more than a decade now. I know that every time you want to take a shit, you gotta fill in eighteen goddamn forms and an FDNY lawyer has to sign off on every one. I don't get how you can just decide we're playing this game and I just have to go along with it."

"What part of it don't you understand?" Andy asked.

"Like shouldn't I have signed something? Where's— Who's supervising you and what you're cooking up here?"

She laughed. "Who's *supervising* me?"

"Are you FBI or NYPD?"

"Neither," she said. "I'm freelance."

They stared at each other.

"I was commissioned on this job by a high-ranking official in the FBI," Andy said. "We've worked together before. He used to freelance, too, but he went straight. There were times when he acted as what we call 'over-watch' for me. He supervised, or watched over, me. But this isn't like that. Part of my conditions for accepting the job were that I'm not overseen. He's handled some background paperwork for me and funded this whole thing but that's it."

"So you just get to do whatever you want?"

"It's not a matter of 'getting to.'"

"But where did you train for this? Like, Quantico?"

"No."

"Then where?"

"Nowhere. I'm not official. I'm not on the books."

"That . . ." He balked like he'd encountered a bad smell. "I don't buy that."

"It's not for sale," Andy said. "It's reality. What? You think every major law-enforcement case in this country is solved by the books? By following protocol?" She laughed. "You're delusional."

Ben said nothing.

"Okay. Imagine this. You got a guy in . . . I don't know, Chicago," Andy said. "A lead detective. He picks up a missing-child case. The kid's been gone maybe an hour, two hours, seen getting into a car that's identical to the one belonging to the local kiddie fiddler. The detective picks the guy up, finds he's got scratches on his arms and leaves in his hair. He drags the guy in for all the official stuff. Interview, with the lawyer present. Search of the guy's known addresses. All that time-consuming and barely useful shit. But he turns up nothing. This detective, he feels like the kid is out there somewhere. Alive still, maybe. The clock is ticking. He lets the guy go. Watches him. But he's doing nothing. He's at home watching Cocomelon and eating Pop-Tarts."

Ben was rubbing his stubble, hiding his face in his palms. "I don't know if I really want to hear this."

"The detective's got two options," Andy says. "Bring the guy in. Do all the official stuff again. He could even employ an *official* undercover. Which will take time, and money, and approvals, and forms, and lawyers. Someone who will chitchat with the perp in the holding cells, try to get a disclosure. Or maybe the detective takes the second option. Doesn't bring the guy in at all. Goes off the books, instead. He has someone, a specialist, come in. It might be somebody he already knows, or someone who's recommended to him. The specialist might enter the pedo's home and beat the shit out of him. Take him to a warehouse somewhere and waterboard him until he gives up where the kid is. Now, something like that would completely destroy the detective's case against the perp. But it would get the kid found, wouldn't it? And if nobody ever knew about how things really played out, the detective could reverse-engineer the finding of the kid and take credit for it. He could tell everybody that the perp's story about being waterboarded was complete nonsense."

Ben looked shell-shocked.

"On a longer-term case, say a murder where it's pretty obvious who the suspect is but nobody can prove it, a freelance specialist works in all kinds of ways." Andy shrugged. "They would be free to do all sorts of unsanctioned things that would corrupt an on-the-books job."

"Like what?"

"Like drugs." Andy sipped her beer. "You take drugs as a police undercover and the job goes down the toilet, immediately. All a lawyer has to do is argue that you were inebriated when you heard the guy confess to the crime or say where the body was or whatever."

"What else?"

"You name it." Andy put her beer down and threw her hands up. "Participate in crimes. Beat people. Endanger people. Entrap criminals. Allow them to commit crimes you can fuck them with later. When I get hired for these jobs, I take a good look at them first. Decide how I want to run things. And if I decide I don't like the case, I say no. Sometimes I do that even after I've begun. I walk away. Nobody's going to fire me. Nobody's going to cancel my fucking pension. Sometimes, like if I've been hired privately, the people bringing me in don't want the perp to go to jail. They want other forms of justice."

A coldness came over Ben. His body seemed to stiffen. Andy shrugged, pressed on.

"I can also fuck the suspect if I want. Or fuck his friends. Can't do that on a by-the-book job. It's a big no-no."

Ben nearly spat out his drink. "You've . . . you've fucked suspects to solve crimes?"

"I fuck who I want, when I want." Andy rolled her eyes. "You can put your rosary beads away, Ben."

"And you do the same thing once you have the information that you need," Ben said. "You just . . . reverse-engineer the police finding the kid or the body or . . ."

"You really think *that many* bodies have been found in this country by people out walking their dogs?" Andy asked.

"Don't you get like, annoyed?" Ben cocked his head. "These cops who hire you. They get all the credit for solving the case. You're in and out like a ghost. Nobody ever knows you were there."

"I don't do it for the credit," Andy said. "Half the time, that's the only reason I'm brought in. Because someone wants to save time and money and scoop up all the credit."

"So why do you do it?"

"To find people. To catch bad guys."

Ben shook his head. "This sounds . . ."

"Ben, Ben, Ben." Andy put her hands out. "I hate to break it to you, honey. But the cops, the FBI, the government . . . they *do* this. They just bring people in to *do things* sometimes."

He raised an eyebrow.

"Depending on how corrupt the organization is," Andy said, "sometimes this is their main way of doing things. Think New York in the fifties. Think Washington in the sixties. Think Baltimore in the nineties. A clandestine

undercover operation is pretty pedestrian compared to some of the stuff that
has happened in modern America, Ben."

"But what if it goes wrong?" he said. "Our case. If it goes right, nobody
knows about it. That's the same if it goes wrong, right?"

"Just don't think about that."

"Oh, okay, I just won't think about it." Now he rolled his eyes. "Great
plan."

"Ben—"

"Look. It's three A.M." He got up. "Do you think we would have finished
banging each other's brains out by now?"

She didn't answer, because he was already dumping his beer bottle on
the counter and heading for the shower.

Ten minutes under the steaming faucet, his hands pressed to his face, the
hot water running over the top of his head and down his back. Ben turned
it all over in his mind, the embarrassing incident with Kenny, the last phone
call from Luna's brother-in-law Edgar, the shaken and sick look his girlfriend had given him after both of those interactions. In laying it all out
for Andy in the dining room, Ben had been forced to take into account the
complexities of his connection to Luna. All the moving parts. Because it
was never clearer to him than it was in that moment, that one of the characters that featured in the story he'd just told had stolen Luna and the boy.
But who was it? He felt paralyzed with exhaustion, yet taut with urgency to
get it out. Would the next thing he said reveal to the "specialist" where his
lost family was? Or would it be the thing he said after that? When would
the deciding beat come?

He stepped out of the shower and almost ran into her. She was standing
before the mirror in the small space, raking her hair up into a ponytail, as
naked as he was.

"Jesus!" He covered himself. "What are you *doing*?"

"I'm going to catch a couple of hours here," she said. She bent and
opened the drawer in the vanity and plucked out a still-boxed toothbrush,
clearly aware of exactly where to find one. "I'm tired, too. And if this was
real, I'd probably wait until sunrise to get a cab."

He snatched a towel from the rack and dragged it around his waist.

"I mean why the fuck are you *naked*?"

Andy turned toward him. "Ben." She cocked a hip. "You think we're going to get through the next few weeks without knowing what each other looks like?"

He was staring at the ceiling. "I hadn't thought that far ahead," he said. "But like, surely . . ." He had no words.

"Look at me," she said.

"No. Get out."

"Fucking look at me!"

"Why?"

"Because you need to know about this," she said, gesturing to her arm. He glanced quickly, caught sight of the scar. Big, grisly, a chunk missing from her upper arm on the left-hand side. "You'll need to be able to talk with authority about it. About my tits. My ass. My pussy. Those things might come up in conversation. And if you get it wrong—*if you get any of this wrong, Ben*—it could cost us both our lives."

He stared at his feet, shook his head, had to laugh at the ridiculousness of it all.

"I'm sleeping in that bed with you tonight."

"This doesn't make any sense!"

"It makes perfect sense," she said. "We need to play this *as close to the truth as possible.* At all times. That's how we get away with this, Ben. By playing it out. You have no idea if Engo is going to turn up here, ten minutes from now, and knock on the door. Do you? You have no idea if he'll suddenly drop by, because he went home with a woman from this side of the bridge and he's hoping to catch a ride in to work with you in the morning."

Ben was silent. She had a point. It had happened. Engo was so desperate, he'd driven out of state for pussy. He'd turned up on Ben's doorstep at ludicrous hours for all kinds of reasons over the years—business ideas, religious awakenings. The guy was crazy.

"What are you going to tell him," Andy asked, "when he walks in and finds me on the couch and you in the bed?"

He shook his head, stared at her feet.

"Ben," she said. "Grow the fuck up."

That did it. He lifted his eyes to her. Looked her over, briefly, got an impression. She was hard and lean and there were more scars. He wondered if they were from the job, from gunshots or knife fights or car accidents. He looked at her abs and wondered why she'd done that to herself, why she'd shredded off a good five pounds of fat since he saw her last and worked her body until it was a statue of skin-covered steel. It occurred to him that see-ing her now, naked, unmasked, it was almost as though he knew less about her than when he'd first laid eyes on her. Like she was actively stealing away those few clues he'd been able to scavenge about who the hell she was.

He gave up. Rehung the towel.

She looked him over and then turned back to the mirror and started brushing her teeth.

"Not bad," she said, her words slurred by foam.

In sheer bewilderment, Ben went numbly to the bed and crawled into it. He thought about leaving the lamp on for her, and then didn't. When she slipped in beside him, he lay frozen, turned away from her, watching the lights flicker on the distant apartment blocks. He listened to her breathing, until it slowed and steadied, and then he turned in the glow of the city and watched her sleep.

He peeled his shirt off and dropped it on the wooden bench, stared at it, dazed.

Ben had been on duty for thirty-one hours straight. The shirt was so laden with the evidence of how he'd spent that time that it slithered off the wood and pooled on the floor like some half-liquid, half-fabric creature. There was grease and oil on it from servicing the station engines, piss and shit and disinfectant from scrubbing the station bathrooms. The shirt carried ash and food and extinguisher fluid from a restaurant fire, burned rubber and metal filings from a warehouse explosion, dust and cobwebs from an attic he'd crawled into to free an old man with dementia—the guy had climbed up there to hide from the Viet Cong and scratched the fuck out of Ben's arms as he tried to drag him out. Ben brushed mystery grit from his chest hairs and looked in his locker for a clean shirt to wear home on the B train, but there were none. It was his fourth straight day on rotation.

An alarm sounded, and Ben jolted hard, his body scraping the bottom of the barrel for reactive juice and finding only adrenaline and cortisol and liquid dread. Because as the station's probationary firefighter, if he was in the building and the call came, he was on it. Fuck your thirty-one hours. Ben looked across the locker room and saw that the alarm was just a guy from the medic squad's phone. The stocky firefighter had been napping on the bench and snapped awake at the sound, took the phone off his lap and silenced it.

The adrenaline hit ate up everything Ben had left. He eased himself down on the bench, leaned forward, rested his head against his locker door, and closed his eyes. That was a mistake, and he knew it. The metal was cool and flexible, bent slightly, cradled his brow. He let his shoulders sag. A whole-body shutdown. Ben wondered if he would survive this. It was ten times worse than what they'd done to him as a building-site newbie over in Queens, before he'd found out about his brother and become an instant sorta-dad. Wondering if he would survive being a noob—a probationary—firefighter terrified Ben, because the truth was that he had to survive it, for the kid. But he was reaching malfunction point now. He literally needed to take a minute just to get up the strength to walk out of the goddamn building and he wasn't even six months in.

"Hey!" someone barked.

Ben was on his feet, robotic, the ability to rise coming out of nowhere. He wondered if he'd actually been sleeping, sitting on the bench with his head against his locker like that. The guy in front of him now, a beast of a man, wore the kind of boiled-blood expression that made him think maybe he was.

"Why the fuck are you so tired?"

Ben had never laid eyes on this guy. He'd have remembered. Just the volume of his voice made his eardrums pulse.

"I asked you a question!"

"I just." Ben gestured to his locker. Looked at his filthy shirt on the floor. "I don't know."

"You don't know?"

"I'm the probie." Ben shrugged.

"I didn't ask who you are." The guy edged closer. There were veins in his thick neck that were standing out. They made Ben think about snakes swimming in red milk. "I asked why the fuck you're so tired. Are you moonlighting?"

"What?" Ben laughed. He actually laughed. The sound got choked off pretty quick when the guy cocked his head like a giant killer clown in a bad horror movie. "I'm just coming off my shift, I guess."

"You guess?"

"I'm sorry."

"You're sorry?"

Ben felt delirious.

"How long have you been on duty?"

Someone crossed the back of the locker room, another medic. Eyes wary. Gone in seconds. Ben couldn't signal for help.

"Are you deaf? How. Long. Hav—"

"I pulled a double." Ben wondered if he should put his shirt on. "And then, uh . . . uh . . . Some guy from night watch called in sick."

"So you just came off a triple shift?"

Ben's stomach was hard, ringed with bands of pain.

"Answer the question!"

He couldn't.

The guy walked off. His stride was long, fast, and he was headed right for Chief Warrens's office. Ben jogged up behind him, grabbed the big guy's biceps and got bounced off the wall for his efforts. It was like being bucked off a bull.

"Get the fuck off me, probie."

"Listen, listen, please—" Ben got in front of him. "Sir!" Ben had managed to stop the bull before he broke down the doors to the hall. "Don't. Don't say anything. Please. I need this job. Okay? Okay? I got a kid. My brother. He-he-he's fourteen.

I just got custody. I've only been stationed here three . . . three . . . three . . . three months. I haven't even got my ticket."

"Get out of my way," the big man growled.

"I-I-I—"

"You what?"

"I need—"

"You're so tired you can hardly string a fucking sentence together."

It was true. The words were cascading out of Ben's mouth. Exhaustion and raw terror. The big man barged past him. Suddenly they were in Chief Warrens's office, the lean fire chief rising from behind his desk.

"What the hell?"

"Is this your noob?"

Ben figured he must be dreaming. He was shirtless, wild-eyed, standing in his chief's office. The big guy, who was obviously a chief too from the sheer gall with which he'd thrown open Warrens's door, stood there full-arm pointing at him.

"Matt, what the fuck are you doing here?"

"Forget why I'm here. I just found this probie practically comatose in the locker room." Matt's mean lips flicked spit as he talked. "Are you overworking your pro-bationaries again?"

Wade Warrens's chest inflated. His eyes flicked to Ben, back to Matt.

"What I do with my firefighters is—"

"Oh. Please. Don't say that it's none of my damn business." Matt shifted for-ward, his feet never leaving the ground, a heavyweight boxer edging in for a jab that would drive your eyeball clear through the back of your skull. "Don't you dare say that, Wade. Because the probie is telling me he just worked a triple shift, and I believe him, because the kid's so fucked up he can't even talk right."

"Matt," Wade warned.

"It looks to me like you're pulling the same dangerous shit you were pulling when I was here," Matt said. "Grinding the probies down until they throw up or pass out because you think it's old school. That's not old school, you stupid, small-dicked, no-good son of a bitch. That's the kind of shit that will get somebody killed."

Ben watched the two men, his mind tightroping the edge of reality, thinking about a comic book he saw once where King Kong had a fistfight with a T. rex. He tried to lock in to the moment, to decide if he'd really just heard someone call Wade Warrens "small-dicked."

"Did you just send this kid into the warehouse fire down on Eighth Street?"

"I don't answer to you, Matt."

"You did. Didn't you. You backed up one of your own crew members with this half-bagged little prick."

"Matt, get out of my fucking office!"

"I'm gonna have your badge this time, Wade," Matt said. "That's a promise."

He turned and walked out. Ben just stood there, half naked, dirty, hollow, a plane-crash victim on a deserted beach. Only Matt's voice from the hall could unstick his feet from the sand.

"Catch up, probie!"

Ben followed Matt back to the locker room, pulled another stinking shirt on in the icy, aftershocked, postapocalyptic silence, because he was just guessing what he was supposed to do now, and none of it mattered anyway. Other guys in the station had heard the commotion. Probably every guy. They were watching Ben and Matt unabashedly as Ben packed his bag and then the big man led him out of the station, down the stairs. They went along the street to a Toyota minivan parked with one wheel up on the curb in a no-parking zone yet inexplicably ticketless. Ben climbed into the front passenger seat beside Matt for some reason, scooting his feet down into a pile of kids' toys and take-out containers. Matt was muttering furiously to himself now, fishing in his pocket for his phone, firing off a half-dozen texts, searching in the overstuffed center console for a packet of cigarettes and a lighter, all while somehow pulling off the curb and squealing into the traffic.

". . . old school my ass. Just a bunch of fucking . . . shriveled-dick bitches . . . trying to feel like big men by pushing probies around . . . Noobs! Like you can't make a noob piss his pants just by lookin' at him . . ."

They were on the road. Ben gripped the door handle and tried to figure out how he was going to afford Kenny's school supplies now. Matt fell silent, drove hunched over the wheel, the car ceiling too low for him. The temperature in the vehicle leveled out like a heater had been switched off. Ben figured after they hit Midtown that Matt had forgotten he was sitting there.

He hadn't.

Matt parked the minivan in the driveway of another firehouse. Ben was staring right at Engine 99. Matt reached over and opened the glove compartment, fishing in the detritus there, raining receipts and scraps of paper over Ben's knees. He came out with a piece of paper that had a number already written on it. Slapped that piece of paper into Ben's chest.

"Call that number tomorrow morning," Matt said. "Engo will get your paperwork started."

BEN

.

"Family meeting," Matt said.

Ben turned his phone over on his thigh. His corner of the car went dark. He felt Jakey shift in the seat behind him, heard Engo give a grunt of intrigue. They'd all been sitting in the car down the street from the jewelry store for about fifteen minutes before Matt said the words, but that was routine. Matt would say "family meeting" right in the middle of a shift, and what it meant was to shut up and pay attention because he'd worked out what he was going to say, and it was serious, and he was only going to say it one time.

"We gotta replace Titus," Matt said.

Engo groaned from the seat.

"Shut the fuck up, Engo," Matt said.

"You knew it was coming," Ben agreed.

Ben had been thinking about it, too. About how Matt's size and reputation for sudden violence, and what had happened to him on 9/11, bought the guy a lot of special treatment. Matt's crew were never pulled up on uniform sloppiness, the occasional bout of unshavenness, or the stink of alcohol that came off them on some early-morning shifts after big fires. Nobody seemed to mind that Jake had been a probie well past the nine months he was supposed to take to get signed on, and that Matt was keeping him on low pay and a dog leash just to see how long he could before the kid cracked. The rest of the firehouse staff kept away from Matt's guys, sharing the almost sacred ritual of the firehouse dinner together and generally leaving Matt's crew to do their own thing. Since the accident that took Titus, Matt's crew had been riding without the appropriate number of team members on their engine, initially so that they could enjoy a grief period and then, as the weeks dragged on, because nobody wanted to pressure Matt to replace Titus. That meant they'd ridden short on second-due jobs and on callouts to get cats down from trees, which happened to every crew sometimes. But they'd also done it on the kind of jobs where being shorthanded was illegal and frankly dangerous, like the fabric-store fire. Everybody was waiting for someone from Command to show up and walk into Matt's office and tell him he needed to stop beating around the bush about getting his crew remanned. But that hadn't happened yet. Because whoever's job that was, he had to know he might as well walk in front of a moving freight train as do that.

"It's too late to hire somebody new," Engo said. "We've adapted. In the old days, they used to give you a new guy the next day. None of this 'grieving period' bullshit. That's how they should still do it, if you ask me. Shows you that people are replaceable."

The car fell silent, all of them waiting for Engo to tell a story he'd told a thousand times already.

"We used to have painter's tape on the lockers, you know," Engo said. "Back at the Forty-Second."

"With your names written on in marker," Ben sighed.

"Yeah."

"Because that way, you could just rip the name tag off when a guy died," Ben said. "No point getting a proper nameplate printed up. Bolted on. The painter's tape and the marker was a reminder: A guy could die any day on the job. No one's permanent."

"That's exactly right," Engo said.

"We know, Engo. *We know.*"

"We're all nice and comfy operating as a four-man team now," Engo whined. "Suddenly we're at five guys again? We'll be tripping over our own feet, double-handling everything. It's dangerous is what it is."

Jake braved a contribution. "It'll probably be clunky for a while."

Everybody shouted for Jake to shut up at the same time. Ben thought of dogs barking behind fences.

"There's more," Matt said. "We just got a new job."

"What new job?" Ben looked over. Matt was chewing gum, his jaws popping. Ben could smell the nicotine.

"I'll tell you all at the barbecue Saturday. It'll take some explaining," Matt said. "Point is, right now, we got another guy coming. We keep everything quiet till we figure out if he can be trusted or not. It had to happen. You can't ride short forever."

"Why not? Command can stick it up their asses. They're not gonna tell you, of all people—"

"You're right, they're not." Matt's voice was icy. "But they've sent a good rec. I might as well grab the good guy before someone else gets him."

"Who is he?" Jake asked.

"Just some guy." Matt shrugged.

"Where's he from?"

"Do I look like I give a fuck where he's from, probie?" Matt leaned back and glared at Jakey in the rearview mirror. "You think I sat there on the phone to Command tryin' to find out what kinda soda the guy likes so I can stock the fridge? Jesus!"

"Aww, Lil Jakey wants to know whether the new guy likes his balls tickled while he gets head." The car rocked while Engo leaned over and ribbed Jake. "You just want to make a good first impression, don't you, Jakey-boy?"

Ben turned his phone back over while Engo made dick-sucking noises and Jake fought him off. He was waiting for Andy's next text, trying to make like he wasn't. Their first exchange, which played out exactly as her script had dictated, sat on the screen.

Just woke up, he'd texted. *Where did u go? U get a cab ok?*

Got places to be, baby, she'd texted back. *Fun night though.*

Crazy good.

Next time we can meet closer to your place.

Next time, huh?

His text had gone unanswered, as it was supposed to. Ben guessed it would look like he was waiting all day to hear back, sweating on her hard-to-get act. He wondered if Andy had written the script herself. Whether there were other people behind this. *Fifty goddamn people,* he'd suggested in the diner, the day they met. Had he been right? The idea that there were others; undercover officers, detectives, *specialists,* who knew what he was doing made his stomach plunge. He looked out at the night and saw movement in every shadow. Her text came now, right on time. It made his stomach twist again, in a different way, calling up those old memories of him and Luna texting after they'd first met.

You free Thursday?

He had a minute to respond. He put his thumbs to the keys, waited. A thought came out of nowhere, a thin thread spinning downward from a tangled web of wonderings about what Andy had planned for him on Thursday. He saw her lying naked beside him in the bed, her face turned away, the light falling on her lean throat.

He rubbed his face and shook the thought away. He was past the response time by thirty seconds.

Matt was pulling down his balaclava, getting out of the car. "Phones off, people."

"Wait." Ben typed furiously. "Just a sec."

"Speaking of people getting head." Engo popped his door.

Ben sent his text back to Andy and turned off the phone and hid it under his car seat. He pulled down his balaclava and got out with the crew, fishing in his pocket for his miner's light.

"Was that her?" Engo seemed to be grinning, even in the dark, even through the black wool covering his face. "The chick from last night?"

"Shut up. Get moving," Matt said. "This is a job, not a fucking ice cream social."

ANDY

·

She knelt down on the rubber floor mat in the dark, set the camera on a window seat before her, its enormous lens pointed right at the jewelry store's iron-grilled door. Andy expected Ben and his crew along any second now. Fifteen minutes earlier, when they'd pulled up and parked in a moon-shadowed spot outside an out-of-business pharmacy, Andy had been waiting in the street to snap them. She had good pictures of Matt behind the wheel, a thick arm on the sill. Ben in the front passenger seat, his face lit by his phone screen. She'd had to wait until Engo and Jake got out of the car before she could get them clearly. She captured Jake with the hem of his balaclava still up over his forehead, tucking his platinum-blond ponytail into his collar.

It hadn't taken long for Andy to discover what Ben and the crew had planned. A quick tour around the apartment, even before she'd made contact with the guy, told her he was a thief. The first clue had been the number of tools he owned, many of them having no purpose she could readily discover when surveying his belongings. There were wire strippers, micro-screwdriver sets, worm cameras, magnetized camera tripods. There was a lock-picking kit, not the kind a guy's girlfriend might get him as a joke, but the expensive kind, with well-used hooks and forks. Following Engo for a mere day had given her the location of the jewelry store they were going to hit. The guy had all the subtlety of a brick to the face, practically leaning out his car window to check out the place as he drove by on the way to and from the firehouse.

Tonight, Andy had been following Engo again, knowing exactly where he was going and who he was going to meet. She had taken pictures of the men in the car, then dashed down a service driveway, up and along a fire stairwell to the side door of the gym positioned directly across from the jewelry store. To break into this place, she hadn't needed to take any of the elaborate steps Ben and his crew had employed to get into the store. Some gentle manipulation of the deadbolt at the back, and she was in. Two days earlier, when she'd toured the gym pretending to consider membership, Andy had plotted her path through the gym to avoid being picked up by the cameras, which were mainly positioned to capture members abusing the equipment. When she left, she would pull the door shut behind her and flip the deadbolt. No one would ever know she had been inside.

The crew arrived a full twenty seconds after she got herself set up, and Andy started snapping them again. Her camera stuttered and whirred in the dark. It was Matt who clipped off the padlock on the door grille with a set of bolt cutters. Engo and Ben who pushed the grille aside. Matt who raked the front door lock. Andy assumed Jake had peeled off from the group to keep watch, probably from the rooftop of a building on her side of the street.

As the front door of the jewelry store opened, Andy watched the men pause. This was the critical moment, the first potential failure point in their plan. Andy figured Ben, the known tech-head, had bypassed the store's security system somehow. That move had probably been facilitated by the fabric-store fire two blocks over, which she knew the men had attended. So if whatever Ben had done that night—inserted a bug, rerouted the store's call-out system, whatever—was in full operation, the men's entry now should be soundless. Unremarkable. No flashing lights. No screaming alarms. The men waited. Then at once, they moved. Andy smiled at the professionalism of it. The cleverness. No one but herself and the crew would know the shop had been robbed until the following morning, when the staff arrived to open up.

Andy watched the men enter the store through her lens. They had rolled the grille back across the doorway, and closed the glass door behind themselves, and a less experienced undercover specialist might have had to down tools then. But in her work Andy compromised on nothing, and her lens was the kind that could pick up the individual feathers on pigeons pecking at bread crumbs on the street from the balcony of a fourteenth-floor apartment. She knelt, swiveling gently to adjust her aim, picking off parts of the men through the grille and the glass doors as they raided cabinets. She captured Ben's wide shoulders twisting as he worked a crowbar into the lid of a display case. Engo's mangled three-fingered paw in the silicone glove, heaping necklaces into a black cotton bag. The camera had infrared, but she didn't use it, didn't need to. There was a soft glow inside the store from the headlamps strapped around the men's foreheads, worn over the balaclavas.

Andy saw as she snapped away that the bulb of each lamp had been duct-taped so that only the barest slice of light showed, enough to illuminate their work, but not enough to alert anyone who might pass by on the street.

They'd thought of everything.

She clicked and clicked.

Andy sat back on her haunches in the cool dark of the gym, admiring the crew's many precautions, the contingencies and safeguards that, as she counted them off, began to border on neurotic. The taped-down lights, the balaclavas, the plateless car borrowed or stolen for the specific purpose of driving them to a pre-scouted spot fifty yards down from the jeweler's. Andy felt an affinity for the crew, then. Not an uncomfortable one. She enjoyed taking down clever marks. The challenge thrilled her. She felt that this job was a good match, a meeting of similar minds. Andy, too, was overprepared. Slightly neurotic. Ready for anything.

So she was just as surprised as the men she was watching when the shadowy figures appeared at the front of the jewelry store.

BEN

.

A shape, big and hulking, wandered into Ben's peripheral vision and stopped in the street. His head whipped around, and the shape split and sharpened through the blur of sweat in his eyes. A man and a woman. The guy was digging around in his pocket, the lady was looking down at the ground. Ben had a linen bag in one hand and a velvet display case full of engagement rings in the other.

"What the fuck?" Ben hissed.

Like clockwork, Jakey in the earpiece. "It's okay. It's okay."

"What in the name of *shit* would make you think this is okay?" Matt had appeared from the back room, was beside Ben and assessing the threat. Engo was across the U-shaped display cases, clutching a handful of men's watches. "Who the fuck is that?"

"Dog walkers," Ben said. He watched the man in the moonlight, a pear-shaped, tall guy. The guy pulled a poop bag from his pocket like a black magician's handkerchief and flicked it open. Ben couldn't see the dog behind a parked car. Even as he was saying the words, he didn't believe them. Not for a second. "It's okay. It's just dog walkers."

"I saw them come in," Jake said. "I was waiting to tell you until I had a better—"

"Abort," Matt said. He took the case from Ben's hand and dumped it on the counter. "Now."

Ben did as he was told, headed for the back room. It was Engo who slammed a hand on the rear door before they could get through it.

"Wait, wait, wait." His voice was muffled by the balaclava. "We're flipping out over nothing. We're right here. *We're right here!* Let's just finish this!"

"You see a fucking dog walker in this street at any point in the last four months?" Matt was a huge black cloud choking the air out of the room. "No. You didn't. I know you didn't because I read all your notes. We know every motherfucker who comes in and out of this street, all night and all day."

"It's two A.M.," Ben agreed. "Who's walking their dog at this time of the morning?"

"Night-shift workers."

"Fuck that. We're out."

"Jakey"—Engo touched his earpiece—"you see anybody else out there?"

"There could be a street parade for all I care, I said abort!" Matt seethed. He was saying it, but his feet were planted, and Ben could see why. The boss had cracked the safe while he and Engo raided the front of the store. Not even "cracked it." Just "opened it." They knew the code from the bug Ben had planted, which had coopted the building's CCTV system and fed it to the crew. A year's worth of footage, including that belonging to the camera overseeing the safe as the manager opened and closed it every day.

The safe door was hanging open. Six rows of black velvet boxes, six rows of paperwork, a single chrome-plated revolver.

"There's nobody else out here," Jake said. "There's just the couple. They're walking on. Slowly."

Ben, Engo, and Matt all watched each other, sucking and huffing the same dry, empty air, the safe yawning open, full of uncut stones. Ben felt the need of the men again, the same way he had under the floorboards that night. Matt's child support. Jakey's gambling problem. Whatever the hell Engo spent his money on. He didn't trust them, not then, not any time lately. And this was the worst moment to let their needs decide their next move.

"We're good," Matt said. "Let's load up and move out."

ANDY

.

She took out her phone and dialed, her eye still on the camera, watching the darkened doorway to the back room of the store through which Haig, Roderick, and Fiss had disappeared. When Newler picked up, she knew the answer to her question. He'd connected too fast. She asked it anyway.

"Are you up on Haig and his crew right now?"

There was a pause. Andy ground her back teeth.

"It's an insurance policy," Newler said.

"For *fucksake!*"

Andy was so angry she was momentarily blinded. Green clouds tunneled her vision. She backed off the camera and began dismantling it by feel, her cell phone clamped between her ear and shoulder.

"I'm not an idiot, you know. I looked ahead," Newler said. "Played out the possibilities. I'm thinking: What if Haig didn't murder the woman and her kid? What if his crew didn't, either? What if they had nothing to do with the shooting of Officer Ivan Willstone? What if I've brought you in as an undercover, and you fish around for a few months, and you discover there's nothing here that interests you? You get tired of my shit, and your sudden unceremonious departure spooks the crew. Suddenly I'm fifty grand in the hole and I look like an asshole, because I can't pin anything heavier than a parking ticket on these guys."

"*I'm* gonna spook the crew?" Andy had to tell herself not to scream the words. She shouldered her backpack and blinked away the rage clouds. "You just sent an eyes-on team in as *dog walkers*! What is this, *grade school*?"

"You can insult my tactics all you like. You're the one who didn't notice my team following you this week, or setting up tonight. You haven't noticed the guy I've got planted under a car at the end of the street, have you?"

Andy glanced up at the buildings above her as she exited the back of the gym. She saw no signs of a team overlooking the jewelry-store robbery, but that didn't mean they weren't there.

"This is not what I agreed to," she snarled. "I came into this with you, Tony, with *one condition*. I work alone, and unsupervised!"

"I'm not comfortable with that."

"All right, I'm done." Andy shook her head. "I'm walking."

"You're not gonna walk when you know there's a kid in the mix."

"*Fuck you*, Tony."

"Yeah, yeah."

"What are you gonna do if Jake Valentine spots one of your guys?"

"That's your problem, not mine," Newler laughed.

Andy was so distracted by her own anger, she banged her elbow on a rail of the fire stair on her way to the street. The sound seemed to clang on forever and ever into the night, the pain rattling through her as she held the phone hard against her ear.

"There's another possibility," Newler was saying. "You fall for Haig, or one of his guys, and you let them walk. I need something in hand in case that happens."

Andy gripped the phone so hard she heard the plastic case creaking.

"We both know it's possible," Newler said.

Andy threw the phone against the wall beside her. It shattered in a spray of plastic chunks and splintered glass.

BEN

.

You still good for tonight?

Ben typed the message and hit Send, sat on the couch in the squad room and stared at the screen for a moment or two, in case she came back immediately. He knew she wasn't coming back to him immediately, but he figured it made a good show for Engo, who he could sense was reading his screen over his shoulder. The night before, when Ben had sat with the team in Matt's basement popping stones from their settings, he'd made sure to check the phone a few times for texts from Andy, even though they weren't scheduled. He figured it would convince the guys he was distracted by it, by wanting her and wondering about her. Maybe he wasn't going to be so bad at this whole undercover thing after all.

Truth was, he really hadn't stopped wondering about her. So he was playing it close to the truth, then, he supposed. Like she'd said he should. Not for a second had she left his mind, not since he rolled over the morning after she slept beside him and found her naked figure gone from the bed, no sign of her ever having been there.

He'd slept beside plenty of women in his life without knowing a thing about them, not even their names.

But it had never felt dangerous before.

"No nudes yet?" Engo asked.

Ben turned around on the couch, threw him a look across the squad room. Engo raked his greasy hair behind his ears and sighed.

"Suppose it takes a few days."

Jake was all over his own phone at the end of the couch, chewing his nails, which meant that either he was setting up a feeding frenzy for his loan sharks now that he had some chum to offer, or he was already begging for fronts for new bets. Matt came charging in from the chow room with a plate of pancakes and a giant coffee mug, heading for his office. Matt always came into the building the back way, so he didn't have to pass the

NEVER FORGET memorial and the wall of the fallen. The pictures, the uniforms. Titus Cliffen now last in the row, with his smug smile.

Ben looked back at the end of the couch and saw that Jakey had vanished, the door to the engine bay swinging. Ben remembered those days, when you could hear your chief's footsteps from a mile away, pick them out from the gait of a hundred other men. Matt had rescued Ben from Wade Warrens in his probie days, sure. He'd never docked Ben's pay. Never outright hit him. Never overworked him. But he was an asshole in other ways, because that was the law of the jungle. Back then, Matt had thrown things at him, pushed him over in sewer canals, blasted him about the littlest things in front of other officers. A loose strap. A badge worn crooked. And if there was ever a welfare check and the front windows of the place were crowded with blowflies, Matt sent Ben in.

A car under a bridge with fogged windows and a suicide note on the hood?

Matt sent Ben.

A tent fire in a homeless camp, the crazies fistfighting over whose fault it was?

Matt sent Ben.

It was the rules. It was tradition.

A decade and a half later, Matt's footfall still made Ben a little uneasy.

When the door Matt had charged through flew back open, the uneasiness switched gears into outright dread. Matt pointed right at Ben's face, which didn't help.

"You! Here! Now!"

Ben went. Engo came along, just to watch the fireworks.

When Ben reached the hallway outside the squad room, standing there in the white morning light with her bunker gear uniform on a hanger on her finger was the woman he knew as Andy.

Matt gestured to Andy, his small black predatory eyes glittering at Ben. "What the fuck is this?"

Ben looked at Andy. Her mouth had dropped open and all the color had drained from her cheeks. She let her shoulders slump so that her backpack slid down to one of her wrists, and her bunker jacket wilted on the floor.

Ben gaped, reaching inside himself and coming up with nothing but the truth. "I have no freakin' idea."

"You're Andy Nearland?" Matt asked Andy. He lifted a clipboard, held it up so both Andy and Ben could see. "*You're* the fucking new guy?"

Engo burst into laughter behind Ben, startling him.

Andy's eyes were big and confused. "What are you doing here?" she asked Ben.

"Me? I work here! What are *you* doing here?"

"Andy Nearland." Matt tapped the clipboard hard, still in denial. "Says right here. The new guy's name is Andy Nearland. That's not you. That can't be you."

"It is me." Andy eased a strained sigh. "I'm Andy. Andrea Nearland."

"Did you know about this?" Matt wheeled on Ben.

"What? No!"

"I must be going crazy, because to *me,* she looks a hell of a lot like the broad you picked up at that bar the other night."

"She is," Ben said. They all stood there, the silence cracked only by a huge wheeze from Engo as he sucked in more air to laugh again.

"This is just amazing!" Engo hacked. "Where the hell's Jakey? He's got to see this!"

"Get into my office. Both of you."

Matt stormed down the hall. Andy picked up her things and walked beside Ben, two kids on their way to the principal's office, their mouths tight and minds racing. It was suddenly all making sense to Ben. Why Andy was ripped as all hell. Where she'd been for a week. He looked back and made sure Engo had gone from the hall before he grabbed her biceps.

"You can't do this," he said.

She tugged her arm away. "Don't fucking touch me," she snapped. There was something indignant and unfamiliar in her eyes, like somehow this really was their second meeting ever. "This has nothing to do with you."

"I'm serious," Ben hissed. "You can't work here. You're not a trained firefighter. You'll never pass as one."

"Hurry up!" Matt bellowed from his office, two doors ahead of them. They passed a pair of Ladder 98 guys, who looked Andy over with interest.

They traversed the wall of aftershave and nicotine-gum stink that permeated Matt's office. The giant was sitting behind his steel desk, an angry king trying to decide who he should have beheaded first. Ben sank into a chair. There was sweat running down his temples. Andy looked bloodless.

There was a plate of pancakes and a mug of coffee rapidly cooling on the edge of the desk.

"This is a setup," Matt said. The words made Ben's stomach plunge. That devastating finger lined him up like a shotgun barrel, pointing right between his eyes. "You picked her up on the weekend. You got talking. She told you she needs a job. You made a call to someone in Command."

"That's not true." Ben's mouth was dry as bone. "I didn't even know she was in the job, Matt."

"Don't lie to me."

"You think I know people in Command?"

"You, then." Matt pointed the Finger of Death at Andy. "You set this up."

"I had no idea he worked here." Andy shook her head. "I had no idea he was FD. We didn't talk about that. We didn't *talk* about anything." Her face flushed, a rush of pink that was quickly gone. "Jesus." She held her head. "I don't need this."

"Neither do I." Ben looked at Matt, tried to decide if the big guy was accepting his performance. He was doing it. He was acting. It was all moving so fast, but he was keeping up. He'd been blindsided, and he thanked God Andy had known to do that, because most of the terror and confusion he was feeling right now was real. "Matt, this is not a setup, man. It's a ridiculous fucking coincidence."

"Doesn't matter." Matt pushed the clipboard with Andy's name on it aside. "I don't have couples working together in my crew. Never have. Never will. Shit goes down, and you're trapped somewhere? He'll abandon his post to come get you. I've seen it happen. It's dangerous. It's not how I operate."

Andy was still as a stone now. Ben's chest ached. Neither of them spoke.

"So I'm sorry, *Andy*. Which is a stupid fucking name for a chick, just so you know." Matt shook his head. "But you're not working here. I'm going to put in a call to Command and have you reassigned somewhere else. Vacancies are tight but there'll be a workaround. Go home."

Nobody moved. Andy was staring at a spot on the bottom edge of Matt's desk. Ben didn't know what the plan was. Had never known what the goddamn plan was. He gripped his chair like a guy on a roller coaster waiting for the thing to bottom out at the end of a sickening plunge.

"Ben," Andy said. "Get out."

Ben looked at Matt. In an absurd few seconds of silence, the two men played mental Ping-Pong, trying to figure out if this woman had the authority to order Ben out of Matt's office. Then Andy lifted her head and Ben saw a look in her eyes that could melt marble.

"Get," she said. "Out."

ANDY

.

She waited until the door had closed behind Ben before she spoke. "I *need* this job."

Matt's features softened. Andy didn't know for sure that those were the exact words Ben Haig had spoken to Matt Roderick the day the chief rescued him. But she could guess. Andy had picked through Ben's FDNY personnel file, read between the lines, knew the story. She knew Matt had snatched Ben from the abusive work environment he'd been stuck in under Warrens, and she wanted Matt to remember the day he'd stumbled across Ben now, what a brilliant find the young man had been. She wanted Matt to remember the desperation. The exhaustion. The fury. The righteous vindication he'd felt when Haig began proving himself as an invaluable member of the crew, as both a firefighter and a criminal. She rubbed her face hard with her hands.

"Please, just hear me out."

"No." Matt put a hand up. "Honey, I get it. But you gotta understand: You don't want to be here. You'll get no respect. Most of these guys? They spend every spare minute trying to figure out how to get into the pants of the lady firefighters. We got this one guy Engo who makes life a nightmare for every girl who comes within sniffing distance of him. He's like a terrier humping a table leg. When guys in this job find a way to get what they want from you, the regard for you as, like, a human being? It fucking *swan-dives*. So you'd already be starting from subzero here."

"I get it," Andy said. "But—"

"I ain't finished," Matt growled. "I've got pull around here, okay? So I get to pick my guys. I get to say yes or no to whoever they assign me. That's a privilege I earned." He tapped his meaty chest. "And I run an all-male team. Maybe that makes me a sexist asshole, but I've managed girls before and I'm no good at it. Now there's a station up in the Bronx run by a—"

"I can't be moved again," Andy said. She drew a rattling breath, lifted her chin, defiant but on the edge. "If I'm moved again, I might as well quit."

Matt paused. He'd been about to tear a sticky note off a pad.

"This is my third station in a year," Andy explained. "I'm not from New York. I'm a transfer from San Diego. Hopefully, that's all my file says about my work history. HR said they'd be able to keep my story off the paperwork so that the whole mess didn't follow me out here."

"What 'mess'?"

"There was a . . . a problem. Out in SD." She watched Matt's eyes. "With my station chief."

Seconds passed.

"So," Matt said. "Spit it out."

"Things went bad with me and him. Real bad."

Matt waited.

"Sexually bad."

Matt's brow lowered.

"He wasn't 'on me like a terrier on a table leg,'" Andy said. "He was completely professional. Warm. Friendly. Everybody loved him. Me and the two other females, we were treated very well there. It was a big city place with a good reputation." She pretended to lose herself in the memories. Stared at her feet. "Anyway, the night it happened, I was three years in with this guy. So it was completely out of the blue, both for me and for the people I reported it to."

"What was out of the blue? What happened?"

"Christmas party." Andy tightened her jaw. "I think he put something in my drink. I woke up and tried to fight him. Broke his nose. He told investigators I got drunk and took a swing at him because I wanted a promotion."

Matt massaged his heavy brow. Took a while to find the words. "Well, I'm sorry."

Andy nodded.

"Who is this guy?"

"I'm not gonna say."

"He does all that to you and you won't burn him?" Matt's eyes sparkled with buried rage. "You're crazy. Tell me his name. I'm not askin' ya."

Andy just sat there. More empty seconds. Something changed in Matt's features again, curiosity fighting to the forefront. He reached for the coffee on the edge of the desk.

"Doesn't matter. I can't help you anyway."

"Yes you can," Andy insisted.

"No, I can't."

"Chief, this guy chased me all over San Diego. The investigation came back 'inconclusive,' not 'unfounded,' so he was pissed. I was moved a bunch of times. Every time I settled somewhere, he'd pop back up wanting to have a little chitchat with my boss, chief-to-chief. I was basically run out of town. I've moved to the other side of the goddamn country to get away from this thing, and that won't mean shit if I can't get another job."

Matt drank his coffee. All the fire had gone out of him. He was thinking. Andy let him think. Eventually he shook his head, but it was with regret this time, not disgust.

"I meant what I said about the couples thing." Matt shrugged. "I don't do that. Nobody does that. It gets people killed."

"Look, there's nothing between Ben and me." Andy let desperation creep into her voice, pretending to have seen a mirage of hope on the dark horizon. "You gotta believe me about that. It was a mistake. I just arrived here last Tuesday, okay? The shitty apartment I rented was supposed to be furnished, but it's not, and I'm still fighting it out with the landlord. For the first three nights I was here, I was sleeping on a yoga mat on the goddamn floor. I went out Friday night just so I didn't have to stare at the walls anymore. I saw Ben, and yeah, the idea of sleeping in someone's actual *bed* got the better of me." She let her hands slap down on her thighs, defeated. "It was just supposed to be a one-night stand."

Matt folded his arms.

"I checked with the bartender if the place was a firefighter hangout." Andy huffed. "I Googled, too. This was the last thing I wanted."

"Why didn't Ben tell you he was in the job as soon as you started talking?"

"Probably because he knows that's the biggest turnoff a girl could ever hear."

"It is?" Matt balked. "That's news to me."

"Literally the only thing that's attractive about firefighters is their bodies." Andy sat back in her chair. "You stink too much, drink too much, and spend all your time around toxic males playing hero games. You're shift workers. Jesus."

Matt shook his head.

"Please don't make me go back to HR and tell them that I screwed up the first posting they've managed to get me," Andy begged, "because I went home with one of the crew."

The chief blew out a humorless, disbelieving laugh.

"It's going to get around anyway that you did that. Half the station will know by now. By next week, all of Midtown will."

"I don't care," Andy said. "I'll have money in my bank account by then. I can shake off the reputation with hard work."

Matt cocked his head, appreciated her. "You sure got a bad sign hanging over your head, woman."

"I just need help," Andy pleaded. "*Your* help, Chief."

Matt was quiet. Then the alert tones started, three fast tones that indicated a job had come through. Shouts from the hall. The warbling PA system. Matt stared at Andy, and Andy stared at Matt.

"Ah, fuck it." Matt waved an arm at the door. "Our engine is in bay five."

BEN

·

He watched Andy all the way to the scene, riding in the front with Matt, his eyes locked on the rearview mirror. She'd obviously had some kind of training. Andy had her bunker gear on and her fixtures fastened quicker than he'd ever seen it done, and her hand went automatically to the pussy bar on the ceiling as she hauled herself into the seat behind his, like she'd pulled herself into a fire engine just that way a thousand times in her life already. She sat beside Engo, listening distractedly to whatever he was shouting in her ear, never once meeting Ben's eyes in the mirror. Ben couldn't hear Engo over the siren, but he could guess the older firefighter was giving her the same speech he'd given Titus and Ben and Jakey when they'd joined. Two sales points: First, that Engo was the real alpha on the team and that new members should defer to him on everything.

And second, that you don't talk about September 11 around Matt.

Not for any reason.

Not ever.

Dispatch had been vague about the callout. Male, fifties, trapped in a roof cavity. Ben counted five security cameras as he walked up the steps of the four-story brownstone with potted topiary on the spotless porch. The double doors opened into a foyer with a twenty-foot ceiling that was hung all over with mistletoe. A live Christmas tree sat in a giant pot in the corner, filling the air with the scent of pine.

"What the hell is all this?" Matt said, towering over the small woman who had greeted them at the door. She was dressed in a bloodred skirt suit. Pearls and French-polished nails. She was in her sixties and scowling. "Lady, it's August."

"Not in this household." The woman thrust back her shoulders. "I'm hosting an early celebration with my grandchildren. And I'm afraid, despite my intentions, that things have gone slightly awry."

Ben turned and spotted two children in the room off the foyer, sitting on a chaise lounge. They'd obviously been told to stay put, but to them that meant butts on the seat and nothing else. Every part of the young blond boy and girl seemed to strain toward the door, their eyes bulging from their heads, trying to take in the arrival of the fire crew. The little girl was leaning over so far Ben thought she would topple off the couch.

"My son announced last week that his family will be spending the coming holiday season *alone* this year, in the *Maldives*," the woman was saying. She spotted Engo's paunch and grimaced. "It was my daughter-in-law's choice, of course."

"Sorry to interrupt." Andy raised a gloved palm. "But is there an emergency here or not?"

"I'm getting to that."

"Get there quicker," Matt demanded.

"It's the gentleman I hired to play Santa Claus." The woman twitched indignantly. She raised an unsteady finger toward the roof. "He assured me the chimney was wide enough."

Ben and Andy took the fire stairs in silence to the roof. It was a nice view. To the south, a slice of downtown. To the east, a sliver of the river, storm gray and moving between two other blocks of brownstones. He dumped his gear on the concrete and went to the chimney on the southwest corner. There was a double black iron grille leaning against the chimney stack. Only darkness inside. Andy leaned over beside him and bellowed down the hole, "Saint Nick! You in there?"

The reply was downtrodden and muffled. "Yeah."

"Can you breathe?"

"Yeah."

"I'd tell him to hold tight, but I think he's got it covered," she said, leaning back. Ben watched her dump her own gear bag and unzip it.

"Are you a firefighter?" he asked. She didn't answer, kept unrolling gear. "Hey. I'm talking to you."

"Don't start. We've got a job to do."

"Oh, I'm starting." He grabbed her arm and pulled her up, held her, so she had to face him. "You are not undercover here as a goddamn Walmart checkout girl, Andy. This is life-and-death shit. You can't be doing this."

"Keep your fucking voice down. There's a civilian down that hole and Jake and Engo will be getting set up right underneath us."

"You can't—"

"I can do it, and I am doing it, Ben." She pushed him off. "Jesus. Why do you think it took me a week to come on board this case? Huh? I was retraining, that's why. I was researching and I was training, and I've had better-quality training for this role than you got in the academy, I can tell you that much."

"Who trained you?"

"A guy out in Delaware. You want his number? You want to call him, see if he covered 'Try before you pry' with me?"

"Have you ever done this before?"

"I was on an undercover job maybe five years ago," she said. "The marines. I took the full course at the academy, then served for six months. They were trying to catch a commander for raping a seaman recruit."

Ben squinted at her.

"That set me up for this role in two ways: I got a shitload of firefighter and search-and-rescue training, and I learned how to shed body fat like a fucking cancer patient."

"That was five years ago." Ben shook his head. "Look, I don't care how much experience you have. A lot has changed in half a decade, and you've never served in the department. There's a big difference between putting out fires on a navy ship and putting them out in warehouses and apartment buildings."

She grabbed a flashlight from her vest and flicked it on, shone it down the chimney. Ben just stood there with the warm, heavy breeze stirring his discomfort.

"Who *are* you?"

"You keep asking me that." Andy clicked the flashlight off. She started unrolling rope and tackle from her gear bag. "I don't know what kind of answer you're looking for that you haven't already got. I'm an undercover investigation specialist. People hire me to go places, take up an identity, get deep inside the lives of other people. I dig around. I find stuff out. It's really very simple, Ben."

"Who do you work for?"

"Right now, the FBI. I told you that."

"But other people hire you sometimes?"

"Yes. We've talked about this."

"Were you there the other night?" Ben asked. When she didn't answer, he stepped closer. "At the jewelry store. The dog walkers."

"I wasn't there, Ben."

"You can't bullshit your way through this with me," Ben said. "You said it yourself. We're supposed to be working together. I want to know why you do this. I want to know your real name."

"Ben!" It was her time to stand and take his shoulders. "Wake up, would you? There's a fucking dude dressed like Santa Claus stuck ten feet down a hole." She gestured to the chimney beside him. "Can we talk about this later?"

He didn't get to answer. She went back to the chimney and leaned over and looked in while she clicked the radio on her shoulder.

"Chief, Andy on the roof," she said. "I've got eyes on. He's pretty wedged. All I can see is beard and wig. I'm gonna see if we can get a rig around him and haul him up."

"B Team's good to go here if we have to cut the fucker out," came Engo's voice. *"Looks like the chimney's only single brick with no liner. We can cut through the side and pop him out into the attic."*

"Don't try too hard on the haul up, Andy," Matt said. *"Part of me thinks this rich bitch deserves to spend some money having her chimney repaired, and I know a contractor who might give us a taste."*

"Aye, aye, Matt," Andy said.

"We're ready to make a mess," Engo said.

"Sounds like you're adjusting to the five-man situation with grace and ease, Engo." Matt's voice on the line was crackly.

"Well, it's really only four and a half, right?"

Andy rolled her eyes. She tossed Ben a heap of rope, which he caught against his chest. "It begins," she said.

He stayed the hell away from her for the rest of the shift. It wasn't hard. He guessed she was trying to do the same thing, demonstrating to Matt that "Andy" wasn't going to jeopardize her new job by continuing her thing with him. Ben hid in the storeroom doing the equipment count Matt had threatened to cut his head off if he didn't do a whole three months earlier. He glimpsed Andy now and then. She was covered in a thin sheen of sweat and engine oil, traversing the hall or the bay row with Engo trailing after her.

Jake slipped into the equipment room sometime in the late afternoon and closed the door behind him.

"If you're about to give me a tip on the next jump at Belmont Park: Don't," Ben said.

"I'm not." Jakey sat on a crate of oxygen filters. "I want to know what's going on with the new chick."

"Last I saw she was changing the oil in bay two."

"No, I mean like, you and her." Jake's blue eyes were swimming with good intentions. "How are you gonna be together without Matt finding out?"

"Jake," Ben sighed. "Everybody's going to forget what happened Friday night, me and Andy the fastest of all. Okay? In fact, I think I already forgot. By accident. I was pretty drunk."

"So you're not gonna, you know." He waved a hand. Ben's heart was lightening by the second.

"No, Jake."

"Would you have?" he asked. "If she hadn't ended up being the new guy?"

"I don't know. Maybe."

"You'd been texting."

"Yeah."

"So all that's over now."

"Jake, are you trying to get my permission to go after her?"

"No, no—"

"Because you might have to go toe-to-toe with Engo on that."

"She's not my type."

Ben marked off a row of boxes of gloves he'd just counted. "Then what's your sudden interest in my romantic life? You got a hard-on for me, Jake?"

"I just think, you know, it's sad." He stared at his feet. "Maybe you coulda had something."

"I'll get over it."

"What did you tell her?" Jake said. "About your apartment."

Ben remembered the last time Jake had been there, maybe two weeks earlier, the kid swinging by to drop off a fifty he'd bummed off Ben so he could get phone credit. The quiet dismay in his face when he saw the place was still arranged as it had been when Ben's pseudo-family was there.

"I didn't tell her anything," Ben said. "It didn't come up. Maybe she figured I was married with a kid and they were somewhere else that night."

"What are you *gonna* tell her?" Jake asked.

Ben stopped counting boxes of gloves. He stared at the clipboard in his hand, the numbers in columns, his "atrocious" handwriting.

"The truth," he said. He looked over at the young probie with his Barbie-blond ponytail hanging over his shoulder, his eager, upturned face full of secondhand unrequited angst. "They ran out on me."

ANDY

.

She was sitting at the little table in Ben's kitchen in the dark, tapping away at her laptop, letting the glow of the street and the dim white screen relax her aching muscles as she worked. Andy had known that her first day on the job would be a tough one physically, but the emotional strain was the surprising part. She'd gotten completely swept up in her mask's story about needing a spot on Matt's team, the injustices that had hunted her here to New York, her rock-bottom hunger to start over. She'd spent the day working her ass off around the station, hoping for a callout to a fire so she could demonstrate to Matt that she wasn't just good at puzzle jobs, she was good at real crises, too. That time would come. Now that she was "offstage," and back to being *her,* her mind thrummed the stuttering replay of what she'd said and done. Looking for slips. Holes. Mines. She had to keep pushing it away as she tried to focus on her real mission.

She hit Play on a recording saved on the laptop, an interview she'd already listened to a hundred times.

HAIG: I'm trying to tell you that this is a serious situation. I'm not overre-acting here. I'm living with this woman, okay? We're not just dating. I know her. I know her life. So when I tell you she's actually missing . . . like, she's in danger. You've gotta—

SIMMLEY: See, that's what I'm getting hung up on, Mr. Haig.

HAIG: What?

SIMMLEY: The whole "she's in danger" thing.

HAIG: Why?

SIMMLEY: Because there's absolutely no evidence of that.

HAIG: You're trying to tell me she just dropped her entire life? Her bank accounts, her passport. Gabriel's medications.

SIMMLEY: People do that. It's more common than you think. They get bored of their lives and they up roots and let the wind blow them away.

HAIG: That's not what she did.

SIMMLEY: Look, your version of this? It just doesn't happen. Okay? You're suggesting that she and the kid have been abducted together, and they're maybe dead or being held somewhere. . . . That *doesn't happen.* Now, murders happen, sure. Murders of mothers. Murders of kids. But for them to get picked up and abducted, both of them, by someone they don't know? Something like that is so rare. I mean, it happens once in a generation.

HAIG: But—

SIMMLEY: Your insistence that the case come to me in Homicide was over-the-top, Mr. Haig. And I gotta be honest: That request was only granted because you're a first responder. Joe on the street would have been told to go fuck himself. So now that we've talked this through, I'd like to bump your case back down to Missing Persons until there's evidence of foul play.

HAIG: What if it was someone she knew?

SIMMLEY: Excuse me?

HAIG: You said mothers with kids basically never get grabbed by strangers. But that's not what I think happened here.

SIMMLEY: We've been down that road, Mr. Haig. You said her family have cartel ties. News flash: Half of Mexico has cartel ties.

HAIG: It wasn't her ex's family. They didn't kill her and they didn't send her home.

SIMMLEY: Why are you so sure about that?

HAIG: Because they wouldn't have kept it quiet like this. If they were unhappy that she was knockin' boots and maybe raising his kid with a gringo, they'd have made a show of the whole thing. They'd have kicked the shit out of me and made sure I didn't come looking for her.

SIMMLEY: You seem to know a lot about how bad guys work.

HAIG: Well, I've been around some. I'm still around some. And Luna was, too. You should look into that.

The door to the apartment opened. Ben slid in, carrying a grocery bag against his chest. He yelped when she set her wineglass down with a clink on the tabletop.

"Jesus, fu—" He gripped his chest. "You're like a fucking ghoul, you know that?"

"I hope there's milk in that bag. We're out."

"What are you doing here?" He fished an AirPod out of one ear. "Sitting in the dark like a goddamn serial killer. You heard Matt. He's going to hang us from the town square if we continue this."

"Oh we're going to continue it," Andy said. She picked up her glass and swirled it. "Our lust for each other cannot be extinguished, not by threat of job loss or Death by Matt."

Ben heaved a sigh, kicking open the fridge to load stuff in. "I'll need a minute to get my head straight on this. Because it sounds like you're trying to tell me that we're people who are not having a love affair, who are *pretending* to be people having a love affair, who are *pretending* to be people not having a love affair."

"Sounds straightforward enough to me."

"You didn't have to get onto the crew." He was angry now, throwing things onto the shelves in the fridge. "Being my sudden love interest, that gets you plenty of access to the guys."

"Not *immediately*," Andy said. "Not *today*. Imagine that, we go home together and suddenly I'm picking you up from the station the next afternoon? No. I had to get into your personal life *and* into your work life immediately. Luna and Gabriel are missing, Ben. This is a flash-boil job, not a slow-simmer job. The only way—"

"You can't—"

"The only way to do it," she cut him off, her voice low and full of warning, "was this way. I achieved a lot of things, doing it like this. I had a private conversation with Matt in his office, in which I disclosed some things. I was vulnerable. I showed him that I was in pain. He likes that."

"He *likes* that?" Ben scoffed. "You don't know this guy."

"Yeah, I do. I studied him. I studied you all. I knew he'd flip on his policy about couples if I rolled over and showed him my belly. And making him do that—making him bend his rules because he likes me? That'll come in handy later."

"When? For what?"

"It's better if you don't know."

"I think you're a crazy person." Ben flipped open a cupboard, started shoving boxes onto the shelves. "You're an adrenaline junkie. You enjoy the danger of the undercover work, and you thought you'd up the stakes endangering other people's lives as well. If you had to go undercover as a brain surgeon, would you do that? Would you train for it in Delaware and then start cutting people up?"

Andy just smiled and sipped her wine.

"What could you have possibly gained from being at the station today?"

"I went through all your lockers," Andy said.

Ben paused, a hand on a box of Cheerios, the box half on the shelf.

"I searched Matt's office. I photographed his work diary. I downloaded the contents of his work computer."

Ben put the box on the shelf, shut the cupboard door.

"When?"

"When I was marching around looking busy as all hell."

Ben looked at her.

"I've tried to get into Matt's computer myself." He tapped his chest. "It's password-protected, and the credentials have three security points. You'd have needed to run an algorithm on that for a day, at least, to get the password. Without anyone noticing you were doing it."

"You might be a super computer nerd, Ben, but you're also dumb as a brick sometimes." Andy sighed. "Matt's password is written on a Post-it note stuck to the picture frame to the right of the monitor."

"Well . . . fuck."

"There was nothing of interest on the computer, or in the lockers," Andy said. "I mean, Jake's got a small quantity of ecstasy in his, bagged for distribution. But I assume that's just a favor he begged from someone to pay a loan shark with."

Ben was silent.

"I'm not crazy, Ben," Andy continued. "I'm a specialist. This is what I do. This is my life."

Ben leaned on the counter, worked his brow. "I think my brain is melting."

"So put some ice on it, and while you're at it, put your walking shoes on." She got up and pushed her laptop closed. "We're going out."

They got a cab to East Orange. Ben didn't even ask why. He was slumped into his corner of the seat against the door, an elbow up, chin in his hand. It was a pose she'd seen a million times, one that screamed disconnection. She always hated this part of the case, when her host started pulling away, because it meant she would have to throw him some kind of lure. If Ben decided she was the enemy he would follow his instincts, stray back toward the familiar. His brotherhood of thieves, though untrustworthy, were more predictable than she was. And warmer. And funnier. Andy sighed and glanced at the plexiglass screen in front of her, grimy with the handprints of passengers. She could barely see the driver, who was muttering on a hands-free call in Hindi.

"This time last year I was in Utah," she said.

Ben looked over. She gave him a second to peel himself away from his thoughts and get back in the cab with her.

"Place called Caineville," Andy continued. "Middle of nowhere. Fields. Mountains. Mormons."

"What was the case?"

"There was a rich family there. Good old boys. Bourbon distillers for six generations." Andy watched a group of corner boys suss out the cab as they approached the shadows of the park. "Mom, Dad, two six-foot-tall daughters in the household. Twins. The girls couldn't stop in town for gas without half the male populace falling over themselves to get at them. They were cut out of the same cloth as French fashion models. But even if they were butt-ugly, whoever got the job of husband was going to come into a lot of money. The game was on."

Ben was listening, watching her.

"The father was a known asshole," Andy sighed. "The wife flinched every time he made a sudden movement. He controlled the local law enforcement. The sheriffs. The judges. Everything. One day the wife goes missing. Feeling was that maybe he'd gotten drunk and snapped, killed her by accident. She'd agreed to drive the girls into town, even after the father had said he didn't want them going out at night, what with them getting so much attention and being only sixteen. The wife was last seen dropping the girls off and heading back out of town toward the homestead."

Against the storefronts, Ben was only a silhouette, still as stone. She went on.

"I was called in—"

"By who?"

"The wife's sister," Andy said. "She had money, too, and she wouldn't let it go. I went in as a housekeeper. Without the wife around, the house was a sty. I scrubbed a lot of toilets, and those people paid a lot of money, so that I could bring them home a bag of bones."

"How did she get ahold of you?"

"Cases come to me along a grapevine." Andy shrugged. "A person gets frustrated by police. They think outside the box. Maybe they approach another police department, like you did. Or they speak to a lawyer, or a private investigator. Eventually they find someone who knows someone who knows me."

"Why did you take my case?"

"The bureau is interested to know which heists you were talking about in the letter." Andy turned to him, watched his eyes carefully.

"I never talked about heists."

"Come on, Ben."

He shrugged.

"Specifically," she went on, "the bureau has a hard-on—a huge, rock-solid hard-on—for a crew who robbed a private residence in Kips Bay last year."

Ben's face was unreadable. He stared at the back of the seat in front of him.

"An off-duty police officer got shot," Andy said. "Whoever solves that is going to be swimming in glory for the rest of their lives. It'll open political doors. It'll grease palms all over the city. The case is a year old. It's frozen. If my handler can use me to solve it, he'll be able to pick a political direction and snowplow his way toward it without any resistance whatsoever."

"What does he want to be? Mayor of New York?"

"He wraps this up well enough, he could run for fucking president."

Silence fell between them. The city rolled by.

"I didn't ask you why the bureau took my case," Ben said. "I asked you why *you* took my case."

Andy settled back in her seat. Answers danced on her tongue. How much truth should she give? How much was safe? She needed Ben to keep participating in the job. But she also needed to protect herself. Ben Haig, and his life, spread before her. A deep pit of humanity she could easily fall into.

But the words just came.

"You shouldn't have had to give up your crew," she said carefully. The car rumbled around them, a siren wailed somewhere. But to Andy, the silence was icy. Loaded with dangerous potential. "The police should have taken your concerns seriously. They should have looked for Luna and Gabriel properly."

Ben didn't answer.

"Now you're going to go to jail," Andy said, "your whole crew is, whether I find them or not."

"And you feel sorry for me."

"No." Andy looked at him. "I don't feel sorry for you. You're a thief. You're a criminal. You chose this life. You continue to choose it, every day."

Ben gave a smile. She could see little of it in the passing streetlights, but what there was seemed sad.

"But Luna and Gabriel didn't choose to be some lazy cop's afterthought," she went on.

Another silence fell, but Andy felt a sudden desperation to fill it, because she knew what was coming next and it was too close to the truth. When he started speaking, his words were like hammer blows to her heart.

"Is that what happened to you?" he asked. "Is that why—"

"We're not talking about me."

He nodded, dropped it. A rush of gratitude flooded over her.

"So how much time do we have?" Ben asked.

"For what?"

"Finding them. Before you or your boss get tired of all this and just arrest me. You said it yourself: They're not here for Luna and Gabriel. They're here for the heist where the cop got killed. They could grab me and put me in a room and beat the shit out of me and make me confess to that any time they want. Or they could catch me on something else, make me flip on my crew and point the finger at them for it. I know you were there the other night, watching the jewelry-store job."

"You do, huh?"

"Yeah, Andy, I do," he said. "Because when I asked you about the dog walkers earlier, you didn't say 'What dog walkers?' like any normal person would."

"That wasn't me," Andy said. The words just fell out of her mouth. Fury at Newler, at what had happened between them in the past and the raw, wild ridiculousness that it hadn't changed him at all. Andy had to force her face into a neutral mask, to stop her lips from curling back over her teeth. "It was the agent who hired me. He just wants to make sure you're all stitched up on something in case you try to bail. It won't happen again."

"I'm not gonna bail," Ben said. "I tried to find them, Andy. I did everything I could think of. I fucking begged that cop. I begged him. And now it's come down to this; I can find out what happened, but I've got to pay this price. I've got to give myself up, and my crew up. And I decided I'm going to pay it. Because I have to believe there's a chance they're still alive."

Something in her face must have told him how little hope of that she believed there was. He had been looking at her, but he cut his eyes away, resistant, defiant.

"I have to know. They're my family. *I have to know.* And that's worth going to jail for. It's worth putting everyone in jail for."

"Will it still be worth it, if all I'm bringing you is a bag of bones?"

"Yes."

"What if Matt and the guys are innocent? Will you sacrifice them, just to know?"

Ben paused. Then he nodded.

Andy watched the street roll by. She didn't believe him for a second.

BEN

·

The bar was narrow, dark, spotted with colorful fairy lights strung beneath the countertop and the shelves behind. A little curiosity sparkled in him as to where the hell he was, why she'd brought him there, but his mind was so filled with other questions that a logjam had formed and none of them were coming out. She held his hand and led him in and slid into a little booth lined with sticky red vinyl, set him there and went to order the drinks. He watched her back and tried to imagine her on her knees scrubbing the toilets of some asshole bourbon maker while she tried to pin the guy for murder. He wondered if she'd been scared out there alone in the big house in the dark night, with the crickets, the farmhouses full of barrels and stills, the well-dressed killers. A fox sleeping among the hunting hounds. It made sense now how the hell she slept beside him so soundly that first night in his and Luna's apartment in Dayton, because of course, her work had probably taken her to places where she could well wake to find a shotgun pointed at her face and a drunken good ole boy at the end of it. Or a drug lord. Or a terrorist. He supposed Andy had decided that Ben was a known quantity, once she'd dug around in his life long enough. But at what point had she decided that? What had she seen in his belongings, or in his eyes, that had convinced her?

And was there something on her skin or in her eyes that could make her known to him? Because that was all he had. Her body, sliding into the booth beside him, cuddling into his side. He didn't even know her real name.

"What happened with Engo and his wife in Aruba?" she asked, taking his arm and draping it around herself like a shawl. The question came like a slap, so out of tune with what she was doing physically that he struggled to focus on it.

"Do we have to—" He shifted up.

"Yeah." She held the arm in place. "Because we're out in public. We play it as close to the truth as possible. I told you that." She leaned up and kissed his mouth, and something in him stirred in its sleep. "So. Aruba."

Ben gripped his whiskey. There was a fly drowning in it.

"Nobody knows, exactly. Engo hasn't come right out and said."

"But what do you know?"

"I know he went there on vacation the same week as his ex-wife." He fished the fly out of his drink and gulped some to take the edge off. "She went missing two days after he flew in. You must know that, too. I mean, you would have seen the police reports."

"I want to know what Engo's said about it."

"Look, Engo is a freak," Ben said. "He would play it up like he killed her, just for the . . . the street cred. He wants everybody to think he's a dangerous motherfucker. It's like the thing with his missing fingers. He has all kinds of stories about how he lost those. But the guy used to be a builder before he joined the fire department. He probably just ran over them with a circular saw."

"Have you and the guys asked him about it?"

"Sure." Ben shrugged. "When we get drunk, every now and then. The song will come on. You know the one . . ." He struggled for the tune. Some heavy-metal shit was playing on the box at the back of the bar. "'Aruba, Jamaica . . .'"

Andy nodded.

"He starts dancing, or gets all glassy-eyed, and one of us will say 'Come on. Just tell us.' He's heavy on the suggestions. He was harassing her. Marlene, that is. Calling her day and night. Texting her hundreds of times. Leaving things on her porch. He told me one time he was turning up to her job at Macy's and causing problems, and her boss chased him away. So he went to the guy's house and did some things to scare him."

"What things?"

"He had little kids. Engo just let the guy come home one day and see him in the driveway, talking to the kids. That was enough to get Marlene fired."

Andy was watching him. His arm had slipped down to her ass and was just wedged there between her jeans and the vinyl while she leaned her elbow on the table. They could have been any other couple deep in conversation, maybe about their relationship, maybe about their futures. Not about some maybe-murderous loser, some poor man's Jeffrey Dahmer. Ben had a bad taste in his mouth and the whiskey wasn't clearing it.

"So she takes her savings and books a trip to Aruba with a couple of girlfriends, and he follows her," Ben continues. "Stays in the same resort.

She's going out for early-morning swims, like, just after sunrise. One day she never comes back in."

"You must have accused him," Andy said. "In the beginning, after Luna went missing. Even if Engo has never come right out and said he murdered his ex-wife, he's admitted to stalking a woman."

"I got him drunk." Ben nodded. "Blind drunk, several times. He never changed his story. Never said anything weird. And, I mean, I'd like to think that means he didn't do it. But he never admitted to killing his wife, either, when I questioned him about that. And I'm talking on-the-floor drunk. He'd tell you anything."

"Did you ever ask Jake?"

"Even if Jake was involved, he'd never tell me. Not even drunk."

"Why not?"

"Because he knows I'd kill him."

"What about Matt?"

"I'm not stupid," Ben said. "You ask Matt the time of day and he'll fire-breathe your face right off your skull."

Ben closed his eyes, and took a deep breath. The music was pumping now. He could get right to the edge of a fantasy that he was with Luna, if he tried hard enough. It was a Saturday night, and Gabe was in at his *abuela*'s, and they were at some clean, cute place on the Jersey shore and not some shithole in East Orange of all the places in the world.

"Why are we here?" he asked finally.

And then the reason dropped down right in front of him, onto the other bench seat in the booth, lumping a well-thumbed glass of what smelled like bourbon on the table. Ben looked at Edgar Denero's mean little eyes. Then he turned his gaze from Luna's brother-in-law to Andy, and saw, just for a second, the real her. Before she put the mask on. Before she feigned surprise. She was watching Ben almost apologetically, because she knew—had to know—that what was about to happen would be very, very bad, and she'd been the one to set the whole thing up. She was squeezing his fingers with one hand and feeding him to a rabid dog with the other, just so she could watch how hard the thing bit.

All Ben could do about it all was smile.

Edgar put his elbows on the table and leaned forward, giving a lopsided grin that made Ben's heart ache. That was Gabriel's grin. Ben had never met Luna's ex, but he'd seen pictures, and even as the guy had been wasting away from cancer he'd had that same cheeky slanted mouth. He guessed all the Denero men did.

"Well, look who it is!" Edgar reached across the table and slapped Ben's shoulder. "How you doin', Benny boy?"

Andy was deep in her bewildered and slightly unnerved new girlfriend façade, peeling away from Ben, her eyes big and cautious. "Hey. Who's this?"

"Yeah, Ben, who *is* this?" Edgar gestured to himself. "How the fuck you gonna explain who I am to the new squeeze?"

"She's not the new squeeze," Ben said. It was all he could think to say. Because he was trying to get his head right, to figure out what his story would be, about his missing girlfriend and her kid and her angry brother-in-law. He was suddenly thrust onto a stage, and it was Andy who had thrust him there, and he was so angry about it he could barely speak at all. "She's just a friend."

"Oh! Right! Cool! Sure looked like you were getting friendly, from what I could see from over there." Edgar pointed to the end of the bar, to a dark corner, where an empty stool stood next to a huge Hispanic guy in a plaid shirt. The big guy was watching Ben and Andy and Edgar's table with interest. "Look at you, Ben, making new friends so fast after Luna and Gabriel disappeared. You don't waste any time, do you?"

"'Disappeared'?" Andy shifted away from him on the bench. Searched his eyes with hers, huge and bewildered. "Ben, what's he talking about?"

Ben glanced toward the door. There was another guy there, clearly one of Edgar's friends, leaning against the jamb with his arms crossed. Ben felt the hairs on the back of his neck stand on end. He knew he could take two guys without much of a problem. But three, no. And there might have been others, too. The bar was suddenly full of people, a wash of newcomers trying to find places in the other booths. He felt like they were all watching him. Judging his acting skills.

"Luna and Gabe aren't out of town," Ben said to Andy. "They're missing."

Andy's eyes widened.

"He told you they were out of town? And you went for that?" Edgar threw back the last mouthful of his drink, looking over Andy's body. "Real piece of work you got here, Ben. You two deserve each other."

"Watch it," Ben warned. He gripped the edge of the bench under the table, his knuckles straining and popping with effort. The fear and the fury were warring in his chest, tightening everything. All he was getting from Andy was the scared-girl act, but he looked at her anyway, tried to figure out if she'd planned a way out of this for him. With effort, he reached over and gripped her fingers, tried to get her to feel his desperation. She yanked her hand away.

"What you gonna do about it, white boy?"

"Nothing. We don't need to get into this right now, Ed," Ben said. "We can just leave."

"Let me tell you about this guy." Edgar pointed at Ben's chest. "*This* guy: He comes around my shop the week after Luna and my nephew disappear, and he's wanting to search my place. Talk to my guys. He wants to check out my CCTV. He wants me to go in and give a statement to police. And tonight, I look over and I see this?" He threw his hands at them. "You for real, bro?"

"I'm for real." Ben nodded.

"Amazing. Amazing. Hey, don't get me wrong. I understand. I saw your ass when you came in, honey." Edgar looked at Andy. "Ass like that, I'd fuck you all over the house. Has he fucked you in my nephew's bed yet?"

Ben tried to get up. Andy swept an arm across his chest, forced him down. The drinks rattled on the tabletop. People stared.

"Easy. Easy! Just keep it together." Andy's words were high and tight and her eyes were scared. "Let's just go."

"Where are they, Ben?" Edgar's teeth were locked together. "Did you bury them?"

"Did *you*?" Ben asked. "You're the one who's always bragging about your fucking cartel connections. Did you finally break your cherry, Ed? Or did you puss out again?"

"What the hell are you even talking about?" Andy was gripping his arm, her nails sharp. "Can we just go? Please!"

"Let me tell you about *this* guy," Ben said. "Ed had big cartel dreams. He always wanted to be a gangster. But they had no use for some cheese-dick mechanic from fucking Queens. So one time he's fixing a car and he finds a human tooth under the grille. Sees there's a hit-and-run in the newspaper. He goes groveling to the local scumbags with a tip about where they can get some easy extortion money. You had to beg for a spot, didn't you, Ed? You have to suck any dicks to sweeten the deal?"

The guy by the bar and the one by the door were watching Ben, their eyes hungry. Fuck it. Ben might have been speaking his last words. He was going to make them good ones.

"The cartel gave him an invite." Ben smiled at Ed. "But he wimped out when they asked him to kneecap some guy. Couldn't pull the trigger. Pissed his pants instead."

"We're going." Andy was dragging at him. "Come on."

"That's what I heard, anyway. You piss your pants, Ed?"

"I'm gonna make you piss your pants, you little bitch." Ed was rigid as a rock. "Because I been thinking about you. All that huff and puff you came into the shop with? It blinded me. It blinded me to the fact that it might have been *you*, man. I remembered that Luna had called me, maybe two weeks before she went missing. Wanted to see if I could get her a gun for a friend."

Ben felt Andy freeze beside him. All the sound in the bar drained away.

"Maybe the gun wasn't for a friend," Ed said. "Maybe it was for her."

The guy from the door was there, reaching right over the top of Andy to grab hold of Ben's shirt.

Ben let him drag him up, and Andy let herself be knocked to the floor, and then the two of them were being shoved out of the door of the bar and off the stage.

ANDY

.

He'd been in a few fights in his life, that much had been clear long before Andy ever met Benjamin Haig, when all he was to her was an outline of a person, a bare sketch. Child Protective Services records showed that every time they removed Ben from his parents and placed him in a group or family home with other boys, the placement didn't last. The kid fought. The care workers, and probably a handful of well-meaning defense lawyers, had managed to keep Ben's criminal record clean until he was twenty-one. But then came the litany of bumped-down and pled-down assaults, batteries, angry scraps. Always in bars. The booze weakened the chains that locked up the animals inside Ben. The assaults stopped a week before Ben filed for custody of his younger brother, Kenny.

Andy did the screaming, crying girlfriend dance, struggling and twisting in the door guy's arms. But what she was really doing in the alleyway beside the bar in East Orange was carefully watching a skilled combatant fight for his life. Ben let himself be led into the dark behind the dumpsters with his hands up and his palms out, one biceps in Ed's hand and the other in the biggest thug's death grip. He made like he was still hoping to talk his way out of it all, and the strategy earned him the first swing. Ben smashed an elbow into the giant's nose and shoved him against the bricks, turned and donkey-kicked Ed Denero in the stomach, folded him in half. Then Ed locked him up in a tight grapple, and the giant recovered too quickly, and Ben was in a headlock, long seconds passing while Ed pounded his ribs. They picked him up and dumped him on the wet concrete like trash. He balled up against the kicks, waited, struck out again at just the right moment, sent the giant's knee sideways at a sickening angle and then rolled and popped up onto his feet, his tread light, fists up. Ed tried for a wild haymaker and Ben broke his nose. Except he made the mistake of coming in too close to deliver a shot to the ribs, and Ed came out of nowhere with a broken bottle scooped off the alleyway floor.

Mistakes and triumphs. Grunts and cries. Ben fought dirty; gouged eyes, used the glass, the walls, the concrete, the edge of the dumpster. Ed gave up and the guy who was holding Andy went in, but by now he'd watched Ben in action and was half-hearted and nervy about it, took a few swings and seemed to bend with relief to Andy's screaming that she was gonna call the cops.

When it was all over, Ben was sitting against the wall catching his breath and bleeding from a big gash in his forehead, and Andy was watching Ed and the door guy try to heave the semiconscious giant into a car across the street. She wasn't ready for the cold, dark fury in Ben's eyes when she came over. She offered a hand and he ignored it, turned and spat blood on the ground.

"Oh come on." She sat down beside him in the muck and blood and glass on the alleyway floor. "What did you want me to do? Go to Edgar's shop? 'Hi, I'm Ben's new girlfriend and I have a few questions, if you don't mind.'"

"Fuck off, Andy," Ben said.

"You saw that reaction. Edgar Denero could well have ignored the two of us just now. If he and his cartel buddies had had anything to do with Luna's disappearance, it would have been a relief to see you moving on with someone else."

"So you used me as bait?" Ben asked.

"Luna and Gabe are missing, Ben," Andy said. "I need to use my time wisely. This was the fastest way to see if I needed to focus any of my time on Ed Denero and his crew. I knew he had a share in this place." She gestured to the bar. "And that he'd be here tonight. So I ran a little experiment."

Ben didn't answer. He was holding his ribs, which were probably cracked. Andy reached over, and the gesture made her freeze. They were alone. There was no acting now. Yet she'd found herself reaching out to put a hand on his arm. He hadn't noticed, was trying to get to his feet. The blood was running down his neck and into his T-shirt.

"Luna needed a gun, just two weeks before she went missing," Andy said. She followed Ben to the mouth of the alley. "Come on. Let's go home. We need to search the apartment again, and see if she managed to get one. See if it's there."

Ben turned to her, the pink neon sign outside the bar making the blood on his face a whimsical, heavy purple.

"Andy," Ben said. "Fuck. Off."

She decided to walk for a while before getting a cab, took some ugly road away from the bar, trading in the stink of gas stations and a twenty-four-hour KFC for the bright lights and the directness back toward home. Andy wasn't afraid of walking in the dark, but she wanted to drift into her own thoughts rather than having to keep alert for anyone who might dare to bother her. She was thinking about what might drive Luna Denero to try to acquire a gun. She was the mother of a small, handsy, curious child. And she had a big, capable, and apparently doting fireman in her household, a man who was familiar with protective violence. A gun in the house had apparently seemed unnecessary to Luna, at least to protect from danger coming from outside that house. What had changed her mind? Had something happened? Indeed, was Edgar Denero's idea that the gun had been to protect Luna from something *inside* the house, from Haig himself, valid?

Andy walked in the soapy, rainbow-streaked soup drizzling down the driveway of a car wash. Branch Brook Park spread its arms slowly before her as she approached. She decided she would stop on the edge of the park and get a cab to the street where Luna had vanished.

Haig had done a good job narrowing down the CCTV footage of Luna traveling along Washington Avenue in Dayton, heading for her ex's mother's house to drop Gabriel off. Haig had gone door-to-door along Washington, noting down the names and statements of every shopkeeper, cabdriver, homeless person, and bystander he spoke to, what they had to say about the night Luna went missing, what they saw. No one had anything useful. They hadn't noticed the car, the woman, the kid, anything out of the ordinary. Luna's car had entered Washington Avenue and gone by a liquor store at 7:12 that night, was captured briefly on the storefront's CCTV. She would presumably have driven by a row of cafés and boutique clothing stores, a Best Western hotel, an apartment block. But her car had then failed to appear on the CCTV Ben had managed to track down at the end of Washington Ave., where it met Hansel. That whole intersection was covered by a camera fitted at the front of a furniture store. Luna's car went into Washington, and it never appeared to leave.

Haig was convinced, it seemed, from the amount of notebook space he'd devoted to Washington and what had happened to Luna's car, that this was where the incident that stole her and her son out of his world occurred. It made sense. Luna drove into the street. Never drove back out. Andy hadn't told the man so, but she knew things weren't as cut-and-dried as all that. There were plenty of variables, because CCTV cameras weren't magical windows to the absolute truth. They were operated by humans, and humans made mistakes. They wired them wrong, angled them wrong, entered their setup data wrong, rendering time and date stamps obsolete. And, sure, it *looked* like it was Luna's car slowly rolling through the channel of parked cars on either side of the road on one-way Washington that fateful night. It made sense for her to have been there at that time. But it was possible the car *wasn't* hers, just an identical one belonging to someone else. The plate wasn't visible in the video, and coincidences happened.

Andy was going to go there anyway, walk the street herself, take a measure of the place.

Then her phone rang in her pocket.

"You see the report?" Newler said in greeting.

Andy bit back a string of vitriol. It took her a minute. "How did you get this number?"

"The jewelry-store owner's reported nine hundred k in losses. There were uncut diamonds in the safe, which account for about half of it," Newler said. "Those guys are smart, you know. They took a bunch of shit they're never going to bother moving. The watches and the engraved pieces, all the traceable stuff. Makes it look like amateurs hit the store and got lucky with the safe being left open or whatever."

"Newler," Andy said. "I asked you a question."

"And I don't have time for dumbass questions, *Andy*, or whatever it is at the moment." He gave a soft chuckle. "You think I can't get your number?"

"Have you thought about what'll happen if one of them gets ahold of this phone?" Andy's teeth ached. "You are jeopardizing my safety."

"You don't seem to be getting it," Newler said. "I have to stay on top of you. Because I know what you're like. You'll puddle around in this thing with the crew looking for the bodies of some woman and her kid, when there are—there are *real goods* on the table here."

"Real 'goods'?"

"I've looked into this whole thing now. I think that I can tie Matt

Roderick's crew to some of the biggest hits in New York City in the last ten years." She could hear the excitement reverberating in his voice. "I've got my researchers on it. We've got about five major, *major* heists that we're looking closely at. There were fires or evacuation-level emergencies in and around these premises in the months before they were robbed. Some of them, Matt's crew responded. Some of them, they're not on the books, but they may have been offering support. 'Second due,' they call it. And all that? That's *beyond* the murder of the cop, Andy."

"'The cop'?"

"Willner."

"It's Willstone, you fucking psychopath." Andy tried to breathe, tried to rein in the fury. "You sound like a kid listing off what you want for Christmas. You're so excited about what this case could do for you, you can't see that there are human lives involved in it; one of them mine."

"Don't try to sell me a sob story on it," Newler said. "I know you. The real you."

Andy said nothing.

"These guys have stolen from powerful families, okay? *Politically connected* families. You love these kinds of cases, where everything and anything is at stake."

Andy had entered the park. She was walking in the blackness between streetlamps shrouded in foliage. Green and gold, black water moving soundlessly beneath a concrete bridge.

"You're thinking about it, aren't you? The power. The possibilities."

"No," Andy responded.

"You tell me you're on this case because of the people, the kid, the human lives," Newler said. "But I've always been able to read the writing on the wall with you. I got your message loud and clear when you chose your mask."

"What?"

"'Nearland,'" he said. "Andy Nearland. Near. Land. You're trying to come home. You've been out in the cold, black, windy sea and you're finally near to land, and you want to come in. It's okay to say that to me. I'm not going to throw up everything we've been through. You can come home."

She had to laugh out loud at that one. "Jesus, Tony. Listen to yourself."

"Tell me I'm wrong."

She lifted her face to the night, gave an angry laugh. "Right now, I'm trying to tell *myself* not to walk away from this case," she said. "Because I really want to find Luna and her son. But I also really want to fuck you and your political aspirations and your dreams of me coming home, Tony. I want to leave you standing there with nothing but your shriveled little balls to put on a plate when these powerful people come to dinner."

The silence on the line was deep, suffocating. For a second she held the phone and her own breath and braced for his rage.

"You could have had all this," Newler said. "I offered it to you. You turned it down so you could play cops and robbers with the lowest forms of life you could find. I don't get it, you know that? I just don't *get it. I don't fucking get it!*"

His screaming made the line crackle. She pulled the phone away from her ear, reconnected with the night. A homeless guy on a thin, rusty racing bike was approaching, rolling across the bridge. The bike was saddled on either side with grayed fabric bags stuffed with belongings. The basket on the handlebars, also stuffed with items, was adorned with a cardboard sign. GOD BLESS. Andy listened to the radio blasting from the basket as he approached and passed. The beat rising, cresting, falling away. Kesha's "Blow."

"I'm going to save you," Newler was saying when she raised the phone again. He'd taken control of himself, just barely. "I'm going to stop you punishing yourself like this and bring you back, if it takes everything that I have in me, Da—"

"Don't!"

Andy stopped. She was shaking all over suddenly, a shudder that didn't end.

"You don't get to call me that name," she spat.

In the background of the call, she heard Kesha's "Blow."

She turned, looked back into the woods on the other side of the bridge, toward where the cyclist had disappeared. Streetlamps, pockets of gold light in the blackness. Nothing moved.

BEN

·

ndy arrived about a minute and a half after he did. Must have been out there, waiting for him to get there, timing it perfectly. Ben guessed that it was supposed to be a dead giveaway to Matt and everybody at the house that Ben had given her a lift in his car most of the way and she'd pretended to walk from the Oyster Bay station. Donna was still making a performance about his face, trying to get ahold of his head to look at the stitches. All Matt's wives had been tiny little ladies, probably chosen in the hopes that he'd have a normal-sized kid one day, so to get a good look Donna was either going to have to drag Ben's head right down against her ballooning belly or pin it against the enormous kitchen island. So he resisted as much as he could. Matt was nearby in a struggling Hawaiian shirt, the only person who seemed like he fit properly in the room. He made the high ceilings and the triple fridge look appropriate.

"Doesn't matter, doesn't matter." Donna was waving at Engo and Matt. "The guys'll get them. Dirty motherfuckers, bashing up my Benji. Matt will take the guys down there this afternoon and find 'em. The local cops will know who the bastards are."

"You kiddin'? Forget that. This afternoon I'm gonna be asleep." Matt pointed at the leather lounge, which was the size of a limousine. "On that couch. In front of the baseball. You let yourself get jumped, Ben, that's your problem. It's not gonna ruin my day off."

"He'll get 'em, Benji, don't worry."

"I keep telling you, there's no 'getting' to do." Ben took Donna's hand down from where it was stroking his hair. "I got them already."

"Sure you did." Engo joined in the hair-stroking. "Shhh."

"Get off me, you prick."

Then the front door opened and Andy walked in. She was wearing a black linen off-the-shoulder dress and sandals, and she'd swept her inky hair up so that it piled on top of her head like a bundle of glossy ribbons, showing the shaved under-bit. Donna squealed when she saw her. Matt and Engo exchanged a look, probably about the timing.

"Is this the new guy?" Donna waddled over with an arm around her pregnant belly like the baby might fall out of her skirts any second if she let go. She thrust her other arm out to hug Andy. "Oh my God! Hi! I'm Donna! I'm Matt's wife!"

"Hey." Andy gave her the awkward cautious hug people give pregnant women and showed a palm to the semicircle of men. "Hey. Where's Jake?"

"Mowing the lawn."

"What? You got Jakey out mowing our lawn?" Donna looked toward the double doors Andy had come through.

"I told him to do the neighbors' first."

"Matt!"

"He's the fucking probie, Donna. That's how it works. He wants to drink with my family in my house he earns it." Matt hadn't taken his eyes off Andy. "More importantly, why aren't *you* looking at *him*?"

The question split the air. Everyone was still. Matt had one Finger of Death poked into Ben's biceps, the other pointed straight out from his beer bottle at Andy's face.

Andy looked from Matt to Ben.

"Why aren't I *looking* at him?"

"He's beat to shit." Matt jabbed Ben with his finger again. "You spotted it when you walked in. No surprise on your face. None. You come in and you say nothing at all about it. And now you won't look at him."

"I'm looking at him right now."

"No, you're not."

"Matt! Stop it! You're being weird!" Donna said.

"Well, I mean, I just . . ." Andy feigned helplessness. Ben watched her mouth working, trying to form words. "I-I-I don't know. I guess I was gonna ask what happened. Like, eventually."

"After you found out where Jake was?" Matt said.

"Uh, yeah?"

"You wanted to know where Jake was more than you wanted to know why—"

"I mean—"

"You were there," Matt said. "Weren't you?"

"I was where?"

"On the scene. When it happened. That's why you weren't surprised."

"No. No. No."

"So you're telling me you walk into a room and Ben's standing there looking like he just got scraped out of the wheel well of a Mac truck and you don't say 'Ho! What the fuck happened to you'? You say 'Where's Jake'?" Matt's neck and chest were the color of raw steak. He turned to Ben. "She was there. You two hooked up last night."

"We didn't—" Ben began.

"We just had a drink. One drink!" Andy put her hands up in surrender. "I mean, we-we-we had to talk about it. Right? We had to talk about the game plan. How we're gonna work together and not, you know . . . *You know.* Be together."

"It's simple!" Matt barked. *"You start by not being together!"*

"Matt! Jesus!" Donna slapped his hand down from Ben's biceps. "Calm down! Everybody's trying to have a good time! You're stressing me out!"

Engo had worked his way around the circle to Andy's side. Ben hadn't noticed, until the guy stroked his hand up the back of Andy's arm in a way that gave her a full-body shudder.

"Is that how you got these bruises?" Engo murmured. "Did they hold you down?"

"No. I didn't see him get jumped." Andy moved away from Engo. "He went out to the alley to have a cigarette. I was inside. Can we move on?"

"Yes, we can." Donna shot Matt a warning look that could have killed a horse. "What are you drinking, Andy? Wine? Scotch?"

Ben tried to get away from her. They fell into the usual Saturday-at-Matt's thing: Engo and Matt arguing about the barbecue, Matt's two teenage daughters from his second marriage taking selfies by the pool. Ben went over and had an awkward, one-sided chat with the girls for a little while because that's what you did, knowing they'd fade out on him eventually and he'd be off the hook. Somewhere beyond the fences in the painfully sunny suburban wonderland of Long Island the sound of a Weedwacker told him Jakey was halfway through earning his first beer of the day.

Ben was sitting on an outdoor lounge chair messing around on his phone when he overheard Andy and Matt coming together in the sliding glass doorway to the kitchen. She'd escaped Donna's clutches and was probably headed for him, but he didn't look up. Kept his eyes on his phone and his ears pricked.

"Matt, listen."

"What?"

Ben heard Andy give a stressed sigh. Her voice was low. "There really isn't anything going on with Ben and me."

"Oh, wonderful. Good to know. I'll sleep easy."

"I know you bent your own rules to bring me on, and I'm not going to take that for granted."

"You're sure as shit not gonna take it for granted." Matt's words were sharp but his tone had softened. Donna must have been watching. "Because it's not granted. Not one bit. I get wind you're up to anything that's going to put my crew in danger, and I'll fire your ass so fast your kids'll have scorch marks. You're the new guy. You get that? That makes you one shade above a probie to me."

"Right. I got it."

"Now get out of my face before I make you wash my car."

She came and sat beside Ben on the adjacent lounge chair, turned toward him, wary eyes watching Matt and Donna through the big doors.

"Having fun?" Ben asked.

"Don't move. I'm gonna slip two things into your hand," Andy murmured. "Put them in your pocket."

"What are they?"

Andy put her bag on the floor at her feet and reached in, fished around and came out with a big pair of sunglasses. On her way back up she tucked two tiny objects into Ben's palm, which was curled on the edge of the chair.

"One's a button camera, and one's a GPS tracker," Andy said. Her voice was light. She settled in the chair, an arm up behind her head, watching the girls by the pool. "The button camera you're going to put on your shirt and wear into the room when Matt takes you to split your jewelry-store cut. I assume that'll happen today."

Ben had to force his mouth not to sneer. "I'm not wearing a fucking wire, Andy."

"It's not a wire."

"If they find me with something like that, they'll kill me," Ben said. The tiny items in his clenched hand were heating up, becoming soaked in sweat, but he didn't dare pocket them. "And then they'll kill you. Because I'll give you up in a goddamn heartbeat, just the way you did to me last night."

"Wow, sounds messy." Andy grinned at him, reached over and clinked his drink with hers. "I guess you better not get caught, huh."

"What's the tracker for?"

"I don't know," Andy said. "You might just find an opportunity that I haven't uncovered yet. I've already tagged Matt and Donna's cars on the way up the driveway. I got Engo's car last week. Jake's motorcycle is a bit trickier. He washes it by hand. Very thoroughly. I might have to secret one into the foam padding inside his helmet."

They sat in silence. Somewhere, a leaf blower was powering down.

"If one of these guys killed Luna and Gabriel," Andy said carefully, "they may visit the bodies. Or if they're being held somewhere—"

Ben pocketed the items and held a hand up. They watched Engo hanging over the pool fence, talking to Matt's daughters. The two girls were recoiled on their towels, their legs tucked under and their mouths downturned.

"Did you ever get the sense Luna knew what was going on with your crew?" Andy asked. "Finding out, getting nervous that she knew too much and the guys were going to come for her . . . It might have inspired her to go to Edgar and ask for a gun."

Ben shrugged.

"How did she react when Titus Cliffen died?"

"What do you mean?"

Andy smiled at him. In his reflection in her sunglasses, Ben could see himself. The grief stubble was making a resurgence. He rubbed his face.

"You think Titus found out what we were doing." Ben nodded, trying to keep his face light even as his head filled with darkness. "So we rubbed him out?"

"He was only on your crew for four months," Andy said. "Then he falls through the floor of a burning bike store and is killed instantly. The accident-investigation team opens and shuts the case with zero complications in forty-eight hours. No one on your crew takes any grief time. No one goes to the funeral. I read the reports, Ben. Matt had decided to give you a little impromptu training session in active command on the street that night. He and Engo and Jake went in with Titus. Did Matt keep you out of the loop deliberately, because he considers you to be the bleeding heart of the crew? Or did you okay the hit, as long as you didn't have to do the dirty work?"

"Matt lets me have street command sometimes if he's bored or he just wants to go in. He's been doing that for a year or so, okay? The guy has to retire one day, and Engo is too wild to take over Engine 99. You'd know that if you read all the reports, not just cherry-picked the ones that make us look like a pack of killers," Ben said. The words felt like pieces of glass sliding up his throat. "What happened to Titus wasn't a setup. They didn't kill him."

"So why not go to the funeral?"

"Nobody went to the funeral because the family wanted to do their own thing. And yeah, nobody took any time off, because Titus was a jerk."

He looked Andy square in the sunglasses.

"He was a college-educated prick who wanted to lecture us all the time on politics. He only became a hose jockey to piss his rich daddy off," Ben said. "Nobody was tight with the guy, not even Jakey. Titus was treading a fine line with Matt with all the political shit, so he was going to wash out of the crew in a couple more months anyway. The way Matt told it, Titus shouldn't have been on that floor alone in the first place but he'd doubled back against Matt's orders."

"But you can see where I'm going with all this," Andy said.

"Sure. But what I don't see is how Luna could have found out what we've been doing, without me *knowing* she'd found out. She was never around the crew without me being there as well."

"Did she come to these barbecues?"

"Yeah, her and Gabriel both," Ben said. "Gabe loved the pool. Couldn't swim. Didn't stop him trying."

"This is a big house. It's in Oyster Bay, for God's sake. On top of that, Matt's got three ex-wives to pay alimony to."

"So?"

"So did Luna ever ask you how the hell he affords it?"

"No," Ben said. "She probably figured he got money from 9/11. Therapy money. Loss of wages from the time off. Whatever."

"Was she right?"

"No. He never claimed anything. Never took any time off. I only know that because I overheard another chief getting into him about it one time, about how he should. Right before Matt threw the guy down a flight of stairs."

Jakey appeared at the glass doors, sparkling with sweat and dusted with grass clippings. His knees were stained green. He sat beside Ben on the end of the lounge chair and huffed a sigh and clinked beer bottles with him.

"Between the glitter sweat and the ponytail, I can't tell if you're Edward Cullen or Lestat, Jakey," Andy said.

"Pfft. Lestat. Give me some credit." Jake caught Ben's side-eye. "Vampire books. She likes them, too."

Ben wondered if that was the first genuine thing he'd ever learned about Andy. He punched Jake right in the joint of his shoulder, a signal they'd established early after they'd met, Ben telling Jake he had done a good job on something. "You do the pool filter, Mr. Book Nerd?"

"Not yet. I'm hoping Matt forgets."

"Gotta do the pool filter."

"Poor ole Jakey," Andy lamented. She rubbed his arm. "It won't last forever."

"It's okay. He's put me through worse." Jake shrugged, then looked at Ben. "Did you have to mow Matt's lawn too, when you were a noob?"

"No." Ben smiled, remembering. "He was married to Christine when I was a probie. They had an apartment in Tribeca. I had to get there early and take Kaylee and Sharon out in the stroller for a couple of hours so they could get some alone time." He pointed to the teenage girls. "I'm the only reason they have a third kid."

"I'd rather take out babies than mow lawns," Jake said.

"Yeah, it's okay for a probie detail. You're a chick magnet. Young guy in a park with two babies and no wedding ring? Come on." Ben smiled again. "But then one of them has a blowout in her diaper and the other one throws up all over your lap and it's not so great."

They laughed together, the two criminals and the woman planning to put them both in jail. Ben felt sore and sick and a little like he was floating outside his own skin, the minicamera and tracking device in his pocket threatening to fall out on the floor and end his life. The stitches in his brow itched, probably drawn too tight. He'd done them himself after he got home from the bar, was out of practice with stuff like that.

Matt appeared at the doors. "Family meeting," he said.

Ben hit the bathroom while Engo and Jake headed downstairs to the basement. He stood in the glow of the makeup lights, fished around in the cabinet as silently as he could to find something to cut the thread on the button of his breast pocket. His hands were shaking. Images flashing before his eyes, of Matt or Engo or Jake trying to hug him in the office and feeling the tiny box in his pocket, asking him what it was about. He supposed Matt would choke him out right then. No sense in letting him leave and get to his stash and head for the hills. They'd probably come downstairs as calmly as possible and tell Donna that he'd fainted and to go wait out front for an ambulance. While he was gone they'd lure Andy up to the office and put her lights out, too.

He cut the button off and pocketed it, slipped the fake button onto the shirt in its place and clipped it into the tiny box. The thing was no bigger than his thumbnail but it felt like it weighed a ton, seemed to him like it dragged the whole front of the shirt down.

Ben gripped the sink and tried not to throw up.

ANDY

.

o I'm holdin' the steering wheel," Donna was saying, white-knuckling an invisible wheel with one hand while she held a glass of alcohol-free champagne in the other. "And I'm just *cryin'*. I mean bawling my eyes out. That's how helpless I was. I just froze, you know? Meanwhile the smoke is pouring out of the hood and over the windshield."

She made a billowing motion with her arm. Andy sat there grinning, the marble top of the kitchen island cold on her forearms.

"And this guy just appears out of nowhere, and he's banging on my window. 'Lady! Your car's on fire! Are you out of your mind? Open the door!'"

"Is this the craziest meet-cute I've ever heard of?" Andy wondered aloud.

"Ten minutes later I was sitting on the hood of his car a little further down the highway, and he was writing me out a phone number for this guy he knows who could get me a good deal on a new car," Donna said. "I remember it like it was yesterday. Matt was wearing a black guayabera shirt and chinos. And the fire and smoke all behind him? Urgh. God. I'm getting hot flushes just thinkin' about it. The car blew, of course, just like he said it would. Pieces flew all over the highway. And you know what? He didn't even flinch. I'm thinking: Either this guy is hard of hearing or he's the biggest badass I've met in my life."

Andy leaned her chin on her palm, appreciated Matt's wife. She was a skilled comical mime, might have made a good actress at some point. Pretty, if weathered by a rough Jersey childhood and a couple of years married to the biggest badass the girl had ever met in her life.

"*Is* he a badass?" Andy asked curiously, playing with the stem of her wineglass. "Or did the Towers just make him numb to everything?"

Donna's head swiveled, checking for her husband. "Oh, shit! Babe, we don't talk about that in this house."

"I know."

"As soon as my mother heard he'd been a part of all that? She tried to warn me off him." Donna's voice was barely above a whisper. "My mom remembers that day. I was too young. She's like: 'A man goes through something like that? He's a walking bag of problems for the rest of his life.' And she was right. Matt *is* a walking bag of problems. The nightmares. The rage. The paranoia. His exes all tried to warn me, too, but I didn't listen."

"Paranoia?" Andy leaned in. "What's that all about?"

"He thinks he's gonna get cancer from it." She shook her head. "Always getting me to feel his neck. 'Can you feel a lump? Is this a lump right here?'" She pushed her fingers into her jugular, poked around. "He thinks he deserves to get it. Because everybody who went into the Towers paid some kind of price, right? The guys who didn't come out. The guys who got the cancer afterward. When's Matt gonna get called up to pay his share?"

Andy didn't answer. Donna rubbed her belly, looked at the round dome of it stretching the front of her dress.

"Especially him, of all people," she said. "He says he should pay the biggest price of all."

"Why?"

"Because he lost everybody. His whole crew. There are plenty of guys around still who were there, but not many of them lost *everybody*. So people give Matt a little extra, because he was the only one left from his station."

"Jesus. How did that happen?"

Donna leaned in now. Andy could smell her breath, the fake champagne and Doritos. "Not a lot of people know this, okay? I had to get him fall-down drunk just so he'd tell me."

"Okay."

"Matt was part of the North Tower response. They got prior warning about the collapse. The calls were coming through like crazy after the South Tower went down. *Mayday! Mayday! Everybody get the fuck out!* It was like *Drop your equipment and go!* His whole crew were there, trying to help the people who were trapped or injured and couldn't walk. Nobody was leaving. There was a consensus. We're staying to help these people. The guys didn't know the other tower had gone down; you couldn't see it through the smoke. They didn't believe it was possible, a thing like that. So they heard the calls but they decided they were staying no matter what."

"But Matt didn't stay."

"No. Matt grabbed some lady off the floor and just ran," Donna said. "Took him an hour to get up to the forty-first floor. Ten minutes to get back down. He lost everybody. Even the station probie. He kills himself about every part of it, you know? That *this* guy stayed, and not him. That *that* guy stayed, and not him. That the fucking probie stayed. He even beats himself up about which woman he grabbed on his way out. Because there were two to choose from, both lying on the floor just by the fire stairs. He picked one and not the other. Turns out the one he didn't pick was a mother with three kids."

"Jesus."

"And so now, everywhere you go, it's like *Never forget! Never forget!* All Matt wants to do is forget that day. He says: That's the day he found out he's one of the bad guys."

BEN
.

Matt lumped stacks of thick bound notes onto the green moss of the pool table. Because they were mixed and used, they were crumpled and sized differently. He shoved four each toward Ben, Engo, and Jake. Light poured in from the ground-level windows looking out across the deck toward the pool area. Only twenty feet away, Matt's daughters sunbathed while their father split his crew's takings.

"It's a hundred k each, after the fees."

Nobody said anything, because Jake needed whatever he could get to stop the loan sharks from slashing his Achilles tendons, and a hundred grand would keep Engo deep in hooker pussy and moonshine until the next job, and Ben was wearing a fucking *wire*. There was a bit more than a hundred left stacked in the bag Matt drew the funds from, and Ben assumed the fence had already taken his cut. Then there was the laundry man, and whoever Matt had needed to pay not to look too closely at how both fires started in the fabric store.

"Half the nation's chiffon supply went up in flames so you could waste that money, gentlemen, so be wise." Matt zipped up the bag. "Try to hold on to it through the weekend, Jake."

"What in the hell is chiffon?" Engo squinted.

"It's a fabric, dumbass."

"And how do you know that?"

"I got one daughter through prom already and two more on the way." Matt jerked a thumb toward the windows. "How do you think?"

"I also know what chiffon is." Jake shrugged.

"What? How?"

"Project Runway."

Ben raised a hand.

"What! You're fuckin' with me," Engo balked. "You too?"

"I surprised a woman with a dress once," Ben confessed. "Put it on the bed before we went out. Left a note. Like they do in the movies."

Engo sighed. "Surrounded by fuckin' homos here."

"Did it work?" Jake asked. "The dress thing."

"Oh, it worked all right."

"Enough. We need to talk," Matt said.

"About the new job?" The hope in Jake's voice was unmistakable, even though he was still counting his take.

"No. First things first." Matt pointed the Finger at Ben's chest, right at the button cam, which made his balls shrivel up into hard little pellets. "We all know the story about you getting jumped by a bunch of pricks over in East Orange is bullshit. You're not an idiot. You'd see a crew of stickup punks coming a mile away."

Ben said nothing.

"Luna's brother-in-law's gone legit. He just bought into a bar there." Matt widened his eyes, waiting, daring Ben to try to hold out. Engo had his thumbs in his suspenders, was looking down his nose at Ben like he was some TV sleuth, like Sherlock Holmes or whoever would be caught dead in suspenders stained with cocktail sauce and tan shorts.

"I had no idea about the bar," Ben conceded. "Neither did she. We just got unlucky that it was Edgar's place. Seriously unlucky."

"There's a lot of bad luck going on in this relationship," Engo mused. "Anybody would think you're trying to do your best impression of Jake at the greyhounds."

"She's just a black cloud," Jake said, calling on the old firefighter metaphor about people being white or black clouds. Attractants or repellents for bad luck and big fires. He was still counting his money. "Not me. I just won ten k at the greyhounds last week."

"So Edgar and his people spotted you in the bar," Matt said. "Took you out the back and rolled you?"

"He was pissed to see me out with someone else so soon. He figures I must have had something to do with Luna and Gabe going missing." Ben let his shoulders slump, tried to look helpless. "So either he had nothing to do with her going missing, or it was a hell of an act."

"How did he know you and Andy were *together*, though?" Engo said. "Why couldn't you have just been work buddies?" He didn't let Ben answer. "See. You two were all over each other in that bar. I knew it. More lies, Matt."

"Is that true?" Matt asked Ben. "Are you two still on? Because not ten minutes ago she stopped me upstairs and said—"

"We're not on." Ben glared at Engo. He knew Engo was taking the piss, but he felt real danger coming off Matt; pulsing waves of heat. He needed to act. But it felt like his face was moving of its own volition, not backing up what he was saying. He couldn't keep his hands still. He hoped to pass it off as nerves as his crew members grilled him.

As close to the truth as possible.

"Ben—"

"I like her, okay?" Ben focused on Matt. "She's hardcore. Tough. She's been through some shit in her life. I could tell that about her, even that first night, when we basically didn't talk at all. But last night at the bar, before Edgar spotted us; she told me some things. Like what happened in San Diego."

"What happened in San Diego?" Jake asked.

"Shut up," Matt snapped. "He's not done."

"I think Andy's really cool." Ben shrugged. "And she needs a break right now. So we talked about it and we figured maybe, you know, down the road . . . she could transfer to another station. Quietly, so it doesn't look like she got the boot. And then maybe, after that . . ."

"You could be together."

"I don't know. Maybe."

"This is so romantic." Engo tried to put his hands over Jake's ears. "Stop, Benji, you're gonna make Jake cry."

"I don't even know if it'll pan out," Ben said. "We just know we're holding off for now, like we *said* we would. That's the truth. I don't know what Edgar picked up between us. But we're holding off."

"What does *she* think happened?" Matt asked. "To Luna and Gabe?"

"She thinks the same thing as me," Ben said. "Nothing. No fucking idea."

Engo squinted. "Are you telling me this whole situation isn't a giant turnoff for her? Jake said that Luna and Gabe's stuff is still in your apartment."

"I sold it like Luna walked out on me."

"What do you mean, you 'sold' it to her like that?" Matt took one of those heavyweight boxer's half steps toward Ben, which put him within swinging distance. Ben's throat felt tight. "That's what happened."

Ben said nothing.

"I've always had other theories," Engo said. He snapped his suspenders, deducing. "Could be she's in witness protection. She got wind of this thing we're doing, and she's in a safe house somewhere. And the cops are about to come down on us like a ton of bricks."

"Do you think that's possible?" Jake looked pale.

"Look." Matt was trying to keep it cool, but his teeth were flashing a little too much between his lips. "We can't be in a situation here where you don't trust us, Benji, and we don't trust you."

"I know that."

"We can't have you lying to us," Matt said. "No lies. Not even about something as trivial as whose puss you're in."

Matt reached out and poked Ben hard in the chest. The Finger of Death, just an inch to the right of the button cam. Ben concentrated on staying upright. He could think of nothing else. When the big guy backed off it was like someone had taken a boot off his sternum.

"All right. Agenda item number two," Matt said. "The next job. Hold on to your helmets, gentlemen. This is a big one."

Andy appeared beside Ben as he stood at the edge of the pool, just beyond the huddle of men at the barbecue. He was watching Matt and Engo argue over when to flip the steaks. The flames danced gold on their shiny red faces, happy demons searing blooded flesh. The sun had started going down. Ben was holding on to his drink like it was a life buoy and chasing one long breath with another. The moment in the cellar, when he'd hung back and slipped the GPS tracker into a pocket on the side of Matt's black duffel bag, played over and over in his brain. Because that was it, now. He'd completed his first assignment in his bargain with the devil. If Matt found that tracker before, or during, or after he'd taken the bag wherever he was going to take it, he'd know someone in his crew was a rat. Ben felt sickened by the cleverness of it, the skill and experience it had taken Andy to know to give him the tracker before he went down to the cellar. The bag would go to a couple of meetings with Matt's people, revealing who they were to Andy and *her* people, and then it would presumably go to where Matt kept his stash, thereby revealing and closing off his runaway route.

Ben wondered where in his own life Andy had placed trackers, because surely she had. To look at her now, standing beside him with her sexy linen thing hanging off her unscarred shoulder and her hair loose and falling down, a little tipsy, or so it seemed, from the white-wine deep'n'meaningful session with Donna—she fit perfectly into the scene. A chameleon. All her wicked plans were coming to fruition.

Ben asked himself who the real devil at the barbecue was.

"Enjoy your little meeting of the gentlemen's club?" Andy asked him. "Anything I need to know?"

"You can watch the tape," Ben said flatly. He'd disconnected the button cam from his shirt and shoved it now into her hand. They passed a look between them, and she covered it with one of those perfect smiles.

"Well, that was fucking stupid."

"I'm running dry on patience," Ben said. "You need to get—"

"Smile, would you?"

"No, I'm not gonna fucking smile," he leaned in and murmured in her ear. "You need to get moving on Luna and Gabriel. All this shit about the heists. You're wasting your time. If you don't find them, I won't cooperate with you. You'll have us for the jewelry store, and that's it."

"It's all connected, you idiot." Andy's smile had turned hard. "I'm working both cases at once here! I'm—"

"You're too focused on making your case."

"I *have* to make my case, or I—"

Donna called Andy. She threw him a look and she wandered away, and Jake came up beside him, said something about her. That she was cool, or the like. Ben didn't hear it, didn't take it in, because his ears were throbbing, the pressure of the secrets forcing their way upward from the bottom of his belly. He'd said what he said next before he even realized it. It was up, and out of him, and in the air, uncatchable, before he could stop himself.

"She's not who she says she is," Ben said.

The two men looked at each other. Jake confused. Ben stricken, stiff. The smell of seared steak burned suddenly in Ben's nostrils and he thought for a moment of all the charred bodies he'd seen in his career, the way people curled up like spiders or burst open down the middle like overcooked hot dogs.

"Are you lookin' at my daughters, Jake?" Matt asked.

The chief was standing by the younger man, a plate of meat resting on his palm. Jake looked up, then back the way he'd been staring—toward the poolside where Matt's daughters were lounging in the last of the sun. House cats on a stoop.

"What?"

"You heard me. Were you checking out my daughters just now?"

"Wha— I— No, Matt. No. Absolutely not."

"'Absolutely not'?"

"No way."

"Why?" Matt cocked his head. "You don't find them attractive?"

Jake's mouth opened and closed. He looked at Matt's daughters. Tore his eyes away. Shielded them with his hand. There was nowhere safe to look.

"You're trying to tell me my daughters aren't hot enough for you?"

"Matt, lay off the kid, huh?" Ben said.

"My own daughters? You would 'absolutely not' check them out? 'No way'? They're that hideous?"

"Matt."

"Jake, answer the fucking question," Matt said.

"They're beautiful." Jake's voice was gravelly, forced through a shrinking windpipe. "Really beautiful."

"How would you know that unless you'd been checking them out?"

"I-I-I just— I just— I just—"

Matt's face broke into a grin. He wrapped his free arm around Jake's neck, crushed the probie against his chest and kissed him on the top of the head. "Jakey, I'm just fucking with you. Get a grip, would ya?"

Matt released Jake and drifted away to where Donna and Andy were setting the outdoor table. The probie put his hand out in front of himself, the fingers spread wide. Ben could see the hand was trembling hard.

ANDY

.

t was midnight before Andy got to her apartment. She was drunk. Not sloppy, but there was only so much tipping of her drinks into Matt's garden, or down the sink, or into the pool that Andy could do before someone started to notice. Donna had decided Andy was her new best friend, and she wanted intense conversations all evening, eye-to-eye, the consumption of alcohol unavoidable. So Andy bumbled into the bare, dark space and went to the bathroom and stuck her fingers down her throat, threw up what was in her belly so she could try, at least, to work. The windows were small but curtainless, and the summer night sky over Hell's Kitchen was dirty orange and cascading in. She put one light on in the bathroom but left the rest of the house bathed in tangerine.

She fitted her AirPods in and stood before the mirror, wiping her makeup off while she listened. The recording from the button cam on Ben's shirt was playing for the second time. Some of it she had listened to on the train on the way home already.

ENGO: We don't take commissioned jobs, man. That's the whole point of what we do. Nobody knows our gigs, because we choose them ourselves.

MATT: This is a one-time-only thing. It's big enough that we can make an exception.

BEN: Who's the contact?

MATT: No one. He's not someone in the life. He's straight. Just a lawyer who's flirting with breaking bad.

ENGO: No.

BEN: Absolutely not. I'm with Engo. It's a "no" from me.

JAKE: I've got to say, I'm—

MATT: Shut that hole in your head, Jake. Nobody asked you.

BEN: We have a system. Why would we screw with it?

MATT: You're right. You're right. We have a system. We've always said: We all have to vote "yes" on a job for it to go ahead. Even this moron here. But you haven't even heard the whole story yet. You assholes don't get to enter a vote until you know what the job is.

ENGO: This lawyer. He's talking about these wills. That's all very hinky, man. If you forge a will, the family are gonna notice it. You've got to have multiple people witness for those things.

MATT: Okay so, look. Let me just explain it. Give me a fucking minute here.

BEN: Go.

MATT: It's like this: The rich guy had multiple wills. He wrote them all out by hand. He would amend things, change things, get pissed at the kids and cut them out, then next week he's putting them back in. You know how rich people are. So this lawyer's working for him. He's getting these wills every six months or so. The lawyer would approve the new one and file the old ones in his records.

BEN: Okay . . . ?

MATT: So there are three versions of the will that interest us. The most recent three. In the first one, the oldest one, it says that the old man's baseball card collection is supposed to be split equally between his children. Right? The collection was specifically named in the will. The will says the collection is in a safe, in the old guy's office in his house on the Upper West Side.

ENGO: Mmm-hmm.

MATT: Then suddenly, the lawyer gets another version of the will from the guy. Because the old man got spooked, right? A couple of break-ins in the neighborhood. He decides it's stupid to keep such a valuable collection in his own house. So he puts the cards in a safety-deposit box in a facility in Midtown. He puts a couple of other things in there, too. Jewelry and whatever. So he amends his will. The second will just says: "The contents of the safety-deposit box at blah blah location must be split equally between Little Johnny Fat Fuck Junior and all his brothers and sisters." The baseball cards aren't specifically mentioned in the second will.

JAKE: Heh! Little Johnny Fat Fuck.

ENGO: Shut up, Jake.

MATT: Then a *third* will comes. The last will. The current will. And . . . Wait for it! The will mentions *both* the contents of the safety-deposit box *and* the baseball card collection.

BEN: Okay but . . . does it say that the baseball cards are *in* the safety-deposit box?

MATT: No. It doesn't.

ENGO: Ohhh.

MATT: Yeah. It just says "I leave them the contents of the safety-deposit box" and "I leave them the baseball card collection."

ENGO: It's like . . . an error.

MATT: Sort of. I mean, it's true. He's leaving them both of those things. But the way you read it, it doesn't say that *one is inside the other.* That's what got the lawyer to wondering about all this.

ENGO: Right. Because if you read the three wills in order, and you don't *know* that the guy moved the baseball cards *into* the safety-deposit box, it *reads like* those cards are still at the house. Like they stayed at the house the whole time.

MATT: Yeah.

BEN: And nobody else knows about this? Nobody has spotted the error on the will? Not even the witnesses who signed it?

MATT: Apparently not.

BEN: They're gonna figure it out. The kids.

MATT: How?

BEN: By going to the damn safety-deposit box after we've hit it and looking in and seeing no fucking baseball cards. That's how. If the cards aren't in the guy's office at the house, and they aren't in the safety-deposit box at the facility, and the safety-deposit box facility has just been robbed . . . It doesn't take a rocket scientist.

MATT: We're not gonna hit the facility. We're going to get in and out without anybody knowing anything's been touched.

ENGO: How?

MATT: Oh Jesus. *With a fire, you stupid asshole!*

BEN: I don't like this.

JAKE: If we—

MATT: Jake, I'm going to kill you right here in this cellar in a minute. I will bury your body under the pool.

ENGO: It might be a go, Ben. The wills, the way they're written. They *disguise* the fact that the baseball cards were ever in the safety-deposit box. If we can get in and out of the box without anyone knowing it's been touched, the whole *theft* is disguised, man.

MATT: See?

BEN: How are you going to make it look like the box is untouched if there's been a goddamn fire in the building?

MATT: We'll get to that.

ENGO: Point is, that if the cards were never in the box, and the box was never robbed, the kids have no reason to look for them there when they discover that they're missing. When the old man dies, they're going to expect them to be in the safe in the house.

MATT: It's good, right?

ENGO: This is the cleanest fucking job I ever heard of. There's no crime scene. The safety-deposit box is going to be locked tight. Untouched. The kids are going to be sitting there trying to figure out how the cards got robbed out of the house. Or if the guy sold them or gave them away on the sly. Jesus. The house cleaner better start looking for her own lawyer.

BEN: This is not clean, Engo. Are you nuts? The lawyer knows about it. This guy is not in the life. How do we know he's not a cop?

MATT: So we vet him.

ENGO: What about the cards? How do you move something like that?

MATT: We'll work it out.

ENGO: When does this have to go down? I mean—

MATT: The old guy's on death's door right now.

BEN: Jesus Christ, it's like I'm speaking in tongues. Why are we even— We don't do commissioned jobs! We don't do this kind of kiddie shit! And I mean, baseball cards? Fucking *baseball cards*? Are you serious? What are they even worth?

MATT: Eight point two million dollars.

Someone banged on Andy's door. She pulled her AirPods out, put them on the bathroom sink, went out and stared at the door in the dark of the little hall. A dozen possibilities shuttered through her mind. Neighbors. Peddlers. Lost partygoers. She could hear the distant thumping of a get-together on one of the upper floors. When she considered that it might be Newler, that he might have followed her home, her stomach lurched. She went to the door and looked through the peephole, pulled the door open until it clunked against the chain thick with Landlord's Special cream paint.

"Surprise," Ben said. He was leaning on the doorframe. Eyes bloodshot, glazed. Andy unlatched the chain, realizing there was a gun in her hand only when the drunk firefighter pointed to it.

"Expecting someone else?"

"How did you find me?"

"Check your back pocket," Ben said. He walked in, brushed past her. Andy slipped her hand into her jeans and pulled out a GPS tracker. "I stood in the street and watched the building and saw which light came on fastest after you arrived home."

"Sneaky motherfucker," Andy said. She guessed it sounded humorous, but it wasn't. Newler's presence, even the unrealized potential of it, still sizzled on all her exposed skin.

"Hell yes, I'm sneaky." Ben was standing in the middle of the bare living room, taking it all in. The boxes stacked against the wall. The mattress on the floor with its pillow and sheet set, the rumpled duvet. "I did tag Matt's stash bag. Then I changed my mind. I went down to the cellar and took the tag back out. Paired it with my phone. Put it in your pocket."

They both stared at the lonely mattress in the middle of the floor. The empty rooms beyond.

"What's in the boxes?"

"Thrift-store stuff." Andy waved at the boxes absentmindedly. "First thing I do when I get into a role. Hit a bunch of thrift stores. Buy all the character's personal belongings."

"Look at you. You've even organized them." Ben was looking at the tape on the tops, the marker labels she'd written on the sides. KITCHEN. BATH-ROOM. BEDROOM. CLOTHES. "Like you really did just fucking fly in from San Diego."

Andy said nothing.

"Where are your actual things?"

"What actual things?"

Ben stared at her. "Your . . . your *things*. Your personal belongings."

"There aren't any."

"But where's home base?"

She gestured to the bed. "Here."

Ben's eyes were suddenly clear. "Why the hell do you do this to your-self?" he asked. "What happened to you, that you want to live like this?"

He looked sad. And the sadness cast a line down, threaded it through her sadness, the heavy, deeply sunken one, and tried to haul it upward out of the blackness into which she'd drowned it.

She snapped the thread.

"Ben, are you here for a reason?"

"Well, yeah. I'm here to tell you to get your ass into gear and find Luna and Gabriel," he said. "Because I want my fucking family back."

"You said this at the barbecue."

"And I don't want to do the job. I don't want to rob a goddamn safety-deposit-box facility. I'm going to get myself or someone else shot or burned to death, and I'd much rather go to jail."

"Baseball cards." Andy nodded, grateful for the turn in conversation. "It's smart. I did a little light Googling. For that amount of money, you could be looking at pre–World War I cards. No serial numbers. Easy to fence."

"It's not happening," Ben said. "We'll be in jail by the time the old man dies. Because you're going to find Luna and Gabe and end all this."

"I'm working on it."

"No, you're not!" Ben was suddenly looming over her, his back to the fire-stained night. A broad-shouldered, beer-scented silhouette. "You're wasting your time trying to wheedle your way into the crew. It's the robberies you're interested in. You and your boss. Because millions of dollars' worth of burglaries makes headlines. Dead Mexican mothers and their kids don't."

He sat on the edge of the mattress suddenly. Just plopped down. It was softer than he expected. He had to rock himself forward so he didn't tumble over backward.

"Let me tell you a story." Ben groaned as he righted himself and gripped his cracked ribs. "I had this cop up in Paterson. I was living there for a while with a foster family. Guy hauled me in from the street. I was . . . I don't know, fifteen? He was trying to bust me on a bunch of damage some punks did to a car yard. Looked like a kid's work. Windows broken. Cars dented. Spray paint."

Andy sat beside him on the edge of the mattress. She put the gun down on the carpet.

"The guy says"—Ben jerked a thumb over his shoulder, imitating, remembering—"'Oh, guess what? We actually got your mom in holding right now. Marissa Haig. That's your mother, right? We just picked her up for soliciting. How funny—mother and child both in the same station at the same time. Weird. Anyway look, kid, we'll do you a favor: We'll help your mom out if you just admit to a couple of things here for us.'"

"Ben," Andy said, "I think you should go home."

"So I say," he carried on, his words slurring, "'Okay, I'll admit I was in the area. I maybe saw something.' And the guy's like 'Great. Great. We've taken your mother out of the drunk tank, she's away from the crazies and she's in her own private cell. Tell us more.' The guy got me to admit it all. Step by step. While he gave my mother dinner, let her have her phone call, had her charges bumped down. But guess what?"

"She was never there," Andy said.

"She was never there."

"Ben," Andy said, "I'm not stringing you along on my search for Luna and Gabriel so that I can tangle you up for the heists. I'm not an indolent, conniving beat cop trying to score easy-solve numbers by railroading a defenseless teenager."

"Uh-huh."

"I'm an experienced undercover specialist trying to find a missing mother and child. And I'm not going to bust you, or let anyone else bust you, until I've done that."

Ben was looking right through her.

"I need to get as close as I can to Matt, Engo, and Jake," she said. "I need them to trust me. I need them to accept me. This is what I do, Ben."

"Why?"

"Why what?"

"Why do you do this?"

"You need to go home." Andy stood. "You're drunk, and I'm tired, and I've said all I'm going to say tonight."

"Fine." Ben got up, toppled, almost fell on the bed. Andy watched him as he struggled out of his boots. "It's bedtime, then. Excellent."

"What are you doing?"

"I'm going to bed," Ben said. "That's right. That's half the reason I came here. Because I know where you live now, Andy. So it's payback time. This is what you get. You want to be my undercover girlfriend? You want to play charades? Well, now you're the one who gets to have a naked stranger force their way into your goddamn bed. Let's see how you like it."

He tore his shirt off and his jeans and climbed onto the bed, dragged the blanket over himself while Andy just stood there, mortification pulsing through her. She waited, giving him time to drop the game and get up and leave. But the seconds passed, and she watched the lump at the top of the bed rising and falling as he breathed.

"Ben," she said. "I get it."

Nothing.

"You've made your point," she tried.

He didn't move.

"This isn't funny!" Andy yelled. She kicked the mattress. "Get out of my goddamn bed!"

Ben didn't stir. She was twitching with anger, watching the city lights, trying to think of her next move when she heard him begin to snore.

The second day after a proper beating was the worst. Andy knew that from experience. So she wasn't surprised by all the groaning and wheezing when Ben started to wake, the hangover teaming up with the aftermath of the bashing to force him back down into the pillow a couple of times. Andy sat near him on the edge of the mattress in the morning light, drinking coffee, thinking about the nightmares that had plagued her in the dark hours.

She'd been back there. Twenty-two and untainted by what was about to happen, sitting behind the counter of her parents' gas station in the desert south of Sheffield, Texas. Listening to Kanye West. She recalled now that her biggest worry in the world had been whether she was ever going to make it into a life and a city where she frequented places where gold diggers hunted rappers for their money. Where there were nightclubs and skyscrapers and subways, where she could have friends she hadn't met on MySpace. She'd remembered the college chemistry textbook she'd had on the counter that night, and the magazine tucked inside it. Brad and Angelina and their domestic bliss in Kenya. Cover under cover, in case her father came in from the house attached to the back of the gas station and tried to check on her. So many of the details of that night had been stored away somewhere in perfect detail. Others were invented. In the dream, Andy saw the headlights of the first car coming down the road. In real life, she hadn't seen the men who would destroy her until they were already out there by the gas pumps.

She'd snapped awake, drenched in sweat and struggling to breathe, at

3 A.M. Ben hadn't stirred, but she braced herself now for him to say something about it.

The nightmares hadn't come in years. Why were they back now?

Ben sat up, rubbed his eyes and reached over and took her coffee out of her hand like it was for him. Didn't even question why it was half empty. She let him have it. She cut over him before he could ask her what she was afraid he would ask.

"Time to get up," she said.

"Why?"

"I think I know where we can find Luna's car."

BEN

.

She walked beside him with her head down, her arms folded, watching the sidewalk pass beneath her feet. He was learning that the best kind of stuff came from Andy when he allowed her these long, silent times, so he'd ridden beside her in the Uber to the front of his apartment in Dayton in silence, and now he walked in silence, too, watching the colors and expression change in her face as she argued with herself. Or plotted or planned, or came up with lies. It was cooler than it should have been, and windy, and she was walking too fast. He knew that he'd unsettled something in her by turning up in her private space the night before. Felt strangely guilty about it. Sure, Andy's apartment was set up like the rest of her charade, so the idea that someone could penetrate it had obviously crossed her mind. But she was disturbed now. Off-balance. He had the odd instinct to comfort her, this woman he didn't know at all, who was experiencing some anguish he couldn't possibly guess at.

They were standing on the corner of Washington Avenue before he realized it. Andy stopped and turned and took a hair band out from her jeans pocket, swept up her hair. To an outsider, it might have appeared like they'd paused to do that—to allow her to get her hair up out of the wind. But her eyes were on the liquor store on the corner.

"On your mission to find out what happened to Luna," Andy said, "you door-knocked this street. You were looking for CCTV footage. Trying to discover what people had seen that night."

"Right," Ben said.

"You got the guy in the liquor store to let you look at his camera feed," she continued. "It showed Luna's car driving along this street toward Gabe's grandmother's place at seven twelve P.M. About five minutes after she left your apartment."

"That's right." Ben pointed to the corner. "She turned and—"

"Don't point. We're not solving a crime; we're heading out to breakfast."

"Okay." He shoved his hands in his pockets. "She turned and headed up here. I'd dropped Gabe off with her before. It was normal for her to go this way."

Andy walked. Ben followed. After a few feet, she slipped an arm around his.

"Oh," he sighed. "So we *are* back on?"

"If anyone's keeping an eye on us, Ben, they'd have seen you stay at my place last night."

"If that person who's keeping an eye on us is Matt, you better call an ambulance now," Ben said. "Because he's about to come grind me into the sidewalk like a cigarette. I said we were holding off."

"He'll get used to it."

"Mmm-hmm."

They stopped at a café. Andy took a laminated menu from a stand on the street and pretended to peruse it.

"The next piece of CCTV you managed to get a look at was from this café," she said. Ben glanced inside. The guy who'd let him come into the office at the back of the café and watch the feed wasn't there. There were a couple of young waitresses in black aprons swirling around, lifting chairs down from tables, setting out napkin holders. The place wasn't open yet.

"Luna went by at seven thirteen P.M.," Ben said. He caught his reflection in the windows of the café. He looked like walking dog shit. "I got a better angle on the car. She was alone in the front seat. Gabriel was in the back."

Andy wrinkled her nose at something on the menu, replaced it and took his hand and walked on. "The only other piece of footage you got was from the furniture place on the corner down there at the intersection." She looked ahead.

"Right." Ben couldn't see the shop. A row of cafés and clothing boutiques stretched before him. "No sign of Luna. It took a lot of convincing, but the woman who runs the store let me check through the whole day and the next day. Luna never went by."

"So whatever happened to Luna, it happened on this street," Andy said.

"Maybe." Ben shrugged as they stopped to peruse, or pretend to peruse, another menu. "Or the cameras were wrong somehow."

"Possible. But let's assume they were not. How did her car get out of the street?"

"I thought maybe someone put it in the back of a truck," Ben said. "But no trucks big enough to load a car into an enclosed cabin went by. Not in the two days I looked at. And by the third day, I was out here walking the street looking for her car, getting the footage. No trucks. These apartment blocks here? I checked their parking lots. I had to sneak in to do that, because none of the residents would let me beg my way in. But I did it. The car's not there. Same with the hotel."

He nodded to the Best Western hotel dominating the center of the street. The circular driveway, where a cab was just pulling in.

"The hotel wouldn't give me CCTV," Ben said. "They've got policies. Privacy. So I just snuck in. I went down to the parking lot, scoped it out. Her car wasn't there. I checked the loading docks and the staff parking. And I checked again a week later. Walked all four levels. Not there."

"I walked them, too," Andy said. "Yesterday. Before I followed you to Matt's place."

Ben stopped.

"The car's not there," she confirmed.

"So what are you getting at?"

"I'm getting at how the car could possibly have *been* there," Andy said, "without you seeing it."

Ben stared.

"Let's sit."

Ben felt his legs give way as she pushed him into an outdoor chair. They were at a café directly across from the Best Western. He tried to focus on the menu she slid under his fingers, but his eyes kept flicking back to the stained cream exterior of the four-floor building, the uniform red-and-green curtains hanging in every window. A stain-disguising, chaotic, triangular print. On the second floor, a guy with a business shirt undone to his round belly seemed to be staring right back at Ben, brushing his teeth.

"Before it was a Best Western," Andy said, "that used to be a Marriott. The land was acquired and the hotel was built under the Marriott brand, and that's what it opened as. The owner was a guy named Raymond Fresco. Longtime hoteling family."

"So?"

"So, the Best Western we're looking at right now has a few more interesting features than your regular Best Western," Andy said. "Because a whole bunch of money was sunk into it when it was created. Before it went bust and changed owners. Raymond Fresco was trying to create a hotel that would appeal to international travelers coming into Newark Liberty who didn't necessarily want to feel like they were staying *at* the airport. What he didn't realize is that people aren't dumb enough that they're going to book a nice hotel just outside the airport limits. You're either resigned to the aircraft noise, and you stay at the airport, or you get somewhere nice in the city."

"You're losing me here." Ben held his head. The waitress had come by, and he looked at her pleadingly. "Coffee, please. Black. Strong. I'm talking jet-fuel strong."

The waitress smirked and took Andy's order and went away. Andy pulled Ben's hands down from his skull and held them.

"The reason you didn't see Luna's car in the Best Western parking lot three days after she went missing may have been because it was underneath another car," she said.

"Underneath?"

"The hotel has hydraulic parking stackers. On the very bottom floor."

Ben frowned.

"Underneath twenty of the parking spaces on the bottom level is *another* parking space," Andy said. "A hydraulic lift tilts the top car backward, revealing a hidden space underneath. When the bottom floor of the hotel parking lot is full and all the cars are level, it just looks like a regular lot full of parked cars. But there's a hidden layer underneath. Raymond Fresco installed the hydraulic system to add an extra twenty spaces because he wanted the hotel to be able to accommodate everyone's car if the hotel reached capacity."

Ben's mind raced. He felt sick.

"You can see the parking out here is terrible." Andy gestured to the street. "It's one-way. What fine hotel doesn't have space for everyone's car? Fresco didn't have enough money to add a whole other level to the hotel lot but he had enough to add a row of hydraulic spaces."

"Do you *know* the car isn't down there right now?" Ben's chest felt tight. "Can we go look?"

"No. I'm not sure it's not there right now," Andy said. "It may be. But we can't look. And chances are, it isn't there."

"How do you know that?"

"I *don't* know," Andy said. "I don't know any of this for sure. I'm working on it. But I have a theory. See, the only people who can access and operate the hydraulic stacked car spaces are the valets, right? So Luna would have had to give her car over to a valet for it to have ended up in a hidden space. But the stacked spaces are the *very last* spaces the valets would have used that night. Because it's a pain in the ass to get a car out of the stacked space. The hotel would need to have been at capacity for my theory to work."

"*Was* it at capacity that night?"

"It may have been." Andy nodded.

"All this may, may, may." Ben gripped his head. "Nothing's for certain."

"Not yet," Andy said. "You've got to be patient."

He let out a long breath.

"I've found social media posts suggesting there was a wedding at the Weequahic Golf Club that night," Andy said. "It's one street over, across the park. Makes sense for a lot of the guests who didn't want to fork out and stay at the club to have been staying at the Best Western instead. And the wedding started at six P.M. So by the time Luna rolled along at seven thirteen P.M., the parking lot under the Best Western would have been pretty full. She may have ended up in a hydraulic space."

"So wait . . ." Ben pressed his fingers into his aching eyes, trying to block out the light, the noise of the street. "Luna gave her car to a valet. It went into a hidden hydraulic space. Two days later, when I came looking for it, it was still in that hidden space?"

"Possibly."

"What about seven days later?" he said. "When I checked again? Would the valets have just let it sit there?"

"I don't know."

"We have to go look!"

"We can't," Andy said.

"Why the hell not?"

"Because you've accepted that Luna ran out on you." She patted his hand, smiled. "And we're just a pair of firefighters having breakfast on their morning off."

Ben took his hands from hers, clasped them hard between his knees to stop himself from hurling his cup at the wall. "We have to tell the detective. Simmley."

"We can't do that."

"Why? *Why*, Andy?"

"Because as far as Detective Simmley knows, the case went away. Only me and Newler, the guy who hired me, know it's being worked on right now. And that's how it's going to stay. For your safety, and mine."

"But that's not true," Ben said. "The dog walkers."

"Those people who you saw in the street, they'd be a surveillance team of Newler's," Andy said. "They wouldn't know the full picture. And the cop you targeted with the letter—Johnson. Once he handed your case over to Newler and the FBI for a check-over, he'd have been told to walk away."

Ben wrung his hands. "So when are you going to go look if the car's there?"

"I'm working on it."

Ben gripped his head again.

"I don't think it's there." Andy pulled his hands down. "But I'm not sure what their policies are. I've been watching the valets, and there's one who's kind of shifty-looking. A little weak. I'll need to do my research, see if he's got a background I can use. I'm planning to approach him, tonight maybe, and see if I can get some information out of him. About whether someone came back for the car after a week. About how long the hotel would allow an unclaimed car to sit in its lot if someone didn't come back, and which towing company would have picked it up if the owner couldn't be located. I would assume they'd give an owner a week to claim their car."

Their coffees came. Ben snatched at his, gulped it. It was too hot but he didn't care.

"If no one came back for the car after a week, would they have called the police?" he asked. "I mean, they've got the towing fee to try to recover, right? And the days it sat there running up a parking tab."

"Maybe."

"We gotta get the guest list for the hotel," Ben said. "And the valet sheet. They'd have written up all the cars they booked in."

She just sipped her coffee and looked over the rim at him. Ben sighed.

"Okay," he said. "Okay. I'm sorry. Turns out you're not just baiting me. You're not an insolent beat cop."

"Indolent."

"Whatever. You have been working on this the whole time."

He stared at his coffee; it tasted like acid on his teeth. He could see gathering storm clouds beyond the café's flapping awning reflected in it. Grave imaginings were swirling in his mind, about Luna meeting someone in one of the rooms in the hotel above them, about that meeting going bad somehow. Luna strangled on a bed. Gabe drowned in a bathtub. Their bodies loaded into suitcases, wheeled through the lobby or downstairs to the parking lot.

"Why did she come here?" Ben asked. He couldn't look at Andy. Didn't want to see the knowing in her eyes. Because she would have an idea. She'd have seen this a lot, throughout whatever dark travels she'd been on before she wound up with him. Women who had secrets; those secrets getting them killed. "Whatever she was doing that night—why'd she have to keep it from me?"

He finally dared to look at her, and again he thought he caught a flash of the real *her*, whoever she was. She looked like she was genuinely sorry for him. Like she was feeling the hurt and confusion coming off him, and the hands that were holding his now were trying to cradle that hurt, ease the weight of it. She'd told him in the cab before she organized to have his ass beat that she wasn't sorry for him. That he was a thief. A criminal. But Ben was almost certain that before she turned away, something connected between them. A shared longing, sparking, sizzling, being hidden away.

Thunder rumbled somewhere, and the wind lifted Andy's ponytail off her shoulder. He watched it tangle in the breeze, had a vague memory of her body next to his in the bed, a nightmare quickening her breath. He'd lain there and listened to the dream coursing through her body until it peaked with a gasp and a jolt and a trip to the bathroom to wash her face. An hour or so later, when a second storm broke on the plains and wildlands of her mind, he'd reached down between the sheets and gripped her sweaty palm until it passed.

He jogged up the steps to his front door before looking at who was standing under the awning, taking shelter from the rain. The shoulders of Jake's T-shirt were damp, and he had glassy, hungover eyes.

"What are you doing here?" Ben brushed the rain out of his hair. An icy thump hit his sternum, as he imagined Jake having seen him part with Andy on Washington Avenue only minutes before. But oh, she was good. So good. Little snatches of chance, coincidences and alignments, could sink them, and Andy knew that. If Jake had indeed seen them around the corner, he'd have seen them holding hands. Arms linked, maybe. "You been waiting long?"

"Nah, nah, I just got here." Jake watched him buzz his way through to the foyer. "I was over at my mother's place mowing the lawn."

Jake's mother had a small place over in Metuchen, Ben knew, about a half hour away from where they stood, a property he and his sister had inherited and didn't seem to be able to agree on selling. While Ben's place was kind of on the way home to Harlem, where Jake had a share apartment, Ben had so much on his mind that it took him a second to put together why Jake was there.

"I was about to send you a text. I need a favor."

Ben stopped dead. "Don't tell me."

"Well . . ."

"Jake." Ben turned, lowered his voice. "You just got paid a hundred grand yesterday. Don't tell me that it's all gone already."

Jake swiped back his damp hair, his cheeks were rosy.

The humidity in the stoop had spilled inside. New York's stinking heat sliding languidly around the streets like a great yellow snake, squeezing out all the breathable air.

"You got a fucking problem." Ben shook his head. "And that's—"

"It's not what you think."

"—that's a problem. For all of us. These dirtbag loan sharks you're dealing with: How long before they start wondering where the hell you're getting all this money from? They're gonna find out you're dirty. You could bring us all down with this, Jake."

"I know. I know."

"You've got to go to rehab. They have groups for this. It's an addiction."

"I've stopped." The kid held his hands up. "I stopped a while ago."

"Bullshit."

Jake shoved his hands in his pockets and looked toward the doors like he was considering throwing the whole favor in. "The hundred k from yesterday was supposed to get me square with *everyone*. I just forgot about the vig on one loan. It's only five grand."

Ben opened his mailbox and raked the mail out, stuffed it in his back pocket. He was muttering to himself, so angry the words were actually coming out. About how much five grand would have meant to him when he was Jake's age, when he was trying to raise his little brother on food stamps and cash construction work.

"Five grand," Jake pushed. "And then—"

"And then what?" Ben slapped the elevator button. "You're penniless until next payday. So it's not really five grand, is it, Jake? It's five-five. Because you know that if I'm nice enough to loan you money, *again*, to stop you getting your toes cut off, I'm probably nice enough to make sure you don't have to wash windshields for lunch money as well."

Jake stared at his wet shoes.

"But you weren't going to ask for the extra cash," Ben said. "You were going to wait for me to offer. We've done this dance so many times, I'm starting to feel like I should just tell you where my stash is and you can go help yourself when you need to."

"Benji, can I have the money or not?" Jake whined. "I feel enough like a piece of shit."

"I don't have it with me."

"What?"

"I left my cut at Matt's. I didn't go home last night."

Jake frowned, then one brow lifted. Ben tapped the elevator button twelve more times in rapid succession.

"I can't go to Matt's," Jake said. "He said if I ever come to him asking for money again, he's going to grind my bones into powder and snort them like cocaine."

"So I'll send you a bank transfer."

"Cash is better."

Ben just looked at him. Jake winced. "Okay. Thank you. Thank you, Ben. I owe you one." The elevator doors pinged open. "Oh, there's a dude up there waiting for you."

Ben froze in the threshold of the elevator, a blue strip of lights inside each door marking his presence. He turned around. "What dude?"

"I don't know. Some guy. Like, a buttoned-up guy. I tailgated one of your neighbors through the front doors and went up and he was already there, so I came back down and waited outside." Jake gestured to the street. "It was awkward. Two dudes standing in the hall waiting for you like that."

"A 'buttoned-up' guy?"

"Yeah."

"He say his name?"

"I didn't ask."

Ben let the elevator doors slide closed on Jake. He put a hand on the wall and tried to suck in air as the numbers ticked upward, but no oxygen was reaching deeper than the top quarter of his lungs. And then it was the top five percent. His mind was swirling, trying to decide what would happen if Jake had just seen a cop standing waiting for him at his apartment. Or the guy "Newler," who Andy had mentioned. Surely it was one of them. Surely that was who was waiting. And there would be no convincing Jake not to tell the others, Engo or Matt, or he'd make it clear that there were secrets he was keeping from the crew. *No lies. Not even about something as trivial as whose puss you're in.* Who would Jake assume the guy was? Or would he not assume at all—would he ask him about it next time they spoke? Would he ask him in front of Matt and Engo?

Ben was unsteady as he exited the elevator and turned down the hall. He had to force himself around the last corner, his legs numb and vision clouded with red throbbing panic as he laid eyes on who it was standing there.

"Oh Jesus," Ben said. Suddenly the breath came. He sucked in a chestful of sweet, precious air. "Kenny. What the fuck?"

"'What the fuck' right back at you." Kenny was trying to frown, but the Botox or surgery or whatever the hell he'd done to his brow wouldn't let him. He looked Ben over like he was a homeless guy staggering in from the street. "You look like shit."

Ben went to the door and unlocked it. His brother smelled as he usually did these days: like a new car. A new Italian car. Ben had a weird impulse to hug him but didn't. The days when they hugged and Kenny smelled like cheap deodorant and pimple cream were long gone.

"What are you doing here?"

"Just joining the queue of people waiting to see you, I suppose." Kenny came into the apartment and popped the collar of his business shirt, and the cuffs, which was something he did whenever he walked into a room. Ben didn't get it. "Who was the little punk with the ponytail? Is he responsible for the black eye?"

Ben went in and pulled two coffee mugs down from the cupboard, and then he put one back up, because fuck Kenny. "You have a key. I don't know why you didn't just come in here and wait."

"Didn't seem appropriate, given how we left things."

"Why are you here?"

Kenny was still fiddling with his shirt. "I just came to, uh . . ."

Ben stopped what he was doing, looked Kenny right in the eye.

He had stepped in as a pseudo-father when his brother was fourteen and he was twenty-two. He couldn't possibly figure how many times he'd said sorry to Kenny in his life. He'd said sorry for not being able to rescue him out of the system when he was eighteen and legally old enough to take custody of the boy. It didn't matter that Ben hadn't even been told about Kenny's existence until he was nineteen. Or that it had taken another three years to *get* that custody. He was sorry, and he told the kid that. Over and over. He was sorry about what happened to Kenny in those four years. He was sorry that he'd ignored Kenny completely for another eight years after he had him, because he was in and out of the apartment like a ghost working his ass off to keep Kenny fed and clothed and happy through high school and then college so he could do something with the natural smarts he had. He was sorry that even though Kenny was a walking rags-to-riches story, the pain was still there. He made a shit ton of money, and the pain was still there. He was one of the state's most sought-after plastic surgeons, and the pain was still there. Ben had done everything he could think of, and the pain was still there, and he was sorry about that.

Kenny had never said sorry to Ben for anything in his life. Nobody ever had. But that didn't stop Ben standing there now, in the kitchen, looking at Kenny, wondering if today was going to be that magical day.

"So what happened?" Kenny said. He was looking at Ben's face.

Ben set the coffee maker off and used the seconds to fish around inside his brain for something that would satisfy his brother.

"Went to a garbage-fire callout," he said. "The guy didn't want us to put out his fire until all the trash was burned up. He grabbed the hose. I grabbed it back. Things went from there."

Ben smiled at the lie, felt a weird kind of pride. The story was appropriated from a callout he had attended once, a guy who had really fought him for the hose. In real life not much had happened. The guy had spat in his face. Ben had kicked him in the nuts. He'd spent the next four hours sitting in the ER having blood drawn for AIDS tests and the like. *As close to the truth as possible.* He was getting good at this whole undercover thing.

"You do those stitches yourself?" Kenny asked.

Ben felt his forehead. "They're fine."

"They're too tight. Let me redo them."

"No."

"It's what I *do*, man." Kenny laughed.

"*What do you want*, Kenny? Fuck!" Ben set the milk down on the counter hard.

Kenny shrugged, adjusted his collar. "Luna's not back yet, so I hear. And I just wanted to say that I . . . I really regret what happened. With me. And her. And you."

"Uh-huh, thanks," Ben said. "Jeez. You better sit down. That was the closest you've ever gotten to a real-life apology. You must be exhausted."

"I'm sorry I haven't come to see if you were all right," Kenny said. "To help."

"Wow. Who is this person? What did you do with Kenny?"

"I don't know if she told you . . ." Kenny gestured at him. "But Luna sort of cleared the air with me about it. So if you're thinking that she ran away on you because of what happened between us, then—"

"What do you mean she 'cleared the air'?"

"She emailed me."

"When?"

Kenny fished around in his back pocket for his phone. Ben was surprised he could get the device out, his pants were so tight. No idea how he got it in. Kenny scrolled with a manicured thumb.

"I mean, I don't know the exact date she left you. I just remember it was a week before that. Assuming you told me right away."

"I did tell you right away. I'm worried she's been fucking murdered, Kenny."

He tried to frown again. Failed. "Surely it's not that."

"Show me the email." Ben did what he could not to snatch the phone out of his brother's hand. In close proximity, he could feel Kenny looking closely at his face. The guy probably studied faces and breasts the way house painters studied shutters on old buildings. Ben ignored him and read the email from Luna's work account to Kenny's.

> I just wanted to tell you it's all good between us. There's no hard feelings.

"I could just take those out real quick and redo them." Kenny reached for Ben's face. "I've got a kit in my car."

Ben slapped his hand away. It was sickeningly soft and covered in some weird substance. "What did you write back?"

"Nothing." Kenny shrugged. "I didn't know what to say."

"And you didn't think you should tell me about this?"

"I figured she would," Kenny said. "Then, I wondered if she had. Ergo: This delightful exchange we're currently having."

Ben sighed and handed the phone back. Kenny was still eyeballing him.

"You're gonna end up with a big ugly scar."

"I hope I do," Ben replied. "Whenever we're in the same room from now on I'll show it to people. I'll say 'Look. My brother did this. Kenny Haig. Eight years in med school, and this is his work. He's a butcher. Call *Dateline.*'"

Kenny smiled his weird, plumped-up smile and Ben tried not to smile his unaltered one back.

"Seriously, though," Ben said, putting as much space between them as the kitchen would allow. "I want to tell you something. It was always cool between us. Even with the, uh, the thing that happened. So if you coming here was also about us—"

"I know. I know."

"I'm being real, though. I'm trying to say that if anything happens, in the future, uh . . ." Ben waved a hand. Kenny stared, not getting it. *Willfully* not getting it. Ben had no idea why it was so hard between them. It was like they spoke two different languages, and they were trying to communicate in a third that was unfamiliar to them both. "I'd rather you didn't sit around wondering if it was all cool between us. Because it is. And it was. And it will be."

"Okay . . . ?" Kenny said.

". . . When it happens."

"When what happens?"

"Jesus, Kenny, I'm just talking in hypotheticals!"

"Why? *Why* are you talking in hypotheticals?"

"Look, if I have to go somewhere, and I . . ." Ben struggled, stared at the ceiling. "What if I went into a coma, for example? If that happened, I wouldn't want you to come and visit me, Kenny. I'd want you to go and live your life. You don't owe me anything for what . . . for what I've done for you. College and all that. Okay? So if anything happens to me, I don't want it to drag you down as well. That's not right."

Kenny just stared at him.

"Just say you understand," Ben sighed.

"But I don't."

"Kenny!"

"Okay! I understand!"

"Are we done?" Ben asked. "Is that all you wanted?"

"Yeah."

"Go, then." Ben flapped a hand at the door. "Go find somebody to put tits on."

Kenny smirked and went to the door. "Love you, man."

"Yeah," Ben called.

He grabbed his phone and called Andy.

ANDY

·

She was an hour early, and she traversed the neighbor's darkened yard to get to the back gate of Newler's property. When she announced her presence by tapping on the glass of the doors opening onto the deck, Newler glanced up from where he was perched on a kitchen stool and gave her a resigned kind of look. Like he was disappointed she didn't trust him enough to turn up anywhere or any way that he expected her to anymore. He came out onto the deck and gestured to a seat at the huge oak table, but she stood by the pillar instead.

"When he arrives, I want these lights off." Andy pointed skyward, to the lights in the awning that covered the entertaining area and the beginnings of the lush gardens beyond. "He'll sit there. I'll sit here."

"Why?"

"So I'm in silhouette."

"He's just a homicide ghoul from Midtown," Newler tried to say. But Andy held up a hand. They waited, Andy tapping on her phone, Newler smoking by the edge of the lawn, the tension shimmering across the thick summer air between them. The rain had broken the heat briefly during the day, but it was creeping back, flowering in sweat on her ribs and the back of her neck. In the garden, things sang and cried. Crickets, frogs, night birds.

Ben had called twice during the day. She'd texted him back that she was busy, with a winky smiley face in keeping with the game, but there was no stupid little yellow cartoon face for what she was feeling then as a text came through from him.

Important re: Luna.

She eased breath between her clenched teeth, turned the phone off, watched Newler go inside and greet Detective Nick Ryang from Seventeenth Precinct Robbery/Homicide. At the instruction on where to sit, the guy rolled his eyes. He was the typical working homicide cop. Baggy eyes, sagging belly, chewed nails, and a chip on his shoulder about being made to accommodate a younger woman. Andy sat in the shadow of the interior lights and pulled her ball cap low.

"I don't like smoke'n'mirrors bullshit," Ryang said.

"We're not gonna keep you long, Detective." Newler sat at the head of the table. "My associate just has a couple of questions about the shooting that aren't covered in the paperwork."

"I'd also like a full run-through of the investigation," Andy added. "In your words."

"And I'm just supposed to sit here and do that on face value?" Ryang squinted at Andy's silhouette. "How do I know this isn't a setup for some adorable IA surprise party? I put my best guys on this, and I don't need them all tied up for the next year and a half giving depositions."

"I'm not from IA," Andy said. "And you know that, because if you genuinely thought that was what you were walking into, you'd never have agreed to come here tonight. All this bluster is about making sure Newler knows that you're pissed, and you're inconvenienced, and he owes you a favor for this. So tell him that you know that, Tony." Andy flicked her hand at Newler.

Newler nodded. "I know."

"Happy?" Andy leaned back in her chair. Ryang sighed and cracked his knuckles, smoothed the tabletop with his palms like he was really weighing it all up and not just sulking.

When he finally got to it, he told her the story. Of the enormous penthouse apartment on Lexington Avenue in Kips Bay, two blocks east of the Flatiron Building and above a Book Bonanza store, with a private elevator opening into the foyer off the formal dining. The "Singaporean gangster asshole" who was never there, who hadn't wanted to answer questions about what was in the safe or let police search the apartment after the theft was discovered. Andy sat and listened to the tale about the off-duty police officer, Ivan Willstone, who'd been leaving a karate class one block over in Midtown, and who'd been found in the side street behind Book Bonanza with a double tap in the chest and his gym bag emptied on the concrete beside him. All Ryang and his team had been able to ascertain in the first twenty-four hours was that two shots rang out in the side street at around 11 P.M., and those in the surrounding apartments had been too busy, or tired, or anti-police, to call it in until 1 A.M. when somebody got a case of the guilts.

Officer Willstone's body had been discovered twenty yards down the street from his car, in the direction heading *away* from the karate school. With his belongings strewn on the ground, and his wallet and phone missing, it was assumed he had made it to his car, then been beckoned farther along the narrow, pedestrian-only section of the street and mugged.

"Officer Willstone fell between two dumpsters that were attached to a construction site when he was hit," Ryang said. "So anybody who heard the shots and got off their lazy ass long enough to glance out the window wouldn't have seen anything anyway."

"So when did you learn about the safe robbery?" Andy asked.

"Eight days after we found Willstone's body in the street," Ryang said. "The homeowner, the Singaporean guy, flew in on business from Geylang. Apparently he's in the country once every couple of months, keeps the penthouse apartment as a bolt-hole for business and a fuck pad, but it goes empty in between. He says he arrived and discovered the safe missing, and while he was asking his neighbors if they'd seen or heard anything, he learned about the shooting in the street. Heard it was on the same night. Wondered if the two were related."

"Okay," Andy said.

"I call bullshit on that, personally," Ryang said. "The apartment was wired up with more cameras and sensors than a modern prison. He would have known he was being robbed the *moment* someone entered his apartment. But what do you know? He says all his tech blinked out about a half hour before Willstone's shooting. Nothing was caught on film."

"If nothing was caught on film, how does this guy know the robbery was the same night as the shooting, and not the night after, for example?"

"Exactly." Ryang shrugged.

Andy thought about Ben Haig crawling under the jewelry store on West Thirty-Fifth Street, accessing the subsurface electrical exchange, implanting his security-obliterating bug. Haig hadn't told Andy that's how the crew had blinked out the security at the jewelry store. But a glance at the amount of tech magazines Haig had on his bookshelves, and a quick tour of the maps of disused subway tunnels under the jewelry store and the fabric store, had set Andy's imagination wandering.

She looked at the detective across from her, measured him. "So you're assuming whoever stole the safe took it down to the street behind the Book

Bonanza. Willstone approached them while they were loading it up," Andy said. "But you have no witnesses. No other footage."

Ryang scoffed. "I don't need either. It's a pretty solid assumption."

Andy didn't comment.

"If we'd known the safe had been stolen *that same night,* I would have gone down a completely different avenue of investigation." Ryang was stabbing the tabletop with his finger now, his eyes searching the darkness beneath Andy's ball cap. "As it is, I had my guys looking for muggers, or for someone who would have wanted to target Willstone personally. I turned this man's life upside down looking for suspects. His wife's, too. There's stuff about the Willstones' world that I wouldn't have had to dredge up if I'd known he just got unlucky stumbling into a robbery in progress."

"What kind of stuff?" Newler asked.

"Oh, you know, the regular shit." Ryang ran his hand through his hair. "Affairs. Debts. Kinks."

They all fell silent. The night creatures chorused on.

"Tell me about the Hurst tool," Andy said.

Ryang sat back. "It took a forensic nerd to tell us that's what it was. All we could see from the crime scene, *when we finally got access to the apartment,* was that the safe had been lifted right off the spot it was bolted to. To us, it looked like someone had wheeled in a crane and picked the thing up off its housing."

"What do you mean?"

"This safe was bolted to a concrete slab." Ryang made a circle with his thumb and index finger. "Bolts this round, solid steel, drilled down about four inches. The Jaws of Life—the Hurst tool, whatever the fuck you want to call it—it doesn't only cut. It also spreads. Someone jammed the teeth of the device in between the bottom of the safe and the concrete slab. The gap was about a half inch wide. They turned the machine on and spread the gap until the safe popped right off the concrete, bolts and all. The forensics lady was able to tell us it was a Hurst tool from the shape of the cracks in the concrete."

Andy leaned her chin on her palm.

"We were thinking firefighters," Ryang said. "I know that's crazy. But we looked into it anyway, and everybody came up clean. I really liked that theory. I mean there was even a fire in the building six months earlier.

Kitchen fire, two floors below. Whole-building evac. Two teams of fire-fighters. One covering Kips Bay, one in support. About twelve guys total. I wondered if, you know, maybe while they were putting out the fire the team took a stroll around, got into the guy's apartment. Noticed the safe. Decided to come back."

"So you looked closely at the crews who responded to the fire?"

"Yeah, and they're all stand-up guys." Ryang shrugged. "One's a 9/11 first responder, for chrissakes."

Andy said nothing.

"Also, the hose jockeys, they have this thing called a thermal lance," Ryang said. "Cuts through steel like butter, would have had the safe off the slab before you could say 'Abracadabra!' So why would they have used the Jaws of Life, if they had one of those they could use instead?"

Because a thermal lance would have been messier, Andy thought, remembering her training. *And louder.*

"So I dropped that idea," Ryang went on. "Turns out you can get a Hurst tool just about anywhere. Body shops use them, and so do junkyard salvagers and demolition guys. EMTs, too. Most of the big ships down on the Hudson carry a set to cut anchor chains with, in case of a snag. There was also the construction zone two doors down, the one that had littered the side street with dumpsters and equipment. I couldn't get a solid answer about whether they had one or not. None of the guys working on that site spoke English. You can buy a Hurst tool on eBay, for chrissakes. It was a dead end."

Andy gave Newler a wave, went to the edge of the deck, and stood looking at the garden as Newler saw Detective Ryang out. Her thoughts had her so tangled that she was standing staring at the lawn when he arrived back beside her, though she'd intended to slip away. The gold garden lights hit angles in his face that reminded her of the evening they'd met. The alleyway behind the homeless shelter.

"You need to get Ben Haig on tape confessing to this," Newler said. "Then you need to get him to discuss it with his crew. Get that on tape."

"Sure, I'll have it on your desk Monday morning," Andy quipped. Newler gave that awful elongated sigh. "Haig won't budge on the robberies until I make headway on Denero and her son. That's my priority right now."

"It shouldn't be."

"Well, it is." Andy put her hands in her pockets so he wouldn't see her clench her fists. "It's possible Luna and the boy are alive and in danger. Ivan Willstone is dead. I can't help him right now."

"But you can help yourself." Newler stepped off the deck and came in front of her, stood on the grass. He was at her eye level now. "This can't really be your long-term plan, can it? Wandering around the countryside, picking up cash jobs?"

"My long-term plan doesn't concern you."

"There's a way you can keep doing this." Newler's eyes wandered her face. "You like the smoke-and-mirrors games. The acting. The puzzle-solving. I get that. But you can do it *safely*. With a team. With a security net. I know the kind of stuff you've been doing out there, and it's only a matter of time before one of these private clients shorts you, or kills you, or gets you killed, and there won't be a damn thing anybody can do about it. You're gonna get too old for this one day." He laughed. "Don't you see that?"

"Is that your long-term plan, Tony?" Andy asked. "Loop me back in? Get me sanctioned, on the books as an FBI consultant. Give me an office and a team. I'll face the commute on the way home. Try audiobooks to keep my mind busy. I'll cook you dinner, have it ready before—"

"Oh come on."

"—you get home. You can fuck me in the ass once a year, on your birthday."

The meanness had come into his eyes. He worked his jaw softly, chewing on his rage.

"It's exactly what you were offering me back in Pierre Part," Andy said. "Ten fucking years ago. I haven't changed my mind, Tony. Just being around you is a living hell. I wouldn't last a week in the pretty little cage you're trying to put me in."

She turned and walked to the end of the porch and found the stepping stones in the grass that led to the back gate. When she glanced around at him, she expected to see that rage still burning. But he looked like a sad, deflated old man, the empty house with all its lights on sprawling behind his bulky silhouette.

"If you're patient," she said, "I can give you Officer Willstone. Maybe Titus Cliffen. Maybe Luna and Gabriel Denero, too. You'll have multimillion-dollar solves in your name, some of them going back a decade. A crew with this much blood on their hands, and one of them a 9/11 veteran? You'll make international headlines, Tony."

His eyes glittered in the dark.

"But if you do what you did in Pierre Part, you'll lose it all," Andy said. Newler was silent. He tried to turn away.

"Don't you dare turn your back on me," she snarled. "I need to hear you say it. You're going to stop following me. Stop shadowing me. Stop thinking about me, and the stupid little fantasy life we were *never* going to live together. You're going to be a professional and treat this job like any other. Say it."

Still, Newler didn't speak.

"You have to let me go, Tony."

She turned and walked into the dark before she could decide whether her words had landed, whether they'd changed something in him. Because she was just too afraid of what it would mean if they hadn't.

BEN

.

Ben looked at his phone on the edge of the table, tilted the screen toward himself so that it woke. His stomach was heavy with dread. He hoped the other guys at the table couldn't sense it. There was still nothing from Andy. He'd remembered the reverence in her voice and the hardness in her eyes when she'd told him not to go off script. His message to her, mentioning Luna, had been burning a hole in his brain all that day, was searing there now as he tried to pay attention to Matt's scrawlings on the paper in front of them. Matt's cellar yawned around them. He could hear Donna playing Taylor Swift somewhere above them in the kitchen.

"This is Borr Secure Storage, it's one block down from Rockefeller Center. You know, where the FedEx place is." Matt drew a box in the middle of the paper, then added another identical square on top. "It's a two-story place. Level one: foyer, small office, and the boxes. Level two: more offices. Next door, here, on the right, we got an office-supply company. On the left here we got an Italian restaurant. Cristobel's. Two floors each."

Matt added blocks to either side of his original column. Engo leaned over and looked at the three columns of squares, two high.

"I feel like I'm there!" Engo said. "I can smell the cannelloni!"

Jake snickered.

"The safety-deposit box we're interested in is on the first floor of Borr's, back corner, right-hand side, about chest height. It's box 408." Matt tapped the first box he'd drawn with the pen, his eyes sharp and moving over their faces. "I want you all to have that number burned into your fucking minds from now on. Four oh eight. I want you saying it in your sleep."

"Four oh eight, Engo." Ben nudged him. "That's just about how tall you are, isn't it? Four foot eight?"

"It's my dick size," Engo said.

"Ah, yes. Thing's like a carpet python. Long and thin."

"Scaled for her pleasure."

"We want our entry into the facility to be completely organic." Matt's voice was getting edgy. Ben settled in his seat. "So we're gonna come through the restaurant."

"How?" Engo asked.

Matt leaned forward, his pen on the restaurant's first floor like he was pinning the imaginary doors shut. "We call in a gas odor. We respond. We'll arrive on scene and find our multi-gas monitor is faulty. We'll order a whole-building evac as a precaution while we wait for the 98s to come in with their monitor. While all that activity is going on out front, you'll be round the back, Engo."

"Doing what?"

"Pumping the restaurant full of LPG."

Engo laughed. "Nice."

"We're gonna blow the restaurant?" Jake's eyes were wide. "Jesus, fuck. What's on top of it?"

"Apartments," Matt said. A hush fell over them all. Ben looked at his phone, fiddled with it, didn't want to be the one to tap out first. When Jake spoke up, Ben felt a wave of pride. For all the crap they gave Jake, the kid had morals.

"We can't do that. We have rules," Jake said.

"Everybody will be out," Matt continued. "We'll make sure they're out. We have all the time in the world to clear the apartments."

"Well, we don't have all the time in the world," Engo said. "The 98s are gonna want to know why we didn't vent the restaurant as a precaution."

"We'll work it out."

"We can't blow up a restaurant that's underneath an apartment building!" Jake yelled.

"Jake, he's not talking about a nuclear-level blast here." Engo tapped the line that separated the Borr Secure Storage box from the Cristobel's restaurant box. "We just want an explosion that's big enough that it'll blow out this wall and give us access to the storage facility, the lockboxes."

"It's not going to collapse any of the overall structure." Matt followed the lines connecting the restaurant and the storage facility. "This is double brick. This is concrete. This is steel."

"Yeah, but—"

"But what, Jake?"

Jake looked at Ben.

"Variables." Ben shrugged. "Millions of variables. How are we going to contain the force of the blast? What's to say it won't just blow out the front and back and leave the wall to Borr Storage intact?"

"The only reason I'm thinking a blast is what we need," Matt said, "is because I've been into Cristobel's, okay? I've seen the restaurant, seen the layout. The room is divided in half right down the middle, with the back door—where we'll be pumping the gas—right here on the same side as the storage facility. So our half of the first floor will fill up with gas first." He shaded half the Cristobel's box, the half touching the Borr Secure Storage box. "Plus, along this same wall at the back here? You got the freezer room. The coolant tanks in the freezer in there will explode. Then you got the bar. All those fridges at hip height will also blast out. This whole wall is going to come down, leaving the safety-deposit-box room right there, open to us."

"This is going to be a big fire," Ben said. "It's a restaurant. You got tablecloths. Curtains. Carpets. Wooden furniture."

"Yeah."

"It'll be bigger than the fabric store."

"No it won't."

"Yes it will."

"I've thought about this. I've made all the necessary calculations. An LPG blast is going to be big enough to crack the wall, and damage the boxes on this side of Borr Storage, but not the ones on the other side of the room." He shaded the paper, circled, his pen strokes becoming steadily more exaggerated. "So 408 and all those boxes will be perfectly intact. With nothing taken from the damaged boxes, and nothing taken from the unopened boxes, it'll fit our story."

"But a blast that size will—"

"We're talking about LPG, we're not talking about napalm!" Matt barked.

"I don't care if it's methane. It's right underneath an apartment building," Ben said.

"*An empty apartment building!*" Matt's neck was growing red. "You're not hearing me! Open your fucking ears!"

"We've never done this before," Jake said quietly. "The fabric store, that was commercial buildings on either side. Whenever there's been residential places near our jobs they've been small fires or false callouts only. A big blast near civilians? I don't know."

"It'll be fine. In fact, we should consider something a little heavier than LPG, though, if we're getting technical." Engo tapped the paper with his damaged hand. "It'll take half an hour to fill that space with LPG and you're crossing your fingers it'll bring that wall down. If we used acetyl—"

"No."

"If we used—"

"I said no," Matt snapped.

"You're not even letting me finish! Acetylene gas would get in there quicker, it'd have a bigger—"

"Why would a restaurant be full of acetylene gas! They're cooking spaghetti, not welding copper!"

"It won't matter! Your guy on the arson investigations team will—"

"Engo. Matt," Ben said. "Just stop. Stop."

They'd both half risen out of their chairs. Ben and Jake were like two guys outside the tiger enclosure at the zoo, wondering what the hell they were going to do if the jungle savagery they were witnessing spilled through the plexiglass. Nobody spoke for a solid minute.

"So." Engo turned to Matt like nothing had happened, pointed to the restaurant. "You're out front coordinating. Ladder 98 are on their way to support. Ben and Jake are knocking down the fire. I dash in here, open up box 405, take the cards."

"It's 408, you motherfu—"

"I'm fucking with you, Matt, I'm fucking with you. I know it's 408."

"Don't fuck with him, please!" Jake begged.

"Box 408 will survive the blast, like I said." Matt exhaled long and hard. "It's on this wall. Opposite the blast zone. There's no way any of these boxes will be damaged. It's too far."

"So we'll need a key," Engo said.

"Keys," Ben pointed out. "Those safety-deposit boxes, they need two keys. One from the owner, and one from the facility. So you'll be digging around at the front of the store trying to find the key for 408."

"They're in cabinets marked by number. It won't take long."

"But it'll take time," Ben insisted. "And who the fuck knows how we're going to get the old man's key."

"The lawyer," Matt said. "I'm working on it. That's the next phase. We're in this phase now." He stabbed the paper a bunch of times with the pen, peppering the boxes with jagged dashes. "There are *phases*, you dumb pricks!"

"I got a question." Jake raised his hand and Matt's nostrils flared. Ben set his legs, in case he had to throw himself on top of Jake to stop him from getting choked out. "Where the hell's Andy during all this?"

"Crowd control," Matt said. "I'll keep an eye on her."

"But what if she—"

Matt snapped the pen in half with his thumb. Jake slid his chair back.

"No, really, though," Engo said. "Where's Andy? It'll look weird if she's not in there."

"We could make sure she doesn't come along." Jake shrugged. "Keep her busy with something at the station."

"You could bang her so hard the night before that she can't walk straight and has to call in sick." Engo nudged Ben in the ribs.

"Jesus, man."

"It's not bad, though," Jake said. "Get her to call in sick. If you put Visine in someone's food—"

"Oh, here we go. I wondered how you lost your virginity." Engo nudged Jake now.

"It doesn't knock you out, it just glues you to the toilet." Jake rolled his eyes. "We did it to a guy at the academy."

"You stupid fucks are trying as hard as you can to make sure this doesn't go down." Matt was gently trembling all over. Ben thought of buildings before they collapsed, the way they shivered and swayed. "If you had any brain cells to rub together, you'd realize that this job is the perfect *last* job."

They watched Matt grapple with the monster turning inside him. After a few moments, he pointed to the ceiling, beyond which Donna was clattering pots and pans to a song about broken hearts.

"That's my last wife," Matt said. "That's my last kid. This is my last job."

Ben felt Jake stir beside him. The probie's throat had tightened, his Adam's apple shrinking against his collar. Matt noticed the reaction.

"Yeah." He nodded, knowing. A disappointed judge handing out his sentence. "Sucks to be you, Jake. But you had enough time to put together a proper stash, like the rest of us. You should have been stacking notes away all this time somewhere nobody would ever suspect. The last ever place you'd have anything to do with. A nice old nest egg. The fact that you blew it all on bad dogs and lame horses and rigged poker games is not on me. It's not on any of us."

Jake didn't answer.

"We've all got rainy-day money." Matt pointed the Finger of Death around the circle, let it hover over Ben. "This tight-ass here probably has the biggest haul among us. Ben was raised by junkies and foster carers so he's a trained scavenger. I've seen him tuck a quarter into his wallet. He's like a squirrel. Look at him. He hasn't bought anything new in a decade. His clothes are older than some of my kids."

Ben looked at his own shirt.

"You've been an idiot," Matt went on, lining Jake up with the Finger. "You got one job left. This one. And I say this with all the love I can possibly muster for you right now, Jake. Do not go solo. You're too stupid. You're not built for it."

"You'll try to rob a bodega, slip on a banana peel, and get jacked up," Engo agreed. "You'll try to roll on us to save yourself, and Matt will have to bury you under his pool."

"I'll feed you to Donna," Matt sighed. "That woman ate a cake this morning for breakfast."

"A cupcake?"

"No, a whole cake." He gripped an imaginary dinner-plate-sized object. "Baby shower cake she's supposed to take to a party tomorrow. Sat at the counter. Cut it into eight slices. Ate them all, one at a time."

Ben's phone rang on the table. He put a hand on it, but Engo's was already on the device. Electricity charged through Ben's veins, his whole arm and shoulder spiking with panic, the lightning cracking through his chest.

"Oh, ho!" Engo yanked the phone out from under Ben's hand. "Look who it is."

They all stared at the screen. Andy's name pulsed and flashed, reflected in the deadly black orbs of Matt's eyes.

"You should answer it on speaker, Ben." Engo held the phone aloft, pushed Ben in the chest as he reached for it. "I want to hear you talk dirty to her."

"No, no, no. Give me the fucking phone, Engo!"

"I've been waiting days now for the nudes." Engo laughed, stood up. Ben came after him. "Not one. This time of night, you think if we answered on FaceTime we might get lucky?"

Ben knew his raw, trembling panic was showing on his face, that it was twisting something curious in Matt. The big man at the table cocked his head in that awful way he did when devils were whispering in his ears and the cauldron in his mind was boiling mischief. Ben punched Engo in the sternum, hard, then grabbed the phone when his arm came down. All the breath left Engo's chest. The older man coughed, had to steady himself against the wall by the pool table.

They all knew the hit was too hard and Ben's voice was too high as he pleaded for the phone. The very veins in his arms and neck were standing too taut on the surface of his skin. He'd blown it. Matt put his hands flat on the tabletop.

The phone stopped ringing. Matt pushed the drawing of the heist aside and pointed at the device.

"Call her back," Matt said. "Put it on speaker."

ANDY

·

ndy looked at her failed call to Ben, the red bubble on the screen.
She sighed and slipped into her car, shut the door. In the distance
she could see Newler's house over the wall of cypress trees. The lights
were turning off, one by one, rising upward to what she presumed
was the master bedroom. Though she hadn't entered the house, looking
through the deck doors she'd seen worrying signs about her old partner's
life. One stack of books on the side table in the living room. One dent in
the couch. One set of scuff marks in the decking, beneath just one of the six
outdoor chairs. She imagined him sitting out there flicking spent cigarettes
into the wet bushes and staring at the distant lights in the dark, fancying
himself a tortured Gatsby on the dock. Fear of what Newler was becoming
put a recklessness into her.

She started typing out a message to Ben.

*The script is there for a reason. Delete this message, and your last,
and do not—*

BEN

.

'm not gonna do that." Ben kept his grip on the phone, though all he wanted to do was crush the thing in his fist. "I don't know why you would want me to, Matt."

"Because you're so twitchy," Matt said. "Too twitchy. I don't like it. Open the phone and call her back. Put it on sp—"

"No."

"Put it on speaker. I ain't asking you."

Matt's voice was low, deadly. He was snake-coiled and lethal. Ben had seen him like that only once, maybe twice ever, and it had put the fear of God into him. Actual fear of actual God, like what Matt was about to do was bigger than a man's intent, the workings of something far more inevitable. An avalanche. A cave collapse. The silence in the room offered Ben not a shred of inspiration on how to wiggle out of this, no relief from the wild panic thumping in his brain. He had no plan for what he would say to Andy when she answered. Because of course she would assume he was alone. She would ask him about the last text. *Important re: Luna.* Best-case scenario, it would look like he'd been discussing his missing girlfriend with his current girlfriend. Which wasn't the story. Wasn't the script. Worst-case scenario, Andy was going to be pissed that he'd gone rogue, and she'd cut in over the top of him before he could stop her and she would say that. Reveal that. That there was a fucking *script.* That this was all a game.

Sweat was running down the back of Ben's calves into his socks. The energy in the room was too dark now. They had to be suspecting that what was on the line here was more than a secret relationship. Ben could *feel* it, the knowledge buried in all three of them, waiting to be unearthed.

Andy is an undercover.

Ben is her rat.

The last sand covering these terrifying truths was being shaken off behind Matt's, Engo's, and Jake's eyes.

"Matt—"

Out of nowhere, Matt put a Glock on the table. Just lifted his hand from out of view and put it there on its side, the barrel pointing right at Ben's chest. Engo burst out in laughter.

"What the fuuuuu—"

"Shut up." Matt looked at him. Engo's laughter snapped off. Matt's eyes slid back to Ben, languid. Like he was under the influence of something or someone else. Hand of God. Hand of Lucifer. "Open the phone."

Ben told himself he would get through this. He punched his code into the phone, right there, in front of everyone. The gun sat pointed at him, Matt's hand resting near it.

"Open the messages."

Ben didn't move. Matt reached over and took the phone. He went right to the messages and opened them. Engo leaned over to read. Jake was rigid in his chair, watching Ben.

"'Important re: Luna,'" Matt read.

They all looked at Ben. He could feel that cold sweat now sticking his shirt to his back.

"What does that mean?" Matt asked.

Engo was watching the screen carefully. "She's writing back," he said.

Ben felt a bolt of pain in his core, toward the back, like he'd been poked hard. It was now or never, and Engo's grin of delight did it—gave him what he needed. The grotesque wetness of his teeth. Ben leaned over the table and looked Matt defiantly in the eyes.

"Call her," Ben said.

Matt made the decision. He put a finger to his lips, glanced at Engo and Jake in turn. He made the call and tapped the speaker option on.

Andy came on the line first, cut over him, as Ben knew she would.

"You really are trying to fuck this thing up, aren't you?"

Ben had three gun barrels trained on him. The Glock, and Matt's eyes.

"I'm not," Ben said. "I promise you, Andy, I'm not." He watched the others, tried to look resigned. Defeated. "Just let me explain, okay? When we . . . When we were in bed last night . . ."

Engo's mangled hand flew to his mouth.

"When we were together, and I said Luna's name." Ben pretended to struggle. Shook his head, humiliated. "It . . . It was just out of habit, okay? I wasn't thinking about her while I was having sex with you."

Engo gave a low groan of delight. Matt reached over and gripped his arm to silence him.

"I'm not trying to fuck things up between you and me," Ben continued, staring at the ceiling, praying to God or whatever the hell was up there to help Andy to understand the situation. That he was compromised. That they weren't safe. "I like you, Andy. Okay? It's important that you understand that. Okay, yeah, I said her name. And that's fucked up. Really fucked up. But it was an accident. There was nothing behind it."

Silence on the line. Ben's head was swimming. Ten long, painful seconds passed. He counted them, wondering if they'd be his last on earth.

Finally, she spoke. "How do you do that?" Ben felt the tension in the air split. "How do you *accidentally* say one woman's name while you're fucking another one?"

Engo couldn't hold it together. He went to the windows to laugh into his hands.

"I don't know."

"*I* know." Andy sounded tired. Pissed. Like every girlfriend he'd ever crossed before. "It's because all her stuff's still there in your apartment, Ben. Her clothes are in the closet. Her makeup is in the bathroom. The only thing about the scenario that was different for you last night was me being under you and not her."

Ben wiped sweat off his brow.

"In the beginning, it wasn't that weird," Andy ranted on. "But it's getting *weird*, Ben."

"Okay. I'm sorry."

"I don't know where Luna went but she's gone. She's *gone*, okay?"

"Yep."

"How long are you going to wait for this woman to show up back in your life? Because your dick has moved on, that's for sure."

"I'm sorry, Andy."

"That's one word for it."

"Do we have to talk about this over the phone?" Ben looked around the table. "Can I . . . Can I just come and see you?"

"Maybe."

Andy hung up. Engo was wheezing, crouched by the pool table, hanging off the corner pocket. "Oh man," he laughed. "Oh maaaan!"

"So you *are* still fucking her," Matt said. Ben didn't nod. He didn't have to. Matt didn't have to tell him to get out, either. The message was clear, and Ben didn't waste any time hanging around in case it inspired Matt to start digging a place for him under his pool. He slunk to the stairs and went out the back and took the side passage to his car, the sounds of Engo's laughter and Swift's crooning following him all the way there.

Someone drove over the pipe on the road, and the buzzer sounded. Ten seconds later, a dusty Camaro pulled up at the first pump, and Dahlia glanced out the gas station doors at it without really seeing the vehicle, captivated instead by Brangelina in Kenya, a photo shoot in W *magazine. What insiders were saying about Jen's rage and torment, her unrequited yearning for her own Domestic Bliss. The sound of the TV drifted through the thin door to the back apartment, competing with the hum of the fridges. Her parents' quiet, comedic dissection of the news had drained away as* The Office *stole their consciousness, and that had been Dahlia's sign that it was safe to switch over from her chem assignment to the trash mags. The car pulled in and just sat there idling, and the twenty-two-year-old took no notice.*

It was maybe thirty seconds before the guy got out. He walked to the bumper of the car, stood there facing the rusty sunset, his hands hanging by his sides. He was there another minute or two before something icy tickled the back of Dahlia's neck. Her first thought was that he was watching the sunset. Then, that he'd perhaps seen something out there in the desert. But some deeply rooted alert system in her core told her he was standing there just slightly too long, and too still. Nobody traveled this road who hadn't seen a Texan sunset a thousand times before. And there was nothing out there to look at. Nothing for hundreds of miles.

That's when she went around the counter and over to the automatic doors. They bleeped and slid open, and she saw the blood.

It was running down the back of the man's neck in a thick, red-brown smear to his mid-back, where it butterflied out on the white cotton of his singlet, spectacular wings of red and pink. A contact stain, from where he'd been pressed against the driver's seat. The backs of his jeans black with it, where it had pooled as he sat. Dahlia stepped closer, her whole world wobbling and tilting, and traced the blood landscape back up the man's body to his head. The sandy-blond hair at the rear of his skull was dark with blood and a whole hank of it was hanging down, still attached to flesh and bone, a round door into his skull that had been blown almost completely off its hinges by the bullet.

"Oh," Dahlia said. The word used up all her breath. She sucked another chestful and used it all again on another single word. "Jesus."

"Mom?" the guy asked. He turned and looked through her. Dahlia could see where the bullet had entered his hairline; a dark, round hole. His eyes, bloodshot

and sliding around, moved right over her like she wasn't there. "Mom? Are you home?"

Dahlia turned and ran so hard she misjudged the counter, banged it as she went by, knocked over a stand of novelty fridge magnets. They scattered on the floor. She yanked the door to the apartment open. Her dad had leaped off the couch before she could get the words out.

"Help-help-help!" she screamed.

The guy was in the store by now. His legs were shaking hard. Dahlia's father caught him, lowered the guy to the linoleum. "Holy fuck, what happened?"

"I don't know! He just pulled up and got out and—"

"Get a towel. Rina! Get towels!"

Dahlia's mother had made it to the edge of the counter. She spun and rushed back through the door to the apartment, came out with her arms full of towels. The guy was seizing on the linoleum, back arching, sneakers squeaking, Dahlia kneeling there holding him. She felt her mother come alongside her. Rina carefully shut the door in the guy's skull with shaking, already blood-soaked fingers, pressed it there with the towel. Dahlia gagged. Then her mother gagged. Then they carried on, swathing the head together like they were frantically wrapping a last-minute Christmas present.

"Shaun, we gotta call 911!" her mother shouted.

Dahlia's father didn't answer. She looked up and saw why. Through the automatic doors, the silver-haired and sunbaked Shaun Lore was holding open the passenger-side door of the Camaro. Another guy was spilling out of his seat; a red, liquid human, legs twisted in the footwell and wet arms hanging over his head. This guy wasn't moving. Dahlia noticed for the first time that the windshield of the Camaro was blown out. Her father's boots crunched on glass as he came back into the gas station, leaving prints, making the doors bleep again.

He pointed to the twitching guy. "Leave him," he said. He grabbed Dahlia by the biceps and yanked her up. "They'll be here soon."

"Who?"

"Whoever shot these guys," he said. "The back seat of the car is full of cash."

"What?"

He was shoving her, hurting her, his hands vicious with a parental terror. "Go to your room, Dahlia. Hide in the closet. Rina, go with her."

"We can't leave him!"

"Get in the fucking closet! Now!"

They went. There was so much blood, Dahlia smeared it all over the door and *walls and the closet handle just getting to a hiding spot. Felt angry and heartsick over the guy with the hole in his head and her father out there in the store doing useless things like locking the doors and turning the lights out while he bled and bled.*

Then Dahlia felt them coming. Her father's words had brought them to life, summoned them, and now the beat of their dark hooves was in her neck and chest. Whoever. Her mother clutched her, hushing her, the two of them awkwardly kneeling on her sour-smelling shoes, the dust in the bottom of the closet making her eyes itch. They knelt and panted and whimpered and listened to the hellish orchestra of Shaun's last moments.

Shaun Lore. Gas station owner. Husband. Father. Longhorns fan. Secret comic-book nerd. Stoic, mustached, deadpanning pepperoni-pizza-loving daddy-man. He was about to be murdered. Dahlia didn't know it then, and yet of course she did, because she'd heard it in his voice. The finality of it.

Hello? This is Shaun Lore out at the Road Haven. 1081 Dryden Road. We got a shooting here. I need the sheriff now.

Screaming in response. Steve Carell hysterical about something. The Office was still playing in the den.

One's dead and one's just about. I don't care; I care about who's comin' down the road. My wife and daughter are here, okay? Whatever's gone down with these guys, it might not be finished yet. Tell the sheriff to have lights and sirens on because—

"Listen to me." Rina grabbed her daughter. Dahlia felt her mother's hands on her cheeks, warm with sweat and blood. "We've got to keep calm."

"I can't keep calm!"

"Baby, baby, baby, listen! If your daddy's right," Rina said, "whoever's after those guys is gonna get here long before the sheriff does."

"Mom! Please!"

"That man can't have been driving far with a hole in his head like that. If they didn't take care of whoever was after them, then—"

"Stop." Dahlia was gripping her mother's neck, her hair, didn't know whether to hug her or gag her. Because she knew. It wasn't a matter of if, but when. Whoever was coming. "I can't hear it, Mom. I'm scared. I'm scared!"

"We're not gonna be scared right now, baby. We're gonna be smart."

They heard a clatter. Shaun tossing the phone on the counter. The clumping of his boots, then the shunting of the shotgun from under the counter. Rina and Dahlia held each other, sticky-fingered, dry-mouthed, wide-eyed and blind. The pipe buzzer sounded. A car engine turned off. Two car doors popped open and shut, quietly, calmly. Boots on the glass, slow, confident. The credits were rolling on both The Office *and Shaun Lore's life.*

Open up.

No. I can't do that. I can't do that, okay? I'm not lookin' for trouble, and I'm not lookin' for violence, guys. So take the car and go. The sheriff is on his way.

Open. The doors.

Back away, mister. I will fire. We don't have to do this.

"Oh God, Mom!" Dahlia held her mother, gripped her shirt in both hands. "Please, please, please, please. Don't let them kill him, God, pleeeeaaase!"

Footsteps at the back of the house. A bucket clanging. A broom toppling, hitting the bricks. A door handle jangling.

One last chance to open the doors.

A gunshot, loud and roaring. Two more, softer, popping. A pistol. The women screamed, the shots pulsing in the tiny closet. Dahlia heard her father's gurgling cry. The sound of it lit something in Rina. She grabbed Dahlia's wrists and peeled the young woman from her body.

"I'm going to go out and lead them away from you."

"What! No!"

"Use the distraction to climb out your window, Dahlia."

"Mom! No! No-no-no-no-no! Don't leave me here!"

Two more shots, closer than the first, inside the gas station. Not shotgun shots. Pistol shots. The boots, still slow, taking his time. Rina slid aside the closet door. Dahlia's throat was so dry, her words rasped out like growls.

"Mom, don't leave me!"

The door to the laundry being opened from inside. Whoever had murdered Dahlia's father had crossed the living room on the carpet in silence, and was now letting his partner in through the back. Canned laughter and piano music. Dahlia raked her mother's fingers with her nails as the older woman pulled her hand away.

"You'll be okay," she said as she reached the door. "I love you."

Dahlia crawled out of the closet, went to her bedroom window, knocked scented candles and statues of angels onto the floor as she climbed through. A wind chime caught in her hair, pulling strands free. The night air was warm. Behind her, the voices and the gunshots were barely audible over her own ragged panting.

Is there anyone else here?

No. Please, don—

Pop. Pop.

Dahlia hit the ground and ran for the horizon. It bounced and shuddered, a red-black and featureless brush mark. Whimpers and cries escaped her, tears streaking from the corners of her eyes and into her temples. She heard the window she'd escaped from shuddering as Whoever shoved it open further. More pops. Her shoulder was shunted forward by a flaming-hot poker, sending her tumbling in the sand.

ANDY

·

She woke on Ben's couch, and the dark curtains of the nightmare dropped around her, a man looming up instead, silhouetted against the blue-lit ceiling. Andy reached up and grabbed Ben's shoulders, recognized the feel of his big hands on hers. She didn't even realize she was crying until she tried to speak and all that came out was hard sobs.

"Whoa! Whoa! Whoa!" Ben gathered her into his chest. "It's me. It's me!"

Humiliation washed over her, heavy and prickling. She had drenched herself and the couch in sweat. Pants wet with what she hoped wasn't piss. She pushed him away, all her limbs aching like they had that night as she sprinted into the vastness of the desert toward nothing and away from her waking hell.

"Are you okay? What was that about?" Ben asked.

She waved at him, turned away, trying to swallow or squeeze out the sobs. She had control of her breathing in under a minute. It was her mind that she had trouble reeling in. It was out there, floating in the past, a battered kite caught in a storm. Loop by loop, she had to pull it in. Remember the apartment. The assignment. The man she was with, and not the people she had lost.

"Did you just get in?"

"I've been here a few minutes," Ben said. "I saw you were sleeping, so . . ."

She nodded, wiped the tears away.

"'Important,'" she said.

"Huh?"

"'Important re: Luna.' What did you actually want to tell me?"

"Are you o—"

"I'm not talking about it," Andy said. His silhouette on the end of the couch was upright, rigid, alert. "You caught me in . . . in a private moment, Ben. It was a nightmare. It was no big deal. Let's move on now so you can tell me what you wanted to tell me."

His voice was careful. Quiet. "My brother Kenny turned up here this morning."

He told her about the email from Luna. Andy wound her kite all the way in, hand over hand, so grateful that they weren't talking about the storm anymore.

"You think she was making amends," Andy said. "Saying her goodbyes."

"Maybe."

"What happened between those two?"

Ben gave a short, sad laugh. "It's so stupid."

Andy watched him lean back against the couch.

"He's always wanted to pay me back," Ben said. "For putting him through college. For taking him on. But he just can't figure out how. He gets the guilts sometimes and gives it a try, but he's always wrong. Like he bought me a Porsche once. What the hell am I gonna do with a Porsche? He'll turn up with an expensive coffee machine. Or a lead into a job I'd rather kill myself than do."

"Okay."

"He invited me out to lunch, and I brought Luna and Gabe along without telling him. We've never really talked about that kind of stuff. Girls. Relationships. This was going to be the first woman I'd introduced him to, really. But it was a mistake to bring them without checking first. Because Kenny had a little surprise of his own. He was trying to set me up. Some client of his. An Instagram model."

Andy nodded.

"Luna blew up. Kenny blew up. The client woman blew up. Gabe burst into tears." Ben shook his head. Andy could see the smile tightening his cheeks. "I'm sitting there, the only person at the table who's managing to keep it together."

"So she wasn't apologizing to Kenny with the email. She was just saying—"

"'We're all good,'" Ben said.

They both sat, thinking.

"Why would she suddenly say that, a week before she disappeared?" Ben asked.

"Because she knew something bad was coming." *She was either being scared, or being smart,* Andy thought.

"I gotta go." Andy glanced at her watch, rose from the humiliatingly damp couch. "We're on duty in five hours. I would lecture you on the script—"

"I've learned my lesson."

"And I'm too tired to do it."

"Just stay here." Ben waved a hand toward the bedroom. "You'll add an hour to your sleep time."

Andy stood there in the dark. His face was in shadow, unreadable, but a rush of tingles spread over the backs of her arms, a phenomenon she passed off to the nightmare. She told herself that she'd done unnecessary things with hosts before. Laughed with them, joked with them, ate with them when she didn't need to, because she wasn't a robot. She was a human. She felt things. Humor. Loneliness. Exhaustion. Sleeping beside Ben Haig now when she didn't really need to wasn't any different from a thousand times she'd relented to her humanity with a host before. It wasn't crossing any lines. They weren't lovers. He had no idea who she was.

She showered and climbed into the sheets in her panties, noting he was wearing boxer shorts as she peeled back the covers. He was turned on his side, facing away from her, already asleep.

The hours climbed toward sunrise and she lay awake and stared at the shadows on the wall.

BEN

.

omeless people crowded the engine at the scene outside the abandoned high school, open-mouthed and hollering walking dead. Matt got down from his seat and batted one guy away like a fly, made him slide on his ass on the wet pavement. The four-story building on West Fifty-Second was well past due to become overpriced apartments. It was already leaking curtains of black smoke from three windows in the front. Matt parked close in so they could access the upper floors with their smaller, mobile ladder until a ladder truck arrived. A guy with shoulder-length hair so greasy it was a solid mass tugged at Ben's jacket as he started flipping open catches on the side of the truck.

"Yo, man, this is an insurance fire." The guy pointed to the building. "It's a setup. The owner's been trying to get us all to move out for months, and—"

"Get off me. I'm trying to work here." Ben pushed the guy aside, tried to keep his grip gentle. The guy staggered and kept coming.

"My bad. My bad. I'm just tellin' you, if anybody gets hurt here today—"

"This is attempted murder!" A woman butted in between Grease Helmet and Ben. Her eyes were yellow with liver damage. "Mr. Sanders knew the building was full of people! He's been threatening to burn it down since Christmas!"

"We don't give a fuck who lit it," Matt barked. He banged on the side of the truck with a gloved mitt like he was trying to scare off wild dogs. "Get out of the way so we can put it out."

The woman wheeled on Matt. The socks pulled up to her knees were full of holes revealing scabbed red sores. "Hey! You can just pipe the fuck down, buddy! Somebody gotta know what's happenin' here!"

"What's happenin' is you're just begging me to blast that rancid homeless stink off you with a fire hose." Matt took a shuffle-step toward her. "Ben, get me the twenty bar."

"Okay! Okay! I'm movin'!"

Jake jogged back from his loop around the building, shutting off power and gas. "Some of the locals are saying there's kids on the top floor," he said.

"How many?"

"Two." Jake shriveled as Matt approached, like it was his fault, like they were his children. "Maybe. Can't confirm. Some people are saying Child Protective Services took the kids last week but others are saying they're still up there."

"Where's Mom?" Ben asked.

"MIA."

"Has anyone seen the kids today?"

"Not sure."

"Well, thanks for that pile of useless, hysterical, steaming bullshit, Jake." Matt jammed three pieces of nicotine gum between his jaws. "Ben and Andy, you're on the ladder. Get your asses up there and look for anything with a pulse. Jake and Engo, hit the first floor and work upward."

Ben shouldered his Halligan bar and climbed up the back of the engine, put the ladder up against a window of the third floor of the old school. He could smell gasoline and human waste on the breeze. The black clouds of smoke on the first floor were billowing piss-yellow and brown as Jake and Engo began to force their way into the wall of flames. He was bending to grip the ladder when Andy snuck in front of him and went first.

A thought hit him from out of nowhere, so sudden and wild it almost flashed across his eyes: Andy popping the window at the end of the ladder to access the school building without checking it for backdraft. The flames bursting out, killing her instantly, toasting her like a marshmallow on a steel skewer. He felt a wave of guilt at the relief the vision gave him. Because there were no happy endings on the horizon, he knew. Either Luna had left him by choice, or she had been taken. If Andy died now, he might bask in the not-knowing for the rest of his life, lunatic-happy. But the nonsense fled him as his boots left the safe ground of the fire truck and met the rungs of the ladder. Andy had already busted out the window to the third floor, and he was tugging on his mask and climbing into the blackness with her.

The first room on the second floor was a smoke tank. Ben climbed in the window and followed the wall with a gloved hand, huffing rubber-flavored oxygen, swimming through depthless black and brown murk, nothing to focus on but tiny specks of ash floating past the mask. He kicked and shoved aside anything that came into his path—tables, chairs, cardboard boxes—feeling for the second window along the row. He could hear the distant pops of Andy smashing out windows along the east wall with her Halligan. All the while as he worked, he braced for the sickening sensation he'd experienced a hundred times before, of his boot landing on something that was just the wrong kind of soft and heavy. A body. He bashed out a window and kept going, his spirits lifting slowly as the smoke thinned. Sweat was rolling down his chest and belly, already wet in his hair under the helmet. Engo's voice was on the radio, defiantly calm for what he was saying.

"Watch out for the central hallway, team. It's about to go."

Ben turned toward the sound, a deep crunching as the floor of the hall outside the classroom gave way. Gold light from the flames surging upward, hungry for air, sparks and cinders swirling. Lit for a second was a pathway he could take between the upturned tables, the outline of an old whiteboard, and Andy gripping her way along the back wall, knocking down posters and artworks pinned there.

"You got anything up there, Benji?"

"Entry room's clear of civilians, Matt."

Ben watched in amazement as Andy stepped back and took a run-up, launched herself across the flaming crevasse made by the collapsed hallway. She landed in the entrance of another classroom. Ben went to the door and was stopped by a wall of brown smoke, a billowing response to Engo or Jake down below trying to subdue the flames. He gripped the doorframe, stepped out on a beam he'd barely glimpsed that ran parallel to the wall, and used it to step carefully across the gap. Andy was nowhere. He felt a sucker punch of terror to his belly. No windows had been vented. The smoke was thinner here, but Ben couldn't see Andy where she was supposed to be, outlined against the yellow looms he knew were windows leaking sunlight into the smoke sea. Something ran over his boots. A rat. Tiny taps on his steel-capped toes. He turned right, found a doorway to a storeroom connecting two classrooms. There he ran into her. She was ripping open lockers, shoving over boxes.

"Kids!" He heard her voice through her mask and his, even against the roar of the fire downstairs. "Kids! Are you here?"

"Jesus, Andy!" Ben grabbed her. He gripped the jaw of her mask so she was forced to look at his eyes. "What the fuck are you doing?"

"What do you think I'm doing?" Her eyes were huge. "I'm looking for the children!"

"We don't *know* they're here!" Ben barked. "It's unconfirmed! We gotta vent! That's our job!"

"But—"

"No buts!" He shoved her against the wall, trying to knock some sense into a senseless situation. "Fight the fire!"

He was furious and the anger made him clumsy. He went to the windows and smashed them out, all of them, so mad he almost threw his Halligan out of one and into the crowd below. Whoever the hell had trained Andy, they'd done a good job. She was convincing with the tools. Confident in the flames. But she didn't understand the subtleties, the unwritten laws, the knowledge that came only from bitter experience. You don't waste time trying to find victims you don't know for sure are there. Ben had learned that one the hard way after being on the job for only a couple of years. He'd almost got himself crushed to death by a falling roof beam searching too long for a teenager in an apartment fire, only to learn the kid was half a city away at a friend's place.

"Second room is clear," Ben reported.

They went through the connecting art-supply storeroom, into another classroom, this one bare. There were things hanging from the ceiling here— papier-mâché sculptures of butterflies or birds long since split or moldy or vandalized by the homeless. They vented, but the smoke was getting thicker as the fire took a room on the east of the building that must have been full of accelerants.

"Ben and Andy, I'm gonna get you guys down with the ground team," Matt said. *"Approach from the rear west."*

Ben turned to make sure Andy was following him. She wasn't. She was standing by the whiteboard, holding a teddy bear in her gloved hands.

"They're here, Ben," she said.

"We gotta go."

"No. They're here! I know they're here!"

"Andy, it's a fucking school! There's probably—"

Then he watched as Andy did something that made the hair stand up on the back of his neck.

She took her mask off.

"Kids!" she screamed. *"Kiiiiids!* It's Mommy! Mommy's here!"

"Put your fucking mask back on!" Ben rushed her, grabbed the mask. She was already coughing, her eyes squeezed shut against the searing smoke. Three more breaths and she'd be out cold.

"Kids! It's Mommy! It's Mommy! It's Mommy! Come to Mommy!"

Ben shoved her mask back on. She sucked oxygen, but she was basically blind now, her eyes filled with airborne ash. She wobbled, gripped him to steady herself. He was about to drag her out of the smoke-filled school when he saw a door at the end of the room pop open, the end opposite the storeroom. He hadn't even known the cupboard was there. The door was so covered in student art it was completely camouflaged. A small dark shape was moving, bent double, through the smoke. He heard the choking voice trying to push out words against the suffocating clouds.

"Mommyyyyy?"

Ben ran and grabbed the child, threw it over his shoulder. With his other hand he shoved Andy toward the hidden storage cupboard, where she bent and felt around and came out of the swirling blackness with a sagging bundle in her arms. Her eyes were clearing, but it wasn't enough. He'd have to guide her. Ben held the kid with one arm and Andy's hand with the other and led her toward the back door of the classroom.

It turned out the child in his arms was a girl. Ben didn't know that until he was handing her to an EMT and saw her filthy little Hello Kitty! T-shirt and her soot-coated face. Andy had a boy. He was unconscious. His legs were so bruised and swollen they made Ben think of drowning victims he'd pulled out of the Hudson. There was a woman at the edge of the crowd standing watching the children being loaded into the vans and Ben knew, just *knew*, she was the mother from the way she was rocking forward and then back on her heels. Like she wanted to go to her babies but she also didn't want to spend the next twelve hours in a small room with an investigator trying to explain the condition those babies were in. Matt tried to grab Ben on his way to the woman but for once the big man's strength was nothing against his fury, against a molten magma rage that had been boiling since *he* was the kid crying himself to sleep in a closet and hiding from the sound of sirens while his mother was Fuck-Knows-Where with Fuck-Knows-Who.

Ben grabbed the woman by her rail-thin, track-marked wrists right there in front of everyone, and a groan of protest went up from the homeless and the civilians who had gathered at the edge of the scene.

"Where *the fuck* were you?" Ben roared in her face. He shook her, resisted the urge to squeeze her skull with his gloved hands. Someone tried to haul him off. His helmet clattered on the cement. "Where the fuck were you, huh? *Huh?*"

Matt's hand clamped down on the back of Ben's turnout coat like a steel claw picking up a toy inside a skill-tester machine, just about lifting him off his feet. "Okay. You said your piece. Drop the drama and get back into line, Benji."

The fire was out. Ben was swimming in sweat and fury inside his bunker gear. Fury at the woman. Fury at Andy. He couldn't get his breathing under control. They all knew it. Were all staring at him. Jake's mask was up on his head and his helmet was under his arm, face pink and wet, like a guy who'd just finished a grueling game of high school football. They were all ignoring Andy, who was bent double and rinsing her eyes and mouth and nose with a water bottle someone had handed her. Ben seemed to be the only person who wanted to go over and shake the shit out of her, too.

"What did you do?" he growled. "You took your goddamn mask off? Are you insane?"

"Ben," Engo said. "Lay off."

"Lay off?" he barked. "I had two kids and a *blind* firefighter up there!"

Andy spat water on the concrete. "You woulda had a sighted firefighter and two dead kids if I hadn't taken my mask off."

Ben bit his tongue so hard he tasted blood. It was weird to hear Matt chime in as the level head.

"I'm gonna reconfigure things a little," Matt said. "Until our friend here gets his head screwed back on. Engo and Andy, you two go back up through the second floor and check for reignition sites and bodies. Jakey, sweep the first floor but stay visible."

"Shouldn't we shut down the scene?" Andy asked. "I thought I smelled gasoline in there."

Matt balked at the question, shook his head. "Who the fuck you talking to, New Guy?"

"Sorry, boss."

"Ben, you're gonna stand here and get debrief practice."

"Fuck off. I don't need to be babysat," Ben snapped. "I'm fine to go back in for cleanup."

"Again, I don't know who you assholes think you're talking to, but this ain't a committee." Matt tugged on Ben's shoulder strap when he tried to walk away. "Do what you're fucking told. Ben, stand here. You guys, fuck off back inside."

Ben relented, stopped beside his boss, and watched as the firefighters on his crew returned to the burned-out shell of a building while he stood there like a toddler in time-out. Engo turned back and winked at him, and there was something about it that gave Ben a sense of unease, almost heavy enough to smother out the anger in his chest.

ANDY

·

H e was too close to her. That should have been all the warning she needed. But Andy was mentally whirring, the adrenaline rush from the fire and the weight of the smoke-choked infant in her arms roiling her stomach. She was simultaneously dizzyingly high and suffocatingly low. Her eyeballs were on fire, tears running freely as she tried to keep up with Engo's grumbling chatter.

"Used to be, before the Towers, before all the new regs, that you only used your tank if you needed to," he said, kicking over the burned-out skeleton of a wooden table. "Because guess what? Sometimes you're in the mess for more than a half hour. And backtracking so I can swap out a tank is more dangerous than sucking in a little burned plastic. You think I'm gonna leave Jakey to do a one-man floor clearance because I'm worried about getting dioxins in my lungs? Honey, I smoked my first cigar when I was seven and a half years old."

"Engo," Andy said.

"I feel alive sucking in smoke. I'm serious. I'm a freak. It gives me energy. The Native Americans do smoke ceremonies. They breathe it in on purpose. How come when they do it it's culture, and when I do it I'm an insurance liability?"

"Engo."

"What?"

"I want to talk to you." She stopped, stood in the still-steaming room with him. "About Ben."

The older man was suddenly cackling, a heavy hand on her shoulder. "Woman, listen to me. You gotta understand. When a guy's about to shoot his load, he's not thinking straight. Okay? Now, I know what you're like. When girls are about to come they got half their brain thinkin' about the guy, the other half thinkin' about what they're makin' for dinner, and the *other* half thinkin' about some bullshit their mother said to them eight years ago that they're still angry about."

Andy stared at him.

"Guys aren't thinkin' about *any of that*." Engo swept the air with his gloves. "It's just music in there. Chaos. Destruction. Little bits of electricity smashing together. There *are* no words. If we manage to say anything at all, it's a miracle. So he said the wrong name. Big whoop. You gotta get over it."

"I'm over it," Andy said. "What I'm not over is that you all know about it."

"So?"

"I'm gonna get fired." Andy tried to look pleadingly at him. It was working. He was softening, being drawn in. "And I can't have that."

"You'll get another posting," Engo sighed. He'd stepped closer to her now. She could see his deep pores, feel his breath on her upper lip. Sourness of old sex recalled from the memory cells in his belly. "You're not the first broad in the job to get under a guy, Andy."

"There's more to my story, though," she said. "There's stuff Matt doesn't know."

"What stuff?"

"Worse stuff. Things I did back in SD."

Engo's radio crackled. A single burst of static. Andy looked at it, reached up and felt for her own, wondered why she and Engo weren't on the same channel. Her first instinct was that she had somehow slipped off the operations channel on her own radio. Then she watched the older man click back onto ops.

"You can tell me all about it later," he said. He swung his arm back. Andy felt all the breath leave her as Engo punched her hard in the stomach.

He dragged her across the floor by her boots, got her down the hall and into a room at the back of the building before she could unhitch the spasm in her diaphragm and suck in air. She screamed, turned over, kicked at him. Andy knew how to fight, but the oxygen tank and the hundred-pound bunker gear made it nearly impossible, made it like she was wrestling in mud. Engo flipped her onto her belly, put a knee into her backside and pressed down on the oxygen tank and wrenched her left arm behind her. Andy screamed as she felt his bare fingers fishing around at her shoulder for her radio.

"What the fuck are you doing? Stop! *Stop!*"

He laughed. A dark, low laugh Andy had heard before, one full of an evil confidence, experience. She ripped the tag off her PASS device with her free hand, just to do something, just to feel like she wasn't completely helpless, the immobility alarm emitting a squealing sound as Engo un-buckled her radio from her chest and put it on the ground beside her face.

"Engo, stop! Please! Please!"

"Yeah," he said from somewhere above her. "I'm gonna need you to cut that out. I don't want words. I just want screaming."

He yanked her wrist down, pinned her hand between his knee and her belt. Andy's eyes bulged and her howling mouth gaped against the floor as his hand worked its way into the collar of her jacket, his fingers finding the subclavian pressure point deep behind her collarbone expertly. He pushed down. The pain rocketed through her, electric and blinding, drawing gut-tural screams that were well beyond her control.

Somewhere past the white noise of her agony she heard Engo click his radio.

"Jesus-fuck, Matt! Andy is 10-45 here. Urgh, God. She's— She's— Hang on! Hang on! Matt, she's slipped down a-a-a collapse point in the floor back here. Rear of the building, east. She's hanging off a girder."

There was no response. Engo's fingers worked up and down on the pres-sure point. Andy could feel the pain band-sawing back and forth from her jugular all the way down her twisted arm. She fought the need to vomit, trying to get up the strength in her thighs to roll him off her back. Her free arm swung across the floor, pushing papers around, scrabbling at her pants and jacket, trying to find something, some weapon, or a handhold. There was nothing. His knee was crushing her fingers, making the bones grind together.

BEN

.

He saw Jake's eyes through the broken front windows of the school. The kid looked pale, startled, even from a distance of thirty yards; then he turned and disappeared into the dark forest of charred structural wood like a frightened deer. Matt gripped his radio, his eyes hard against the sunshine.

"*Engo, give us a sitrep.*"

"I'm going in." Ben threw his helmet on.

"Forget it." Matt grabbed his shoulder strap again and yanked him back. "You're acting deputy chief on this scene right now. Jake's responding."

"*She's cut her leg on something, Matt. Fuck me, I think she hit an artery. There's blood everywhere. Jake, don't come from underneath. The floor's still collapsing.*"

"*Where should I go?*"

"*Arrrrgghhh! Hang on, Andy! Hang on! Jake—come up the stairs on the west side and cross over the third-floor hallway.*"

"*Ben! Bennnnn!*"

Andy's voice on the radio lit a fire in Ben. He looked at Matt. Looked deep into the older man's eyes and saw the same rigid blankness there that he had seen the last time he was acting deputy chief. Ben had been alone on the street then, practicing hold of command from outside the fire scene, when his boss emerged from the flaming doorway with *that* look on his face. Too calm. Too empty beyond the oxygen mask. Matt had been retreating to swap out tanks. Ben had been watching him load up when he got the call from Engo that Titus wasn't where he was supposed to be, that no one could find him, that he thought he heard a scream from the floor below.

"Fuck this," Ben said now. Matt tried to grab at him but he shoved him off. "I'm going in."

Ben could hear her screams from the third floor. The peal of the PASS alarm. He followed Jakey's boot prints in the dust, leaped up the stairs to the second floor, taking them three at a time, his whole body shaking with guilt. Because it was there again: the vision of Andy being torched as they entered the school, the sweet relief that had warmed his bones. He was praying now, actually praying for her as he ran, her screams getting louder and louder. Engo's grunts were barely audible over the earsplitting noise of her wails. Ben was only feet away from the door to the room they were coming from when the older man's individual words broke through Ben's tortured thoughts.

"That's right, baby. Scream. Scream. Scream for your boyfriend."

Ben stumbled into the room. Jake was standing in the corner, watching Engo roll off Andy, the sweat-drenched woman looking like a kid playing dress-up in her oversized suit and gloves. All the capillaries in her eyeballs had burst, and wild, wet, demon-red eyes looked up at Ben for a moment before she turned and vomited on the floor.

Engo got to his feet and grinned. Ben didn't know whether to follow his desire to go to Andy or to lunge at Engo. Before he could do anything, Andy pulled herself together and threw her gloves off and came at her attacker. She got in a good, solid shot to the mouth. Ben heard the impact of her knuckles on Engo's teeth.

"You stupid fuck!" Andy reared back for another blow, wobbled on her feet, still reeling from the pain. "You stupid, ugly *fuck*!"

"Jesus." Engo only had to back off a couple of steps to get out of her swing range. He cupped the blood gushing down his chin. "You busted my lip!"

Ben went to Andy. She was shaking in his arms. The collar of her turn-out coat was open and a big blue bruise in the shape of two fingertips was erupting at the side of her neck, blood rushing deep into the traumatized tendons under her collarbone. Ben recognized the marks. Engo's favorite party trick. Andy was struggling with the PASS alarm on her belt, trying to shut it off.

Matt was in the doorway now, leaning, filling most of the frame with his shape. He was chewing fresh gum, and the look he gave Ben of quiet, fatherly disgust made him shrivel up inside.

"You, you, and you." Matt pointed to each of the men in turn. "Continue the scene clearance."

Then the big man pointed the Finger of Death at Andy.

"You, go back to the station. Empty your locker. You're out."

She knew the counter guy was interested in her. He had a hungry look. And for someone in her position, that could go badly—had gone badly a couple of times as she was blown up the East Coast by the winds of fate. Dahlia had been in the homeless shelter in the Bronx for three days, and she'd barely moved from the bunk they'd assigned her. It was a bottom bunk, farthest from the door and in a dark corner. A sweet spot, the sweetest spot she'd found since she left Georgia. She wasn't giving it up. But there was the guy. His curious, bright eyes. Any guy who was interested in a reed-thin, hollow-eyed girl who refused to give her name, who refused to shower, who had blisters on her feet the size of baked beans, was dangerously whacked. She'd gone to the bunk in the corner and curled up like an old dog crawling under a porch to die, and if that kind of helplessness turned the guy on, he was trouble. Dahlia waited until he wasn't on shift before she got up on the third day to get some air, maybe scope out an emergency exit.

Turned out he wasn't on shift but he was there, waiting for her in the back alley behind the shelter, spent cigarettes littered all around his shoes and one wasting away between his knuckles. The hair at his temples was growing silver, and he stroked it like it made him self-conscious as she came to the door. Gearing up for a speech. She tried to retreat but he stopped her pretty quick with "I know who you are."

Dahlia froze in the doorway. Ahead of her, one of the volunteers was trying to cajole another human tumbleweed with a belly the size of a BOSU ball into the doctor's examining room. The guy was sobbing and clutching a filthy pillow under one arm.

"You're Dahlia Lore."

The sound of her name made her somehow weaker than she already was. Her brain told her to run but her legs folded instead and she sat heavily on the concrete step.

"Let me tell you what I know," the guy said. He flicked ash off the cigarette. "Nine months ago you walked into Commander Aaron Ferdakis's office in San Antonio, Texas, and put a binder in front of him. A heavy binder. It slammed down on his desk, made a loud sound. You told Ferdakis it was a research file. It was everything you'd managed to dredge up about the two men who murdered your parents, Shaun and Rina Lore, in the three years since their deaths."

Dahlia drew the sleeves of her hoodie down over her hands. The man, his words—they were making her want to tuck into a ball. Cover up. Disappear.

"You'd given Ferdakis and his guys three years to make some kind of headway on the case," the counter guy said. "Then you took matters into your own hands. You couldn't understand, at first, what was taking the San Antonio PD so long. They had the car that arrived at the gas station that night. They had IDs of the two men who died there beside your parents. They had fingerprints. DNA. Bullet casings. No, they didn't have CCTV footage of the shooters. All the footage was lost when they burned down the gas station with your parents and one of their victims inside. But what they had should have been enough."

Dahlia wiped her eyes.

"But with a little bit of asking around, a little bit of common sense, you tracked them down soon enough," the counter guy continued. "Jude and Michael Hogan. Brothers. Drug dealers from Galveston."

He came and sat beside her on the step, flicked his cigarette away and fished out a new one. Shook the pack at her. She was so run-down, the nicotine hit her like a lightning bolt to the brain. She could feel its fingers working into her skull, prickling over her scalp and down the back of her neck.

"What you did in tracking down the Hogans wasn't what impressed me, Dahlia," the man said, exhaling over his shoulder. "It was entering their lives like you did."

Dahlia smoked and listened to the commotion inside as two attendants now were teaming up to get the big boy-man with the pillow seen to. From what she could hear, it sounded like he had an insect in his ear canal. Or claimed to have. Getting him into the on-site doctor's office was proving difficult. There was talk of trying to convince him to go to a hospital.

"Are you with me?" the counter guy asked.

Dahlia nodded, but she wasn't with him at all. She was trying to lock on to something, anything, to take her away from memories of that night at the gas station, of the years after. Hunting the Hogans. Sliding, snakelike, into their worlds; first as a shitkicker at the auto wreckers where Jude spent most of his time and then as a waitress at a diner down the block from where Michael lived. Neither of the men had recognized her. Sure, she'd dropped a stack of weight, changed her hair, shriveled and hardened the way those left behind after homicides do. She was physically unrecognizable from the photograph that had featured in the newspapers briefly. But she supposed, in the end, what protected Dahlia as she spied on the Hogans was simply that neither Jude nor Michael expected her to be there, smiling timidly and handing them coffee or stacking rumpled sheets of metal *in their own wrecking yard. They expected the terrified girl they'd fired at as she bolted into the darkened desert to be gone from their lives forever.*

"How do you know about the binder?" she asked the counter guy, who wasn't a counter guy at all. Her voice was flat. It seemed like it would take a whole-body effort to lift it.

"I had a listening device in Ferdakis's office," the man said. "Inside the lamp. The whump of the binder on the desk nearly unstuck it, so thanks for that." He huffed a smoky laugh. "Nearly blew my whole operation. I've been watching the commander, clocking up his ties to people like the Hogans. He's got a stable of drug dealers, importers, cooks. The Hogans are small fish in his world. Or they were. Until you killed them."

Dahlia said nothing.

"You're twenty-six." The guy was looking at her now. "You're twenty-six fucking years old. You ran a one-man undercover surveillance operation on a pair of murderous drug dealers for a year without being discovered, and you compiled evidence of their network that led you all the way up to the commander of one of the biggest police departments in the state of Texas."

Dahlia stared at the embers in her cigarette.

"Are you even listening to me?"

"Yeah."

"No you're not." He leaned against the doorframe. "You're tired. I get it. Shit, you've been on the run for months. And doing a good job of that, too. It took me this long to find you. And you're probably scared. That takes a lot out of you, being scared. You're probably thinking I'm here to arrest you for killing the Hogans."

She looked at him.

"I'm not," he said. Swiping at those white streaks again under her gaze. "I mean, we should get rid of the thirty-eight. I don't know why you're still carrying that around. But hey, it's like I said: You're twenty-six. You're incredibly smart in some ways, and incredibly dumb in others. You seemed to believe Ferdakis was just going to put his hands up in surrender the moment you walked in there with all that evidence of who he was and what he'd been doing. Like 'Oh shit, kid! You got me.'"

He laughed. Dahlia didn't.

"So why are you here, then?"

"Because I want to work with you," the guy said. "You're special. You're raw talent. What you did—the investigation, the undercover work—you did all that *on pure fucking instinct. I mean, Jesus. That's unheard of. Imagine the kind of weapon you could be if someone gave you a little training. Lots of training. That's what I'm offering. Dahlia. I want to take you and make something of you."*

"Make what of me?"

"A specialist," he said. "Someone who does this. Someone who knows how to change shape, slide in, find out information. You've got the gift, and you must have enjoyed it, to run the operation that long."

She said nothing.

"We'll have to start with that redneck accent. That's why you stopped talking altogether after Georgia, huh? That twang is like a siren."

She was feeling it now. The ever-so-slight lift. Chemicals coming together in her exhausted bloodstream. Lights turning on in her brain. She'd been shutting down since she put a bullet in the back of Michael Hogan's head in an empty Walmart parking lot a year earlier, having already popped his brother as he lay sleeping in his apartment. It had felt like a completion. The achievement of the only thing she'd wanted to do since her parents died. When Tony Newler started speaking to her in that damp back alley in the Bronx five minutes earlier, she'd been almost dead, a dry husk of a plant lying deflated in a pot. Now the very tips of her roots had smelled water and were twitching beneath the soil.

"Who are you?" Dahlia asked.

Tony turned to her and smiled a smile that filled her with warmth then. A smile she would grow to despise.

"What—you mean, today?" he asked.

ANDY
.

ndy thought now about the Newler she'd met that night behind the homeless shelter; the leaner, younger, more nervous version of the one she had to deal with now. She sat in the car down the street from the Best Western in Dayton and wondered about him and how he'd spent those three days posing as a volunteer care worker and surveilling her in her bunk. Watching her closely enough to know she still carried the .38, her ticket to prison, if she decided to go that way. Closely enough to know that it was suicide or jail or an out for her, and he had maybe the only out that she'd ever want to take.

Dahlia, who today was Andy, tapped the bottom of the steering wheel and wondered if Newler had been in love with her then already. Or if that came sometime later, when he was teaching her to walk like a lawyer from Michigan or talk like a ferry worker from San Francisco or suck down picklebacks like she'd been doing it since her teens in New Hampshire. While the two of them were posing as newlyweds in the Florida Keys, or real estate agents in Utah, or strangers on a train platform in Illinois. Had his love for her been obsessive then, when she was drawn and weak and curled in a ball with her backpack hooked onto her chest and her sleeping arms cradled around everything she had in the world? Or had it grown that way when he tried to make her settle down into a steady, stable, state-sanctioned life in New York? He'd tired of the freelance life, having fallen into the job himself as a bartender in his midtwenties, selling snippets of conversation between local drug dealers to the local cops for twenty bucks apiece. That had been his great love, the watching, the listening, the pretending, the quiet knowing. Now she was his great love, and he'd decided he wanted to go to Quantico and begin a new chapter, and oh, how convenient and wonderful it was: His little project Dahlia fit right into that vision.

He'd tried to marry her, tried to sell the idea of a child to her.

And she said no.

Andy watched the valets at the Best Western, shook her head, tried to veer wildly away from that doomed thought train before she got to Newler's punishment for that no. When she saw Dammerly Tsaba emerge from the revolving doors at the front of the hotel she got out and straightened her wig and glasses and pantsuit in the reflection in her car window. Her brain wanted to settle into other dark thoughts, into the stomach-plunging humiliation of this morning on the floor of the burning school under Engo, into the day spent resting up, treating her aching shoulder and her blooded eyes at her apartment. But she corralled her thoughts back to the matter at hand as she walked across the street toward the hotel.

Up close, Dammerly was everything Andy expected him to be: a vacuum-seal-tight encasement of an upstanding citizen suctioned around the more degraded, more villainous man that rotted covertly inside. He was like the hotel itself with its brightly lit, spacious, and immaculate rooms online that were really dark, cigarette-stink-riddled boxes shot with a fisheye. Dammerly's prison tattoos were peeking from the neck of his blazer, and his nameplate was scratched and askew. The bottom half of his face broke into the smile he was paid to give as Andy approached under the gold entrance lights. But his flat gaze picked over the still-bloodshot whites of her eyes. The power stride had him unnerved from twenty feet out.

"Ma'am, welcome to—"

"Dammerly Tsaba. A word?"

Andy flicked her head toward the dark side of the driveway, away from the safety of the valet's desk and the cameras. Tsaba knew what was up, clocked his colleague at the other end of the entryway and wandered into the dark with her, swinging a set of keys compulsively by his side.

"Ma'am, something wrong with your service? Are you a guest of the hotel?" Tsaba asked hopefully.

"Cut the crap, Dammerly," Andy said. "I'm Tylee's replacement."

"Oh. Man." Dammerly huffed a long sigh, let his head hang back against his collar. The recent parolee stared at the stars over New York just starting to peep through the purple cloak of evening. "I knew this was coming. She get fired or what?"

"She got cautioned." Andy folded her arms with difficulty, her bruised subclavian tendons screaming at the maneuver. "The New York State Board of Parole couldn't prove the two of you were fucking, but they sure knew something was going on when they tried to double-check Tylee's last five sign-offs on your residence and discovered you moved out of the apartment two months ago. They don't look too kindly on relationships between parole officers and their charges, Mr. Tsaba."

Dammerly put his keys in one pocket of his blazer and pulled his phone from the other. "I gotta call her."

"You'll do no such thing." Andy pushed the phone down. "I didn't come here tonight because I wanted to give you a heads-up before you end your shift, go home, and find she's taken a shit on your side of the bed. I came here to get my cut."

Dammerly's head snapped up. He looked like he wanted to laugh but didn't. "For real?"

"For real," Andy said. "Hey, your girlfriend's had a terrible day. She nearly lost her job because the board knew something was off between you two. But what *you've* got to lose, Dammerly, is far worse than that. So if you want to keep parking cheap cars and pocketing dollar bills from out-of-town businessmen, you better give me my end. Or maybe you want to go back to Queensboro Correctional with all your registered-sex-offender buddies and—"

"Will you keep your fucking voice down? Jesus!"

Andy shrugged, put her hands in the pockets. The suit was cheap, faded at the cuffs, bought off the thrift-store rack that afternoon. Andy had wondered if someone similar to the woman she was playing now had once owned it—someone just smart enough to get a salaried government job but too dumb and impatient to keep that job, work at it honestly for decades, slow-broil it into something that paid enough that she could buy herself new suits just before the old ones fell to rags. Someone like a parole officer who squeezed her charges for petty cash, a lowlife who enjoyed making other lowlifes squirm.

"How much do you want?"

"A thousand bucks will get you to the end of your parole period without any more red flags."

"Oh, fuck me."

"You've only got three months left and then I'm out of your life. That's a bargain."

"I don't have that kind of money."

"Maybe your girlfriend does."

"She's not my girlfriend, man." Tsaba grimaced, made a tinny, hissing noise through his teeth. "We hooked up a few times and she's been letting me crash on her couch so I could sublet my place and save money."

"Look at me." Andy pointed to her face.

He looked.

"Look at my teeth." She grinned. "They look white?"

"Uh, yeah?"

"They are. And that's because I don't eat bullshit, Dammerly. I got nice white teeth because I don't sit around all day eating bullshit."

"Okay. Okay."

"Stop trying to feed it to me."

"Okay. Jesus." He glanced at her red eyes and Andy saw him consider a comment, then drop it. Smart.

"I'll have the cash in my hand when I come back a week from tonight." She tapped her palm with an index finger. "No excuses. You're late or short and I'll file a report saying I smelled alcohol on your breath during our friendly little chat tonight."

He flinched as though slapped. "Man, who the hell are you?"

"I told you. I'm Tylee's replacement," Andy said. "You'll get an email five minutes from now with all the change-of-case-management details. And while we're talking computers, I'll have your staff log-in for the hotel."

"What?" The man took a step back.

"*What?*" Andy took a step back also, put her hands out, pantomiming his confusion. "You still don't get it, do you? You're under the thumb here, Dammerly. You and Tylee done fucked up. I'm your daddy now. Okay? So I'm not leaving here empty-handed. I want your log-in. Access to the hotel's room and valet booking system."

"What do you want that for?"

"*Information*, Dammerly." Andy leaned in, smiled, like she was speaking to a child. "You think I got to where I am in the world without knowing what a piece of information is worth? I'm surprised *you* don't know what it's worth. Piece-of-shit career criminal like yourself. You got access to every check-in and check-out and room-service order and parking charge attached to this place going back *years*. Phone calls to and from rooms. Credit-card payments. Names on visitor lists. Bookings at the restaurant. What are you, an idiot?"

Dammerly twitched, looked browbeaten and three inches shorter than he should have been. "No. I'm not an idiot."

"Jury's out on that one, hon." Andy got out her phone and opened up a page in the Notes app. "The log-in. Right now."

BEN

.

nfinite swirls and slabs of white, shards of headache-inducing gold, echoes of feet in hard shoes. Ben kept his head down and tried to move painlessly through it all, every part of him exhausted, the Guggenheim's weird endless circular ramp seeming like a torture device designed for someone who'd had a rough day. Andy had been gone before the crew arrived back at the station after the school fire and wasn't answering texts. Ben had steadfastly avoided Matt by taking over some of the cleaning duties in the station kitchen with the night crew, who were doing a big chili cook-up before coming on duty. Dishes, suds, blackened pots. No one hung around him. They scraped and dumped their plates guiltily and left. It suited him just fine.

Now he was wearing a monkey suit and calculating how many swirls of the gallery he needed to do to get to the figure of Matt, who was standing in front of some sculpture mounted on the wall. Hairy black intestines, bulges and pockets of spray-painted burlap and chicken wire. Sea creature or human colon? The sculpture reminded Ben of burned air-conditioning exhaust hoses, their blackened coils and frayed edges. The Evil Slinkie, they called it, a trap built to ensnare probies. Matt looked from the sculpture to Ben and pointed at him not with the Finger of Death this time but a tiny glass of champagne.

"What? You don't own a tie?"

"No. But nobody's going to notice. I'm in and out."

"The champagne is free."

"I don't even know what this shindig is raising money for." Ben glanced at the crowd gathered at the bottom of the massive spiral. Suits and sparkly dresses. "I dumped a twenty in a bucket on the way in. I could be contributing to the Dogfighters of America. You come to these things?"

"I get invited. All the chiefs do. Donna makes me come if she gets to the mailbox before me."

"You like it?"

"Sure. We come, I drink too much and refuse to make small talk, we fight all the way home. It's a real treat." Ben could feel Matt watching him, eyes boring a hole in his temple. "You're gonna get over the Andy thing. Fast."

"'That's an order,' huh?"

"You proved to me today that you're a dangerous combination, you two," Matt said. "Just like I predicted. One scream from her and you dropped everything. Abandoned your post. In the army, they'd shoot you for that."

"Mmm-hmm."

"You're not gonna hit Engo."

"Oh yes, I am."

"He was acting on my direction. The test was my idea."

"He really banged her up. Her shoulder—"

"She'll be fine. He's done that stupid pressure-point thing to Jake." Matt rolled his eyes. "Remember? At that funeral. Jake was lifting sandbags two days later. I needed Andy to be really screaming."

"You're sick." Ben's ears were on fire. He could feel the fury in his throat. "I should have dropped the two of you, right after."

"You're funny, you know that? You should do stand-up."

"I could do it right fucking now." Ben's words were icy. Something hot flickered in Matt's eyes. "Fuck up this whole thing for you with the lawyer, with the baseball cards."

"Try it." Matt smiled. They watched each other, that awful smile playing on Matt's lips, Ben thinking about how that would play out. Publicly, with Command learning a firefighter had dropped his 9/11-first-responder chief in a public art gallery. Or tried to, and got his skull fractured for his efforts. And privately, with Matt never having had a swing taken at him in his life without paying it back tenfold. "That's what I thought."

"Fuck you," Ben sneered.

"What's to say it wouldn't have gone the other way, Ben, if I kept her on the crew?" Matt leaned in. "You guys break up six months down the road. Maybe she cheats on you. One day a staircase falls on her and she lets off her PASS, you hear it and think, *Fuck you, bitch. You deserve to have your ass hairs singed off.*"

"I don't want to talk about this anymore." Ben grabbed a champagne off the tray of a waiter walking by because there seemed to be nothing else on offer. "Where's the lawyer? Mr. Ick or whatever the fuck."

"Ichh."

"I want to do this and get out of here."

"Should be here any minute."

They walked on a little, Matt leading. Stopped by a white canvas with small yellow squares painted all over it. Ben could see some of the pencil marks under the yellow squares.

"You have any idea how easy it would be to forge that?" Matt pointed to the painting.

"No."

"What about what it's worth?"

"No, Matt. I don't know that either. I don't sit around googling what modern art pieces are worth so I can feel like a piece of garbage. Why do I want to know that I earn peanuts endangering my life every day to save innocent civilians, while guys who went to art school make millions of dollars painting little yellow squares?"

Matt smiled at him. Matt loved rants.

"I know what it's worth." The chief showed Ben his phone, the Google page. "Five point three. You believe that?"

"Why do you care?"

"Why do you think, dumbass? You have the painting forged. You set up a gas leak. Cut the power, lights, everything. Waltz on in. Do the old switcheroo. Fence the real painting and bank the bucks."

"I'm sure it's not that simple."

"Might be fun finding out, though."

Ben looked at him. "This is all bullshit, isn't it? This job being your last one. Donna being your last wife."

"Donna is my last wife."

"Yeah. You kinda said that three times already."

That spark again in Matt's eyes.

"All I'm saying is, I think you've got a bug for capers." Ben shrugged. "No different from Jake. Every time he goes all in on something, he knows he's either gonna live it large for the next three weeks or take a hit that might end up killing him. You're both mainlining the danger and you're not gonna quit because you just wake up one day and decide to."

"Oh and you're not the same?" Matt snorted. "You're not mainlining the danger?"

Ben didn't answer, because of course he was. Some unevolved part of his brain still got off on the unpredictability of the jobs. It was a boot-pounded track cut into his mental forest when he was a kid and he had no idea if his mother was going to come home at night cuddly and sorry and full of promises or high and frantic and paranoid that CIA agents were following her on motorcycles. Or at all, even. Matt's brain was almost certainly crisscrossed with the same toxic rabbit runs. Chasing the self-loathing of seeing their criminal handiwork in the newspaper the day after, the internal wretchedness that followed any interaction with a cop at all, of which there was a daily supply. Engo was hooked on their extracurricular deeds because his mother was probably Aileen Wuornos and he'd had to eat seven other fetuses in the womb just to be born, like a tiger shark. They all knew why Jake kept coming back: because when Jake tasted something he liked it was all-you-can-eat for eternity. Nobody knew or cared why he was like that, because probies were only half human anyway.

A man appeared beside him, taking the Yellow Box Painting Appreciation Society membership to three. Ben looked at the lawyer, at his sunspotted and bald scalp and his yellowed irises and his dusty suit, and snarled at Matt.

"You gotta be kidding me. This is the guy?" Ben turned back to Ichh. "Has your client got room in his hospital bed, Father Time? Because you two could save a lot of walking around for the nurses. They get sore feet, you know."

"Yes. Well. That's part of the reason I'm doing this, Mr. Haig." The lawyer sipped a beer he'd scored from somewhere, licked foam off his upper lip. "If I weren't so busy, I might very well be on my deathbed, alongside my client Mr. Freeman. I have pancreatic cancer."

Ben looked at the painting, held his champagne. He wasn't a cancer connoisseur but he knew Patrick Swayze had had the pancreatic kind and it hadn't ended well. He would have said something comforting but he was too far in to back out right away so he just said to Matt, "Oh good, he knows our names."

"He could have found out easy enough," Matt said. "I thought about calling us Mr. Pink and Mr. Brown and Mr. Green but I'm not an asshole."

"Matt—"

"And he knows my name already," Matt said. "I came recommended."

"By who?"

"Does it matter?"

Ben chewed his lip. Because yes, it did matter, but he could put the pieces together himself anyway. Matt had three ex-wives and a lot of assets to hide so that he didn't have to disclose them during divorce settlements. Whoever had recommended Matt to Ichh probably knew there was some plan afoot, but would be kept at bay by the dirty work they'd done for Matt. Ben pinched his brow and tried not to feel afraid. The lawyer watched him, waiting to be verbally assaulted again. Somebody came onto a microphone downstairs. Muffled pleasantries and modest applause. "So what is this, huh? You lived your whole life by the book and now you want to do something dirty before you kick the bucket?" Ben asked the lawyer. "Don't tell me. The trust fund. Harvard Law. Fancy-schmancy charity fundraising things at art galleries. You're bored out of your mind. Have been your whole life. You've decided you want to feel a tingle in your prick just once before you meet your maker."

"Not exactly." The lawyer stared into his beer foam. "I went to Yale. And my life is, at present, full of unwanted adrenaline-pumping action."

"It is?"

"I find myself in the midst of an all-out war with my ex-wife over our wealth and assets. She's going to 'take me to the cleaners,' as the expression goes. Every time the phone rings, my heart is in my throat."

Ben watched the little man examining his drink.

"If she were kind, she would just delay it all," Ichh said. "Wait for nature to take its course. But she was never kind."

"You're a lawyer," Ben said. "Can't you defend yourself?"

"She's a lawyer, too. A better one. *She* went to Harvard. But it's the genetic propensity toward unkindness that makes her so successful. She won't stop until I'm skin bare. She'll take the pigeons nesting in my roof gutters, and all their droppings, too."

"The guy's got a kid outside the marriage." Matt nudged Ben's elbow with his own. "Wants to make sure the boy is set up after he's in the ground and his ex has come and taken all the blue out of his toilet water."

"From what Mr. Roderick tells me, you might be able to relate to that?" Ichh looked at Ben with those big, dry, chemo-ravaged eyes. "Having sacrificed so much for your brother?"

Ben turned to his boss. For the first time in their relationship, Matt shrank a little. "It just came out."

"You can save all the chumminess for Matt," Ben said to the lawyer.

"You've got more in common with him than me. He also has exes who would love to see him mangled in a heavy-machinery accident."

Matt choked on his champagne, recovered, and hacked out a laugh.

"Talk to me about the key," Ben said. There was more applause downstairs. "Where is it kept?"

"My client keeps everything of real value in a safe in his home office, and to my knowledge the key to his safety-deposit box in Borr Storage is in there." Ichh gave an uncomfortable shuffle of his feet. "Mr. Roderick floated the idea with me of taking a picture of the key, from which you could make a forgery."

"You can do that, right?" Matt nudged Ben. "You take the photo, get the dimensions, get your guy Paxi over in Jersey to machine up a replica key in his workshop."

"It's not that straightforward. But okay."

"This forgery," Ichh went on, "would hold the place of the original key while you used it to open the safety-deposit box on the night of the . . . the, uh . . ."

"The burglary," Ben said.

"I can't even say the words." Ichh sighed. "But I don't think that will work."

"Oh. So you're the ideas man now, huh?" Matt nudged Ben again. "He's the ideas man."

"It's just that I've dealt with the Freeman family for the last thirty years. I've seen the children grow up. They have a lifelong skepticism . . . uh, a mild hostility, even, toward me."

"Why?" Ben asked.

"Well, I suppose every time their father has decided to scratch their names off the will, I've been his obedient servant in that quest." Ichh shrugged.

"That'll do it," Ben said.

"I feel I may be able to convince the eldest son to allow me access to the safe, without his father present," Ichh said. "It'll take a story. Some contrivance about needing to fetch or peruse a piece of paper from the files stored there. But I just cannot see that I could convince him of two separate incidents of access. One to take a photograph of the key, one to swap that key out for a forgery."

"Do we even need to do this?" Ben looked at Matt. "A key's a key, isn't it? If we make a forgery that's that good, it'll work in the freakin' lock."

"We can't risk that," Matt stated. "We can't risk you being a millimeter off and the thing not working on the night. And it has to look real-deal. They're not just simple keys like you'd unlock your house with. Some of these private secure storage fuckers are paying twenty k a year for the boxes. For that, you get pretty-looking keys. I've eyeballed one and they look like they have a long round stem like an antique clock-winding key and a flat head with the Borr logo embossed on it. I didn't see what the teeth looked like."

"Oh great," Ben said.

"We'll just get a different model for the forgery," Matt said. He pointed at the lawyer. "You take the forged key in, access the safe once, and swap it out. It'll have to be modeled off a real key from Borr Storage, just not Freeman's exact key. Nobody's going to look at the forgery and recognize that it's not *identical* to the original one just by sight. It just needs to be a Borr Storage key, so that nobody glances into the safe and finds the key's missing while we're gearing up to do the job. After the robbery, you make your second excuse to get into the safe. You can wait until the old man dies and you've got to execute his will. That's when you put the original key back."

"Sure," Ben said. "But how are we gonna get a Borr Storage key to model the forgery from? Do we know any other clients of that facility?"

"Engo can lift one from someone's pocket or their car or whatever," Matt said. "I've already got him on surveillance at the facility. I'll tell him to watch for an opportunity."

"He steals someone's key, and he'll have to do it covertly and drop it in the gutter when he's got a picture," Ben said. "The whole appeal of this job is that there's no burglary at the facility. There's no crime. Some random person gets pickpocketed outside the facility a week before the fire, and—"

"I know. I know."

The two firefighters looked at the lawyer. The smaller man had a strange expression on his face, standing there, watching them discuss the next phase of their criminal plan with all the ease and familiarity of men coming up with dinner arrangements. Ben knew what it was. It was a mixture of intrigue and disgust. He'd seen the same face on people driving by prisons, watching men in the yard through the fences. He felt his hackles rising at the idea that now that their business had been ironed out, Ichh would try to launch into more casual, curious chitchat about "the life" and how long Ben and Matt had been in it. He imagined the little lawyer gently pressing

Matt about why he broke bad in the first place. Why he stayed that way. Whether the rumor he'd heard, that Matt was a 9/11 first responder, was true. Ben looked over the railing and wondered if the lawyer would survive a fall from this height.

He was walking to his car when Andy called. That morning they'd discussed greetings they'd share on the phone that indicated whether it was safe to talk, so he said "Hey babe" in greeting rather than "Hi, Andy."

"I'm going to tell you an address," she said. "Can you meet me there? Just do a couple of tours around the neighborhood first to make sure you're not being followed."

"What is it?"

"It's a tow yard."

Ben felt his mouth run dry. He listened carefully to the address as he walked a block down and into a private parking lot. "What about you?" he said when she was done. "Are you okay?"

"I'll be fine," Andy said, and hung up.

He clicked the key fob a long ways out, just because it was in his hand. He didn't notice the guy standing smoking against a pillar until he got close. The guy was thickly built, with white wings in his hair that Ben had seen a few times in gangster films, only these looked real rather than painted in. He was getting tingles of instinct about the guy as he slipped into the driver's seat, but played them off as dread or terror at what he might find in Luna's car. The man was just a man, standing in a parking lot, probably waiting for his chatty wife to quit making small talk over at the charity thing and meet him at the car so they could fight all the way home.

Ben pulled out and drove away without giving the guy another glance.

ANDY

.

Ben pulled up at the gates of Belafonte Towing, northeast of Summit, and barely had the engine off before he was striding toward her in a suit with an open collar. The breeze off the Passaic River was carrying a fishy sourness toward her mixed with engine oil from the yard. Andy was so mentally tangled in the ruse she'd had to play to get Dammerly Tsaba to cooperate with her, and the whole separate one she'd played on Nathaniel Belafonte to get unsupervised access to the tow yard, that she just watched Ben coming toward her and was unguarded against the thought that he looked good. There was a wrongness to the combination of the beautiful navy wool suit that Kenny had probably bought him against his will and the smudgy bruise under his eye and the cut in his forehead. It was the same dark partnership of opulence and violence that action-movie lovers thrived on. Andy examined the thought and resisted the urge to give herself a hard slap.

"Are you okay?" he asked again as they came together. "Jesus, look at your eyes."

"I said I was fine. Where were you?"

"Meeting with Matt and the lawyer about the job."

"You might have told me that." She gave a regretful click of her tongue. "I would have given you the button cam."

"I know. That's why I *didn't* tell you." Ben looked her over. Seemed to want to question the pantsuit but didn't. "You'll have enough on the crew from the meeting in Matt's basement. And there's no point in coming after the lawyer. He'll be dead by Christmas. Can we just do this?"

Andy led him into the yard. Their shoes crunched on wet gravel. A row of semitrailers had been backed in against the trees lining the river, and beyond them sat a row of squat, sturdy tow trucks. Andy took out a set of keys and unlocked a cyclone fence into a second yard. These were the repossessed, reclaimed, and dumped cars the Belafontes were probably hoping to sell once their rightful ownerships had been established.

Luna Denero's car was in the farthest corner of the lot. Ben spied it and ran there. Andy raced after him. "Ben! Ben. You can't touch it."

"Why not?"

"It's a crime scene."

"Tell me you didn't bring me here just to stare at it from the outside." He stopped at the bumper of the car and wheeled on her.

"Cool it, cool it." She put her hands up. Andy tugged a pair of disposable gloves from her back pocket. "I'm going to open it up. You just can't get in, okay?"

He nodded, and she pulled the driver's-side door open. Andy reached in and hit the roof light with her knuckle. Ben's eyes roved around the car, and Andy observed him closely as she opened the passenger side and both back doors. Luna's car was filled with the kinds of things a busy mother collected in her vehicle. Takeout wrappers, toys, children's clothes, water bottles, carefully collected sticks and leaves. Ben walked around the outside of the car, leaned in, and squinted when she opened the glove compartment.

"Anything weird? Anything out of place?"

"No." His mouth was twisted. "Not really."

There was a little blue backpack wedged between Gabriel's safety seat and the front passenger seat. Ben did two laps of the car, looking at it several times, before he stopped and pointed at the bag.

"Can you?" he asked.

Andy pulled out the bag, dusted cookie crumbs off its exterior, and unzipped it. Ben looked in as she shifted aside a handful of pencil drawings and a lunch box and showed him the bottom of the bag.

What he saw made him sit down right there on the gravel of the tow yard. He cradled his head in his hands.

"What?"

"The nail."

Andy backed off and tilted the bag in the car's dome light, looked in. At the very bottom, a dark, rough shape. She pulled it out. It was hard and heavy in her hands, square, the cold feel of it in her palm reminding her of the butt of a gun. Andy came toward Ben, but he turned his face away sharply. She waited. On the banks of the river, something moaned, a night bird in the trees.

"We saw a, uh, a video on YouTube." Ben cleared his throat. "Magnet fishing. Gabe and me. You get a powerful magnet and you attach it to the end of a rope and just chuck it into the Hudson and see what you pull up. People film themselves doing it and they put it on the internet. The kid wanted to try it out, so I made it happen. I was, uh . . ." He rubbed his nose on the back of his hand. "I was half worried we were gonna come up with a gun or a syringe or something. I mean, it's New York."

Andy sat on the gravel in front of Ben. The gold light from behind him was making the rims of his ears glow red.

"We hauled in half a bucket of junk, and then there was that." Ben pointed to the rusty nail in Andy's hand, finally showed her his face. His eyes were wet. "It's a railway nail. An old one. Gabe was just . . . He couldn't handle it. He was so excited. He wanted us to pack everything up and go home to show Luna, right then and there. We'd only been out fishing half an hour."

Andy examined the nail.

"He wouldn't have left it behind," Ben said. "Luna—she wouldn't have *let* him leave it behind. That nail went everywhere with us. If we— If we drove twenty minutes to go pick up Luna from work, and Gabe realized he didn't have the nail with us in the car, he'd make me drive back and get it. Like he would *lose his freakin' mind.*"

Andy nodded. She put the nail back in the bag, zipped it up, wedged it in the spot in front of Gabe's seat. By the time she had closed the car up completely, Ben was on his feet, standing in the aisle between the vehicles, staring unseeing at the bumper of a hotted-up black Escalade. They started walking together toward the street.

"What happens to the car now?"

"My boss will claim it. It'll be forensically examined."

"So it came here from the hotel? It had been inside the hydraulic parking space?"

Andy nodded. "It went there the first night. Was there for six days before the hotel had it towed. Luna put it in under her own name. Gave her driver's license."

Ben walked, his arms folded and his head down.

"I have a log-in to the hotel's intranet belonging to one of the valets," Andy said. "I've managed to gain some information that helps. But I was hoping for more. There's no CCTV access, for example. But I can access the check-in and booking sheet from the week she went missing. Luna paid for parking at the Best Western that night, although there's no room or restaurant booking under her name. I want to show you those lists and see if you recognize any names, in case she was meeting with someone you know."

"Okay." Ben stopped at the gates to the tow yard. "I'll wait for you to lock up and we'll convoy back to my place."

Andy felt a flicker of something guilty and painful in her stomach, something she told herself was not desire. "Look, I'm tired. So are you. Let's take this up in the morning."

"Tell me the log-in details." Ben pulled out his phone. "I might be able to work my way into the back end of the hotel's systems with it. Get the CCTV. Maybe there are incident reports. Emails I could look at."

"Right. I forgot you're the tech-head," Andy said. She remembered the bug Ben had most likely placed at the jewelry-store robbery. The one that had accessed, pillaged, and then knocked out the security systems. While she read out the details, she thought about the bug that had shut down the cameras in the apartment in Kips Bay. She held her phone next to his so he could copy the log-in details. "Where'd you learn all that stuff?"

"A teacher. Some high school somewhere. I can't remember." He waved a hand dismissively. "The guy tried to help me out. He knew I wasn't going to hit a home run with the jocks so he put me in with the computer nerds."

"You never wanted to go into that?"

"No."

"Why not?"

"Because that's a normal-person job," he said, his eyes on the screen. Andy felt a hard twinge in her chest at the knowledge that being placed in a stable, predictable IT job was as destined to work out for Ben Haig as it would be for her. That the thing that made him thrive in a high-stakes environment where he could be burned or crushed to death any day in a fire, or killed by his psychopathic boss, was the same thing that made her want to spend her days walking a high wire over being discovered and killed for infiltrating a possibly murderous crew of thieves. They weren't normal people. What had happened to them had ruined them for desks and emails and team meetings.

"Don't stay up all night doing that. You're on duty tomorrow."

"Fuck that. I'll work the case tonight, you work it tomorrow during the day," Ben said. "You're off the crew now. You've got free time."

"Ben, I'll be getting myself back on the crew one way or another," Andy insisted. "I meant what I said. I'm not just chasing a cold case here. I'm trying to bring down a crew of thieves. I need to be as close to the planning of the Borr Storage job as I can be."

They stood facing each other, their hands in their pockets, the hard white moon making shadows of their bodies on the pavement.

"It's not just about that, though, is it?" Ben said. "If we're really honest with each other."

Andy waited for it to come. Ben watched her eyes.

"You want to know if we murdered Officer Willstone."

Andy drew a long breath before she answered, let it out slowly. "Now why would you say a thing like that?"

"Because it makes sense," Ben said. "The longer and harder you go at this, Andy, the more I get to thinking there's more in this for you than a few heists. You might have been able to sell it to me in the beginning that that's why you're here. Because you really care about Luna and Gabe, and the heist stuff is all bonus material. But, come on. Someone hired you. They paid good money for you. They're not going to do that for burglaries, and a Mexican mother and her child."

"What do you know about Willstone?"

"I saw that case. Of course I did. There was talk all around the station. Whoever did it used a Hurst tool."

Andy felt her mouth run dry. "That detail wasn't published in the papers."

"You think cops and firefighters don't talk? We had detectives crawling all over us. Every station did. They told us why. It's because a set of Jaws was used."

"Did you do it, Ben?" Andy asked. He shook his head, started to walk back toward the car. She got in front of him. "Look at me and answer the question. Did your crew do that robbery? Did you kill that officer because he walked up on you?"

Ben leaned into her. She could smell champagne on his breath. He jabbed her in the breast with his index finger. She looked down, realized he was poking the top button of her shirt.

"No camera. I'm surprised."

"You have to understand something," Andy said. "You made a bargain with the FBI: You'd give up your crew for the robberies if we find Luna and Gabriel. But you never said you'd confess to a murder."

Ben said nothing.

"Exchanging ten years of jail time might have been worth it to you, in the beginning," Andy continued. "You find them, dead or alive, and you pay the price you deemed fair. But if I find out that you and Engo and Jake and Matt murdered an off-duty police officer? You'll be paying a lot more time than you've originally bargained for, Ben. You'll be looking at life on the inside."

He just watched her.

"Will it still be worth it?" Andy insisted. "Or are you going to bail out? Will you stick around long enough to know what happened to your family, and then run?"

"Are you holding back on finding them so you can take me for Willstone's murder?" Ben cocked his head. "Is that what this is?"

"No. I wouldn't hold back on finding a mom and her kid who might be in danger, Ben. And fuck you for suggesting that I would."

"I can see it, though. You stick by me and the crew until we've done the Borr Storage job. You parlay that into a confession about Willstone. Put Jake, Engo, and Matt in different rooms, see which one cracks first. Suddenly you've got a string of high-stakes heists *and* a cop-murder confession in the bag. Fuck the woman and her child. They're a garnish."

"That's not what I'm doing." Andy gestured at the gates to the tow yard. "You can see where we are, right? I brought you here, to the car. I'm working the case, Ben."

He stared up at the moon. It made his face look pale purple, the stitches in his brow like painter's brushstrokes.

"We used to lie on the couch together and watch all those YouTube videos," he said. "Me and Gabe. One after the other. The internet would lead us around. First it was magnet fishing. Then it was science experiments. Then it was facts about animals. I hardly watched them. I just used to love feeling him lying on my chest. I used to pretend I was a dad, you know? But one time, we watched this video about tarantulas. You know sometimes they team up with frogs?"

Andy frowned.

"It's true." Ben nodded, his eyes drifting down from the moon to her face. "In the Amazon. Frogs and tarantulas make a deal. The tarantula protects the tiny frog from predators, while the frog protects the tarantula's eggs from whatever might want to eat them. The frog and the spider both live in the same burrow."

"Ben—"

"What do you think happens to the frog, after the tarantula's eggs hatch?" he asked. "After he's stopped being useful and there are three dozen hungry mouths to feed?"

Andy didn't answer. Couldn't answer. She watched him get into the car, start it up, and pull away. The strange flickerings of desire that she'd felt only moments before had mutated into revulsion.

There was no security system outside the apartment building in the Bronx, save for an elderly man with a walking stick and milky eyes who watched Andy all the way up the cracked path. The man didn't speak as she shunted open the heavy glass doors, walked through the foyer toward the yard out back. The air inside the building was thick with the smell of cooking oil and the sounds of competing televisions. At the rear entrance, another old man sagged in a plastic chair, this one asleep, a paint can full of cigarette butts almost overflowing by his slippered feet.

Engo was standing on the fold-out steps of a sun-scorched trailer sitting in the middle of the yard, listening as a man and woman argued before him. He had the look of an overworked night judge hearing a car-repayment dispute. When he saw Andy coming, his eyes flashed. He pointed to the man and the woman in turn.

"All right, all right, all right," Engo said. "You, buy a set of headphones and watch your porn with them on. You, tell your kids to grow up. Your boys are eight and ten now. If their minds are dirtied up by a little groaning coming through the air vents they better stay the hell off the streets." He waved the warring neighbors away. "Now scram."

Andy came to the edge of the light flooding through the trailer's grimy push-out windows. She stood there with her hands in the pockets of her hoodie. Let Engo enjoy his moment looking down on her.

"Don't I know you?" Engo said. "We used to work together, right?"

"Can I come in?"

"Oh, hell no." Engo laughed. "You seen yourself in the mirror? You look like that demon child from *The Omen*. You might be here to stick a knife in me for getting you so good with that viper bite."

"I just want to talk." Andy put her hands out. "I need your help, okay?"

The potbellied overlord lingered on the steps and weighed his decision for a while, enjoying every last inch of the three-foot height difference as the seconds ticked by. Andy thought of the obtuse little mustached man who answered the big doors of Emerald City. Eventually Engo went inside, and she all but crawled in through the tiny door after him.

Inside, there were objects crammed into every space, the paraphernalia of a man who owned and operated and acted as super for a low-rent apartment building. A toilet cistern leaned against the lower cabinet doors of the kitchenette, and fly screens covered in an oily brown substance were stacked in one corner. An upturned milk crate served as a guest chair. Andy sat and Engo sank into a human-shaped groove in a filthy gray corduroy recliner.

"Before you say anything"—Engo swept the air with his hands—"it wasn't my idea to have me put a hold on you today. That was all Matt. He came to me and asked me what I could do to incapacitate you without major physical injury so that we could run a little test on Ben. And sure, I mean, he was asking the right guy." Engo laughed, popped his chest. "That subclavian pressure-point hold? That comes from the Japanese. The samurai came up with it. Not the assholes you see in the movies. The real ones. In my twenties I trained with a couple of them in Tohoku. Nice area. You know it?"

Andy opened her mouth to answer.

"The Japanese know a whole lot about pressure points," Engo said before she could. "Not just pain ones. The pleasure ones, too. You got a point between your thumb and index finger there. I grab a hold of that wrong, and you won't be lifting your arm for a whole month. There's another inside your ear canal, though. I get that just right and the orgasm will make you rethink your entire *life*, honey."

"Engo, I didn't come here to—"

"I can't give you your job back," Engo cut her off. He showed her all eight fingers, leaned his head against the grease spot on the recliner's headrest. "Sure, I told you when you first arrived that I'm the go-to man at the station. Matty wears the boss's helmet, while I'm the true heart of the crew. The guy on the ground. And I stand by all that. But I don't have any part in staff relations. That's just a headache I don't need."

"But you have Matt's ear, Engo," Andy said. "You could at least tell him what I've said here tonight."

"Look, you can *say* whatever you want"—Engo shrugged—"it was Benny Boy's *actions* that signed your marching papers today, honey. One yelp from you and he was up those stairs like a rat out of a flooded basement. Pe-tow!"

Engo shot an arm through the air, cackling. "And hey, I get it! If I had something like you on the line, I'd get on my horse to ride out and defend my princess, too."

Andy sighed.

"Maybe 'princess' is wrong, though." Engo's eyes were penetrating hers. "You know, you can tell what a woman sounds like in the bedroom by how she screams when she's in pain. I was dating this woman for a while. Cut it off because she had a baby and things got real stale. You know what? She sounded exactly the same in the maternity ward as she did in there." He jerked his thumb toward what Andy assumed was the trailer's bedroom. She didn't look. Engo grinned.

"You must sing a beautiful song in between the sheets, am I right?"

Andy shifted her hands into the pockets of her hoodie. She had to unlock her jaw to speak. "Engo," she said carefully, "I'm here as a fellow fire-fighter. I'm here as a colleague. I've got my hat in my hand. If you think that means you get to sit there and talk to me like I'm one of the crack whores who rents a room in your shithole apartment block, you're dead wrong."

Engo hung his head back and howled with laughter, actually clapped his hands.

"I want you to go to Matt and tell him, from me, that I want back onto the crew," Andy said.

"Oh yeah?" Engo wiped a tear from his eye. "And why should he do that? Why should he take you back on?"

"Because I know," Andy said.

Engo stopped laughing. His smile slowly faded. As the seconds ticked by, a reptilian blankness came into his shiny eyes. "You know what?"

"I know everything."

BEN

·

The succulents were dying. Ben took a break from the laptop screen, looked over at their stringy and browned forms sitting on the shelves by the windows, each in a beautiful planter Luna had made. He tried not to think about the suffering plants as visual representations of his weakening hope. On the screen, the log-in page for the Best Western Dayton's staff account system was reloading.

There had indeed been a way into the system, as he knew there would be. It had been as simple as logging into the hotel's intranet as the employee Andy had targeted with her little scam, Dammerly Tsaba, and working from there. The internal system the hotel was using to manage its staff was pretty standard. Ben had seen it used for hospitality workers before in restaurants, diners, and casinos. He went in and accessed Tsaba's last pay slip, got his employee ID number, and noted down his manager's name on a piece of paper beside the laptop. He then went to the employee profile, where Tsaba could edit his address and personal contact details, and accessed his staff email account. Ben noted that Dammerly Tsaba's staff email account began with "DTsaba," which probably meant his manager's username followed the same format. Ben clicked the option to change Tsaba's account password. He got lucky. Instructions below the box where he could type his new password told him that the password could be as long as ten characters, but there was no mention of a punctuation mark or a numerical digit being necessary. That simple fact would cut the possibilities down from sextillions to quadrillions.

Ben went back to the staff log-in page and entered the log-in username "GFannet," making an educated guess that Tsaba's boss, Gloria Fannet, would have access to the hotel's CCTV system. Tsaba, a lowly valet, did not. Ben flipped the page down, went to a folder on his desktop, and opened a password detection program. He told the program he wanted a password of not more than ten characters. When his program had generated an algorithm, Ben copied the link it provided. Once he had pasted the link into the password box on the log-in page, the program set about guessing Fannet's log-in password from what Ben supposed was about four quadrillion possibilities. The password box filled with numbers and letters scrolling so quickly they blurred gray. Even with the program checking a thousand possibilities per second, Ben knew it could take days to find what he wanted. He looked at the plants again, then decided to get up and dig.

Ben had turned the apartment upside down at least five times since Luna and Gabe's disappearance. He was sure he had been through every drawer, examined every sheet of paper, emptied every container, turned out every picture frame, and felt for hidden compartments in the base of every drawer and cabinet. In Luna's handbag collection, he had emptied every pocket and unzipped every sleeve. But Andy's comment about finding the password to Matt's office computer on a Post-it note right by his monitor had Ben rattled. He didn't want to have missed something in such a mind-bogglingly stupid way inside the apartment, something Andy might have spotted without really knowing what she was seeing, because she wasn't familiar with his and Luna's lives. He set about his mission, hoping to drag the sunrise closer to him through sheer mindless labor.

Ben had completed an exhaustive survey of Gabriel's room, the kitchen, and the bathroom and was sitting on the floor in Luna's room, with the contents of her filing cabinet emptied and spread around him, when a dark realization struck. Ben rose up onto his knees and patted the piles of carefully categorized paperwork around him. There was one for utilities. One for car-related paperwork. One for personal items—the old love letters and photographs Ben assumed all women had tucked away somewhere. There was one for Gabriel's art. Ben's hand fell on the pile from the folder Luna had marked "Certificates." He toppled the carefully stacked pile, exposing her high school graduation certificate, her birth certificate, some awards and recognitions she'd received at various jobs. When the little blue booklet he was looking for did not reveal itself, Ben gathered up the stack and heaped it into his lap.

He leafed through the pile from beginning to end.

Then he leafed through it again.

Then he spread the pile out, fanned the individual pages.

Luna's passport was not there.

Ben went to a pile of papers marked "Gabriel: Certificates." He pushed aside the kid's preschool enrollment, birth certificate, immunization records, searching for the passport.

The little blue booklet slid out from under a Helper of the Week award trimmed with gold filigree. Ben snatched the book up and flipped through it, his hands shaking.

He held his head.

Luna's passport was gone. Gabriel's was here. Ben clawed at his skull, tried to imagine a scenario in which he'd been wrong about Luna's passport still being in the apartment after they disappeared. It had been. It *had* been. He was sure. Five times before, he'd noted that the passport was there in the file full of Luna's certificates. Five times, he discovered the passport, held it, flipped through it, checked its expiry date, made sure it was current. Five times, he'd nurtured the little ember of hope—that could easily have been dread—that wherever Luna was, she hadn't taken her and Gabriel's passports with her. She had not deliberately fled from him. She had not "gone back to Mexico, where she belonged." Ben knew that each of those times, he'd placed the passport back exactly where he found it. Keeping the apartment exactly as it was when Luna and Gabriel disappeared wasn't just a grief ritual. It was a strategy. He was inside a living time capsule, a moment frozen when Luna turned away from the door to the bedroom in which he'd been sleeping off his illness, and he wished her a groggy and weakened goodbye, and never saw her again. The time capsule had been his to examine, yes, but also to preserve for future examination.

And yet it had been disturbed. Sure, he'd had to disturb it himself a few times. He'd had to keep it clean. Keep it functional. But this tiny detail, he was searingly, *achingly* certain, he had not altered. It had meant so much that the passport was there.

What did it mean, now, that it was gone?

Ben stood and looked down at the papers at his feet. A siren wailed somewhere, tickling the highly trained senses embedded in his brain that were addicted to the call. He went to the kitchen table and snatched up his phone to call Andy. As he did, the algorithm scrolling through password possibilities hit a match, waking the computer. The log-in page disappeared, and Gloria Fannet's staff profile popped up.

He was in.

ANDY

·

Engo settled in the recliner, his hands gripping the leather arms, danger dancing in his pupils. *"What* do you know, smart little cookie?" he asked.

"You, Matt, Ben, maybe Jakey as well; you're all crooked," Andy said.

Engo licked a canine tooth. Andy waited, holding his gaze.

"That so?"

"Yeah. You're crooked as a bucket of fishhooks," she went on, shifting carefully to the edge of the milk crate. She painted on her best eager, mischievous gaze. "Matt tried to nail me at the barbecue on Saturday about walking into that goddamn *palace* that he owns and not wondering what happened to Ben. I'm surprised I said anything at all. I was speechless. Property records say Matt bought that place two years ago. You have any idea what it's worth?"

"You searched Matt's *property records?*"

"Even if he got a solid-gold handshake for what he did on 9/11, they sure as hell didn't make the guy a millionaire for it," Andy went on. "His people are firefighters from Rhode Island going back a century. Where does the money come from? And then there's Jake. I had an eye on his phone all that afternoon. He blew six grand on online poker while we were chewing on those steaks."

Engo leaned forward in the recliner. They were almost knee-to-knee, and with that easy, casual shift in position, Andy knew she was now within grabbing distance. She was sure there was a weapon down the side of the recliner, in the built-in remote and magazine pocket. There had to be. She just hoped it was a whomping stick and not a knife or a gun.

"Then there's you." Andy jutted her chin, but didn't take her eyes off Engo's. "You pretend you survive on chicken shit living out here in this trailer and moonlighting as a building super. You cut your own hair and dress like you fell into a dumpster behind a thrift shop, but you *own* the building out there. Property records show that, too. Every apartment, top to bottom. You got to have at least three studios here that are just fuck pads for Craigslist hookers, right? You can tell from the boarded-up windows. Those girls would be throwing you cash kickbacks. Then there's the alley behind us, which is perfect for re-ups for the gangbangers renting the bottom floors. You could launder hundreds of thousands of dollars through this building in a year if you were smart enough."

Engo didn't speak. Andy was talking so hard, she was running out of air. She took a moment to suck in a lungful, heard it tremble with barely contained nerve as she spoke again.

"It's the fires," she said.

Engo's right hand crept up the arm of the chair.

"The insurance fires," she continued.

Engo paused.

Andy nodded, her chin up, defiant.

"At the school yesterday," she said, "the same fire where you and Matt decided to run your little 'test' on Ben and me. That place reeked of gasoline. It was clearly a deliberately lit fire. And yet, Matt didn't close off the scene."

"*Excuse* me?" Engo frowned.

"I could smell the gas. So could you. I *know* you could. You gotta close down a scene when you suspect there's been arson. You don't go back in for cleanup! Everybody knows that. You gotta leave it for the cops. But Matt didn't preserve that scene. And I know why. It's because he wanted to get me out of the way. He sent me upstairs with you so you could babysit me, while he sent Jake back to the ignition point to make sure there was no evidence of the accelerant left over. Matt wanted to make absolutely certain the arson was covered up."

"And why the hell would he want that?" Engo was grinning.

"*Because he's in on it!*" Andy hissed. "You're *all* in on it!"

Engo rocked back in his recliner. He held his belly as he laughed.

"Wait-wait-wait. So you think we hook up with members of the public," he said, cackling, "and we cook up insurance fires?"

"That school," Andy said. "You got any idea what *that's* worth?"

"You've— You've had—" Engo sucked in a breath, hacked more laughs before he could go on. "Oh, man. Andy. Andy. Honey. You've had such fun on that property records website, haven't you?"

"This is what you *do*," she insisted, edging closer, trying to convince him. "I know it. You hit maybe three, four big targets a year. You find jobs where you know the fire is deliberately lit, and you heavy the member of the public for a cut of the payout. You split the money in exchange for making sure the scene is clean of evidence."

Engo kept laughing. Andy bit her tongue.

"I'm trying to tell you, Engo, that I know what you all are up to. And I want in."

"You want 'in,' huh?"

"I do. Because I have something to offer. I'm crooked, too."

"Oh, I can't wait for this."

"My boss." Andy was trembling all over. The apparent bravery she'd had to muster to present Engo with what she knew was slipping away. "Back in San Diego. I know that Matt told you what he did to me."

"Uh-huh." Engo wiped his eyes. "He slipped you a Mickey and an unwanted good-night cuddle. So what?"

"So he'd been waiting for his shot," Andy said. "That's why it took so long. Four years, and all he could do was make passes. Sleaze onto me. Hope I'd give in. But when I tripped up on the job, and he finally had something to hold over me? That's when he decided to strike. He thought I'd never report him for raping me. He thought I'd be too scared that he would reveal what he knew about me."

"What did he know?" Engo asked.

"I took cash from a burn site," Andy said. "A meth lab blew up, right in Five Points. During the cleanup there was a bag of cash left over in an unburned room. The cops were there on the scene already. The fire was out. I was part of a team just doing grunt work for San Diego PD. We were moving evidence for the cops from the second-floor apartment down onto the street. I had to walk down a long, empty hallway with two plastic grocery bags full of cash in my hands."

Engo smiled. His eyes shone as he listened.

"So I took a stack. It was just under seven grand." Andy eased a rattling breath. "I didn't realize I was on camera. My boss got the footage. He didn't tell me about it, didn't tell anyone. But then, the night of the party, when he . . . when he . . . when he did what he *did* . . . he said he'd hand the video in to police if I ever told anyone."

"This is what you were trying to tell me." Engo nodded. "At the school. You said there was more. There was stuff Matt didn't know."

"Right."

"Jesus, this is amazing."

"I want into your crew." Andy rose to her full height. "Next insurance fire. I want to help cover it up. I want a cut."

"Or what?" Engo said.

"Or—"

He lunged at her. Engo was out of the chair so fast Andy felt the whole trailer rock around her like a boat hit by an unexpected wave before she realized she'd been snatched out of the chair. She was pinned against the flimsy timber-veneer wall. Engo had one of her hands trapped above her, his knee between her legs, a hip driving into her pelvis, leaning all his weight into her. The three-fingered hand gripped her windpipe like a claw.

"Clever little cookie," Engo breathed into her mouth. She tasted stomach acid. "Tell me. Tell me. *Or else what,* Andy? I want to hear it."

Andy drew the pliers she'd brought with her out of the pocket at the front of her hoodie. She swung them up and used them to bite into the soft flesh under Engo's biceps, gripping an inch of skin and T-shirt in the teeth of the device. He instantly let go of her throat and arm, the pain jolting him, drawing a deep gasp from his chest. Andy used the surprise to shove him backward onto the floor in front of the door. She kept her grip, squeezed hard on the pliers, all of her cold mental focus driven into pinning his free arm under her knee and sitting high enough on his chest so that he couldn't flip her off. She was instantly panting, covered in sweat, the two-second-long maneuver she'd been mentally rehearsing for several hours now complete.

"I had a lot of fun on some other websites, too," Andy said. "Am I getting this right? This is the brachii muscle in the triceps. Have I got it? Does it hurt?"

Andy twisted the pliers. Engo screamed.

"They teach you this one in ninja school, bitch?"

"Get off me! Get off me! Pleeeeaaase, urgh get off me!"

"Who's screaming now, little piggy?" Andy twisted and tugged. "Huh? Huh? Who's screaming now?"

Engo howled.

"You're gonna tell Matt to put me on the crew." Andy had to yell above Engo's cries. "Or I'll come back here and give your inbred ass something to really scream about. You understand?"

Andy got off him. Engo curled into a ball, his arm cradled against his chest. She resisted the urge to kick him in the spine before she let herself out the door.

BEN

.

They stood in the back room of the pet store and stared up at the ceiling fan, Engo and Ben shoulder-to-shoulder, Jake kicking things around in the next room, chasing embers and being nosy. The python wasn't one Ben had ever seen before. It was pastel yellow and cream colored, as thick as his forearm in parts, coiled around the stem of the fan like a scaled insulation system. The men had been watching it for five minutes, off and on, while the breeze off the Hudson cleared the room of smoke. The creatures, almost all of whom had survived being suffocated in their tanks, lolled and crawled around on plasticky, half-hearted jungle or desert landscapes. There was a lot of luck in the room for the creepy, crawly things behind the glass here who might easily have been snuffed out by the fire started by an electric bike in the back room of the shop. Ben had seen e-bike fires kill whole families while they slept.

"How did it get up there?" Ben asked, looking at the snake. There was nothing he would deem "climbable" on the ceiling or upper parts of the walls anywhere near the fan.

"They can climb sheer walls, pythons."

"No they can't."

"It's not real, then."

"You can see it's real." Ben gestured to the snake. Jake came in, dusting soot off his gloves. "Why would a place that sells real reptiles have a fake snake wrapped around the ceiling fan in the back room?"

"Family meeting." Matt came through the doorway, not looking at any of it—the snakes, the lizards, a tarantula bigger than Ben's hand walking sadly around in the sand. Because what the hell are reptiles and spiders when you've seen what Matt's seen? "We're a man down now, and that's a problem."

"Why?"

"Because Command is making noises about a guy they've got over with the Forty-Niners. Some annoying pissant that they want me to bring into line." Matt finally glanced up at the snake, seemed not to take it in. "I don't want some new asshole trying to prove himself on the team the same night we take Borr Storage."

Ben hadn't seen or spoken to Andy in two days. He'd texted her, called her, and she hadn't answered, and he hadn't known if that was part of the Almighty Unwritten Script he was supposed to be following. Like if she really was his girlfriend she'd have a thousand reasons to be pissed about what happened at the burning school—that he'd come for her, that he hadn't kicked Engo's teeth in there and then, that he got her dumped from the crew. She was now giving him the silent treatment and expecting flowers. But Ben didn't know if it wasn't the script at all but something real, like Newler had reassigned her or she'd reassigned herself, and he was about to pull off the Borr Storage job after all whether he liked it or not. If that was the case, he was on his own now trying to find his family before he was arrested, and all he had was the CCTV footage he'd been able to scrape up off the Best Western's ridiculously insufficient security system. Someone walking with Luna through the hotel's lobby. He had that, and he had the constant random stomach-plunging feeling the footage was causing him, and nothing else. He wanted to call Andy and scream down the phone, that while the footage told him basically nothing, it told him everything. There were two people walking. Two sets of legs cut off at the knee. One was distinctly Luna's, and one was an adult set with jeans and sneakers.

Whoever was walking with Luna, he or she was hidden from view.

But Ben had the legs.

Gabriel's tiny sneakered feet were not among them.

"What do we know about Freeman?" Engo asked. "The old man. How close to the velvet curtain is this guy? Because if he dies tonight, we *go* tonight. We don't have to worry about some extra punk from the Forty-Niners."

"He's not dying tonight," Matt said. "But he's close."

"How do you know that?"

"The lawyer's got a burner. I've got a burner. He's keeping me in touch as much as he can. But the guy can't be hanging around the old man's bed like a vulture." Matt glanced back up at the snake. They all followed his gaze. The thing hadn't moved.

"We can't move on that place until we have a key." Matt looked at Engo.

"How are you doing on that?" Jake asked Engo. "Do you need help?"

"If I needed help, it wouldn't come from you." Engo rubbed his nose with the back of his hand. There was something going on with his arm. It moved slow. Made him wince when he lifted it. Ben noticed it but passed it off as an old injury that had flared. "I've seen you try to open a jar of pickles, Jake. It's like you've got hooves. You'd be about as good at lifting something from a person without them knowing as I'd be at sneaking into a nunnery."

"What's a nunnery?"

"It's where they keep nuns, fuckhead."

"Don't they call that a 'convent'?"

"I got a key last night." Engo took out his phone.

"You already got a key?" Matt pinched the bridge of his nose. "After all that, you already fucking got one? Jesus."

Engo brandished his phone for the crew. A picture of a Borr Storage key sitting in the palm of his mangled hand. They all bent in and looked. The key was shiny, brass, a pretty thing people paid whole college funds per year to carry around like an extra dick.

"Don't tell me that's the only photo you have of it," Ben said.

"It is. So what?" Engo frowned. "I did exactly as I was told. I lifted the key from some chick who was on the way to her car. I took a picture with it and dropped it in her parking space. She'll think it fell out of her pocket or whatever."

"Engo"—Ben felt his shoulder muscles tightening—"I need to make a 3D-printed replica of that key from the photo. I need to use the printed key to make a mold so my metal guy can make a replica."

"So?"

"So the picture is just of the key in your hand," Ben growled. "There's nothing for scale. I told you to put a quarter next to it so I could get the exact scale!"

"Hey, fucko." Engo smiled. "All this computer-nerd bullshit you're telling me right now? It's all Greek."

"Why did you think we were taking a *photo of the key* in the first place, you moron!" Ben barked. "I can't get a proper scale from your goddamn hand!"

They came together. Matt and Jake pushed them apart. It wasn't the scale. The key. The photo. It was Engo just being Engo, and Ben thought that if he had to tolerate that in his life for just a second and a half more he was going to spontaneously combust. Like he'd just turn to dust and cease to be. Matt backed him all the way into a tank full of scaly things.

"Engo, take a photo of a quarter in your hand and send it to him so he can try to get a scale," Matt ordered. He shook his head at Engo. "Ben, chill the fuck out."

"Well, don't chill *all* the way out just yet." Engo's eyes slid to Ben. "I want to talk about Andy, while we're having difficult conversations."

"Andy?"

"Yeah, Andy. I have some questions about that woman."

Ben's stomach did that thing where it suddenly swan-dived and smashed into his bowels. The Fight or Flight road fork popped up before him and he swung hard left. "Jesus, I wish you stupid fucks would leave her alone. She's out of the crew. What do you want?"

"What's she doing right now?"

"Looking for a job, probably."

"I've been thinking a lot about her the last couple of days," Engo said. He waited, but Ben didn't bite. "About who she is."

Ben felt his spine harden, felt his legs brace automatically, like his body was literally gearing up to run. A sixth sense told him Matt was watching him, had those demon eyes locked on his. Ben wasn't game to glance over and check.

"What do you mean 'who she is'? What are you talking about?"

"You know, it's funny." Engo cocked a hip, then waggled a finger at Matt and Jake in turn. "You two, with your supreme lack of attention to detail, you probably didn't notice it. But the other day? When Action Man here ran in to save his bride at the school fire? I saw something very interesting that I didn't really think about fully until last night."

"*You're* getting into *me* about a lack of attention to detail?" Ben looked at Matt and Jake, his eyes wide. "Is he for real?"

"You had to shut off her PASS device for her," Engo said.

Ben balked. When he spoke, his voice was too high. "What?"

"She set off her alarm," Engo said. "When I grabbed her, when I put her on the ground, she pulled the tag. The alarm went off on her belt. Then, when you two were having your little kissy-wissy afterward and you were checking her boo-boos—"

"Engo, Engo," Ben tried to break in.

"When you were trying to make sure she was—"

"I don't need to hear this." Flight. Ben tried to walk.

"Let him finish," Matt said. His hand grabbed the back of Ben's turnout coat and yanked him to a stop, the alpha dog arresting a retreating pack member in his jaws.

"She was fiddling with her PASS device." Engo licked his teeth, his eyes full of glee. "You had to shut it off for her because she couldn't work out how to do it. I saw her hit the on switch again a couple of times but she didn't seem to know you had to hold it down to shut it off."

Ben couldn't speak. The hatred was so thick on his tongue it was like wax.

"It was almost like she'd been taught how to set the thing off," Engo went on, "but not how to shut it up again. Or like maybe she was familiar with the old style of PASS alarms. The ones without the tags. They had an on and off switch."

"What is your point, exactly?" Ben squinted.

"My point is that the woman seems smart," Engo said. "Real fucking smart. But only in *certain ways*. In other ways, she's not smart at all. I want to know how much of Andy Nearland is capability and how much is cunning."

"Why is this even relevant?" Ben threw his hands up. "You trying to date her, Engo?"

"I want to know who we're dealing with here."

"We're not dealing with anyone. She's off the crew!"

Jake spoke up. "You told me she wasn't who she said she was."

Everybody turned to him. Ben felt hot air ease out of his nostrils. He had to force his fists into his sides so he didn't lunge over there and strangle the young man standing before him, the same guy who had only days earlier bit him for five grand and was now trying to tip him into an early grave. *Jake*, Ben thought. *Jake, I will hammer you into the floorboards under us like a fucking nail.*

"When did he say that?" Matt asked.

"At the barbecue."

"Look." Ben spoke quietly, could feel his lips wanting to pull back over his teeth. "Andy probably didn't know how to shut her PASS device off because she was in shock. One of her own team members had just tried to break her collarbone for no reason at all. And I said what I said at the barbecue, *Jake*, because I'd had a few drinks and I was pissed at her." His voice trembled with anger, fury trying to smother out the fear. "She was needling me about Donna, and I'd had enough."

"Donna?" Matt cocked his head. "What about Donna?"

"She saw Donna patting my hair."

Matt laughed. "Oh, that's funny. You and Donna? Oh wow. Look, Benji, I've seen your dick. It ain't half as big as Donna needs to get her out of bed in the morning."

"Fuck you," Ben spat at his boss. He gave Jake and Engo a look. "And fuck the two of you, too."

He walked to the front of the store, a bigger space lined with nicer tanks and healthier, prettier animals. The survival rate here was higher. The animals were more active, clearer eyed. A gathering of men and women all stopped talking in Arabic and looked at Ben when he walked in. The helmet, the jacket, the boots. Superhero. Supervillain. Ben was about to walk out into the street, was craving a cigarette, but he felt Matt come up behind him and wasn't prepared to leave the Arabs and Matt alone together. They stopped by a tank that was so full of rats the animals were all heaped in a corner sleeping or trying to make a pyramid of bodies to get to the lid. The smell of their piss made his eyes sting. Matt took out a pack of smokes like he could read Ben's thoughts and shook one at him and lit up, eyes on the watchful Arabs like he wanted them to try to stop him smoking in their store.

"How well do you know Andy?" Matt asked.

"What the—" Ben almost threw the cigarette down. "What *is* this?"

"This is Engo coming to me last night at some crazy hour wanting to talk about her."

"He wants to fuck her, that's all." Ben searched Matt's eyes, looking for tiger stripes in the long grass. "Do not put her back on the crew, if that's what you're thinking."

"Why?"

"Because I want to keep hittin' that, and this is neater for me. That's why."

"Engo's got all sorts of interesting ideas about the Borr Storage job," Matt said.

"Yeah. I heard some of them. He wants to use acetylene. The guy wants to make another—" Ben almost said "9/11" but caught himself just in time. "—another Chernobyl. Don't listen to him."

They watched the rats crawling and writhing all over each other. Pink fleshy palms spread on the glass. Little baby rats were getting squashed at the bottom of the pile. Matt's eyes wandered to the tanks on either side. Two big green pythons in one; a mean-looking brown snake in another. Matt's lip was pulled up by an invisible hook. He turned to the scarfed and bearded grouping in the corner of the store.

"You keep the fucking rats right next to the snakes?" Matt asked.

The group in the corner all turned inward, interpreting, dissecting. A man with a goatee spoke up. "They're for the snakes. They're food."

"Right." Matt tapped the glass beside him with a gloved knuckle. "But they can *see* the snakes."

"Matt—"

"They can *see* the fucking snakes," Matt repeated. He tapped the glass dividing the rat tank and the python tank. "The rats can see the snakes they're going to be fed to, through the glass. You don't think that's sick? You don't think it's fucking twisted? Letting the rats see the snakes?"

The group in the corner turned inward again, trying to understand. Matt didn't wait for their response. He gripped the glass at the front of the rat tank and ripped downward, peeled the glass off like it was fabric. Rats spilled out of the tank, dripped on the floor in great brown furry lumps, bolting for the shadows under the shelves and along the walls. The tank was empty but for sawdust in seconds. The store owners watched the rats fleeing everywhere and did nothing.

She walked in and dumped her bag to the side of the doorway, exactly the way he'd told her not to a million times. The house in Pierre Part was small; appropriate for a Fox long-haul trucker and an Amazon factory worker, the latter of which Dahlia had been pretending to be for eight months at that point. The only way Tony could cope with it all—the distant barking of alligators, the steaming dampness lying over everything like a blanket, the clackety air-conditioning unit that overheated and ground to a stop every forty-five minutes—was if everything was kept in order. The guy felt safe in neatness and cleanliness. Tony was standing at the peeling kitchen counter with a glass of paint thinner posing as whiskey in his fist, and when she kissed him on her way to the fridge he didn't lift his eyes, just shifted his mouth sideways out of habit the way a person reaches for a seat belt in a car.

"I think she's ready." Dahlia grabbed a cold bottle of water from the fridge and guzzled half of it, beading sweat just from the walk from car to house. "She's almost ready to tell me where she buried the baby."

Tony had his back to her. She looked at his love handles. Southern food, the role, the monotony of pretending to be out on the highway somewhere between Virginia and Maine when really he was sitting in their bedroom fifteen feet away from where they stood now, watching her feed on a laptop screen. The overwatch pounds. Dahlia sympathized. She'd stacked on weight when she took overwatch duty on their last case. But she'd at least had the novelty of watching Tony run a plumbing-supply store. Dealing with the customers. Answering their queries. Chitchatting with his colleagues. All Tony got to watch was her gloved hands scanning uniform brown and black boxes as they traveled along a conveyor belt in a factory so loud workers mostly communicated in hand signals.

He said nothing now. She chattered on.

"I had a good long conversation with her in the break room," Dahlia said. "You probably saw it. She told me about her father. The abuse. Tony, I'm buzzin'. I think I'm on the edge here. I think Margie's gearing up to tell me about the first baby, you know? A month or two, and I'll get it out of her. How her parents making her give it up was—"

"Dahlia."

"—was too traumatic. That'll open the door to her telling me how she wouldn't have been able to face something like that ever again."

Dahlia got an eerie feeling. It was swimming in the silence of the house, which was not really silence at all, because that didn't exist down here. There was always something moving or fighting or fucking or singing out there on the bayou, or some dirt bikers rumbling through the reeds. Firecrackers. TVs. Cheap houses made a lot of noise, too. The appliances hummed and clunked and the corrugated-iron roof breathed in and out all day like a living thing slumped over the house. Tony had dropped his accent to say her name. It was weird. They always kept their accents, especially somewhere like the South, where picking up and putting down the drawl could be like hefting bags of cement.

She went around and studied his face. "What?"

Tony licked sweat off his upper lip. Stared at the glass. Shrugged. "You were getting too close to her."

Still no accent. Dahlia felt her face twist. "What?"

"It's been eight months, Dahlia," he said. He let that sink in for a while. It didn't. "Eight months."

"Right. So—"

"I'm on overwatch." Tony touched his chest. "It's my job to keep ahold of that balloon string so that you don't float away. And I'm . . . I've . . . Look. I called it. You were taking too long, and that's because you were getting in too deep with Margie. You got yourself into a relationship."

"A what?" Dahlia laughed hard in his face. "You're not accusing me of—of—of—"

"Hell, I don't know, do I?" Tony shrugged. "Friday night? The boil, over at Jimmy's place? You turned your—"

"I didn't turn my camera off," Dahlia snapped. "It malfunctioned."

"It malfunctioned?" Tony's eyes searched hers. "Just as you and Margie snuck away behind the garage?"

Dahlia stared at him. The creepiness she'd felt when he first said her name hadn't eased. There was more. She could smell it. Shivers of dread began in her diaphragm.

"I'm not fucking Margaret Beauregard," Dahlia said carefully. "I'm trying to find out when and how she killed her baby, and where those remains might be. I'm trying to find answers for the Beauregard family and the Peters family and the local PD, who brought us in. I'm doing what I was told to—"

"How do I know that's true?" Tony shrugged a heavy shoulder. Just one. Like he was tired of lifting them. "How do I know we're not eight months into a cute little dyke fuckfest here?"

Dahlia's mouth fell open.

"You said you were bored, back in Portland." He looked her over. "That's why we're here in the middle of the redneck-infested swamplands right now. I've been wondering if maybe you weren't just bored with location, though, Dahlia. Maybe what you meant was that you were bored with me. With us. With solving murders. With the whole goddamn arrangement."

Her jaw was hanging. She breathed wet panic and Southern summer. There'd been no warning. That was the thing with Tony, the most dangerous thing, the thing she'd learned the hard way. He could hide the black, slithering badness deep down under the surface of his eyes the way the swamp hid things even her nightmares couldn't assemble, things that bit alligators clean in half.

"What did you do?" Dahlia asked. She thought of her bag by the front door. Her phone. Margie's number. She imagined going there. Calling her. But she couldn't move. "Tony? You said . . ."

"Look, I'm sorry."

"You said I was getting too close to her. I was."

"I greenlit the arrest about an hour ago." Tony watched her eyes. Seemed to be actively looking for the pain bursting there. "I waited until I knew you'd be on the highway."

Dahlia sucked in air.

"Margaret went for the shotgun under the kitchen sink." Tony sipped his whiskey. "A deputy took her down."

"She's—she's—she's not—Margie's not—"

"She's dead."

"No she's not." Dahlia went to the bag in the corner by the door. "No she's not."

She fell on her knees on the boards, grabbed the bag. The zipper jammed. Dahlia ripped it open, sliced her index finger, knelt in the light from the street pouring in through the mottled yellow glass and tried not to think about a baby rotting in the ground somewhere who would never be found and lifted and rescued from that hole. A baby with no name who deserved a place in the world, a cross, a stone, a plaque, flowers, a notice in the newspaper, something, anything, whatever the goddamn fuck. She knelt and cried in the doorway with her bag on her lap and tried not to think about a mother who made a mistake, the worst mistake a person can make, a mother who deserved to be lifted from the hellishly lightless and airless pit of her own mind like the child she'd put in the soil. They were both gone now. Lost under the surface.

"You were getting too close," Tony insisted.

Dahlia got up. She hugged the unzipped bag to her chest and opened the door beside her, and set about getting as far away from Tony Newler as she could.

ANDY

.

She stood in the shadows of the apartment complex entryway two buildings down and across the street from where Ben was going. Andy leaned against the bricks, watched as Ben instructed his cab-driver to take him on two full laps of the block before he dropped him off. He didn't see her standing there on the corner of that anonymous street in North Ironbound. There was too much active camouflage on offer. Andy was a still figure in a restless landscape of people; drug peddlers waiting on the steps of the apartments next door, one of them idly dribbling a basketball while another handed a hit to an itchy man in a jumpsuit. The drug deals here were open-handed, relaxed, almost friendly, because there were spotters at either end of the street and half the cops in town were on the take anyway. There was an assembly outside the bodega on the corner waiting for hamburger patties to fry on the grill just inside the window cluttered with sales paraphernalia, and kids played near the cab Ben got out of, oblivious or resigned to the fact that they might get popped any minute by a rival gang coming for the dealers across the way. The local church, Andy guessed, would be crammed with candles lit for baby-faced collateral. The sad fact was that drugs brought more money into this neighborhood than the government ever did, so the kids played and the parents lit candles and the dealers bounced their basketballs off the bricks.

When he thought the coast was clear, Ben disappeared inside, using a key to get through the iron-barred foyer door. Andy started after him, but her phone rang in her pocket. She pulled it out, her muscles already twitching.

"Yes?"

"Do you remember that case we had in Littleton?"

Andy shrank back into the shadows of the doorway. A woman with a toddler on her hip and a cigarette in her mouth had come into the foyer to check her mail. She gave Andy a look up and down through the grimy glass.

"Littleton," Newler repeated. "The Harris and Klebold devotee who moved into town. You remember? We played her neighbors. Kept an eye on her, trying to figure out if she was planning to stage another—"

"This isn't a good time to play Memory Lane with me, Tony," Andy said. "In fact, it's never a good time."

"We hadn't been partners long," Newler carried on. "I took the case for us because it was a slow boil. Unlikely to turn into anything. Just a couple of weeks of babysitting a psycho who couldn't walk the walk. We were over-kill, because the local FBI agents were new and nervy. You eased into that role so uncertainly, Dahlia. You were always gripping my hand too hard. One time, you threw yourself at me in our yard just as she was pulling into her driveway. You wanted her to see us kiss."

"Tony—"

"I don't think it was nerves at the idea that you had to play someone who was in a 'couple' for the first time," he said. "I think you were nervous about kissing me. Leaning into me. Letting me hold you. Because you wanted me, even then. Even that early after we'd met."

Andy gripped the phone.

"Do you remember what it feels like to be held by me?" he asked.

"Don't call me again, Tony."

"I can tell when you're scared, you know," he said. It was like she hadn't spoken at all. "You're scared now."

Andy glanced out into the street, hung the phone up before Newler could tell her she was scared of this case and his involvement in it and what it might mean for the two of them. Following her heart. Going backward. Admitting she was wrong. Admitting she'd overreacted about Margaret Beauregard in Pierre Part, that she'd thrown away everything he'd been offering her at the time—a husband, a family, a safe and secure job—over some baby-killing hick she barely knew. Andy could hear Newler like she hadn't hung up on him. Like his lips were against her ear, saying that the offer she'd thrown away was still there.

It would always be there.

It was okay to come in now from the dark, cold sea.

She was so achingly close to safe harbor.

Andy's stomach was churning. She crossed the street, took the keys she'd had duplicated from Ben's set while he slept one night and found the one to the barred door. She let herself into the foyer, and then into apartment number 2.

When she entered, he came into the hall, his eyes wide. His face relaxed as he recognized her, but an ugliness was there. The sneer. The sigh. He went back into the living room, slumped into a plastic lawn chair, the only piece of furniture in the room.

"How?" He put his hands out. "*How?* I checked for a tail. I left my phone and my wallet at the apartment. I hailed a cab, paid cash."

"How do you think?"

Ben patted down his clothes, feeling for a tracker.

"It's in your shoe," Andy said. Ben reached down and pulled off his shoes, checked the sole of each. Still couldn't find it. "In the tongue. The left one."

Ben felt the tongue of the shoe. The tracker was expertly sewn into it. She watched him running his fingers over the invisible seam. "Unbelievable."

"Look, if I had to guess where your stash was without being able to put a tracker on you, I'd still have guessed it was here." Andy looked at the bare walls of the apartment where Ben's mother had been living when he was born. "You have this same instinct with Luna's apartment. Own it. Protect it. Keep it preserved. Find a way to change it. This is not just an apartment for you, and neither is Luna's. They're moments."

"You know what the head shrinks charge for this kind of—what do they call it? Psychoanalysis?" He smiled. "Lucky me. I get it for free."

"Uh-huh."

"You ever played a shrink?" he asked. "Or are you talking from personal experience? Do you own the place where it all went wrong for you?"

"Oh, that's long gone," Andy said, stiffening through the shiver passing through her. "So what do you want to do first? Show me the money or tell me what the hell you've been doing for two days?"

"Me?" he scoffed. "What the hell have *you* been doing for two days? I've needed to tell you shit. *Important* shit. They're on to you, Andy."

"How so?"

"It's Engo." Ben's eyes were narrow, examining her. "He's got some sudden hard-on for you. Did you call him? Did you go see him?"

"What's he saying?"

"He's picking you apart. What you did here. What you said there. Jake and Matt are starting to listen to him."

"It's fine. I'm keeping an eye on it. You don't need to worry about that."

She went and sat on the carpet beside his lawn chair and took out her phone.

"What do you mean?"

"I want to run some things by you that I've dug up." Andy swiped through images in her photos app.

"*How* are you keeping an eye on it, Andy?"

"I've been trawling through bank accounts," she kept on. "That's where I've been. I have a contact who's good with this sort of stuff, but he's hard to get ahold of. He's finally pulled through. This has been lock-yourself-up-with-snacks-type work. Just reading screens. Couple of things I spotted. Matt, first. Tell me what you think."

"I'm asking you questions and you're ignoring me."

"Get used to it."

"Jesus."

"Three days after Luna and Gabriel went missing"—she zeroed in on a picture of a list of purchases—"Matt goes and buys a set of children's clothes."

"Matt's got like twenty-five kids." Ben hardly glanced at the photo, slumped in the chair. "I don't know if you noticed. He knocks up anything that comes within spitting distance. If I was you, I'd go get a test. You've ridden in the same engine."

"Yeah, well, I was able to run the receipt number against the store's records. The clothes were size four to five."

Ben stared at the floor. There was the faint smell of vomit in the air, not quite disguised by the new carpet and the basic paint job. Andy imagined when the breeze was right, the vomit smell inside had to compete with the outside smell of the nearby waste-management site.

"Donna's pregnant," Andy went on. "But aside from that, isn't Matt's youngest kid ten years old?"

"Yeah."

"So?"

"I don't know." Ben shook his head, his stare fixed. "Were they boys' or girls' clothes?"

"I couldn't get that much."

Ben thought. "Okay. So Matt and Luna they . . . They were together. They met at the hotel. He killed her. Maybe she said she was gonna tell me or . . . or Donna about what was going on. He killed her, and he couldn't kill Gabe so he . . . He kept Gabe instead. Didn't have enough clothes for him . . ."

"Do you see Matt cheating with Luna?" Andy asked. "Is that something you can imagine?"

Ben looked at the bars on the windows beyond the lace curtains. "No."

"The guy's got more wives than fingers. Surely he cheats."

"I've never seen it." Ben shrugged. "And he's had offers. We've been in bars and the women know we're FD. They're crawling all over us. None of his wives left him for cheating. Him and Mary broke up because they got married too young. Imogen, he was with her when 9/11 happened so she caught the brunt of that. Christine, he called it off because *she* was cheating."

"There's a first time for everything."

"Where would he keep Gabriel? How would he hide something like that from Donna?"

"I don't know."

"What else have you got?"

"Two weeks before they went missing"—Andy swiped through her phone, more screenshots of bank accounts—"Luna withdrew three thousand dollars from her bank account."

"What?"

"The initial detective, Simmley, he ran Luna's bank accounts," Andy said. "But he probably missed this. She didn't withdraw it from her everyday checking. She pulled it from her 401(k)."

Ben licked his teeth. Looked harder at this screen grab than he had the one from Matt's account. "It was to pay for the gun, maybe. The one she tried to get her brother-in-law to source."

"Maybe. There weren't any big bills around that time? No big purchases?"

"No."

They sat in silence for a while, looking at the figures.

"I have something, too," he said.

"Okay."

"Luna's passport isn't at the apartment. And I got CCTV of her walking with someone in the hotel lobby."

"Her passport is there," Andy said. "It's in the filing cabi—"

"It was. But it's not anymore." He looked at her. "So you saw it in the filing cabinet? When you searched the apartment, just before you met me. When you broke in and did your little recon mission."

"Yes."

"So, I'm not crazy. It *was* there."

"Someone's taken it, or moved it, since I saw it," Andy said. "Who's been inside your apartment since we met? Who had access?"

"A bunch of people have been through there." Ben shook his head, sat with the phone on his knee, playing the vision for himself again and again. "Jake. Engo maybe, just to pick me up. That was the day before I met you, I think. My brother Kenny. But I mean, he just came into the kitchen. I had eyes on him the whole time."

"Who has keys to Luna's apartment?" Andy asked. "Who might have been there while you were out?"

Ben shook his head again, rubbed his stubble. "I don't know."

They sat in silence, shadows of the evening passing over the bare room around them. Andy watched the edge of the light walking across the unused carpet fibers, imagined it was the same light that had played over the furniture that was here when Ben was an infant, in the days before he was first removed from his parents' care. Andy knew it was time for her to make Ben show her his stash, so she could photograph it, and him, a stick to add to the pyre Newler would be building for him. But when she looked at Ben's face, she didn't see the remorseless criminal that he was. The liar, and cheat, and endangerer of innocent lives that he had become. She saw instead a wounded and confused man, swiping the footage back over and over, watching it play out, trying to find within it some clue as to what had happened to his imaginary family. And it seemed as though all the humiliation and justice that might have swirled around that moment—the moment she photographed his secret treasure trove of stolen cash—was already playing out here before her. It would have been cruel to double down on it. Ben chewed his nails, and Andy leaned over to view the screen in his hands.

"This is it? The footage?"

"Yeah." He turned the screen so she could see. She could smell his body, close as she was. Ben had showered after a day of fires. She recognized his cologne. Andy watched the footage a couple of times. The feet walking side by side.

"Those are her shoes." Ben pointed at the screen. Andy could see his finger gently trembling. "I recognize them. They're the ones she always wore to work. They got messed up with clay."

"She might have been carrying him," Andy said. She nodded at the phone. The footage. "Gabriel. I know what you're thinking, Ben. She left the house with Gabe. So where is he? But Luna could have been carrying Gabe on her hip. She still did that sometimes, right?"

"Why was she meeting someone at the hotel?" Ben asked. "With or without Gabe. Who was she meeting, and why didn't she tell me about it?"

"Same reason she didn't tell you about the gun, or the money. Is there any other footage?"

"Of course not!" he barked. "That would be too easy. The parking lot has no cameras at all. The lobby has this camera and two others. Luna and this person, whoever he is, come up out of the elevator and manage to walk right into a blind spot. I can't tell where they go from here." He stabbed a finger at the screen. "That way is reception. That way, the first-floor rooms. That way, the restaurant."

"She's not on the booking list at the restaurant?"

"No. She didn't get a room, either. At least not under her name." The meanness had come into Ben's face again. "There are no names that I recognize on the guest list for that night or any of the nights around it."

Andy thought. She was startled when Ben threw his phone at the corner of the room. It smacked off the wall and bounced on the carpet.

"Why wouldn't they have put cameras in the goddamn parking lot?" Ben's face was in his hands now. "For the love of *Christ*, if they just had cameras in the parking lot, we'd have everything!"

"Ben." She put a hand on his leg. "You can't lose hope, here."

"We're not going to find them." He shook his head. "I mean, look at this. They've managed to thread a perfect fucking path through the camera grid without being seen."

"An *almost* perfect path."

"It's me," Ben said. "I don't deserve to know what happened to them. That's my punishment for . . . for everything. Whatever happened to them, and the rest of my life not knowing what that thing was."

He looked around the apartment. She knew what he was seeing. The wretchedness of his childhood here. The playing out of what the universe had apparently decided he deserved, even before he left the womb. The poverty. The danger. The unwantedness of Benjamin Haig. Andy could almost read his thoughts, about how foolish it had been to think he could have a family of his own, live out his dreams of providing a safe and secure environment for a boy. To heal, day by day, as he did for that boy what had not been done for him.

"The cameras didn't see them," Andy said carefully. "And it wasn't because of you, and what you deserve. Okay? It was because hotel cameras don't work that way."

"What do you mean?"

"They're usually pointed at the staff," she said. "Sticky-fingered waiters and clumsy cleaners are what most concerns hotel managers, not the guests. In my experience, anyway. Hotel patrons don't tend to steal anything because their name is on the room, and they're usually so busy having a good time that they're not taking notice of what there is to take. It's the bartender who works all night for peanuts that you need to watch. The one who has to count in and bag up the money for the bosses every night."

"How do you know that?"

"I ran a hotel for a few months. Place in Boston. Trying to catch a lady-killer."

Andy watched Ben. He'd seemed not to take in the Boston thing, the reasoning, and she was sure he didn't believe what she'd said about what he deserved. He was gripping his scalp, his elbows on his knees, eyes on the floor.

So Andy said, "You can dance, huh."

It wasn't a question. But he raised his head anyway.

"What?"

"Luna was Latina," Andy reasoned. "She spent more than five minutes with your ass. So you must be able to dance."

Ben raised an eyebrow.

"We need to blow off some steam."

BEN

·

She got it just right. And that wasn't easy, because the last time he got in a cab with her and she decided where they went he wound up having to kick the asses of two guys and getting more than a little whupped himself. She picked a place just off Chinatown, and it took so long to get there in the cab that by the time they walked in he was too drunk on a bottle of Jack they bought that he couldn't read the name on the door. It *had* a name on the door, which clocked up more points still, and he got let in without a cover charge and wearing a T-shirt with a hole in it.

He was laughing as they fell into the ladies' room together, actually laughing, with his girlfriend and his kid maybe dead and gone and the undercover cop who was going to put him in a fucking jail cell for a decade hanging off his arm, doing coke off the counter under the mirror, not bothering to watch if she did it, too.

They went out onto the floor together and every woman in the place was looking at him, and maybe word got around that Andy was his sister or something, because those women were slipping into his arms and grinding their hips on his and running their hands up his chest and through his hair and Andy was doing nothing at all about it.

She'd been right, of course, about the dancing. He could move it. Okay so he *hadn't*, in years, no more than to twirl Luna around the kitchen; half because she was the mother of a three-year-old and staying out past ten was her idea of a nightmare, and half because if the guys found out they'd never let him hear the end of it. He'd picked it up somewhere, in some foster home maybe or some school, the footwork, and the rest of it was just having a firm grip on the girl and having eyes only for her.

Andy kept handing him drinks and he kept sinking them, and once or twice he looked over and saw her dancing with some guy, and the rage flickered in him, right in the middle of his chest, like something knocking on his sternum, asking to be let out. And Jesus Christ, could she move it, too. What she was doing was nothing picked up at a school or in a home;

it was slithery and wet and wicked and only worked when she paired up with another woman, because men couldn't move like that. And so she did, a bunch of times. The women came for her like they were coming for him, out of nowhere, beautiful girls with long hair. He went to the bar and stood there and watched because he had to, Jesus he *had* to, and Andy and this one girl worked each other so deeply and so seriously that the girl went for it and gripped Andy's head and planted an unexpected kiss right on her mouth. Nobody saw it coming. Not Andy, or Ben, or the girl herself, and suddenly the three of them were laughing about it, pink and purple light washing over them, the coke shimmering through his brain and making everything glow with hope.

Andy slipped between him and the bar and dragged his arm around her waist, and he bent around her and smelled her neck and hair and pressed his hard cock against her ass because he couldn't figure out who the hell he was supposed to be right now, her partner or her victim, the good guy or the bad guy. It was badness that was in him; hurt and anger at himself for forgetting all about Luna in this moment, guilt about the things Andy didn't yet know about him, fear that she did, in fact, know them and had something terrible in her pocket for him now or in the next minute or the one after that. The music was suddenly so loud he could barely hear his own voice. Had to yell into her ear.

"Is this real, or not?"

She turned and looked at him. He was still pressed against her. She wasn't moving away. Had her arms around his waist, in fact. Ben felt like every cell in his body was on fire. Fever hot, pouring sweat. That sweat mixing with hers.

She was about to answer him when the fucking bartender set up her drinks. Two tequila shots. They threw them back. He thought he caught something in her eye over the top of her glass, a menacing glint that made all the sweat grow cold at once.

When she led him toward the door he followed and wondered what the hell she had waiting out there for him this time; a street full of cops, guns pointed at his face?

He lost time between the bar and the cab, the cab and some random corner where she ordered the taxi driver to pull over and got out. He stood in the cold of the wind off the river and waited, watching rats, while she slid into some cramped and brightly lit bodega. He had his hands stuffed in his pockets, the breeze bringing uncomfortable levels of sobriety into him. They walked and she lit a cigarette, and it occurred to him that he hadn't seen her smoke before. Was *this* real? Not just the feel of her body in the bar, but all of it; the cigarette and her hand wandering down his arm and gripping his hand. He was looking for another cab when something in the lay of the land snapped him back into reality. New York did that to him sometimes. Aligned itself in a particular way like a Magic Eye, the buildings, the angles; this sparkling souvenir shop and that Dunkin' Donuts popping out of the flatness and reminding him of his place on the map. He stopped dead in the street, felt like he'd been hit with a battering ram in the chest.

"What?"

Ben looked at her. Dropped her hand. Smiled.

"Amazing," he said. He actually laughed. "Amazing, Andy."

"*What?*"

"Don't give me that." He kept walking. Because fuck it: if she wanted to do this now, he'd do it. "This is the street. Up here, on the corner. The Book Bonanza. You think I don't know where we are right now? We're a hundred yards from the Willstone murder scene."

She followed, should have had that look on her face like she'd been caught out but didn't. He walked right into the side street, stood waiting for her to join him, looking up at the building etched across the yellow-clouded night sky. There were lights on up there. Ben didn't know which window was the Singaporean gangster's place, and which belonged to the apartment where they'd put out the kitchen fire.

"Okay, so I'm here." Ben turned to Andy. "Lay it on me. Tell me how it went down. Or do you want me to do that? Huh? Because that's the whole point of this. You get me drunk and you bring me here and you see what happens. Okay. Sure. Better get your phone out, Andy, or whatever your *fucking* name is. Here I am, this is me. I'm coming through this door here. The whole crew is. Me, Jake, Engo, Matt. We're wheeling a big fucking safe we just stole down on a trolley."

He went to the big steel fire door at the back of the apartment building, banged on it with his fist, pantomimed pushing a trolley. Andy was standing by, her arms folded, the cigarette poking out from between her fingers, trailing smoke across her unreadable eyes.

"Here we go." Ben acted out the maneuvering of the safe to the back of the van. "We're loading up the van. *Jesus Christ, fellas! I sure hope we're not walked up on by a fucking cop right now. That would be crazy, right? Oh, shit, there's one!*"

He pointed at Andy's chest, his arm outstretched, three fingers fashioned into the shape of a gun.

"Bang, bang."

A slow smile crept over Andy's face. He knew what it was about, could tell from the deep sadness that was badly disguised behind it. Because his angry little reenactment included a couple of things she'd been watching for. The positioning. The angles. Where Willstone had been standing. Which end of the street he came from. The two shots—not three, not one—that had taken him out. Ben stood there fuming and waited for her to ask him how he knew all these particulars, whether he'd heard them on the first responders' grapevine or guessed them wildly or knew them because *it was him*. Because all this time she'd been lying in bed next to a cold-blooded cop-killing monster, the night hours ticking away and the beats of their two hearts getting in sync; one Colgate white and one black as tar. And she didn't ask him. Maybe she couldn't bring herself to shatter that vision of him that she had, as a hero, a firefighter, a scared and grieving boyfriend and wannabe daddy, a good brother, a criminal, yeah, but an otherwise okay kinda guy.

And not a bad man.

Because whoever had ended Ivan Willstone's life, everything that he was and could have been, in this lonely, empty street was one of the bad ones. One of the unredeemable ones. Maybe Andy didn't really want to know that about him. Maybe she liked him enough, not in the fantasy they'd constructed but in the real world, to not want to know.

His phone rang. Matt.

"Are you with Andy?"

Ben looked at her. "Why are you asking me that?"

"Because I'm trying to save myself a phone call, dumbass," Matt huffed. "Fifty-four's got a car rammed into a shopfront on the Square. They're calling a 10-18 for nearby stations in case it becomes something."

"I'm drunk as shit, Matt."

"Did I ask you how you were?"

Matt hung up. Ben started walking to the end of the street without looking to see if Andy was following. A cab was waiting outside a hotel. Ben waved. They slid into the cab together, saying nothing, and he looked out the window and felt numb; no annoyance about the return-to-quarters call that was probably nothing, or trepidation that it might turn into something. The fury from the street behind the bookstore was gone. The hard-on from the nightclub was gone. He might have been sharing a cab with a stranger at that moment for all he felt, and that was bad, because on a completely emotionless level he knew that she was the most dangerous person he'd ever shared a cab with in his life.

Engo was climbing out of his car in the back parking lot of the station. Jake was sitting on his hood, smoking. As the cab pulled away, Ben was walking between them toward the back doors, eyes ahead, looking for Matt.

He heard Andy yelp first. Ben turned in the gravel and caught a glimpse of her in Jake's arms before Engo snaked his arm around Ben's neck from behind and wrenched him backward and all he saw was sky. Ben recognized the squeeze. Engo had tried to put it on him before. Kung fu shit. Ben even knew, on the same cold, rational plane his brain had been traveling along, how to get out of it. Twist sideways. Go for the balls. He even had enough mental power left underneath the booze to remember the sore or weak arm Engo had, the one he noticed yesterday or whenever it was. And yet his world folded in on itself, and slammed shut like a laptop, with only Matt's heavy approaching footfall in the gravel and his words to whisper away his consciousness as Engo pinched his jugular off like a garden hose.

"Her in the back. Him in the trunk."

ANDY

.

ndy struggled on the floor of the portable building, kicked wildly as Jake tried to pull her bunker trousers on over her jeans. Matt was watching, leaning in the corner, head cocked. Ben was coming to, trying to turn onto his back, straining against the duct tape that was half on his wrists and half on the sleeves of his turnout coat, a whip-fast winding Engo had fashioned so he could be there to help Jake dress Andy up and secure her. A cold sweat had broken out all over her, at the planning, the precision involved, the details. They'd bound her once in the darkness of the station parking lot, and now they were dressing her against her will, taking off and then reapplying the tape as they pulled on her uniform, and she was putting it together—the plan, the scenario, looking at the old gas bottles cluttered around the room. The one piece of tape they never removed was the one on her mouth. She talked anyway, because she had to, because the screams came up without her being able to control them.

Ben! Ben! Bennnnn!

Engo pulled her into a kneeling position. Jake dragged Ben up beside her. He was awake now, blinking, shaking off the last of the drunkenness. When Matt ripped the tape off his mouth, Ben gave a howl of outrage and horror.

"What the fuck is this?" Ben looked up at Matt. "Matt? Matt! What the *fuck*?"

"We know, Ben," Matt said.

Ben looked at Andy. His eyes darted all over her—the tape, the uniform, the blood dripping from a gravel-graze on her jaw. Matt slid a gun from the waistband of his jeans and Andy felt her stomach lurch.

"We know you're a cop," Matt said to her.

We know.

Andy wondered if this was it. Or if it would come in a few minutes' time, when the building was stormed by Newler and a team of backups he'd assembled the moment he saw Matt and Engo and Jake subdue them and throw them in the car in the station parking lot. Because she couldn't imagine what would be worse now: being shot on her knees right here on the boards or being caught in the crossfire when that happened, bleeding out in the ambulance on the way to the hospital, Tony stroking her hair, crying his apologies. Andy didn't know for sure that Newler had been watching her that night. The only night she could confirm he'd been following her, being overwatch for her against her will, was the night of the jewelry-store heist. But she'd felt him since the case began, that strange sixth sense rising from a tingling to a burning, a hum to a roar. She had felt his eyes on her in the park in East Orange, like he was closer than the phone call she'd held with him there on the bridge. Once, a million years ago, the sense of Tony Newler being nearby had given Andy comfort. Turned her on a little, even. Now it was going to get her killed. It was going to get them all killed. Over her own moaning and panting and Ben's protests, her ears were pricked for sounds out there in the woods.

"You brought a *fucking cop* into the crew."

"She's not a cop! I swear to God, man!"

"I *raised* you." Andy watched as Matt's big fist trembled around the gun he'd pressed against Ben's head. "I found you in a hole and I dug you out and this is how you want to play me?"

"Matt, Matt, listen to me—"

Andy heard a sound out there in the woods. A twig snap, maybe. Nobody else seemed to hear it. Jake was restless near the open door. His bottom lip was trembling. Andy envisioned him being shot through the doorway, taken out by a sniper. Would that be Newler's strategy? Have a rifleman pop as many as he could before a flash-bang forced entry? Ben was trying to get up, but with his wrists bound it was almost impossible.

I'm not a fucking cop! Andy growled through the tape. Engo came over and she swung around, kicked out at his shins. He went down.

"Get her back on her knees."

Jakey came over.

Don't fucking touch me!

"Benji," Matt said. "There's an out here. I'm *giving you* an out. You gotta take it."

"I don't—"

"Tell us that you turned on us. That's all you have to do, man."

"She's not a cop!"

"Just tell us!"

"Matt, please!"

"Tell us, or I'm gonna have to do this thing. I don't want to do it. But I will."

Ben looked at her.

"I don't want to do this, Ben," Matt said. "Just tell us the truth."

Jakey started to cry.

Ben struggled to his feet. Matt followed his face with the gun, laser-focused, the barrel inches from the bridge of his nose.

Ben breathed. He nodded, short, sharp, decided.

Andy screamed behind the gag. *"The phone!"*

"The phone?" Jake interpreted. His eyes were huge and running tears. "What's she saying? Can we take her tape off?"

"Fuck her," Matt spat, and shook the gun at Ben. "It's you I want to hear from, you conniving piece of shit. Tell me why she couldn't work out how to shut off her PASS device at the school fire. Tell me why I called her station in San Diego and nobody there had ever heard of her. Tell me why she was waiting for you in that bar that night, of all the goddamn places in New York, of all the people you could have hit on—"

Ben was silent.

"You brought in a cop because you think we had something to do with Luna and Gabe."

Still, the silence.

"The phone!" Andy screamed. *"Please, please! Fuck!"*

"What the fuck are you talking about?" Matt swung the gun around at Andy, walked over and ripped the tape off her mouth. The air was thin and cold against her lips. "What phone?"

"Mine!" Andy gasped. She fought the urge to be sick all over the floor, forced the words out instead. "Please. Listen to me, Matt. I'm not a cop! If you just take my phone, and—"

"And what, bitch?"

"Call someone on there!" Andy begged. "I'll give you the code. Open it. There must be— There must be a thousand fucking numbers on there! Call one of them and ask them who I am!"

"I already called half the firefighters in San Diego, you stupid fuck! No one's ever heard of you. You only exist on the paperwork on my end. I couldn't find a single firefighter who would say they'd worked with you."

"Of course they wouldn't admit to knowing me, Matt!" Andy pleaded. Tears were streaming down her cheeks. "I'm blacklisted there. I'm fucking radioactive! If you call one of them from my phone, you'll see."

There was a stillness. Andy sobbed, and the men around her stood and watched, the dynamic in the air changing, shifting, shimmering with tension. Andy didn't know if that was really true, if the great ship was indeed turning around, or if she just wanted to believe it was. She cried while Matt watched her, his eyes icy.

"Get the phone." Matt waved Engo away. He disappeared out the door toward the car, returning in seconds with the phone. Andy recited her passcode. Her teeth were chattering. She couldn't look at Ben.

"Pick someone. Anyone." Andy eased a heavy, shuddering breath. "I'll tell you how they know me. How we met. You can check."

"These might be fakes." Matt's voice was, for the first time that night, uncertain. He scrolled the phone with his thumb as Engo stood nearby.

"Just pick any person, Matt, anyone at all," Andy cried. "Jesus Christ, h-h-how could I fake a thousand fucking people who know me? Go to the messages. Go to my emails. Go . . . go anywhere!"

"Look at her photos," Engo suggested.

"No, I'm gonna call someone." Matt flipped the phone, showed her the screen. "Here. Look. Melanie. How do you know her?"

"We were in high school together. Same friend group. But I haven't talked to her in—"

"Shut up." Matt's fist was gripping the phone hard. "Everybody shut up. When she comes on the line, you talk."

Half of Andy's mind was wandering the dark landscape outside the building, wondering when Newler's team would come and destroy them all. Her hot breath fogged the glassy surface of the phone as Matt held it before her lips. The gun was inches from her, hanging by his thigh.

"Heyyy! Andy?"

"Mel," Andy gasped. "I need your help." Matt lifted the pistol, pushed it against Andy's temple. She winced and struggled on. "I-I-I just need you to explain something for me really quickly."

"What? Andy, what's going on? Are you okay?"

"Don't worry, I'm fine, just please tell me where we met. Right now. Please-please-please."

"Where are you?"

"Mel, for the love of Christ!"

"Where we *met*?" There was a rustling in the background, like someone was sitting up in bed. "We met at South West High. Why? What's ha—"

Matt cut off the call, scrolled again. Andy could see the color had gone out of his neck. In the corner of the room, Ben was standing with Jake, his wrists bound and his eyes fixed on Andy's face, unreadable.

"Who's Bruno?" Matt asked.

"He's a friend of my dad's. He might not answer. He's old."

"Fuck that. I get to choose."

Matt dialed. After eight rings, a gravelly voice answered.

"Yeah?"

"Bruno, it's Andy."

"Who?"

Matt slid his finger off the trigger guard and onto the trigger itself. Andy shook and tried to breathe.

"It's Andy! Andy Nearland! John's daughter! From North Park!"

"Oh, shit! Andrea! How the hell are you, honey? God, what time—"

"Can you please te—"

Matt shut off the call. "I want a firefighter," he scrolled. "Right here. 'Ray E.' That would be Raymond English, right?"

"Yeah."

"That's the guy I spoke to on the desk this afternoon at your old station in Five Points." Matt threw a dark look at Engo. "He claimed he'd never fucking heard of you."

"Call him," Andy pleaded. Matt dialed. The phone rang and rang.

"Oh Jesus," Andy sobbed. "Ray, please pick up."

"How could she fake all these people?" Engo's voice was so quiet, it was barely audible against the wind outside the building. "I mean, that's a lot of names."

The line connected. "Andrea?"

"Ray, it's me!"

"What the fuck, girl? Why are you calling me?" The male voice on the phone lowered to a hush. "I'm on shift at the station right now. If I get caught talking to you I'm mincemeat. What do you want?"

"Enough," Ben snapped. Matt ignored him, flipping through the phone. "What else do you want? You gonna call every single person in the goddamn phone?"

"Shut your trap."

"Please, Matt, I'm not a cop, I swear on my life." Andy shivered.

"You went to Engo's last night," Matt said, his eyes roving over the screen, dark orbs reflecting messages, call lists, pictures. "Tried to get him talking about criminal activities."

"What?" Ben balked.

"I'm sorry. I wanted to be a part of it, that's all." Andy shook her head. "It was so stupid. I'm *sorry*! I won't tell anyone what you've been doing, okay? I swear, Matt. I swear to God. Please don't kill me!"

Matt's eyebrow twitched. His finger was frozen, hovering just above the phone screen. He glanced up at Engo. Engo came over and the two watched the screen. Engo smiled.

"I think we might have been wrong," Engo snorted.

"Everybody's wrong sometimes." Matt slid his gun into his waistband.

"What?" Ben's face was hard. "What's going on?"

"Nothing." Matt motioned to Jake. "Untie these assholes."

BEN

.

Jake went over and snipped Andy's ties. As soon as her hands were free, her attitude changed. She shoved Jake when he tried to help her up.

"Fuck you." Andy spat blood on the ground. She threw a fierce look at Matt, tears pouring down her cheeks. "And fuck you, too. This is s-s-some psycho *bullshit* right here!"

"Psycho bullshit is what separates the men from the boys." Matt winked. "It's what gets you into a crew like this, Andy. Being able to prove yourself if you have to. You cried like a little bitch, sure, but you held your own just now. I could use you."

"What do you mean, 'use' her?" Ben rubbed his wrists. "We're not— No. No. Matt, you can't."

"We need another man on Borr Storage." Matt shrugged. "Engo's right. If she's not in on it, it's another wrench in the works that we just don't need."

"I can't believe this." Ben held his face in his hands. Jake's sniff drew attention to him. He rubbed his nose on the back of his wrist, tried to hide his eyes.

"Poor ole Jakey," Matt chuckled. "He's got a big heart. You want a tissue, baby boy? You want a cuddle? Come here for a cuddle. Come on."

"This was too far." Jake turned away, stared out the dark doorway at the night. "One of these days you're gonna pull something like this and—"

"And what, you're gonna have a cry *and* shit your pants?"

Ben was numb, going to the wall, putting his hands on it to steady himself. He couldn't look at Andy. Couldn't look at any of them. He heard Andy storming outside, sobs still racking her body.

"She can't be on the crew." Ben shuddered when Matt came over. "She can't, Matt."

"I've made the decision already. We need an extra guy for Borr Storage," Matt said. "Engo and I have run the numbers. It doesn't work without a fifth man. When she came to him last night, telling him she was crooked as all hell, and she wanted onto the crew—he thought the same thing I did: either she's a cop, or she's the answer to all our problems."

"Matt, we can't—"

"Don't argue with me." Matt put a big palm up, patted the air in front of Ben's face. "This is neater. It means we won't have to have her babysat doing crowd control while we're trying to pull a heist."

"You're crazy. You don't know her."

Matt shrugged. "I like her, though. I'm not sure I even know why. There's just . . . something there. It's like when I came across your sorry ass over at the Forty-Second. I knew you had a couple of brain cells. Andy's got something we can use."

"She's manipulating you," Ben said. The words just fell out. "She wants you to believe that. She's wanted it from the start."

The boss shrugged again. "It worked."

"But she's not in the life."

"What?" Matt looked him over. "What she told Engo, though . . . About the bags of cash. About her being crooked."

Ben had nothing.

"She didn't tell you?"

"No."

"Oh man." Matt reached up and gripped his shoulder and shook it. "*Man*. You gotta sit that woman down and have a confession session. She told Engo she's dirty before she told you. That's sad as sin."

"She can't be on the crew."

"She's *perfect* for the crew," Matt said. "And it's the perfect time to use her. This is our last job. We don't need to trust her long-term. We get through this, and any heat comes on? We just dispose of her."

ANDY

.

ndy went into the long grass at the side of the portable building, gripped the windowsill, and bent, retched, vomited. They were out there. She could feel them. By her guess, Newler had had maybe an hour to get his extraction team on-site. She'd known him to get better teams together, faster. The problem was, she had Jake and Engo up her ass, smoking, watching her be sick.

"Where's my phone?" She turned to them, put her hand out. "Give me my fucking phone."

"Matt's still got it. Relax."

"Fuck you, Engo!" Andy's teeth were still chattering. Adrenaline. Electricity snapping in her synapses. She screamed so the men out there in the dark could hear her, could tell she was outside the shack now. Alive. Her thighs were chafing in her jeans, wet with piss or sweat or both. "I'm leaving! I'm outta here! Don't fucking follow me!"

"You're never gonna get a cab to come out here," Engo called after her. She walked stiffly back into the portable. Matt handed her the phone, a slightly amused smile playing on his lips. She swiped it from his fist and kept walking. Her elbows and knees were burning, skin off, sticky rawness rubbing against the insides of her clothes as she walked. The struggle in the gravel at the back of the station had torn her up. She fake-dialed as she walked down the dirt road and glanced back, she made sure her voice carried on the wind. "Yes. Hello? I need a cab. One passenger. Now."

Andy gave it fifty yards or so down the dirt road toward the highway before she called Newler. He answered in one ring.

"They're about to go in," he said.

"Call them off," Andy hissed. "Jesus Christ, call them off."

"Dahlia, I have to—"

"You have to do what I say right now, because I'll kill you this time, Tony." She stopped on the black dirt road, the woods around her howling with danger. She could see lights now on the houses on the hill. Her eyes were playing tricks. Making shapes, picking out tiny blinking red lights of rifle sights or radios where there were none. "If you make the call again like you did with Margaret, if you make the call before I'm ready and you get one of my targets killed again, I will come for you. Wherever you are. I will put a fucking bullet in your brain. Do you hear me? Do you understand?"

Silence for a long time, then, "Dahlia, I need to know you're safe—"

"I'm safe. I was always safe. Call them off. Now."

Andy stood in the dark, panting, shivering, her body still hunched because every muscle was pulling inward protectively, a shell trying to close up. Then she spied it. Not a mirage this time but a distinct red light out there in the dark, fifty yards or more into the trees.

The light went out.

She walked on down the road.

BEN

.

She met him at the door of the little bare apartment she'd rented. He got no more than a glance into the place—the labeled boxes of thrift-store stuff were still there, and the mattress was still in the middle of the floor. Then she was in his arms, and he was shoving her hard into the wall right by the door, pinning her hips with his, ramming his tongue into her mouth. She gripped his ass and tugged him into her, groaned into his ear, and Ben could smell she'd showered but the aroma of the woods and the Hudson remained on her, the musty portable, the sweat and blood, not just on her skin but in her hair, in her breath. Maybe it was just memory. Ben pulled Andy's shirt up over her breasts, tore it off over her head. They stumbled and fell into the first room, landed on the mattress. Ben forced her over onto her stomach and worked his fly open while she ripped at hers. Their anger was meeting there on the sheets; hers at the near miss out at the abandoned property, him at the rest of it; *all of it*. Ben tugged her jeans and panties down just low enough and shoved himself inside her, used a handful of her ponytail as one handle, one of her ass cheeks as another, and rode her until he finished, fast, before either of them could change their minds.

Unzipping. Unclipping. Unpeeling. Pulling the layers away. She lay under him and ran her fingers up his cracked ribs, piano keys of pain, flipped his T-shirt up off his head while he worked himself inside her, slower this time, deeper. They kicked their jeans off. He'd seen her body already, but she was revealing a new and different kind of nakedness to him now. Her whispers. Her cries. The way the cords moved in her neck as she twisted away, came for him, seemed to fight it. She wrapped her arms and legs around him, and he fell beside her, and they slept for a while there, tangled.

In the shower, he stood behind her, following the slithers of her hair with his fingertips. His mind tried to wander into dangerous territory. Luna. The men. The abandoned construction site. What Andy, or whoever she was, believed about what happened out there; whether he'd been about to give her up. To tell his crew everything. He kept scooping the thoughts back, shoving them under his desire, trying to blast them out with urgent wonderings about her; about whether he wanted to pin her up against the shower wall now or push her down onto her knees. She made the decision for him. Ben put his hand on the wall under the showerhead and cradled her head against his crotch and sighed.

They woke at the same time, randomly, his breath against the back of her neck quickening, her foot twitching against his shin. The city was humming. Blue light on the walls. Two heads on the same pillow. He slipped a hand around her pelvis, pulled her tight against him. They lay silently, both toying with the idea of further sleep.

Until he said, "How did you do that?"

She turned her face against the pillow. He noticed a scar hidden in her hairline, jagged as fork lightning.

"I recorded them all," she said. "It only took a day. I sat with a couple of actors and ran them through the lines. You can find actors who will do that kind of cash work on the notice boards at arts colleges, usually. But I found these guys on Craigslist."

"Wh . . ." He struggled for words. "I don't understand."

She turned and reached up above her pillow, onto the floor at the top of the mattress. She unlocked the phone and handed it to him.

"Pick someone."

Ben chose a name and dialed. He showed her the name on the screen. Theo.

"Hello?" the voice on the phone said. *"Andy?"*

"This is where I say 'It's me, listen,'" Andy said, her voice still hoarse from sleep.

"What's going on? I haven't heard from you in so long, man," the cheerful voice of "Theo" said. *"Somebody told me you moved out to New York!"*

"This is where I say 'I need your help, tell me where we first met, blah blah blah,'" Andy rolled a hand. "All that stuff."

"What do you mean—"

Ben hung up the call.

"So they're all recordings?" He scrolled the hundreds of names, made them whizz by, an unreadable blur. "*All* of them?"

"It's not as hard as you'd think. You just hook the phone numbers up. You can buy phone numbers in bulk on the internet." Andy stifled a yawn. "That's how the robo-scammers do it. Then I just recorded one-sided conversations with the actors and saved them as the voicemail for each phone number. When we dialed 'Theo' just now we weren't getting a live line. We were getting voicemail. Same as when Matt was dialing the numbers in the portable. None of the phone numbers are attached to real people."

"Jesus."

"I just memorized the conversation I would have with each character. Who that character was to Andy Nearland. Melanie, the girl I went to high school with. Bruno, the friend of my dad's. Theo, a guy I met in the academy in San Diego."

"This is . . ." Ben couldn't speak. "Where did you learn to do this?"

"Newler taught me this one. We had a job out in Palm Springs where we needed him to appear to be this very successful businessman. We dummied up calls to businesses and played them back in front of his target."

"Andy."

"What?"

"This isn't . . ."

She looked at him. He shook his head, the words catching in his throat.

"It's not normal."

She laughed. The mattress shook.

"No I mean, it's . . . it's sick," Ben said. He leaned on an elbow, watched her eyes. "This isn't just a job for you, is it. Normal people don't sit for days and days recording fake phone calls and writing fake text messages back and forth between . . . *between people who don't exist* . . . for a job."

"No," she agreed. The laughter was gone. "It's not just a job for me."

They stared at each other. Ben got that eerie feeling, the same he'd experienced in the cab from Kips Bay, that he was lying beside a very dangerous woman. Someone far beyond what he'd bargained for when he went looking for the help of a cop. A woman unconstrained by cop rules or cop practices. He supposed that was the point of her. She could do what she wanted, whether it was ethical or practical or not. The dark possibilities shook him, stirred something deep down in his core. He couldn't see what had happened to her to make her like this. It didn't play against the darkness of her pupils, and it wasn't written in the jagged scars on her skin. But he was beginning to hazard a guess that whatever it was, it was very very bad.

"What did he see?" Ben asked.

"Who?"

"Matt." He watched her carefully. "After the phone calls. The phone calls, they were a good strategy. But he found something on the phone afterward that made him kind of smirk. He called Engo over to see."

"Do we have to do this?" Andy rubbed her brow.

"Whatever he saw, it was the final nail in the coffin for him. He was convinced, after that."

"I'm tired, Ben."

"I've seen that look on Engo before, Andy."

"I fucked a guy." Andy let her hand slap down on the blanket. "Is that what you want to hear? After that first night, when I made you show your body to me in the bathroom at your place. I went out, I trawled a couple of bars, I found a guy who looked like you. I fucked him and I filmed it on my phone. Made sure his head wasn't in the shot. It's sitting there in my photo app, if you want to watch it, but you did just get the real thing."

"Oh my God."

"I did it for the case, Ben. Matt and Engo, they've got to know a cop wouldn't sleep with a mark just to get a case solved."

"But *you would*!"

. "I would do anything!" she snapped at him. Her eyes were wild now, fierce. "And yes. You're right, Ben. It's sick. *I'm sick*. Once I get into a role, I'm there. I'm in the case. I would do anything, and give anything, to get it solved. Because this isn't just a job for me. It's *my safe place*."

She eased a long, unsteady breath, and the exhilaration of watching it happen shot through him. This was her. The real her, on the edge of screaming, or sobbing, he didn't know what. She was talking to him from deep down underneath her mask.

"If I ever look outside the case I'm in, even for a moment, I'll have to go back to being me. The real me," Andy said. "And I can't do that."

Ben grabbed her shoulders. "Who the hell *are* you?"

Andy wiped a tear from her eye, threw him and the blanket off herself.

"I'm the woman who's going to put you in jail," she said.

He knelt on the bed. Against the windows and the blue night he couldn't see her face anymore, and the shape of her was ghoulish, murky, seeming to shift right in front of him. Changeling.

"I'm going to find them first, Ben," she said. "I promise."

"What good is a promise from you?" he laughed. "I have no idea who you are!"

ANDY

·

Matt was late. He rolled in out of the evening air like a storm, the pressure wave hitting the waitstaff as he strode toward the doors, making them wilt. A server near their booth slammed herself up against a table to get out of his way. He slid in beside Engo and reached his crane arm across him to pluck Cristobel's menu from the holder. It had been two days since she'd seen Matt in the portable building on the abandoned construction site on the Hudson. Two days of silence from all of them, including Ben, while she lay in her apartment scouring hotel CCTV footage, bank accounts, phone records, emails. She knew more about Matt, Engo, and Jake from digging around in their lives; personal things. Engo's taste for violent pornography. Matt's sponsorship of a kid from the Detroit projects who needed funds for attending school. Jake's membership in a choir that sang once a month in a church basement in Hell's Kitchen. Nothing that would tell her whether she sat now with a group of vicious killers or a run-of-the-mill band of skilled criminals, men with the same kinds of secrets and lies fluttering around the edges of their worlds as anybody else.

"This is where we're at," Matt said in greeting. Andy held her wineglass stem on the table before her, glanced at Engo and Jake. "The nurse I've got on the pad at the hospital is telling me they've moved Freeman to stage-six end-of-life care. There are six—"

"What does that mean?" Engo broke in.

"There are six stages total." Matt shot him a thin bolt of lightning from the eyes. "The last stage; he's not conscious a lot. The oldest son is making the decisions now. It's a rich person's hospital, so it's all what kind of fucking lamp the guy wants on when he finally bites it. If he wants music or incense. All that shit."

"Sinatra," Engo said. "I want Sinatra when I go."

"Better stick it on now, then," Matt said. Engo shriveled. "It's time for the lawyer to strike in there. Get the keys swapped out so we're ready to go." Matt looked at Andy. "Where's Ben?"

"That's what he's doing now," Andy said. "I think."

"You're not talking?"

"It was weird enough, me joining the firehouse." Andy widened her eyes. "Now I'm here for this. This is more commitment than you'd get in a marriage."

Matt gave a small, rumbling laugh. Engo leaned across the table.

"I am so here for this," he said. "Tell us everything. Did you fight? Was there make-up sex? This is what we've needed in the crew. A bit of hotness. Something juicy."

"Don't act like you and Jake haven't been blowing each other for years." Matt rolled his eyes, beckoned the waitress over. She snapped to it like a starting gun had been fired. "I see you two coming out of the storeroom with that just-sucked energy."

Jake sighed.

"So this is the wall we're talking about," Matt said when he'd ordered a burger and fries. He reached across Engo again and rapped a big knuckle on the painted bricks. "Half an hour's worth of natural gas pumped in through the back should be enough to split it. Andy, you and Jake are gonna be on the hose at the front making a show for the crowd of knocking down the fire while Ben and Engo go through the wall to get the cards. You two should be in and out before things get hectic at the front."

Andy looked around Cristobel's restaurant, imagined their plan. The grand room she was in now, blown out by a fireball burning hot enough to pulverize every piece of glass in it, to vaporize anything paper—the napkins, coasters, menus, signs—to scorch the carpet and curtains and table-cloths and set them to flame. She watched sad lobsters lolling about the bottom of an otherwise empty tank behind the bar, bubbles rising steadily from an algae-furred tube. If the glass held for some reason and the initial explosion wasn't enough to boil the water in the tank, Andy knew the ensuing fire would have the lobsters cooking in the water within minutes of the blast. She felt like ordering one of them now just so the creature's death wouldn't be so pointless. Then she reminded herself that none of this was going to happen. The explosion. The robbery of the safes. It was a reality only in the minds of the men around her.

"You are very lucky to be a part of this," Engo was saying to her. "And to come in the way you did."

"Oh, yeah, that was a real party out there in the woods." Andy smiled brightly. "I just wish I'd taken more photos."

"If I really thought you were a cop I would have just dropped you with a Halligan in the firehouse engine bay, Andy," Matt said. "I was just doing due diligence."

"That happened to a guy up in Harlem." Engo nodded. "Halligan fell off the top of the truck. Clonked him right on the skull while he was bending down to look at a tire."

"It's nice and neat," Matt mused.

"You seemed pretty convinced," Andy said.

"I wasn't," Matt said. "Cops don't cry like that."

"Oh, fuck off."

"Please, please, don't kill me!"

The men all laughed. Andy sighed.

"You better not think being dragged out into the middle of the woods and having a gun put to your head was the worst thing that could have happened to you." Engo smirked. "Count yourself lucky. You shoulda seen what we did to Jake."

Jake's cheeks and neck were blooming with red spots.

"What did they do, Jake?"

"It wasn't that bad." He looked away.

"I needed him last minute," Matt said. "Like you. It was for a cash thing. I got word that a big-whale poker player was coming in from Washington. Was trying to be smart about it. Staying off campus near the Resorts World but not at the Hyatt itself."

Andy straightened, fiddled with her bra strap, made sure the camera affixed at the second button on her shirt was pointed right at Matt.

"I had a guy all ready to ram the whale's car. But I needed the new pro-bie Jake not to squeal like a little piggy when I bagged the briefcase in the middle of the fire."

"You made out like all the money got burned up?" Andy said.

"That job took more research than you'd think." Engo nodded. The night stretched outside. Office workers heading in. Tourists heading out. He watched them with his milky, bloodshot eyes, sipping his scotch. "It sounds like a smash'n'grab job but we had to source the exact same type of briefcase without a paper trail. We had to make sure the hit was just right. Make sure we didn't kill the guy in the process, or his driver."

"Plus about five grand in sacrifice money to burn up in the car," Matt said, swinging the Finger of Death around. "That came out of *my* wallet because *you're* a tight-ass and *you're* a degenerate."

"Jake, though." Andy looked at the kid.

"I had a detective I know put him in a room for nineteen hours," Matt said.

"Nineteen hours!" Andy looked at Jake.

"It was fine," Jake groaned. "Can we leave it?"

"I gave him an hour before he folded," Engo said.

"I gave him less," Matt chuckled.

"He held out, though." Engo nodded appreciatively. "All the detective was trying to get him to admit was that he'd been on a certain shift with Matt. It wasn't a big thing. But Jakey held out to the end."

"Aww, Jake. You're good for some things, aren't ya, bud? Not many things. But some." Matt kicked him under the table. Jake jolted, rubbed his shin.

"It sounds really tough." Engo smiled over the rim of the glass at Jake. "It wasn't tough, though, was it?"

Jake kept rubbing his shin.

"How many times you throw up, Jake? Five times?"

"The guy ruptured my kidney." Jake frowned. "I had two perforated eardrums."

"Threw up like a little bitch all over his own shoes."

"I threw up last night, Jake." Andy stroked his arm. "It's okay."

Jake nudged her off.

"What did you do to Ben, then?" Andy asked.

"I never did anything to Ben," Matt said. "I didn't need to. You take a wild, starving dog off the street and feed it nothin' but sliced ham, you don't have to worry about whether it's loyal."

"Okay. What about Titus?" Andy asked. The table fell silent. "Don't tell me. You waterboarded him."

Sheet lightning in Matt's eyes. "Titus wasn't in the crew."

"How inconvenient." Andy examined each of their faces. "Must have been a pain in the ass, trying to pull jobs while he was around."

She waited. Engo was playing with his phone. Jake was tearing a napkin to shreds. Matt leaned forward. When he spoke, Andy could feel his dragon breath against her cheeks from all the way across the table.

"You've been in the crew five minutes, sugar plum," he said. "You haven't earned shit. You can pick up your Access All Areas pass when you start proving your worth."

"Bullshit. You can see my worth." Andy felt nervous energy radiating off Jake beside her. "I've been proving it to you this whole time. You knew I was worth something that first day, when you heard where I'd come from. Matt, you got some level of respect built in for anybody who's been through something, because you went through something."

Now it was time for Jake to kick someone: Andy, in the ankle. She didn't flinch.

"And you knew I was valuable when this lil bitch told you about how I'd punked his ass in his own trailer." Andy nodded at Engo.

Engo laughed.

"Matt, honey"—Andy leaned forward—"I'm not afraid of you. *I'm not afraid of you.* And that's got to be the rarest thing in your life right now. The rarer something is, the more it's worth, right?"

Matt sat back and looked at the others. For the first time since Andy had met him, the man seemed like he didn't know what to do or say or think.

"So." Andy straightened, nodded to the waitress for more wine. "Tell me. What'd you do to Engo? You make him take a shower?"

Jake choked on the water he was sipping. The men all fell into laughing together.

BEN

.

I n the video, Gabriel was in his car seat. The same car seat Ben had been
looking at only a few days earlier, the one dusted with cookie crumbs and
spotted with ice-cream stains, Gabe's little ride-around throne. Ben and
Luna were wearing sunglasses. She was driving and chewing gum. The
camera swung to her. She glanced over, gave her Harrison Ford half smile,
on the screen for a second only, two chews. Ben leaned against the bumper
of the old white Chevy in the mechanic's workshop and rolled the video on
his phone back a little, made Luna turn her head, looked at those cords in her
neck. In the last ten videos, Ben figured he had maybe two minutes' worth of
footage of Luna. Why hadn't he taken more? The afternoon sun through the
window was fire in her hair.

"*Say what you just said again.*" The Ben in the video grinned. Gabe kicked
his little legs, sneakers bumping off the front of the seat.

"*Huh?*"

"*About being— About what you wanna be when you grow up.*"

"*I want to be a farmer.*" Gabe smiled.

"*Your people didn't come all this way so you could be a farmer, baby.*" Luna
on the screen again, dropping her sunglasses to look at him in the rearview.
"*Mama didn't raise no farmer. You're gonna be a doctor.*"

"*Maybe that's what he means, Lu,*" Ben laughed. "*He's gonna work for Big
Pharma.*"

"*Right. Okay. He'll be a Pharma bro. I can live with that.*"

"*I'm gonna have lots and lots of chickens.*" Gabe threw his hands up. "*Thousands and thousands and hundreds! Lots of—*"

"*Ferraris?*" Luna asked. "*Is that what you said? Houses in the Hamptons?*"

"*Jaguars,*" Ben said.

"*Yeah, jaguars!*" Gabe gasped. "*I'm gonna have a farm* and *a zoo.*"

Paxi came over from the metal shop and pushed his face shield up on his
head. With the manicured orange beard, he was the medieval knight with
the flipped-open helmet. Ben shut the phone and put his palm out. The key

Paxi handed him was still warm, the edges of the brass still jagged and razor sharp in places. Ben turned the key over in his hand a few times, held it up close, looked at it from afar. Around him, Paxi's garage was quiet. Apart from the Chevy there was a 1934 roadster in pieces in the bay. Ben wasn't a car guy but he'd been fostered by one, once. He knew how obsessive gear heads could get about having the right nuts and bolts and stud heads, or replicas cast and hand-tooled. It was what kept Paxi in beard oil.

"I think the whole border needs to come in." Ben pointed at the key head, showed Paxi the photograph of the original sitting in Engo's palm. The shot he'd taken at the pet store. The two men looked back and forth between the two keys. "A quarter of a mil at best. Do you see it?"

"Yeah, I see it." Paxi nodded. The chubby, pockmarked mechanic flipped his face shield down, his eyes googly in the magnified panel. He took the key from Ben and went away again. Ben sat on the Chevy and scrolled back through the videos. Right back, until he found Gabriel in the pool at Matt's place. The kid had said *"Benji, watch!"* about six times in the first fifteen seconds. The camera never left him. *"I'm watchin', kid! I'm watchin'!"* The vision pulled away after twenty-three seconds, took in Luna sitting at the other end of the pool, her feet in the water, head bowed, talking to Jake. The probie was on the other side of her, in the water, shadow fingers from potted palm trees raking his angular features.

Paxi was back with the key.

"I gotta clean it up, obviously," Paxi said.

"Looks good." Ben nodded.

He was walking down the alley behind Paxi's, traversing a row of hotted-up vehicles with tags in their front windows linking them to the mechanic's shop, when he passed a dark gray BMW with no tag and a guy sitting in the front seat. Ben was ten feet along past the rear bumper, twenty feet from his own car, when he froze in midstride, struck with the realization that the guy in the Beemer was the same one he'd seen loitering in the parking lot down the block from the Guggenheim. He turned, just as the man was sliding out of the car and straightening his navy-blue, nicely pressed shirt and looking at Ben with a kind of regretful resignation that made Ben's insides squirm.

"Haig," the guy said.

Ben thought about his gun, that was resting uselessly under the driver's seat in his car. He slipped the key Paxi had given him into the front pocket of his jeans.

"You must be Newler."

The guy nodded. He was carrying. Ben could see the pistol butt in the reflection in the Beemer's rear passenger window, tucked in the waistband of Newler's trousers.

"It's time to come in."

"You found them?" Ben took a step forward, all caution abandoned. "Jesus, where are they? Are they okay?"

"We haven't found Luna and Gabriel Denero, no," Newler said. "And we're not going to. The terms of the agreement between you and the FBI have changed, okay? I'm here to escort you to my office, where we can sit down and talk about—"

"What do you mean you're not *going to*?" Ben felt like the ground was tilting beneath him.

"That's not a priority of mine," Newler said. "And I'm in charge of this case now."

"Bullshit. Where's Andy?"

"She was too close to this. I'm pulling her off it."

"Does she know that?"

"Not yet. Right now all I want to do is—"

"Get me into custody." Ben nodded. He wondered if the car entering Paxi's was carrying an agent there to arrest the bearded mechanic. If there were people, agents, turning up at Donna's place now looking for Matt. Or at Engo's trailer. "I want to speak to her."

"Of course you do." Newler smiled. "And you know what? You're going to miss her. You two have been close throughout this. But you have to understand something, the person you've been dealing with for the last few weeks isn't real. She got inside your head. She got inside your life. That's what she does. But none of that meant anything."

"Uh-huh."

"She came onto this case in the first place to fuck you, Ben. And that's what's happening now. I'm just making it all happen faster than she intended, and in her absence."

Ben stood there, staring at the buttoned-up asshole with the gun, the buildings with their apartment windows yawning all around them. Something about the guy's words was twisting in Ben's brain. The tone wasn't right. It was too warm. Too deep. Too familiar.

"This is what she does, huh?" Ben asked. "She gets inside your life."

"Uh-huh."

"Gets inside your head."

Newler nodded.

"Fucks you." Ben watched the guy's eyes carefully.

Newler didn't answer, but Ben saw everything he needed to in the way the guy's body stiffened, the way his jaw muscles twitched defiantly. Ben knew the whole story then, could smell it on the wind. Andy, or whoever she was, and this guy, who was probably her romantic partner or even her husband. This guy who'd been watching them two nights earlier on her mattress in her apartment with the curtains thrust open and the city light pouring in, neither of them giving a fuck who saw them. A thought occurred to him, that Andy had slept with him knowing Newler was out there watching, wanting to toy with the man, using Ben as a chess move in some sick-ass game of tit-for-tat between lovers. Now this asshole was going to punish her by yanking her off her cute little missing-mother-and-child case and make her get to the fucking point of it all: the burglaries, Willstone, Titus. The *real* cases. Ben wanted to be surprised but he wasn't. He'd been dodging wild haymakers like this from law-enforcement psychopaths since grade school.

"You must have been watching us this whole time," Ben said. "She said you were. Running, uh, 'overwatch' on us. That's what you call it, right?"

"That's right." Newler nodded. Ben thought about the night out in the woods. The portable building. The test Matt had run on him at the burning school. Tests and games and experiments. Chess moves and mind games.

"You must know about the upcoming job, then. Next month," Ben said. "Over in Queens. The bank."

"I do." Newler gestured to the car. "Get in. We'll go to my office and you can tell me all about it. There may be an opportunity there for us to renegotiate the terms of your cooperation on all this."

Ben walked forward. Put his hands up, the way he had when Ed Denero and his crony led him into the alleyway behind the bar in East Orange. He waited until he was within a few feet, then let Newler reach down and pull the passenger-side door open for him, turning his head in profile to Ben. The firefighter raised his fist, put his whole shoulder into it, smashed Newler in the temple with a savage right hook that dropped him like a dead weight, his whole body whumping onto the asphalt beneath them. Ben looked up at the apartments around them as Newler fought for consciousness, groaning, trying to guard his face from further blows as Ben took his pistol and kicked it under the car. He fished around in the pockets of Newler's trousers and on his belt for cuffs. He found a car key, but nothing else. He felt a little zing of sad humor then, about men who spent so much time behind desks they forgot they were once skilled warriors, law enforcers, who would have seen a smack upside the head from some two-bit thief coming a mile off. This guy had a hand in training Andy, it seemed. She was still the leopard out on the prowl, while this fat house cat had let his claws go blunt.

Ben went to the driver's side of the car, popped the trunk, came back around. He hefted Newler up and dropped him in the Beemer's big, wide, empty trunk, slammed the lid, and snapped the key off in the lock.

ANDY

•

hey met at the rear of Matt's van, parked right out front, stood there while he chewed nicotine gum and rifled around, pushed aside homewares Donna had obviously bought and forgotten were there. There were wicker baskets, muslin wraps, a wooden chandelier. A bag of laundry sagged against the rear seats. The wine had made Andy's head warm. Flashes of Ben's body beneath her as she rode him came now and then, made her stomach plunge. His hands on her hips. He'd disappeared the morning after while she showered again, the tension humming between them, his words ringing in her mind.

What good is a promise from you?

The truth was, she didn't know the answer to the question. She'd walked off on him, afraid that he was right, that she'd not given everything she could to finding Luna and Gabriel, so entranced was she with the case as a whole. Had her instinct to burrow, burrow, burrow into the crew, to embed herself as deeply as she could in the lives of her host and the suspects around the case, blinded her to some aspect of Luna's disappearance? Titus Cliffen and Ivan Willstone's images pulled at her as she dug through their lives. Titus's courtly, stoic photograph on the wall of the station, his eyes fixed on the camera, his rigid, uniformed body screaming of strength and potential. Of dreams and plans. Titus had been barely thirty. Probably on the cusp of getting over his defiance of his father, of dropping the anger and realizing who he was. Willstone's image was friendlier, warmer. He'd taken up the karate class on the encouragement of a cop friend, was reportedly terrible at it, had all the balance and majesty of a baby giraffe on the hard-polished floorboards of the school.

Andy had taken out her phone several times across the two days she worked at the case, prepared to text Ben.

And then she hadn't.

The silence was wire-taut.

She was so lost in the dreams of him that she found herself now standing there at the back of Matt's van, looking at the closed iron shutters over the front windows of Borr, the big polished brass lettering above that shone in the light from the streetlamps. She followed the building up until she saw the apartments that straddled both the restaurant and the storage facility. Someone up there had cluttered their window space with indoor plants. Huge fiddle-leaf figs, palms spread against the glass. In another window, a cat perched, licking a paw.

Matt found what he was looking for, a couple of paper files. He smacked them against Jake's chest. Andy saw FDNY logos on the cover.

"By Monday," Matt said. Jake glanced into the mess.

"What's that?"

A sudden, uncharacteristic jolt of pleasure seemed to ripple through Matt. "These are the new TICs."

"Oh, shit."

"Yeah."

They crowded in, the giant and the lanky, ponytailed boy, shoulder-to-shoulder and smiling as Matt opened the box. For a moment, observing from nearby, Andy might have been able to forget that one terrified the other so badly he probably had irritable bowel syndrome, and nightmares, and cardiac microtears from it, was probably actively rewiring the neurological pathways that governed his self-worth because of it. Working for someone like Matt was bad for a person's biology. Andy knew. She'd been bullied sick plenty of times.

Matt brought the thermal imaging camera out of the box and fiddled with the trigger. Jake fooled with the paper files in his hands, obviously itchy to play with the device, which was shaped like a futuristic plastic gun. To Andy's surprise, Matt turned the camera on and handed it to Jake. Jake swung it around, watched the camera feed to a screen on the top of the device the thermal signatures of everything around them.

He pointed it at Engo, swept it over his body.

"What you got in your pockets, Engo?" Jake asked. "I'm seeing a cold, empty hole where your dick should be."

"You're not looking for his dick, you're looking for cash," Matt quipped.

"There's no money." Engo put a hand over his jeans pocket. "So don't even think about it."

Engo turned to Andy. "You're next, you know. He'll do a sweep on you looking for dimes."

Andy covered her pockets.

"Oh that won't help." Engo dragged on his cigarette. "You don't got it now, you'll have it at some point, and Jake will be right there with his hand out."

"Huh," Andy said.

"Yeah. You've been around, what? Couple of weeks now? You should get a knock on your door soon. Jake asking for a loan."

"Don't do it," Matt told her. "Never do it."

"I won't. I can't." Andy shrugged, blew smoke over her shoulder. "I got—"

"You got four hundred bucks to your name," Matt said. "We know. It was part of the vetting."

"Oh, great. You know I got my period, too?"

"We know you haven't sorted your apartment out yet," Matt said. "Unpack your fucking clothes, will you? Get your life in order. You're living like a teenager over there."

"You broke into my apartment?"

"Come on." Matt watched Jake sweeping the camera around. "Of course we did."

Andy smiled inwardly, but outwardly shook her head, pissed. She knew it had all been worth it. The endless miles walking thrift shops. Peeling price stickers off random junk. Forging bank statements she would leave open on the counter for the guys to find, should they ever vet her. Worked like a charm, every time.

"He'll hit you for money, though," Engo insisted. "He's hit everyone. Donna. Titus. He even hit Luna."

Andy froze. Jake put the camera down.

"You probably raided Gabriel's piggy bank, huh." Engo grinned.

"Fuck you," Jake said. The words were humorless. Almost automatic. Andy looked over at his blank, distant eyes. A tingle ran up the back of her spine.

"You ever hit my daughters for money and I'll put your head in a pot, Jake," Matt said. "I'll cook it until all the meat falls off. I'll feed my family with it all winter long."

Jake thrust the thermal imaging camera back to Matt. Matt put it away and pointed the Finger at Andy.

"Text your squeeze and tell him to get that key swapped out." Matt slammed the rear doors of the van.

Andy nodded, flicked her cigarette into the gutter.

Jake was just standing there staring at it, her cigarette dying, fizzing out in a puddle. His hands were hanging by his sides. It was something about that, the frozen posture of him, his bent neck, that quickened that tingle on the back of her neck, increased a growing uneasiness in the pit of Andy's stomach. Jake turned and walked away, maybe a little too fast. Didn't say goodbye. But neither Matt nor Engo did either.

Andy walked to her car and slid in. She put her hands on the wheel and knew something was deeply, deeply wrong.

BEN

·

Kenny met him on the stoop of the apartment in North Ironbound, hands in his pockets, head down. No amount of fucking around with his face could disguise the discomfort there. Although the guy had only lived in the apartment until he was four, and probably had few memories of the place before he was taken away, Ben guessed it was some kind of animal instinct, the kind that made newborn puppies hate the owner who kicked their mother, even when it happened while they were still in the womb. Kenny probably knew he'd been beaten here. That he'd been locked in closets here. That once their smack-headed mother fell asleep on top of a newborn Kenny and almost asphyxiated him. Even Ben himself only knew those things from the care reports he'd been handed for his new charge when he got custody of the kid. This place had messed them both up in different ways, Ben first, and then Kenny after Ben had been taken into care. Whoever Kenny's father was, he'd probably conceived him here, the way Ben's had, their lives mere mistakes Marissa Haig was too lazy to go and get righted. They were no better than cavities that, by the time she'd awakened to their seriousness, had grown too large to fix.

But Kenny's trepidation was tied to other things, too, Ben knew. His tone on the phone. His whole request that Kenny meet him here.

"What the fuck is this about?" Kenny was shuffling his feet, his tone whiny. "Why here, man?"

Ben didn't say anything. Just unlocked the door and let them in. Across the street, a pair of cops in a squad car had stopped to talk to someone on the corner, and the lead cop had his elbow out the window, laughing. There was heavy rap music playing from the apartment above them, and Ben could hear that it was disguising a fight as effectively as sunglasses disguised fractured eye sockets.

He went to the corner of the first room and peeled up the carpet, lifted the cut boards until he'd laid five planks on the floor. He tried not to look hurried, like he was keeping one eye on his phone for a news report about a firefighter wanted in the city, any information welcomed, pictures of him and his car online. The guy Newler had to get out of the trunk of that car eventually. Ben had grand hopes he'd knocked him out cold, might have bought himself a couple of hours, but after the fight in East Orange he hadn't been at his best. There was a lot to do, and he didn't want to spook Kenny any further by cluing him in to that. Ben slipped into the hole and onto the compacted dirt. The hole was only waist deep. He slid the first duffel bag over, hefted it up, then climbed out. Kenny was standing there in his Hugo Boss looking like somebody just died.

And Ben supposed that wasn't far from the truth. Someone was breathing their last breaths right in front of Kenny. The brother he thought he knew. Ben unzipped the bag and jostled the bundles of cash inside. Kenny stared at the money for a long time, then lifted his eyes slowly, taking Ben in, all the way up to his eyes, probably wondering who the hell he was even staring at now. Ben gave him a minute. He wanted his head to be semi-clear. In the apartment above them, something smashed against a wall and a woman screamed.

"Benji," Kenny said. "What the fuuuu . . ."

"This is what I need you to do," Ben said. "You don't have to remember it all. I've written it down. But I'm going to run you through it now, just in case you have any questions."

"Benji. Benji. What—"

"You're going to take the money," Ben said. "There are five more bags. You're going to take them back to your home. On the way, you're gonna stop by a Walmart or a Target or whatever. At the store, you're going to buy a full set of clothes. Shirt, pants, jacket, underwear, socks—everything. Shoes, Kenny. Okay? You're gonna buy new shoes."

"Why?"

"Take your watch off, take your jewelry off." Ben stared at the money, trying to remember. Because if he missed anything, it was all for nothing. Everything he'd done. Andy had sewn a goddamn tracker into the tongue of one of his sneakers. Who knew what other tricks she had. "You go home, you get changed into the new clothes, you take the money back out again. In the same bags. Do not take your phone with you. Do not take your own car."

"Why are you telling me all this?"

"Because this is my stash, Kenny," Ben said. He watched his brother. "I built this for you."

They looked at the money together. Ben guessed there had to be two million in the bag. Kenny had tears in his eyes. Ben figured the guy probably stood right where he was, looking right how he was, three decades earlier. Crying about something. Dried snot in his nose. Ben hadn't been there, then. He'd been in the system somewhere, no idea that Kenny was even alive and treading that horrible path behind him. If only he'd *known*. Ben felt his nose sting and shook it off, because he'd never cried in front of his brother and never would.

"You're going to take the money and hide it somewhere nobody would ever expect you to," Ben said. "Do you understand me, Kenny? Put it in the last place anyone would think you'd go."

"But I don't *need* this, Benji." He gestured to the money. "I mean, I've got my own money. I-I-I-I'm not—"

"But you *might* have needed it," Ben said. "Or one day, your kids might. *I* might have, or *my* kids might. I did this for both of us, Kenny. For our family line. We were never going to be worthless fucking junkies again, any of us. I started doing this a long time ago, when I found out about you. When I found out she'd done it again. I promised myself it was never, ever going to happen to another one of us."

"Jesus, Benji, what have you been doing?"

"It doesn't matter now." Ben shook his head. "I just need you to understand. You have to protect this money, Ken. Because if you don't, it'll all have been for nothing."

"Is this because of Luna?" Kenny gestured to the money. "Did she— Is this her money?"

"No," Ben said. "It's mine."

"But you're not . . . crooked." Kenny's wet eyes searched his. "You're not a . . ."

"Yes, I am."

Kenny hitched a breath. Somebody beat on a door above them, told the fighting couple to shut the fuck up.

"The police are not gonna find Luna and Gabe," Ben said. "I gave away everything I had, all of this, so that they could find them. But they're not going to. And now I've got to get out, while I still can. I've got a chunk for myself to get me set up somewhere. And I've got one more job to do, to make sure we're all set up, the whole crew, before we have to split."

Kenny gave a sad groan. For the first time, Ben saw his brother in there beneath the too-perfect face. The hands that reached for him were Kenny's hands. Ben hugged his brother, squeezed him, thumped his back.

"I'll call you," Ben lied. "Don't worry."

ANDY

·

She rapped on the wheel, tried to steady her breathing, but the air couldn't get down deep enough, couldn't reach that bottom quarter of her lungs. Her head spun. She tugged the rearview mirror and looked at her own eyes. Come on. Come on. What was it?

The money. Jake had bitten Luna for money. Probably the three grand she extracted from her 401(k) account two weeks before she went missing. But what did that mean? Did that mean he was the one walking with her in the lobby of the Best Western? Andy couldn't see the link.

She turned the new knowledge over in her mind, tried to find the source of her turmoil within it. The idea that Luna had loaned Jake money to cover his debts in itself didn't justify this level of unrest, this almost sickness inside her. Did it? Indeed, if Luna had given him that money, he was unlikely to come to her again for another loan shortly after; say, the night Luna went missing. And she was unlikely to have been so frustrated that he'd not repaid it after only two weeks that she might have asked for a meeting at the Best Western. It was clear that Ben didn't know about the loan, or he'd have mentioned that when Andy revealed it to him. So what *was* it? What had brought to life that spider now creeping along the surface of Andy's skull, its pointed little feet picking holds in the rock face of her scalp?

She put aside the knowledge of the loan. Tried to calm herself. But she couldn't. The creeping was still there, the knowledge that something was wrong. She closed her eyes and remembered Jake standing there, staring at the ground. Shell-shocked into stillness. By something. By *what*? His eyes had been on the cigarette in the puddle. The fire in its tip rapidly cooling.

Heat and cooling. Thermal imaging. The camera. *Cameras.*

Andy snapped upward in her seat. She gripped the button camera at her chest, wrestled it from the buttonhole. She held it in her palm, squeezed it. It was warm. Warm from the heat of her body. But was it *exactly* as warm as her body? Was it hotter? Was it cooler? Or had it taken on her temperature? Had the thermal imaging camera that Jake had been looking through been able to pick out her button camera's slightly different temperature against the fabric of the shirt, the press of her breasts against that fabric? *Had Jake seen her camera?*

Did he know?

Andy threw the camera on the seat beside her and ripped her phone from her pocket. She pulled up the tracking app.

At the barbecue at Matt's, she'd had about a minute and a half to slip the GPS tracker into a tiny tear in the fabric marrying the outer shell of Jake's motorcycle helmet to the interior, forcing the nickel-sized object deep behind the sculpted foam with her pinky finger. There hadn't been time to sew the hole shut, stealing a moment as she was while the rest of the crew relaxed in Matt's backyard. As she tapped into Jake's section of the app now, she saw that her risk had paid off. Jake's little blue bubble was traveling rapidly away from Midtown, down Sixth Avenue toward the Holland Tunnel.

In the minute she'd sat numbly in the car, had Jake called and warned the others? Were they all fleeing now to their stashes? With trembling fingers, Andy pulled up Matt's and Engo's little blue bubbles. They were heading in separate directions, slowly. Matt stopped in traffic up on Fifty-Seventh, Engo traveling at a crawl over on Fifth.

It was Jake who was peeling off toward Jersey, driving at dangerous speeds.

Andy started the car and yanked the wheel and screeched into the street. With one hand, she dialed Ben. He didn't answer. She gave it a minute, weaving in and out of the gentle evening traffic, screaming through crosswalks. She dialed again. Nothing. In the West Village she burned toward crowds, pedestrians leaping out of her way, the bumper of the car bashing a wheeled suitcase right out of a guy's hand, spewing its contents across twenty feet of roadway.

"Jesus, Ben, pick-up-pick-up-pick-up!"

She dialed. The phone bleeped, changed displays, and suddenly Newler and Ben seemed to be in competition on the screen, the contact icons jostling, too many buttons and options. Andy flung the phone onto the seat and drove. Bullying, tailgating, and swerving her way forward, she made it into clear space. She was surging onto the empty road, flooring it into the icy endlessness of the tunnel ahead.

With one hand, she grabbed the phone and dialed Newler back.

"I'm made," she said before he could speak. "Jake Valentine. I'm trailing him now toward Jersey."

"You—"

"Shut up and listen," Andy said. "I need you and your guys to get set up on Matt Roderick and Englemann Fiss. I don't know if Jake's going to warn them. He doesn't seem to have so far, but he might, and they'll split."

"Dahlia," Newler said.

"Don't fucking call me that!"

"If your cover is blown, I need to be with you," he said. "If Valentine is the one who's made you, then he's the most dangerous guy right now. I can't worry about the others. I have to be there with you so you don't try to take him down on your own."

"You are not overwatch on this, Tony." Andy choked the steering wheel. She was driving so fast, drivers were honking at her out of sheer shock as she roared past. "I am making the decisions here. And I just assigned you and your team to Matt and Engo."

"You *assigned* me?"

"Do not let them get away. I've sunk too much into this."

"Where's Ben?" Newler asked. There was a coldness in his voice that made sweat break out on the back of her neck.

"I don't know. He's not answering."

Silence on the line.

"Why is Ben the only guy you're not 'assigning' me to right now, Dahlia?"

She heard it in his voice. The thing that had been there that night in Pierre Part. The dark, jealous beast that twisted inside Newler, that conjured up fantasies about her slithering in the sheets, laughing, with Margaret Beauregard. Only the creature inside Newler wasn't wrong this time. Andy felt her stomach plunge as she remembered the two of them, the curtains open, his fingers in her hair and her lips on his neck.

"I don't know where Ben is," Andy said carefully. "I don't have a tracker for him."

"Is that true?"

Andy tried to breathe. She was traveling at lightning speed, one hand on the wheel, half her mind tangled up in trying to save Ben's life. Because that was what she was doing now, she knew. Trying to convince Tony that she didn't love the firefighter she'd been sharing a bed with. Because it was her love for Margaret Beauregard that got the woman killed.

"Do what I tell you, Tony. For God's sake," Andy pleaded. "Get up on Matt and Engo."

She hung up and dialed Ben. He didn't answer. Andy thought back to the last words they had spoken, tinged with sadness, with hopelessness.

What good is a promise from you? I have no idea who you are!

All along, she knew, she'd given Ben hope. Hope that she'd find his girlfriend and her child. Hope that they'd still be alive. Hope that, as the days ticked down to the Borr Storage job, her priority had been the beautiful mother and her angelic child. His family, the family he'd always dreamed of. But as the clues ratcheted up, and their meanings leaned deeper and deeper into the inevitable, Ben had been losing hope. Andy wiped tears from her eyes, the lights of the cars ahead of her shimmering dangerously in her vision. Oh, God. She hadn't seen it. Hadn't heard it in the timbre of his voice. The hopelessness that he'd be left with anything, *anything,* at the end of all this. Anything beyond a total lack of answers, and a jail cell.

As much as she could feel the knowing inside Jake, she could feel the detachment in Ben now. The unanswered calls were unlike so many unanswered calls she'd made to him before. They seemed impossible, now. Like the number didn't belong to anything. Never had, in the first place.

Jake was slowing. She'd followed him mindlessly, expecting him to head, for some reason, where she'd been going endlessly for days—to Luna and Ben's apartment in Dayton. But he'd turned south, pulled off the New Jersey Turnpike, and stopped behind a brightly lit office block for a company dealing with cargo ships on the harbor. Andy could see them: the huge red ocean liners waiting beneath the cranes for the daylight to come, their smoky sodium lights blocking out the view of Manhattan beyond. There were woods here. Marshes riddled with creeks winding inward from the bay. The smell of the rancid gases produced by the mangroves themselves competed with the trash dumped here—rotting drywall offcuts, old couches, and bags of unwanted clothes soaked and resoaked by the tide. They made spongy, black-molded, and barnacle-encrusted hotels for crabs and maggots and aquatic insect life.

She spotted Jake's bike by the side of a gravel road, flicked her headlights off, and pulled over. Taking her gun from the passenger seat, she stuffed her phone in her pocket and got out. A wave of night noise hit her. The hum of the city sliced through by the song of crickets. A boat horn sounded somewhere, two short blasts. Andy followed the line of soft grass at the top of the embankment leading down to the water. She was twenty yards or more from it when Jake appeared, climbing up from the darkness of the mangroves. He got onto the bike, pulled his helmet on, and kicked it to life. Andy shrank down behind a bush as he sped away, not slowing as he passed her parked car.

She stood in the cold air, torn as to whether to run back to her car and continue pursuit or to go to the spot where Jake had entered the mangroves. Working on instinct alone, she jogged to the place where his motorcycle boots had left deep impressions in the sandy mud.

Andy took her phone out, hit the flashlight, and shone it down the embankment. She could see that Jake's footprints only went two or three feet into the mud. Beyond them, the mangroves seemed uniform at first glance. Crab holes. Ripples and slivers of foam from the long-gone tide. Andy was about to turn away when she saw something that made the hairs along her arms stand on end.

About ten feet out into the mangroves, a patch of earth was bare of the little shoots and roots that stood up everywhere else, an army of tiny soldiers casting long and wavering shadows. The bald patch in the mangroves was oval in shape. Four feet long. Three feet wide. No roots or shoots grew there.

Or those that had grown there had been recently shoveled away.

BEN

.

The lawyer looked all wrong in a hoodie and sweatpants, jittery about the sudden callout. Ben met him on the Upper East Side outside the Carlyle, under the awning. Ben only knew the place because he'd attended a kitchen fire there once, figured the lawyer would know it because he was rich. Ben remembered the fire, people standing on the street crying with worry about the hand-painted murals on the walls. Some woman with an ancient poodle on her lap had sat out the whole fire in a dining room, drinking martinis, unmovable. The panic had receded, morphed into an appreciation for them putting the blaze out, then morphed again into an annoyance for how wet they were getting the carpet while dragging the hose out.

The Carlyle's blaze, and the threat to the fancy art, made the evening news. Two kids died in an e-bike fire up in Harlem that same day but fuck them, the network only had room for so many fire stories.

Ben stepped into the dark outside the awning to meet the lawyer so they wouldn't be on the doorman's camera. The guy had dropped a couple of pounds just in the day or two since Ben had seen him at the art gallery. The cancer was hungry.

Ben put the key in his bony palm and the lawyer stared at it.

"Make the call," Ben said.

Ichh glanced from the key to Ben.

"What?" He surveyed the street, looking for help. *"Now?"*

"No, let's wait for the fall. It'll be prettier then."

"But I can't—"

"Yes you can," Ben said gently. He inched closer to the lawyer. The little man shrank away. "Pick up your phone. Dial the Freeman son. Tell him you need access to the safe *tonight*."

The lawyer looked at his watch. It was big and gold and he had to slide it around his wrist to get it to face up. "But it's eight o'clock."

"You're a smart guy. Yale, right? You'll think of something." Ben let the man see into his eyes, and what he saw in there did more to get him moving than Ben's hand sliding into the weighted pocket at the front of his own hoodie ever could. The lawyer dialed, and Ben pulled out a cigarette and lit it and listened to the call.

ANDY

.

Jake pulled into the parking lot of a Walmart. The lot had just been washed down, and the spaces shone silver and pink in the big red and white lights above the automatic doors. Andy stopped her car and got out and pulled her pistol, moved at a crouch toward Jake. She let her gun hang by her side, watched him rummaging in the compartment under the motorcycle's seat for what she assumed was his phone. When he lifted it, she straightened and aimed the gun at his back, ten feet away and closing in, then in a moment of wild footwork and electric panic she darted sideways and behind a pickup truck as Jake tucked the phone into his pocket. Her breath was coming in short, silent huffs, eyes quick, scanning the lot for onlookers. Lots of cars. No people. Jake walked toward the store, the phone in his pocket, and Andy just kept moving with that weird knowledge knocking around the inside of her brain, finding no purchase. Why wasn't he warning the others? Had he actually made her at all? Andy watched Jake pull up the hood on his sweatshirt as he entered the store.

Jake grabbed a basket and walked with purpose past bedding and linen, stationery, cosmetics, heading for the last aisles. Andy pursued, keeping close to the entrance to the aisles in case she needed to slip down one to take cover. She smelled compost and fertilizer. Jake turned in to an aisle lined with cleaning products in colorful bottles with zippy, flashy labels, and then he was into the garbage bags and trash-can liners. Andy stood at the entrance to the aisle, watching. Jake bent and picked up a roll of trash bags, thought for a while, bent and plucked out a roll with smaller bags. Andy was shifting from foot to foot, watching intensely, so hyperfocused on Jake's hands weighing and comparing the small and large-size garbage bags that she didn't notice him struggle until he silently began to sob.

He was moving slowly by the time he got to Metuchen, pulling the speed down, taking off from the traffic lights long after they'd turned green.

Andy watched him hanging his head under the red lamps, now and then shaking it a little, and the weariness the night brought her bones seemed to combine with Jake's obvious dread, his delaying of his arrival, so that Andy was sunk back behind the wheel as she followed, the whole world pressing in on her.

Jake's mother's house was a tiny weatherboard place in a wide street filled with similar, unassuming little homes that were probably freezing in the winter and boiling in the summer. The grass beyond the stoop was waist high and full of weeds. Jake went up the steps onto the porch and put his bag of Walmart items at his feet and his helmet on a small, cane outdoor sofa. Then he stood at the door for a long time, doing nothing.

Andy slipped out of her car, crossed the street on light feet, and waited in the moon shadow at the edge of Jake's lot. While he stood and stood, unmoving, maybe again crying, she glanced down the side of the house and saw a fat raccoon wandering curiously between the trash cans, nose up, testing the air. Somewhere in the streets beyond, a dog barked. The raccoon paused to listen, then slunk away.

Jake put his hand in the back pocket of his jeans. Andy crept forward until she could hear his soft whimpers: *I have to do this. I have to do this.*

Andy walked out of the shadows, made it to the edge of the stoop before her footfall alerted him.

Jake turned. She lifted her gun and aimed it at his chest.

"Jake?"

The moonlight caught the tears on his cheeks, two silver scars. He nudged the bag, and Andy saw in her peripheral vision a roll of duct tape slide from the open mouth and roll down the porch steps past her feet.

Jake looked at the sky and laughed and wiped his tears. "Oh *shit.*"

Andy nodded. "Yeah."

Jake looked around the street. It was empty, quiet. "Why is it just you?" he asked. Jake pointed to where the button camera had been on her chest. "Aren't there other officers watching you on that thing?"

"We can handle this ourselves, can't we?" Andy asked. "Jake? Honey? Can I come up there?"

He didn't move. She walked gently up the stairs, her aim still true, a two-hand grip.

"What *happened,* Jake?"

The man shook his head.

"Urgh, God, it's so stupid." He swiped at the tears, rubbed his nose hard on the sleeve of his hoodie. "You'd never believe me. Even if I told you, you'd . . . Urgh. This is gonna look like a cold-blooded thing. It's going to look like I *wanted* to do it."

BEN

.

They met on the street outside a dentist, Ben giving Matt and Engo the address, watching them both pull into parking spots that had miraculously opened up right outside, at almost the exact same moment, like it was all meant to be, this whole thing, this whole time.

Matt and Engo got out of their cars and came toward him, and Ben stood under a huge blue neon sign shaped like a perfect set of teeth and thought about how he'd started in when he met Luna trying to create a family, and now he was back here with his real brothers, the brothers he didn't choose, the brothers he was lumped with. A toxic, dysfunctional family coming together now for an impromptu meeting somewhere that suited them all. Crisis talks. Funeral plans. Neutral ground. Disputes over the will. He supposed the Freemans would be doing this soon, sniping across the old man's still-cooling corpse, trying to deduce which one of them had sucked up to the ancient zombie in the last couple of years and sleeved the cards while he was distracted, sold them on the sly.

Engo seemed pissed off, but Matt looked like maybe he'd expected something like this, and was wary of any ripples in the water with his last wife so close to birthing his last baby.

"We gotta go now," Ben said. "Tonight."

"*What?* Why?" Matt looked at Engo, his lieutenant, searching for hidden knowledge of the source of the ripples. "Have you heard from the lawyer? Is Freeman dead?"

"No, but we've got to make this happen tonight or we're going to lose our shot. The keys are swapped out."

"When did that happen?"

"About a half hour ago," Ben said.

"I don't like this." Matt's finger twitched by his side. "Meeting with the lawyer on your own steam? Who said you could do that?"

"It's done." Ben shrugged. "Earlier tonight I had him run a story. Told him to get access to the safe. He did. I met him a second time. He had swapped the keys out, and he's telling me it's all kosher. The son didn't raise any eyebrows. So we're good to go." He held out the key Ichh had given him, let the blue light from the teeth above them smile down on it. Ben had followed the lawyer to the house on the Upper East Side, been ultra-careful to not get the keys mixed up, knowing that while they appeared identical, the one Paxi had fashioned from his 3D-printed mold almost certainly wouldn't fit into the lock at Borr Storage.

"Why have you jumped the gun like this?" Matt insisted, still reeling, his words slowing as his mind raced ahead. "This isn't how we planned it. The lawyer was supposed to be in contact with *me*. I was the one who was supposed to hit 'Go.'"

"You want to figure out who's boss here, Matt, or you want to do your last-ever job?"

"*I* want to figure out who's boss here," Engo cut in. "Because I don't run into burning buildings or high-stakes jobs until that's on paper."

"I just want to be done with this," Ben said. "I want to take some time away."

He hoped that his eyes sold it. That he was tired. That he needed a break. That the grief and humiliation at whatever had happened to Luna, or wherever she had gone, had worn him down so bad that he needed to go stare at a slice of unpopulated ocean somewhere or bury his head in a hotel pillow for a while. Ben was hanging on to that desire, the real desire that he had, for the moment he was planning to tell Matt and Engo both the truth. Once they were in and out of the storage facility, and they'd scored the cards, he would tell them. He would tell them about Andy. About the guy, Newler. About the game he'd been playing with them all this time. But he couldn't tell them now, because it would be his last gift to them, a gift he didn't know and maybe would never know if they deserved, because he would never know which one of them had killed his family. He loved them and hated them all enough that he knew he owed them this, because he'd decided to let fate take hold of it all now. Whoever survived the job and got away, maybe that meant they were innocent. If one of them died an hour from that moment, maybe that was God or the universe or whatever cutting him some slack and doing away with whoever it was. Ben was doing his part now to bring the suspects into the courtroom.

Ben put the key back into his pocket while he waited for Matt and Engo to get their heads together, read the gold lettering of the dentist's name on the glass door of the darkened office. Lots of letters after the name, too. Ben wondered if Kenny had letters after his name, why the hell he'd never taken the time to find out.

"We can't do this now just because you got your panties in a bunch," Engo was saying. "We're not on shift for another six hours."

"So we play it like we always planned." Ben shrugged. "We go into the station. Hang around. If anybody asks, we say we're there to set up a drill for Jake. When the moment feels right, we call in a ladder job. Then we call in the gas job and respond to it, once the truck team are all tied up and out the door."

"I don't buy this," Matt said. His eyes bored into Ben's face. "What's the hurry? You can wait till morning. You can—"

"I know one of you did it," Ben said. Because fuck them. Both of them. Fuck the danger that oozed off Matt all the time and the psychopathic glint in Engo's eyes. He'd been waiting so long to say it out loud, the air rang with the blessed potential of his words and how they might answer them. The knowing. The incredible relief.

Matt and Engo looked at each other.

"I know one of you killed Luna and Gabe," Ben said. "Probably you, right?"

He glared at Engo. Neither he nor Matt spoke.

"I need to do this job so I can get the fuck out of here," Ben said. "So I can cut all ties with you."

Matt shook his head. He closed his eyes, tired, and let all the air out of his lungs.

"Engo didn't kill them, you fucking moron," he said, putting a hand on Ben's shoulder. "Jake did."

ANDY

.

needed money." Jake was trembling all over, staring at the bag at his feet. "I went to Ben's apartment, looking for him. Luna was there."

Andy took another step up onto the porch. The gun was still in her grip, down by her side. "When was this?"

"I don't know. July?" Jake turned, stared into the darkness at the side of the house. He'd pulled his hands into the sleeves of his hoodie, seemed younger again somehow. "I was uh, you know. I was upset. I was down. They were really riding me, the sharks. They were going to do something . . . permanent . . . this time. To me. She uh, she said she'd lend me the money, but Ben couldn't know about it. I'd already borrowed too much from him. She knew he was gonna turn me down."

Jake's face twisted. He shook his head hard to carry on.

"The next time we, I . . . The next time I saw Luna, it was at Matt's," he said. "I maybe had too much to drink. It was hot. I'd sweated my ass off mowing the lawns. My-my-my head wasn't clear."

"What happened?" Andy asked.

"She and I got talking, just chilling by the pool, and I said, you know, I said Ben shouldn't be such a tight-ass about lending me a couple of grand here and there. I always pay it back and Ben's got a lot of money." Jake mashed his palms into his eyes. "I shouldn't have said anything. Because she got curious, I guess. She really latched on to it. Wouldn't leave it alone. Like what did I mean, 'a lot' of money? Why would he have a lot of money? He doesn't seem like he'd have a lot of money. She knew he didn't have it in his bank accounts. So *why* didn't he have it in his bank accounts?"

"She was starting to catch on," Andy said. "To the whole thing. The crew. The crookedness of you all."

"It was like Titus all over again." Jake's eyes were unfixed, roving the dark, his memories, searching for a safe place. "He was like a dog with a bone, that guy. But that's, you know, that's another story."

The young man fell silent. Andy didn't push. She didn't have to. She knew that story. The fire in the disused telephone-exchange building. The chance presenting itself, too perfect to pass up. A fully engulfed building, the crew alone and waiting for a ladder engine to respond as second due. That engine being delayed. The fire growing. Titus and Engo and Matt and Jake inside the blackened and murky maze together, with no witnesses except each other, and a threat much more terrifying than the fire itself dangling over them all: that Titus was beginning to clue in to what they were doing.

That he would talk.

Persistent, and determined, outspoken and inquisitive Titus, a man un-like so many who would have seen the shadows in the waves and got out of the goddamn water. A man who would refuse and stay and try his luck against whatever lurked in the depths. A guy raised not to back down. Ever. Titus, who a team of inquiring officers could easily believe would defy orders and double back inside the fire, simply because he felt he knew better. Andy didn't need Jake to tell her what that scene had been like. Titus's last moments. That look in Engo's or Matt's or Jake's eyes, just before they shoved him over a smoldering handrail into the inferno two floors below. Oh, Andy knew the story all right. It was one she'd heard a thousand times before, one that made sense. What she couldn't decide, yet, was whether Ben had been in on it.

"Did you kill Luna because she knew about the crew?" Andy asked Jake now. "Was it all of you, or just you?"

"No, you don't get it." Jake sniffed. "She . . . She wanted in."

Andy didn't answer. Couldn't.

"With me." Jake tapped his chest. "With my plan."

"What plan?"

"I'd been trying to figure something out for a while. How to get Matt and Engo and Ben's stashes," he said. "I . . . I knew that between them there had to be enough to go. Get out of here. Like really *go*. Leave this life and everything in it." He shot a hand out toward the horizon, gave a sad laugh that was smothered with sobs. "I wanted to blow out of town. Forever. I just had to think of a way to make everyone run for their stashes and show me where the hell they were. I figured I'd make something happen, and then I'd follow them. Come back and raid them at another time, take everything. But . . . I just couldn't make it work."

"Why not?"

"I'd tried to follow Ben to his stash before, but . . ." Jake let his hands flop by his sides. "We pull maybe two jobs a year, man, and half the time he doesn't go. Or he goes ten days later, after the job. Or he goes in the middle of the fucking night. You can't watch the guy for weeks on end. Following Engo is even worse. You watch him for eighteen hours and then he finally gets up and goes somewhere and it's to a strip club for *another* eighteen hours."

Andy smiled inwardly. It was a sad and painful smile. Because in another universe, she might have taught Jake a thing or two about tracking and following people. It was the reason she was standing there at that very moment.

"I knew I had to orchestrate something," Jake went on. "I thought about calling in a tip, maybe, about the cop in Kips Bay. Or one of the robberies. Getting everybody raided. But I couldn't risk myself like that. And then, there was the logistics of it. How could I track them all at once? Who do I follow first?"

Andy watched as Jake vacillated between rational explanation of his plans and waves of emotion. His face contorting, shivering, falling blank.

"Luna said we needed to, uh, to simplify." He wiped his nose again. "We knew Ben probably had the biggest stash, right? I mean, Matt has a lot of expenses. And he hides it in properties. Engo filters it all through his building. You can't get near there. Half the residents are patched gang members. They have lookouts. Wherever Engo and Matt's stashes were, Ben's would be bigger."

"Ben's a hoarder." Andy nodded. "He's a pack rat."

Something moved in the street. Andy and Jake turned. There was silence, stillness, a driveway light on three doors up, someone waiting for a loved one to come home from work. The old porch around them ticked and creaked, still losing heat from the day.

"We thought maybe if she and the kid went missing," Jake said, "Ben would get sketchy. Like he'd worry that she'd robbed him and go check his stash. Or he'd think maybe someone was after him, and *then* he'd go check his stash. Or he'd get raided, right? The police would turn him over a little, at least. Give him a shake. You know how it is, when the girlfriend goes missing. The police, they always, they always, they . . . *zero in*! They were *supposed* to zero in on Ben! And—"

"And they didn't," Andy said.

"He didn't go to the stash to check it, either," Jake said. "He must have trusted her."

Andy ached inside. It was all so perfectly wrong.

"So you had Luna meet you at the Best Western that night. She drove by that place every day on the way to work. She knew the valets would take care of the car."

"I knew the camera system was terrible." Jake nodded sadly. "I scoped it out, after she suggested the valet thing."

The night stretched around them, dark and heavy with foreboding.

"Luna had put Visine in Ben's drink," Jake said. "We did it to a guy in the academy as a prank. You put Visine in someone's drink, they're shitting themselves for twenty-four hours. It was supposed to be just that, but actually it made him real sick. Like, actual sick. We're pretty lucky he didn't go to the hospital, because we needed him to have a terrible alibi. The car would be at the local hotel, he'd have no witnesses as to where he was . . . I mean, it was going to look like Ben was good for it. Perfect for it."

"Where did it all go wrong, Jake?"

"It went wrong two months after that."

"Two months?"

"Luna and Gabriel were supposed to be in the hotel room for, like, a week at best." Jake's lip trembled. "I booked it under a fake name. They were supposed to wait there. The cops were going to come down on Ben like a ton of bricks, and the longer and harder they pushed him, the more likely it was that he'd go to his stash. I mean *he should have gone there! Why didn't he go there?* I was following him day and night. I was sleeping in my fucking car. If it was me, I'd have emptied my stash spreading money around town trying to buy up information. I'd have hired guys to beat information out of people. I'd have put a price on her head, you know? With guys who would kill to claim it. We know people like that. Matt's little black book is full of people like that."

Jake hid in his hands again. Andy thought about Ben. About the route he had actually taken to finding his girlfriend and her child. Through the police. Through Simmley, and then Newler, and ultimately, her. It was all so ironic that Andy wanted to break into tears herself. Because if Ben had just trodden the darker path, the path Jake expected him to, Luna might still be alive.

"I was going to be there," Jake said. "Waiting. Watching. Following. But the, the police took *half a glance* at Ben and then they dropped the case."

"Meanwhile, Ben's busy searching for his family."

"He's hunting for Luna and Gabe like a madman." Jake nodded. "He's . . . he's walking the street. She can see him out the hotel fucking windows. He's *in the lobby*, harassing the managers for footage. Days are passing. Weeks. I'm trying to tell Luna: Just wait. Just wait. Just *wait*."

Andy imagined it. Luna in the room with the kid, the kid going nuts with boredom, having to be quiet all the time. Asking for Ben constantly. Throwing tantrums every time Jake presents himself, tantrums they have to stifle and bribe him out of. Luna pulling her hair out. Jake having to rebook rooms and move them every few nights when the halls were quiet and unpopulated. Luna, Gabe, Jake creeping around the hotel like ghosts staying off the cameras, Luna's belief in a life-changing, mind-bending, once-in-ten-generations payoff beginning to dwindle. Jake switching them to a different hotel. Not having the money to make it comfortable, and not being able to access Luna's accounts so that she could chip in. The nerves making him gamble. Luna trying to control him, hardly knowing him, his lies starting to rack up. Jake coming in with a new promise: that the crew were about to pull another job. A jewelry store. Ben would go to his stash, afterward, surely. He had to. He *had* to.

Jake grabbed two handfuls of his hair.

"It's going to be the biggest payoff of your fucking life!" Jake snarled at the Luna who wasn't there, the Luna who was decaying in her bed of shipping oil and crab shit. *"Just wait!"*

He let his hair go. Opened his eyes. Looked at his hands. They were shaking hard. Andy could see it in his face. All that happened next. When Jake came back to the hotel room one night and had to tell her that yes, they'd pulled the jewelry-store job but no, Ben hadn't gone to his stash yet. Luna saying she didn't believe the plan was going to work anymore. That she couldn't bear the waiting.

That she wanted out.

BEN

•

"He got in trouble moving the body, of course." Engo took out a cigarette, lit it, his eyes never leaving Ben, afraid to miss the deliciousness of the pain dancing in his eyes. "Luna. Okay, she was petite. But that's still a full-grown woman right there. It takes experience to know how to move a thing like that."

Ben eased a hard breath out of his lungs. Barely stopped himself from leaping at the older man, because he knew it wasn't worth it, knew that Matt's spread hand would slam into him like a steering wheel into the chest of a drunk driver as he wraps his car around a telephone pole. Ben swallowed and looked at his boss.

"What did he do with Gabe?"

"He said he took care of that one himself," Matt said. "But by then he'd used up all his available brain cells so he called us in for the mother."

"The *thing*," Ben seethed. "The *mother*. This was someone you *knew*."

"They were all someone I knew," Engo said, almost to himself, staring at his cigarette. The words made all the hairs on the back of Ben's neck stand on end.

"You didn't do anything," Ben said to Matt. "To Jake. Afterward. He was untouched. I'd have noticed if he was beat up. You didn't lay a finger on him."

"Of course I didn't," Matt scoffed. "I knew if I touched him at all, I'd kill him."

Ben tried to turn away. Matt seized him by the collar before he could.

"I told you"—Matt's finger was in his face—"I'm not a kid killer. I meant it."

"But you let Jake get away with it."

"Who says I let anybody get away with anything? Just because I haven't done anything yet, doesn't mean I'm not going to."

"You're a fucking hypocrite," Ben said. "You worked beside him. You let him work beside me. And he *killed a child*!"

"You wouldn't believe the kind of people I have worked beside while I had to bide my time," Matt said. And in his words, and his eyes, Ben heard echoes of all the stories he'd heard about Matt over the years. About a guy who had been a part of the Ground Zero cleanup effort who had taken several extra pairs of boots from a truckload donated by some shoe company to the response effort. The guy selling them on eBay. That same firefighter being seriously injured in a hit-and-run up in Brooklyn about a year later. About the chief who had divided his firefighters between those who had to stay at the firehouse to man everyday fires, and those who had to go down to the Towers and dig for bodies in the weeks after the disaster. That chief pulling names from a hat and writing them on a whiteboard, the Ground Zero column entitled "Losers" and the firehouse column entitled "Winners." That chief getting beaten and left for dead in Central Park in an apparent mugging, leaving him with permanent hearing loss.

About the only guy who ever asked Matt outright why his entire fire-house was up on the forty-first floor of the North Tower when the collapse happened, while he was on the street, feeding an unconscious woman into an ambulance.

That guy ending up being crushed to death when an air conditioner fell on him out of a seventh-story window. He wasn't even on duty. He was walking his mother to church.

"Why did he do it?" Ben asked. He felt tears burning at the backs of his eyeballs but refused, *refused*, to let them form and fall. Bit his tongue to stop it. Locked his teeth to stop it. "Did he say?"

"He didn't need to." Matt shook his head. For once, Ben thought he glimpsed a flash of pity in the boss's face. "Come on, Benji. You go down sick one night, and the first thing Luna does is go meet Jake at a hotel in secret? Then two months later, after she's been completely off the radar with you, he's calling us to help move her body? Doesn't take a rocket scientist to figure out what happened, bud."

"I don't buy it. I don't." Ben shook his head. "There's something else there."

"Well, whatever it is, it was on his end, not ours." Matt jerked a thumb at Engo and himself. "Okay, so we covered for him. We fed you some bull-shit about Luna running off. What was the alternative, Benji? We have another crew member suddenly go down, so soon after Titus? And it's not like we haven't covered for *you*, Ben, under similar circumstances."

Ben saw it. The street behind the Book Bonanza. The way the penlight gripped in Engo's teeth bounced off the enameled surface of the safe and hit him in the eyes. It was dark back there behind the dumpsters, the van like a block of blackness waiting, open, by the wall. Willstone's shape had split off from it the way that water separates a glob of oil from the mass. Ben had heard the cop call out "Hey!" He'd dropped his corner of the safe and turned, slid his gun from his waistband, fired twice with only a single thought in his brain as his body went on autopilot. His family. Not the men huffing and sweating around him, trying to move the stolen safe, but Kenny and Luna and Gabe. Ben hadn't cared who the man was. Whose shape crumpled in half and hit the deck. Man or woman, civilian or cop; it could have been a priest standing there with a baby in his arms. Ben knew only that he wouldn't be caught. Not then. Not that way.

"You had yourself a murdery little brain-snap that could have ended it for all of us," Matt went on. "And we cleaned up *your* mess. We did what was best for the crew. This, with Jake? It was just the same kind of thing."

Ben felt his heart constrict. The threat rang in Matt's voice, a silent warning against argument. He thought about taking his gun from his waistband again now, letting the rage over what had happened to Luna and Gabe take him over, the way the fear of losing them had then. He saw himself murdering Matt and Engo right where they stood. But he was cold. He was numb. He knew what was smart, then, and that was to bide his time. He put his hands in his pockets and looked at his feet and smiled, because Matt was right. In the end, it was the crew above all else. His real family. This pack of killers and thieves.

"Let's get this thing done," Matt said.

Ben nodded. "I'll call the others," he lied.

ANDY

.

His story was out. Andy recognized the phenomenon immediately, the sudden raw emptiness that infected an individual who had just given up everything, who now had no more to give. Jake's confession had poured out of him, and as it had, it left space for what came next. Terror. Andy was on the top stair, level with him, six feet away.

"You can help me, right?" Jake said. "I mean, you . . . you'll need cooperation. About the robberies. About other stuff. I can tell you everything we've ever done."

"That can come later." Andy put her hands up. "One step at a time, Jake. Right now, I want to know what I'm dealing with. Whose body did we just visit out there, near the harbor?"

Jake trembled.

"Was that Luna or Gabe?" Andy pressed. "Is Gabe's body still here? Is that what the bags are for?"

"Gabe—" Jake started, reaching for his back pocket. Andy saw his face turn, whiplash fast, the bullet exploding through his forehead and spraying blood all over the door of the house before the sound of the gunshot even registered in her ears. Andy jolted, her body moving ahead of her thoughts, wheeling toward the source of the shot before Jake's corpse hit the floor. She had her gun pointed into the dark beside the porch and was firing without knowing what, or who, she was firing at. She saw Newler's face lit for a second in the muzzle flash, bloated and shocked and white. Her elevation meant she fired well above his head. He was emerging from the streetlight that fell on the lawn as Andy backed up, still trying to decide if she herself was in the firing line.

"Jesus, Tony, Tony, Tony!" she was stammering. His gun was down. She knelt and held what was left of Jake's head, turned it limply on the ground, felt the weight of it, saw the flatness in his eyes. One of his arms was twisted behind his back. As she shook him, the house keys he'd been reaching for rattled and clunked on the porch, tangled in his fingers.

"Dahlia." Newler grabbed her biceps and tried to pull her to her feet. "It's over. It's over. I'm sorry."

"He was going for his keys, Tony!"

"It had to end," Newler said. "You were too deep in."

Andy let him hold her. There was blood in his hair, on his face, and his clothes were rumpled. He stank of body odor. His grip was too tight, squeezing the air from her lungs, and as she stood there swaddled by him she smelled his sweat and heat and hardness and knew that the final seconds of their lives together were ticking away. She tried to pull away and he held on tighter, and she wriggled and groaned and clawed at him.

"Let me go! You're hurting me!"

"We're not doing this, Dahlia." He let her go, and she felt freedom for a half a second or less before he had her by the throat and the hair. "You're coming in, okay? Look what you just did. For God's sake. You just let yourself almost be taken down by some fucking teenager on a porch in Shitsville, New Jersey!"

"He wasn't going to shoot me!"

"You're so deep in this, you can't even see it. You need me to pull you out."

"Let me go!"

She went for his fingers, though she didn't want to. She wanted to do what was smart. To kick him. To claw at his face. But some part of her, the part that had loved him once, wanted to give him one last chance. But the fingers around her larynx only tightened, and the lightness in her head as the air left her was almost a relief. It made the decision easier. She pushed the barrel of her gun deep into his ribs, so he would feel it.

And she fired.

She sucked in a deep, cold breath as though breaking the surface of the sea.

He fell on her. The grateful breath she'd filled her lungs with became a great balloon of pain crushed under his weight as he staggered forward, not back, as she'd anticipated. The darkness on the porch twisted her sense of up and down, and his great arms were around her again, and before she could stop it they'd collapsed together onto the boards. A white flash as her head hit the wood. Andy heard him groan, or maybe it was her, and the blackness seemed to have extended out to encompass everything—not just the roof over them but the street, too, the nearby houses, the distant stars and the loom of the city. Some cold, clear, calm part of her brain was whispering in that darkness, telling her she'd hit her head bad and needed to swim for the surface of her consciousness before she passed out. Kick. Kick. Kick.

She twisted out from under Newler's dying body and dragged herself somewhere; to the steps, to the rail, to the door, she didn't know. Like a sleepwalker, Andy pawed her way up a wall and stood there wobbling and holding her bleeding skull. A woman was out on the driveway in a robe, trying to speak to her, but all Andy could hear was a hard buzzing in her ears like an electric razor raking over her scalp.

For some reason, she grabbed the keys from Jake's limp fingers and swayed on the wildly rocking floor to the door. She was thinking of getting a towel for her head, or finding a chair to sit in, or turning on a light, or nothing at all; just letting her limbs follow habitual actions as her mind gripped for purchase.

She walked in and turned right and went down on her knees at the edge of the kitchen, and from deep inside her memories she heard the voice of the child inside the burning schoolhouse calling her through the smoke.

"Mommy? Mommy?"

Only it wasn't the voice of a memory at all that Andy was hearing, but a real voice. The small boy rushed from the hallway shadows into the moonlight spilling through the kitchen windows. Gabriel. Thin, tired, wide-eyed Gabriel Denero threw his arms around her neck.

"Mommy?"

Andy held Gabe in fingers wet with her blood, with Jake's blood, with Newler's blood, and heard the distant peal of sirens.

BEN

.

He didn't call either of them. Not Andy. Not Jake.

Matt and Engo seemed to take his word for it that neither were answering. They stood in Matt's office, and Ben looked at the bare walls and listened to the sound of the fire station beyond the door, knowing it was the last time he was ever going to do that. Guys were laughing in the TV room. Probies were gossiping in the engine bays, leaning on brooms, playing shitty hip-hop. Everything was lit with sickly fluorescent tube lights, and that humming paleness falling on the walls and hall threatened to usher Ben right back into the most tenuous of realities, waiting to do the worst job of his criminal career with two men who had buried his girlfriend and her son, hoping the undercover he'd brought in to bust them all was out there somewhere too busy trying to find that woman and her child. Not really caring if she even was.

And then there was Jake, who might show up here any second, Jake who'd destroyed his family, or who Matt and Engo *said* destroyed his family, but for all Ben knew was lying in the same grave as Luna and her son, put there for some reason by Matt and Engo. It was all so fucked up, Ben couldn't keep his mind straight, was fascinated instead by the wood-veneer patterning on the walls of Matt's office.

Matt went round the desk and yanked open one of his drawers and pulled out a burner phone.

"Fuck it," the big man said. Ben knew the tones for 9-1-1. He'd dialed those numbers a dozen times before his balls even dropped, punched them into pay phones, burner phones, home phones. A car phone once. It made him feel tired, listening to them.

Matt made the call about an explosion in an apartment building on Eighty-First near the park. Ben knew it. It was right at the edge of their jurisdiction, as far from the station as anybody from their station could go on a direct assignment. An explosion would mean engine and ladder, maybe a second-due call for the 98s. Lots of rich apartments. Ben thought he heard Jerry Seinfeld lived up there somewhere.

Matt ended the call and Engo popped the door to the hall open, folded his arms and leaned there. They heard the bells coming in fast. A couple of guys even crossed the doorway at a jog.

A guy from the truck, Whistler, got curious about Engo and looked in the door as he went past, shrugging on his turnout coat.

"What are you assholes doing here?"

"Setting up something for Jake," Matt grunted, shutting the burner phone back into its drawer. "Kid's got to graduate sometime. What's the job?"

"Explosion on Eighty-First. Flames in the windows."

Matt sucked air down the side of his teeth meanly, like *Fuck the truck team and their real-ass fires.*

"Watch the stove for us, will you, Engo?" Whistler slapped Engo's arm, turned and jogged on.

Matt jutted his chin at Ben. "Try your girlfriend again."

"I just did," Ben lied. "Jake's not answering either."

"Maybe they're together," Matt said humorlessly.

"Don't tell me Jake's nabbed another one from you, Ben," Engo chuckled. "The Pussy Pilferer strikes again!"

Matt worked his jaw, his wedding ring rapping on the desktop like a wrought-iron door knocker. Ben could see the calculations being made in his mind, about how it would look to the top brass if they attended a suspected gas-leak call while off duty and riding short by two whole crew members. About whether that even fucking mattered, because keeping his job and his reputation meant less than nothing to Matt. Had for years. No man could ever think worse about Matt than he thought about himself. And from here on in, what he was staring down the barrel of was a quiet life trying his best to give himself skin cancer by the backyard pool and dealing with Donna and the baby's mood swings. Before all that, right in front of him, lay a three-way and not a five-way cut of whatever he sold the baseball cards for; minus the fencing and logistics and shut-up money for Andy and Jake. The boss looked at Engo, and then he looked at Ben.

"Fuck it," he said again, and shrugged. He went to the drawer and grabbed the phone, and dialed those numbers.

ANDY

.

Kids were grabby. She knew that from her last case, where she played Kate Towning, daycare-center worker. Peeling Gabriel off her body, his tiny, warm arms and legs locked around her torso, had reminded her of those flustered parents she'd greeted at the door every morning whose kid had decided that any alternative to being snuggled on the couch at home watching *Paw Patrol* in their pajamas was a fate worse than death. Only this child wasn't braving the hellish no-man's-land between the feet of his parents and the warm embrace of Andy in her former mask. He was being sat on the couch in Jake's mother's bare, dusty home, where he'd been held captive for weeks, returned to the terrifying loneliness that Jake had made him accustomed to, because Andy could see neighbors braving the porch and the bodies there, peering in the front windows, trying to see inside. She didn't want to leave the sobbing boy. But she couldn't be taken into custody now, questioned for hours about who shot whom on the porch, and why, and who the hell she even was to either of the men who had died. After kissing him hard on the forehead, and whispering loving and gentle lies, Andy retreated from the boy, out the back door of the little house, and into the yard. While she rinsed her hands under a garden tap, the raccoon she'd spotted earlier ambled around the next property, gunshots and screams and sirens meaning nothing to the beast on the prowl.

BEN

.

There were gawkers in the street, even before they'd parked, the kind of night crawlers a person can find in Manhattan at any and all hours. Homeless people wrapped in blankets. Night workers heading to and from shifts manning convenience stores, vacuuming office blocks, guarding parking lots. A couple of young women in housekeeping uniforms stopped and took up position on the street across from Cristobel's, hands in their coat pockets, and a potbellied delivery guy shuffled in beside them, close but not creepy-close. Matt reported in to Dispatch, and Engo said loudly that he was going round the back to try to find the power and gas mains for the restaurant.

"Ben." Matt put a hand on his shoulder, his voice weird, different, hammed up for the benefit of the onlookers and whoever might have been listening in from the apartments above them. Because Matt hadn't spent the last few weeks giving Oscar-worthy performances to save his own goddamn life. "Get the reader out and do a sweep for gas levels. I'll do the same down this end."

They parted. Ben's breath was coming in short, sharp huffs, sweat already rolling down his chest beneath the turnout coat. The red light from the engine was making the windows howl in every apartment block down the long, narrow street. The curtains were drawn in the front windows of Cristobel's. Ben walked past and pulled out his reader and turned it on, taking samples as he went. His eyes were on the windows across the street, his thoughts dancing between the witnesses who might appear there and Jake. Jake at his apartment, waiting outside the doors, having just come down after encountering Kenny. Had Kenny been seconds away from busting Jake inside the apartment, where he'd used Luna's keys to go inside, to retrieve her passport, to aid his mission to make it look like she'd run off on him? Was that how it all went down? Had Luna tried to buy a gun from Edgar because she was beginning to fear the man she was having an affair with, because Jake was becoming unpredictable, violent, possessive? There was so much Ben didn't know, couldn't know, couldn't decide if he wanted to know. Jake had always been a kid to him. The idea that a kid could kill a kid, that he could take Gabriel's life—

Ben stopped, went to the wall, put a hand on it and closed his eyes. He didn't realize he'd dropped the reader until Matt was handing it back to him, gloved hands forcing gloved hands.

"Keep it together, fuckhead."

Ben's legs were numb. He gripped Matt for strength. "Why did he kill them? Why?"

"I said keep it together."

"I have to call him. I have to know."

"Not now."

"Is it even real?" Ben asked. He was looking at Matt, and the guy was wearing his chief's helmet, and it all suddenly seemed like a costume to Ben. Like the blackened and burned surface wasn't real. Matt hadn't been a chief on 9/11, but he'd have rubbed some of the dirt and ash and grit from the helmet he'd been wearing that day on the one he was wearing now. It was tradition. Superstition. Never clean your helmet. Ben was staring at an illusion, a guy the whole world thought was a hero, a guy who never thought of himself as anything but a coward. How could Ben trust these stories about Jake killing his family? "Was it really Jake, or was it you?"

Matt grabbed a hunk of his turnout coat, seemed to want to punch him but didn't. His eyes slid to the gawkers gathering in the street, the first wave nonplussed by the lack of activity, the second wave rolling in. *"Not. Now."*

Matt let Ben's shoulder go and stood back. He put his hand out. "Give me the key," he said.

"What?"

"The key," Matt demanded. "To the box. You're not right in the head at the moment. I want to give it to Engo. He can be the one who goes in."

"No," Ben said. "We both go in. That's the plan."

"I'm *changing* the plan. Give me the key."

Ben stared at him. Across the street, the delivery guy yelled out, "Yo, dude!" Matt and Ben looked. "What's the drama?"

Matt licked his teeth, ignored the man, got a fix on Ben for a moment. When the big guy spoke again, it was loudly, and into his radio.

"Engo, I got some low gas readings at the front. I'm gonna send Ben up to evacuate the building as a precaution. How's it going back there?"

"Having trouble finding the mains," Engo reported. *"I'll let you know."*

Matt flicked his head toward the small, discreet door to access the apartments above Cristobel's and Borr Storage. Ben walked there on legs that felt like stilts, took a skeleton key from his belt, and slipped it into the panel by the door. The door buzzed and clacked as it unlatched. He pulled the fire-alarm tab on the wall beside the elevator as he went for the stairs. The alarm, a gentle pulsing that would rise to a whooping eventually. There was already a guy in boxers standing with one leg still inside his second-floor apartment, watching Ben come up.

"What's going on?"

Ben looked at the guy. Tried to remember his lines. Tried not to tell him that, in a few moments' time, there would be an explosion right underneath where he was standing that would be so big it would feel like the Prince of Darkness had tried to punch a hole in Hell's ceiling. He was supposed to say it was a gas leak. That everything was fine. That the guy should stay calm. But Ben knew the truth, or had thought he did, and wasn't very sure of anything he'd ever known in his life at that moment.

"Get out." Ben jerked a thumb toward the door down the stairs behind him. "Get out as fast as you can."

ANDY

.

There was still traffic in the Holland Tunnel, but most of it was heading in the other direction, and it was light enough that Andy could swing into the oncoming lane now and then to get around cars that blocked her path. She was aware that she was riding the high wire over certain death. Not just for her, but for the innocent men and women and children in the cars around her, marveling at her as she passed at speeds they'd probably never seen before, certainly not in tight, tourist-riddled New York. She was driving like a maniac and the lights were all shimmery from the blow to the back of her head, and her thoughts were incomplete, unable to run to natural conclusions, because Tony Newler was dead. She'd killed him. She'd blown away the black cloud that had been threatening the edge of her horizon for fifteen years, always out there somewhere, waiting for his moment to finally come on and consume her. Andy had to hope Newler had been as intensely secretive about her involvement in the case as she had been led to believe. That his and Ryang's annoyance at her "shadow games" at Newler's house didn't mean he'd mentioned who she actually was to the grab team he'd set up at the abandoned property on the river. If he had, there would be questions. The ballistics on the porch at Jake's mother's house wouldn't line up, wouldn't sell the experts on the idea that Jake and Newler had shot each other. Gabe, and the street witnesses, would mention a woman.

She'd be hunted.

Andy knew she'd have to get on a plane before the night was through. Go somewhere. Bury herself. She'd done it before, plenty of times, left a mess behind her and questions on the wind. The game just went that way sometimes.

That was if she survived the night.

Her priority now was Ben. Making sure he didn't do something that would make it impossible for her to deliver to him what she'd promised: an answer to what had happened to his family. And a future. He'd have to pay for what he'd done too, sure. The robberies. But in Andy's mind and in her heart, there was still a chance the man she thought she knew hadn't murdered Officer Ivan Willstone, and hadn't been a part of what happened to Titus Cliffen. Andy had to believe that, because she'd felt something as he slept beside her, as he laughed and danced with her, as he gripped her and moved inside her and groaned in her ear.

She'd felt the goodness in him.

She was racing to save that goodness now.

When she'd checked the phone before she left Jake's house, Andy had seen that the little blue bubbles that indicated Matt's, Engo's, and Ben's cars were all assembled at the fire station. As she checked again, entering the tunnel, she saw Engo's car had moved toward Midtown.

Andy knew what that meant.

She held the wheel with one hand and dialed with her other. Ben didn't pick up. There was no voicemail, just a soulless clicking of the call failing.

"I found Gabe!" she roared impotently at the phone. "Please, Ben. Please, please, please. Don't throw it all away."

She screeched into the oncoming lane to get around a semitrailer, darting back in front of the massive vehicle just in time to survive being taken out by a van traveling in the opposite direction. Both horns blared. Andy saw the turnoff to Midtown ahead. She dialed the phone again. Three numbers. It rang twice before it was picked up.

"Nine-one-one, what is your emergency?"

"I'm gonna give you an address," Andy said. "Send everyone."

BEN

.

A little girl in pink pajamas covered in purple unicorns stepped into the light of the hall. Ben froze at the sight of her, alone and rubbing her eyes, her straw-like blond hair flattened on one side from sleep. The girl watched Ben take the last two steps down onto the fifth floor before breaking into a grin. She pointed to Ben's face, waiting for her father to join her from inside the apartment.

"Daddy! Look! Look! Fireman!"

Ben watched the father back out of the apartment with a stroller. There was an infant squawking in a blanket in the seat, unstrapped, booted feet kicking.

"I know, baby. I know." The man looked Ben up and down, pulling a robe around himself. "Where do we go? Across the street?"

"Get as far away from the building as possible," Ben said, his stomach roiling. "Go down the street and turn the corner."

"But my neighbor said it's just a—"

"Do as I say, sir," Ben said.

"When will we be allowed back in? I've got work in the mor—"

"Get out of the building!" Ben barked. He felt his eyes grow wild. "No more questions! Do as I say! Evacuate now!"

The little girl jumped at Ben's words and burst into sudden tears. The man scooped her up against his hip. "It's okay, honey. It's okay. He's just a jerk. Let's get moving."

Ben thumped on doors. "Fire department! Fire department! Evacuate now!"

He pushed into an apartment facing east, left the elderly woman who answered the door standing bewildered in the entryway. He walked to a window at the back of the apartment, smacked the curtains out of the way to get a view to the alley behind. Ben could see Engo's Subaru hugging the wall on the opposite side of the alley, and something about that burned him right to the core, that Engo would try to park his piece-of-shit Subaru as far back from the blast zone as he could so it wouldn't get scratched or the windows wouldn't get busted while he tried to rip off a dying billionaire of eight million dollars. Ben could just see the edge of a pipe snaking toward the back door of Cristobel's.

Ben went back out, past the bewildered and protesting old lady. He barked at the woman to evacuate and waited while she went back into the apartment, emerging with a potted fern clutched under her arm and a sour look on her face. The alarm overhead turned from an eerie bleeping to a more urgent whoop.

"Are they all out?" Matt asked over the radio.

"Yeah," Ben said, though he couldn't possibly know that. Because there was a chance someone was hiding under a bed, or wearing earplugs as they slept, or passed out drunk, or clinically deaf, and they'd be there inside their home when Ben and the crew blasted the restaurant. But fuck it, right? He was a killer anyway.

"Engo, you got the mains switched off?"

"I need a hand."

"You fucking kidding me?" Matt snapped. His acting was getting better. *"Engo, cut the power and gas, now. This ain't your first day."*

"I'll be back there in a second, Engo," Ben said.

He walked down the stairs of the apartment building, got to the foyer, and spotted Matt through the glass entry doors by the mailboxes. The boss was rousting the man in boxers who had since thrown on clothes and was standing barefoot in the street, taking a picture of the fire engine with his phone. Ben went to the fire door at the back of the foyer and pushed his way out.

His heart leaped right up into his esophagus when he smelled the alley-way, like the scent that filled his nostrils had tugged the organ up there on a wire. He smelled garlic. He'd expected to smell the mercaptan additive in the natural gas Engo was pumping into the tubes running beneath his feet, wedged beneath the door of Cristobel's. An eggy, familiar aroma he'd encountered a thousand times. But the scent of the garlic was there, impossibly intense, more intense than a person would encounter at a goddamn garlic farm.

For a second or two, Ben couldn't speak.

"No." Ben went over, gripped Engo's shoulder. The man was bent over a pair of tanks Ben was telling himself weren't maroon colored—sweet Jesus, *couldn't* be maroon colored, *had* to be yellow. "Engo. No. No. No. You're not— That's not—"

"It's acetylene." Engo didn't even look up. "You fuckers wouldn't listen to me, but I know what I'm doing. I know we need a bigger bang to break the wall. In a minute you'll see that w—"

A noise hit him, like a train whooshing through an empty station. Then all Ben's own breath thumped out of his chest as his body hit the Subaru. He fell to the ground, waited for the rushing, thundering, ringing sound in his ears to stop, glass and wood and flaming chunks of ash raining all around him. His helmet was off, one glove was off, and the concrete beneath his bare cheek was so hot he felt the sizzling of his own stubble hairs and skin as he tried to get up. Coughing, wheezing, dragging himself up, smoke shooting from his very lips, the taste of char on his tongue. He saw Engo, a black shape moving in the smoke cloud. Ben knew instinctively that Matt was on the radio, but all he could do was stand there and watch flames roar up out of the great hole in the back of the restaurant where the door and the bricks housing it used to be.

Engo had him by the arm. His face was flash burned, red and raw and shiny.

"We gotta go! We gotta go!"

Ben found his helmet and glove somehow, dragged them on, ran behind Engo back through the open fire door at the rear of the apartment building. He tripped on a rug that ran the length of the room, almost losing it. Engo sprinted through the shattered glass door of the foyer, heading toward the engine. Matt was already laying out hose, something Ben hadn't seen his boss do in over a decade, something it hadn't *been his job* to do in all that time.

"What the fuck happened?"

"What do you think?" Ben yelled before Engo could answer. He turned and gaped for a second at the damage the blast had done to the front of the restaurant. Burning wood and steel fragments were sprayed in a wide arc across the street. There was a flaming dining chair embedded by the legs in the passenger-side front window of the fire engine. The people had cleared out completely; were running, ducking behind cars, crowding into the front doorways of apartment buildings. The glass—a mixture of broken apartment and shopfront windows—was an inch deep and sloshing around their boots like winter snow.

Engo bled the hose and Ben felt Matt come onto the line behind him, and then there was a last sharp tug and they both looked and saw Andy taking up the hose with one hand and trying to right a helmet on her head with the other. Ben recognized the gear as the spare bunker uniform they kept in the back of the engine.

And then Ben glanced down the street and saw two squad cars screeching to a halt in a V shape on Eighth Avenue, and some uptown engine he didn't recognize nosing into the crowd down at the other end of the street. He knew in a second or two what had happened. He knew it all. That wherever Andy had been, she'd looked at her magic little fucking trackers and saw Matt's and Engo's cars, at least, parked back at the station while they weren't on shift. Maybe his own, too. She'd figured the job was on, and she'd called it; it was time to bag them. Him, Engo, Matt, Jakey. She'd called in the cavalry. And in doing that, she'd blown her cover. Now Matt and Engo knew who she was, too, because while Matt had called the dispatcher for backup when the blast hit, the cops and engines they were seeing now got there only seconds later, and the only way that could have happened was if someone called them in before he ever could.

Ben didn't have time to see the bitter recognition in Matt's eyes. Engo had kicked on the hose. He hung on as the older man advanced on the fire, the hose—rock hard and heavy as a human body—swaying in his hands. They beat at the flames, Ben's gaze roving over the fire itself, and the guys from other crews laying hose and tanking up on either side of them. He looked up through the billowing smoke rising fast and rancid brown against the skyline of buildings and saw exactly what he didn't want to see, yet of course did want to see: a pale towel being waved from a window on the sixth floor.

"We still got civilians up there!" Ben roared above the sound of the fire and the water and the sirens. Matt didn't even look to confirm. He got off the hose just as a guy from another crew took it up. Ben watched Matt walk over to a chief from uptown who was standing there trying to get his bearings.

"Civilians up top!" Matt shouted. "I'll send two of mine in."

"My guys are already tanked up. Keep yours on the ho—"

"Fuck you!" Matt's face was blank, rigid, devoid of the emotion that was supposed to be behind his words. "We got here first. It's our save. Put two of your guys on my line."

Matt walked back to Ben before he could get a response. Ben held the hose, eyes locked on the fire, until he felt Matt's tap on his shoulder and a guy slid in to fill his spot on the hose. He was tanked up and sprinting for the broken glass door of the apartment-block foyer before he could catch his breath. Ben locked eyes with Andy for a second before the smoke and heat haze smothered out her image, and he turned and ran into the building.

ANDY

.

She watched Engo and Ben disappear into the smoked-out doorway of the apartment block, then let her eyes travel up the building to the sixth floor, where an arm was hanging from the broken window, waving a towel in slow, desperate circles in the night air. She looked for Matt, but he was gone. Andy dropped the hose, saw the guy ahead of her on the line glance back, his eyes filled with annoyance that she was leaving him and two others with the weight of the hose.

"Hey! *Hey!*"

Andy ignored the calls, darted to the back of her station's engine, and grabbed hold of a firefighter who was passing by. His turnout coat said he was from Battalion 9.

"They're not going for the civilian," Andy said.

"Huh?" The guy leaned in to hear.

"They're not going for the civilian!" she roared. "Tell your chief. Fuck what Matt says. We need more officers up in the apartments!"

Something in her eyes must have told him. Andy watched him sprint away, turned, and reached into her turnout coat to grab the gun hidden in her waistband. It was then that Matt emerged from around the corner of the engine, grabbed her elbow to trap her arm inside the coat. He swung his hand up and knocked her helmet off.

"Lights out, Nancy Drew," Matt said. He grabbed her skull and smashed it against the engine's rear ladder. Andy's legs went. Her last sensation was of Matt scooping her limbs up, bundling her body like a limp bag of clothes, and shoving her into the dark, wet space under the engine.

BEN

·

They went back through the foyer to the fire door, swimming through smoke that was so thick it looked like mud washing against Ben's mask. The alleyway was slightly better, the smoke pouring upward from the blown-out windows of the second-floor apartment where the guy in the boxer shorts had been. The bulk of the fire was up there now, chewing through his carpet, furnishings, slithering through his walls, heading for the third floor. Ben could see the floor of the boxer guy's apartment peeling down into the middle of the restaurant, a collapsed card in a house of cards, half his belongings spilling into the middle of the dining room floor and feeding spot fires there. Incredibly, the wall separating Cristobel's restaurant and Borr Storage was intact, at least as far as Ben could see—maybe fifteen feet into the smoking ruins.

"Mother*fucker*!" Engo yelled.

"Come on." Ben pushed him. They picked their way into the blinding heat and darkness, falling onto their knees before long, crawling beneath collapsed partitions, shoving aside piles of smoking bracken that had been tables and chairs. The floor under Ben's hands and knees was so hot he knew that if he wasn't wearing fireproof gear he'd be burned down to the bone by now. Ben stopped while Engo gripped and shoved a bent and buckled deep fryer out of the way, using all his body weight to bash it aside. There was a crumpled section of the brick wall between Cristobel's restaurant and Borr Storage just where Ben and the crew had hoped there might be: behind the bar, where drill points for plumbing had weakened the structure. Engo beckoned and Ben came up beside him, and the two worked side by side, pulling bricks out of the pile and hurling them into the smoking mess around them. Ben looked back, and through a gap in the rubble he could see spray from the fire hoses out in the street hitting the underside of the collapsed ceiling, chasing flames that were turning and massing in the apartment above. A thin wave of blue and yellow fire was washing over the ceiling, chasing the oxygen spewing into the cavern of the burned-out restaurant.

When they'd made a hole big enough to crawl through, Engo fell on his side and dragged himself forward, using the brick and bits of jagged rebar to haul his body through the oddly shaped gap without snagging the tank or its straps on anything. Ben expected, somehow, that Borr Storage might be untouched by the disaster. But the pressure wave of the explosion had buckled the wall of storage boxes on the restaurant's side, spewing shiny brass drawers and their contents all over the floor. Ben glimpsed stacks of cash, paperwork, velvet jewelry boxes through the smoke now pouring in through the hole they'd just made. The front of the room was darkened by smoke creeping in through the busted glass security doors, around the iron roller shutter mounted behind them, and into the foyer and office area.

"This way! This way!" Engo shouted. Ben pushed past him, followed the darkening smoke toward the office. He went by a doorway and saw that a curtain and a leather couch were on fire now in the waiting area, embers having worked their way into the room somehow, through the tiny slits in the roller door maybe. The whole room was lit red and flashing from the engines outside. Ben rushed to the huge desk dominating the center of the office, yanked out a drawer that was upholstered with velvet and lined with a hundred keys sitting in little special mountings like wedding-gift silverware. He pulled the drawer so hard in his haste the whole thing flew out and spilled the keys everywhere.

"Fuck!"

"It's-okay-it's-okay-it's-okay." Ben pulled Engo up as he bent for the drawer on the floor. He pointed to a label on the front of the second drawer. "That was one to a hundred!"

Ben grabbed the drawer marked "400s" and slid it open carefully, fished out key 408, which was lying in its velvet bed above a brass-plated label. He ran back through the offices. In the seconds it had taken them to retrieve the keys, the fire in the waiting room had reduced a potted palm tree to dust and was crawling across the carpet toward the front desk. Ben knew that soon the smoke easing out of the roller security door would be thick enough to tell the teams outside that the fire had crossed from the restaurant to the storage facility. He and Engo needed to get out of there before someone came through to try to knock down the fire in the waiting room.

"Ben and Engo, I need a sitrep."

"We're on location, sixth floor, trying to locate the civilian," Ben lied.

"Engine 97 sent two guys up there through the back, and they're reporting the

civilian is in their custody and they're on their way down," Matt said. Ben could hear the tightness in his voice. *"Again. A sitrep. Now."*

Ben worked a hand along the rows and rows of brass boxes in the dark, knowing he should find 408 on the right-hand wall in the corner but counting down anyway, from the thousands to the eight hundreds to the six hundreds. Engo was waiting for him in the corner, a gloved finger on the box and his eyes huge in the mask. The smoke was thickening. Ben jammed the key from the drawer into the left-hand slot in the front of the box.

"We must be on the fifth floor," Ben said into the radio. "I thought we were on the sixth. We got another civilian here. Will keep you updated."

"Partial collapse on the first floor is worsening," Matt said. *"Don't descend. Wait for the ladder."*

"Got it." Ben found the key he'd been given by the lawyer in the pocket of his bunker trousers. He took it out, slid it into the right-hand keyhole in the front of drawer 408.

If Engo hadn't moved, Ben wouldn't have seen him. But the slight shift the older man gave to steady his feet directly behind Ben made him slip into view. Ben saw him in the shiny reflection in the polished brass front of the shelf. The image wasn't so great, in the smoke and the darkness, that Ben could see the gun in Engo's hands. He just saw the stance. The planted feet. The arms extended. The hands together and gripped around a black object, that object pointed directly at the back of Ben's skull.

Ben felt a rush of icy clarity hit his body, beginning at his head and racing down his entire being, light-speed fast, like he'd plunged right into the Hudson.

He made a show of turning the keys, twisted his hands but not the keys themselves.

"Jesus! Fuck! It won't . . ." Ben yelled. "It won't go!"

He saw Engo adjust his aim. Ben took a step back, fake-twisted the keys again.

"It won't turn!" He let the desk key go and gripped the lawyer key with both hands. "It's stuck!"

Engo dropped his aim and stepped up beside him, as Ben hoped he would, the gun at his side, his gloved hand coming up to try the key.

Ben smashed him in the mask with his elbow. He used the moment of stunned surprise to grab and twist the gun out of Engo's grip.

Ben stepped back and shot Engo three times in the chest. He went down, collapsed with his head bent forward on a pillow of brass boxes spilled from the busted shelves on the opposite wall. Ben went back and turned both keys in drawer 408, slid it out and lifted the lid. He dumped the contents on the floor, rummaged around, and beneath a nest of papers he found six baseball cards housed in chunky fiberglass capsules. He slid them into the inner chest pockets of his turnout coat and looked toward the offices, where he could hear the unmistakable sound of guys working the roller door open with a Halligan bar. He was on his knees, about to slip back through the hole in the wall into Cristobel's restaurant, when he felt the impact of the bullet in his back.

For a moment, he was in that apartment again, wherever it had been, scrambling through the smoke looking for the teenager who wasn't there, and the roof beam spearing him right between the shoulder blades had fallen again, so full of soundless and complete power it was like he'd been hammered down by the hand of a Titan. He was flat, voiceless, breathless mouth gaping in the mask, the pain coming after the impact, a decent few seconds later, a fiery pain that spread outward from his heart, right to the tips of his fingers.

And then he could move again, and he did move, turned on his side and looked back at Engo and the fucking gun in his fingers, the gun he himself had dropped on the carpet in his haste to open the box with the cards. Taking the shot had been the last thing Engo could manage on the earth. The eyes that stared at Ben through the mask were unseeing. Ben turned again and crawled, whimpering and groaning with the pain it caused him, through the hole in the wall and back into the restaurant.

It was raining ash in big, black, fluttery handfuls as he commando-crawled along the wet floor of the restaurant, thinking if he could just get to Engo's Subaru he might get a second wave of movement and energy like the one that had hit him after the paralyzing pain of the bullet wound receded.

Ben got to the street, pulled himself onto the asphalt, yanked his tank off and let it clank loudly on the ground, the mask a rubbery hellish sucking octopus he had to wrestle from his cheeks. He tasted cold, clean air, knew the fire was being beaten somewhere above him, even as black butterflies of ash landed on his gloves and face. He turned himself over, or no, actually, was turned over and hauled up against the wheel of Engo's car. Andy was there, ripping open the collar of his coat, yanking the jacket apart, spilling the baseball cards in their special cases all down his blood-soaked belly and lap. Her eyes flicked over the cards, eight million dollars' worth of absolutely nothing in her weird upside-down world, giving them half a second of her time before she batted them out of the way to rip open Ben's undershirt and examine the exit wound. He sat there and felt the life draining out of him and wondered, idly, if the items he'd stolen and killed for that she was carelessly kneeling on now were the most expensive she'd ever dealt with, or if she'd spent the last few years doing just this: brushing off diamonds and jewels and stacks of cash to get her hands wet with villainous blood.

When she realized what he already knew, she sat down beside him, and wiped at the tears pouring from her eyes. He only noticed then the enormous gash in the side of her head, right above her temple, directly above her ear.

"I found Gabe," she said. She was holding his hands now, pulling his gloves off, gripping his fingers with hers. He remembered taking her hand in the dark as she slept, and it did something to stave off the strange coldness that was beginning in all his limbs. When Ben tried to squeeze her hands back, he found he couldn't. His head was heavy. His mouth must have twitched, because it inspired a smile in her.

"He's okay."

"What?"

"He's okay," Andy said. "He's alive."

Ben gave a little laugh. She was smiling and crying and laughing above him.

"Jake," he managed. "Was it—"

"Yeah." Andy nodded. "Luna's gone. I'm sorry, Ben. I'm sorry. But she's gone."

Ben wanted to thank her, to laugh more at it all, the horror and meaninglessness of it, but he was so tired, and it felt better just to let her stroke his hair, whoever the hell she was, and hold him.

She must have read his thoughts, because she said, "I'm Dahlia."

Ben thought about the name, held it in his mind, turned it over. He felt it roll from meaning everything, into meaning nothing, into meaning everything again as lights flickered out inside him. He watched the smoke coiling up into the night sky and listened to the sirens and thought that her name wasn't so bad, as far as last things to ever hear went.

ANDY

.

The mess was huge. The way she worked, and the kinds of things she did for people, Andy was accustomed to jobs ending with a lot of covering up to do, a lot of threats, a lot of bargaining. She stood at the window of the hospital in Santa Barbara and watched the highway beyond, red and yellow lights on the 101, feeling tired and ready for the end of it. There was a breeze off the ocean, and the Cottage Hospital, being only three stories high, had windows in the maternity ward that could open, a designer figuring perhaps that the usual rule about postpartum depression and open windows didn't have to apply here. There was an elegant red bougainvillea plant creeping along the edge of the building, and through its dark leaves Andy watched the window of room 302.

In the weeks that followed the fire at Borr Storage, she'd begun to pick at the deeply knotted and tangled last aspects of the Benjamin Haig case, resting up in a hotel under a fake name in Hoboken. She'd watched the news coverage of the attempted robbery of Borr Storage, of the deliberately ignited fire that had miraculously injured no one, of Newler's mysterious murder by Jake in Metuchen and its connection to the events in Midtown. Andy watched anxiously for mentions of her mask's name, or flashes of her visage, or signs that the police would need her assistance piecing together that Jake had murdered Luna and stolen Gabriel, or that Ben's crew had murdered Ivan Willstone and possibly Titus Cliffen. If she could help it, Andy wanted to stay clear of the cleanup, so that there were no questions about what had happened to Newler. About who she was, and where she'd come from, and what dark ghosts lurked across the landscape of her past.

Petal by petal, the flower bloomed. Only one news report mentioned that police sought assistance from an unnamed woman seen by witnesses at the crime scene at Metuchen. Police worked backward through Jake's phone's map app, which led them to Luna's body in the mangroves by the harbor. An arson expert employed by the FDNY admitted, after a week of intense police pressure, to giving a "gently manipulated" report on the fire that killed Titus Cliffen and three other fires on Matt's request. As the days passed, and Andy remained glued to the TV and to her phone, she saw nothing about Andy Nearland and her employment with the Engine 99 crew. She could only think that some colleague of Newler's had scrubbed clean his office and personal effects of his apparent use of a private undercover agent, probably in the hopes of maintaining Newler's reputation and avoiding muddying the police case against the crew.

There was a feast of photographs available to the journalists covering the case—of Ben and the crew in their firefighting uniforms, of Titus in his memorial wall photograph, of Willstone in his NYPD uniform, of Newler in his gray suit. Then there was Luna wrapped around Ben on a beach trip somewhere, little Gabriel digging in the sand nearby. Search-and-recover crews setting up a crime scene at the shoreline in Jersey. Cadaver dogs. A body bag. Then there was the lawyer, Ichh, being led from his office in cuffs. Andy watched their faces flashing on the screen, all of them, as the media and the public tried to piece together what the hell had happened. It hurt to see Ben's picture, because he was invariably smiling, and the starkness of that against her memory of him dying in her arms burned inside her. She'd wondered, as those last seconds of Benjamin Haig's life flickered and fell away, whether she should tell him all of it. About the sheer depth of Luna's deception. But she hadn't. She'd spared him that. And she wondered if she was sparing herself, as day fell into day, from the last truth she didn't have about the firemen and their deeds. Whether the Ben that she had known and held and laughed with, the man who had been so desperate to find the family he'd always wanted, was a cold-blooded killer.

She knew one man who could tell her.

Now and then, Andy had seen Matt's picture beside the iconic blue-sky photograph of the Towers with their trails of black smoke. It seemed that his story as ringleader of the entire mess had been the one the press wanted to tell the least.

Andy knew the search for Matt and Donna was going to be fruitless. While the NYPD, the FBI, and a string of other agencies were doing all the right things, and Matt's uniformed FDNY picture featured prominently on the FBI's most-wanted list, Andy stopped believing they really wanted to find out where he was when she realized no one knew where he had *been*. That, to her, was clear enough. It was obvious, due to the simple fact of where Ben Haig had kept his stash. With Ben so consumed, like Jake and Engo, with what Matt thought and how Matt felt, it seemed sensible enough that Ben hid his stash in a place that gave him pain and sadness because Matt had told him to. It was a good idea. Because that place, the apartment where he'd been born, was the last place anybody expected Ben to go.

Andy only had to apply the same philosophy to Matt to find out where the chief had been.

It had taken some of her classic finessing and manipulation to convince the security team at One World Trade Center to allow her to look at some of their security footage. But in the end, she was given a space in the sleek office walled in by black glass, just down the hall from the ticketing office of the 9/11 Memorial Museum. Someone even brought her a coffee. She sat and clicked and dragged and punched in numbers, and eventually she was able to find footage of a tall, thickly built man in a black ball cap striding down the breezy, tree-lined walkway between the memorial fountains. The footage was recorded forty minutes after Matt had disappeared from the site of the Cristobel's restaurant bombing. Andy watched the figure access the foyer of the offices inside One World Trade with a swipe card, ride the elevators to the forty-first floor, and walk down the hall to an empty office suite. She watched him return from the suite, some four minutes later, carrying two weighty duffel bags.

Andy had then simply followed the trail from there. She discovered the financial identity and accounts Matt had used to rent the empty office space at One World Trade, then backtracked to see whether that identity was connected to the rent or purchase of any other properties. There were closed and emptied accounts, routed and rerouted deposits, creditors and debtors that led to completely fictionalized people. In the end, she was able to follow the trail somewhere else she didn't expect. Not to some distant beach in Barbados, or into the Alaskan wilds, where she believed the rest of the world was searching half-heartedly for Matt. When she hunted him down, she hunted him to sunny Santa Barbara.

Andy put her hands in her pockets and watched the window of Matt and Donna's room in the wing perpendicular to the one where she was standing, waiting for him to come into view again. In the week she'd watched Matt and Donna, or Rick and Sally as they were calling themselves, she'd seen the big man at many windows—at the little house in San Roque that they rented, or the driver's-side window of his truck going suburb-to-suburb as a concreting contractor. Always he was framed there, weary-eyed and anxious, checking, she supposed, for someone like her. Donna having the baby, and the child being by all accounts a perfectly formed, plump, and cheerful infant, only the night before, hadn't eased the tight visage of the man who stepped up to the window now. Andy saw Matt rest his big knuckles on the window frame, watching the distant highway as she herself had done, thousands of lives filtering in and out of the beachside paradise. The marine layer was creeping in, and the red and yellow lights were taking on a smoky, romantic blurriness. Andy watched Matt's eyes drop to the parking lot of the hospital, and fix on her car. It was the missing plates, the rental sticker that did it. She knew they would. Matt stiffened, turned, and disappeared from the window.

She pursued him at a walk, first waiting for him to pass by her door, his heavy boots the only sounds in the otherwise quiet private hospital. She slipped out of the room and followed, was surprised to see him stop at the door to the fire stairs. His pace had been one of determination. The rawness and urgency of the flight response, the need to get as far away from Donna and the baby as he could, so that any danger—angry officers and agents with their guns and their knowledge of his history of violence—would be drawn away. But as she watched, Matt paused there, his hand on the door lever, staring at it. Andy saw a flash of the man Matt had been once: younger, dressed in bunker gear, an unconscious woman slung over his shoulder, that same hand on the door of a different stairwell. The one on the forty-first floor of the North Tower. He'd been fleeing then, too. Andy had a gun on her hip, but she didn't reach for it. She didn't call out to let him know she was there. She just waited, and watched, as Matt slowly took his hand down from the door.

He turned around and saw her standing there in the empty hall. Andy watched as the initial surprise on his face was replaced by a deep, deep relief. It was a loosening, and flushing with warmth, an overcoming of who he appeared to be that Andy knew was much deeper than the knowledge that he didn't have to run anymore. It was a relief that his time to pay a debt he'd wanted to pay for twenty-three years had finally come. He left the door shut, walked back toward Andy, and took a chair against the wall by the vending machine.

She went and sat beside him, and a silence enveloped them, him thinking whatever he was thinking, her noticing that the intense and radiating menace she'd felt in his proximity from the moment she had met him was gone. Long seconds passed. There was no hurry. Andy knew in her heart what was coming: that Matt would tell her and the investigators she eventually escorted him to everything they needed to know about Titus, and Willstone, and the robberies. He would be an open book. He had that way about him now. Andy felt heartsick at what the next few hours would hold, at having to know the truth about Ben, before she dropped Matt at a police station and watched him walk in and hand himself over. There was a needing to know thrumming inside her. There was also a needing to protect herself from it all.

But of course, there was comfort in knowing that the pain wouldn't last. It would be gone when she put on her next mask.

"Boy or girl?" she asked Matt eventually.

"Boy." Matt smiled.

They sat there together, the vending machine humming, the hospital quiet with sleeping patients and whispering nurses. Andy already knew what she was going to say to him. Had been thinking about it for a long time. When she started in, she couldn't look at him. The words came tumbling out, her eyes fixed on the dark linoleum at her feet.

"I know you haven't been to the memorial museum," she said. "I can't imagine you going there. But in one of the exhibits, they have a big phrase on the wall. 'No day shall erase you from the memory of time.'"

She waited. Matt said nothing.

"I know you don't believe that," Andy said. "You believe the opposite. You believe that day, it erased you. Whoever you were before you walked out that door and abandoned your crew, that man, that *good* man, was gone."

Still, he was quiet.

"What I'm saying is"—Andy finally looked at him—"if that's what you really believe, then you have to believe that it can happen again. That this day, or any day, can erase you. A single day can obliterate the badness in you."

Matt smiled at her, his big arms folded and the warm relief still playing about his eyes. "Andy," he said.

"Yes?"

"Just shut up and take me to jail, would you?"

DAHLIA

·

She got off the bus in Morgan City outside a place called the Blowout Lounge. It was three o'clock in the afternoon, and the wall of shipping containers across the street from the little dive bar, along with the levee only two doors down, gave the street a welcome coolness. Dahlia went in and took a seat at the bar, and when the door creaked closed behind her she mused that it could have been midnight out there for the way the paint sealed the door shut against the remains of the day. It was three months since New York, but she gathered a handful of peanuts from the dish the bartender put in front of her and she noted a weird clicking in the side of her head as she opened her mouth to pour them in. Each job left her with some kind of scar or alteration, and they were getting harder and harder to explain. One of these days, the only masks she'd be able to take on would be war veteran or grizzly-bear tamer.

The neon lights behind the bar gave the frizzy graying hair of the woman tending it a whimsical glow, and Dahlia could see a thin sheen of sweat on her sagging biceps as she wiped and arranged things back there. Penelope Brown seemed to hear Dahlia's thoughts, went and turned the air-conditioning up, cursing gently at the remote as she punched and repunched the rubbery and stained little buttons trying to get the thing to work. Eventually the machine on the wall increased its thrumming, and the eternal war with the Louisiana heat took on a new energy inside the little establishment. Dahlia being the only customer of the lounge, if you could call it that, it seemed she and Penelope would fall into conversation at some point. But it took a few good minutes, and Dahlia was happy to wait.

"Where you hailin' from?" Penelope asked eventually, and Dahlia accepted the beer she poured her with a nod of appreciation.

"Santa Barbara."

"Out here for work?"

"Yes, ma'am."

"Must be." Penelope sniffed and wiped her nose on the back of her wrist.

"Only reason a sane person would come to a place like this. How long'll you be in town?"

"Depends." Dahlia sipped her beer. "How long do you think you'll give me to find your missing daughter?"

Penelope stopped dead, peering at Dahlia from behind her greasy half-moon glasses.

"You're her," she said, when she'd regained her composure. "The one the investigator recommended."

Dahlia smiled, rubbed at the clicky spot in the side of her head. Matt's scar.

"Well, Jesus H. Christ," Penelope said. She leaned over the bar. "I'm glad to meet you. I didn't know if you'd come."

Dahlia shook the offered hand. The grip was painful, tight with hope and desperation.

"I'm gonna do what I can to help you out, Penelope," Dahlia said. "But first I'll need to know some things."

"Me first," the older woman cut in. "What the hell do I call you?"

Dahlia sat back and thought about it.

Gave it a few seconds.

Never more than that.

ACKNOWLEDGMENTS

I spoke to a lot of firefighters, both in Sydney and in New York, to fuel the writing of this book. I will keep their identities a secret, as I have been asked to do, because they spoke openly, honestly, and with great vulnerability about what they do. They revealed the good and the bad. The unquestioning openness of these men shocked me (and they all happened to be men, through no design of my own). Some were involved in the rescue efforts after the terrible events of September 11, 2001. Others shared their experience of losing colleagues, of struggling with hostile work environments, of relishing in the joy and heartache that is being a firefighter. They took me into their firehouses, told me their stories, and answered my sometimes difficult questions, based on kindness alone. Any and all mistakes, exaggerations, or flagrant disregardings of the truth about firefighting and its processes in this novel are my fault. And make no mistake: I did not meet, nor hear tell of a single firefighter whose nefarious actions or intentions compare to the men in this book. Matt, Engo, Jake, and Ben are all, thankfully, fictional.

So my thanks go to J, R, N, Chief D and his crew, The Black Prince and his crew, and a number of others. I owe you more cake than I could ever hope to bring you. Stay safe.

I get to do what I do because of the people who have schooled me in the craft of writing at the University of Notre Dame, the University of the Sunshine Coast, and the University of Queensland. Team Fox consists of my long-suffering agents Gaby Naher, Lisa Gallagher, and Steve Fisher, and my dedicated publishers, editors, and others across the world at Penguin Random House, Tor/Forge Macmillan, Suhrkamp Verlag, and beyond. Thank you so much for believing in me.

Finally, Tim; thank you for always holding the fort, never rolling your eyes, being my rock of patience and tolerance. Noggy, thank you for being my teddy. Violet, thank you for being the best kid in the world. It's not easy, but you somehow manage it every minute of every day.

ABOUT THE AUTHOR

Penguin Random House Australia

CANDICE FOX is the award-winning author of *Crimson Lake, Redemption Point, Gone by Midnight, Gathering Dark, The Chase,* and *Fire with Fire.* She is also cowriter, with James Patterson, of *New York Times* bestsellers *Never Never, Fifty Fifty, Liar Liar,* and *The Inn.* Fox lives in Sydney, Australia.

candicefox.org
Facebook: Candice Fox
Twitter: @candicefoxbooks